Cold Steel Rain

G . P . PUTNAM'S SONS

NEW YORK

Cold Steel Rain

Kenneth Abel

Kenneth
Abel
October 25, 2000

G. P. Putnam's Sons
Publishers Since 1838
a member of
Penguin Putnam Inc.
375 Hudson Street
New York, NY 10014

Library of Congress Cataloging-in-Publication Data

Abel, Kenneth.
    Cold steel rain / Kenneth Abel.
      p. cm.
    ISBN 0-399-14662-8
    1. Police—Louisiana—New Orleans—Fiction.
    2. New Orleans (La.)—Fiction.   I. Title.
PS3551.B336 C65   2000   00-035247
813'.54—dc21

Printed in the United States of America
10 9 8 7 6 5 4 3 2 1

BOOK DESIGN BY DEBORAH KERNER

For

my agent,

Philip Spitzer

Nothing stays dead in New Orleans. Not for long, anyway. You get a hard rain on a hot August night, all the ghosts come out. Ride down Claiborne Avenue, past all the muffler shops, discount furniture warehouses, Popeye's Chicken, your headlights catch a wisp of fog twisting up off the pavement like an old Bourbon Street stripper giving it one last lazy bump and grind. Just a glimpse before you drive on through it, send it whirling away behind you, but that's enough to make you feel like some things hang on, refuse to get swept away. They can knock the old buildings down, put up uglier ones, the whole city turning to cinder block before your eyes. But something always gets left behind. "Make a right down where the Dixie Drug used to be," some old guy on the street tells you, his whole hand stuck out, shaking slightly, like he needs all five fingers to point that far, "then keep on going till you get to where they shot that guy last year." And, Jesus Christ, you *know what he means.* 'Cause nothing ever vanishes, this town. You can still see it all, like a dream you wake from, still whispering into the dark.

Danny Chaisson gazed out at the rain-streaked streets gleaming in his headlights. *Like an old love, the one you can't ever forgive.* It drove some people crazy, drove 'em out to California, Austin, or Seattle. But he still loved the place, felt it every day, the way you'd love an old dog that sleeps under the porch, just dragging its weary bones out to get fed. A few years back, the tourist board put a poster up in the arrival terminals at Moisant Airport, a jazz band playing in front of a bearded oak, with the slogan THE CITY THAT CARE FORGOT. Only somebody took a black marker to it, changed it to THE CITY THAT FORGOT TO CARE. The poster hung there for eight weeks before anybody got around to changing it. That was New Orleans. The whole town like your great aunt, an old woman refusing to die, dressing up in her Sunday best every morning just to sit in her bedroom, watch game shows on the TV. *Nobody dies here,* Danny thought. *They just get buried alive.*

He glanced at his watch, swung through the parking lot of an all-night liquor warehouse into an alley that ran behind a row of discount stores. The restaurant was in a run-down strip mall at the end of the alley, a small place with a large glass window that the owners had hung with faded bamboo shades, paper lanterns from Pier One. They'd hired a Vietnamese guy from over in Gretna to paint the name on the window—*Lotus Flower.* Delicate, curving letters, like petals, and below it, a sampan sailing down a river; the guy had thrown the sampan in, no charge. Like he'd felt sorry for the place, tried to brighten it up. Danny'd always liked that picture, the boat drifting away on the dark river, sun fading on its sails.

The place had been a rib joint a couple years back, and they hadn't changed it much. There was a row of booths along one wall, some small tables squeezed close together by the front window. Danny pushed the door open, smiled at the woman behind the register. "You wait up for me?"

The woman looked up from the magazine she was reading. "How you eat, we not open?"

Danny glanced around the restaurant. Two black women were eating soup at a booth near the window, and a guy Danny knew named Dewitt Foley sat reading the newspaper in the last booth, back by the toilets. He was a small-time operator, with nervous hands and a briefcase full of guns at his feet. Most days, he sat in a Greek coffee shop on upper Canal Street, reading his newspaper. Sometimes a kid from the nearby projects would come in, and they'd go out in the alley, lay the briefcase on a garbage can, open it up. The kid would reach in, pick up a gun, trying to act like he wasn't excited just by the weight of it in his hand.

"That's a neat little weapon," Foley would tell him. "Just right, you want to carry it in your pocket, don't want it to show."

And the kid would hold it up, sighting down the alley casually, like he did this all the time, then put it back, reach for a bigger one.

When Foley came back, he'd pick up his newspaper, go back to working on the crossword. Danny'd sat at the counter one day, watched it happen. After Foley left, Danny walked over, picked up the newspaper, glanced at it. Foley'd gotten stuck on twenty-two across: a nine-letter word for "what an optimist sees in the mirror." Danny took out his pen, scribbled in *pessimist,* then dropped the paper in the trash.

Now Foley raised a hand to wave Danny over. Danny looked away, nodded toward the two black women. "Paying customers?"

Phuong glanced up at them, shrugged. "You think everybody like you?"

Danny smiled. She was a small Vietnamese woman, with cheekbones so sharp it made her face look like the stretched head of a drum. *Phuong.* He liked to say her name to himself, the sound of a wire cord snapping back against your fingers. She must have been in her late forties, but he'd never asked. She wore her short black hair pulled back tightly, making her eyes come at you like the glitter off a knife blade. *Phuong.*

"So?" she asked him, taking out a small pad. "You hungry?"

"Nah, I'm not hungry."

"Then why you here?"

Danny winked at her. "Same reason I always come here. See you."

She looked up at him from under her eyelids, smiled. "I tell my husband. You always come in here, flirt with me."

"Tell him. 'Bout time he had some competition."

"He jealous man."

"So am I." Danny reached out, slid the magazine out from under her elbow, glanced at it. *Ebony.* "Soup anywhere close to fresh?"

"He make it yesterday."

"Yeah? What's the occasion?" He glanced over at Foley, saw him watching, anxious. "Okay, I'll take a bowl of the soup."

"That's all?" She shook her head. "You get too skinny. Woman look at you, she not even see you. Look right through you."

Danny laughed. "Tell me about it." He walked back toward the toilets, saw Foley glance up from his newspaper as he approached.

"Hey, my man Danny. How's business?"

Danny slid into the booth. "I got no complaints."

"Yeah, I'll bet." Foley winked at him. He wore the same outfit every day. Suede jacket, jeans, cowboy boots. He was going bald on top, wore a little ponytail in back to balance it off. Made him look like one of those guys who hangs out at the Trailways station, waiting for teenage girls to get off the bus from Mobile.

"That's what I like about you, Danny," Foley said. "You the only guy I know ain't got nothing to sell." He laid his newspaper down on the table, stretched his shoulders lazily. "You're *pure.*"

Danny stared at him. The bell on the front door clattered as the two black women left. Phuong went over, started to clear the dishes off their table. "What's on your mind, Dewitt?"

Foley reached over, grabbed a menu out of the rack against the wall. "I'm hungry. What's good here?"

"Depends. What kind of thing you like?"

"I'm open-minded."

Danny turned, waved Phuong over. "Bring him some soup and an order of tiger prawns." He looked at Foley. "You like it hot?"

"What's hot?"

Danny turned back to Phuong. "Tell Claude to go easy." They watched her disappear into the kitchen.

"You come here a lot, huh?"

"Couple times a week. Since I was in law school."

Foley grinned. "I forgot you were a lawyer. What was it? U.S. Attorney's office, or some shit?"

Danny picked up the menu, shoved it back in the rack. "Assistant D.A."

"Jesus." Foley shook his head. "Things change, huh?"

"But enough about me."

Foley looked at him for a moment, then he smiled. "Just curious, that's all."

"You and the cat."

"Okay." Foley raised his hands, palms out. "You don't want to talk about it, I understand. That's cool."

Danny looked off across the restaurant. "Meanwhile . . ."

Foley sighed, reached under the table, picked up the briefcase and slid it across the table to Danny. "Tell Jimmy we ain't got much time here. He wants to clean up this mess, it better be quick."

Danny looked down at it, not moving. "That what I think it is?"

"You got a problem with that?"

"I might."

Foley grinned. "How much you take in every day, Danny? Really, just between us. What's an average day for you?"

Danny sat back, slowly.

"You ride all over the city, people give you envelopes full of money. You take it back, give it to Jimmy Boudrieux, he goes up to the Statehouse, gets things done. I guess you think that's different from what I got here, huh?" Foley shrugged. "Me, I don't see it." He sat back, rubbed at a scratch on the table with one finger. "You ever squeeze an orange, Danny?" He smiled. "My ex-wife, she always had to have fresh-squeezed orange juice. Every day. Like it's the only thing between her and a brain tumor. She used to come home from the store, big bags of oranges. Bought herself a little electric juicer. I'd sit there, watch her stuff six oranges into that thing, get, like, one cup of juice. Spit the seeds into the garbage can. I told her, 'Jesus, at least take the seeds out in the backyard, see if you can get 'em to grow. 'Cause you keep buyin' all these oranges, we're goin' under.'" He glanced over at the briefcase, his face suddenly serious. "That's what's in that briefcase, Danny. A couple seeds. 'Cause I'm gettin' squeezed, man. And I need some serious juice."

Danny looked at the briefcase on the table. "You done?"

Foley sat back slowly. He stared at Danny for a moment, then he gave a thin smile. "Nah, I got one more thing you can tell your boy Jimmy." He leaned forward, his voice dropping to a whisper. "I know a guy works down at the federal building, says he's heard the Feds have an informant up inside Jimmy's operation. This guy thinks he could get his hands on the guy's name, somebody makes it worth his effort. So you tell Jimmy, he helps me, maybe I can help him too."

Danny looked at him for a moment, silent. Then he slid out of the booth, picked up the briefcase. "Enjoy your dinner."

He walked back to the toilet, set the briefcase on the edge of the sink, took a deep breath before facing himself in the mirror over the sink. *Ah, Christ. Look at you, son.*

His eyes looked tired, and he could start to see his father's face, a guy in his forties, showing up around the edges. Weird how it happened when you weren't looking. Thirty-four years old, and what have you got to show for it?

Your father's face.

He ran some water over his hands, slid them through his hair. *You got to earn your own face. Until then, you're just playing around.*

"You know who you look like?" Helen asked him one night, back when they were first married. She raised her hand, ran it through his dark hair. "That guy in the Southern Bell commercial, used to call home from all those different places, talk to his little girl. You remember? He's standing in a phone booth, rain dripping down the glass, he's got those sad eyes, saying, 'Hi, baby. It's Daddy.' Made everybody cry."

Then she smiled, tugged at his hair. "Only you never call."

Danny winced at the memory. *Let it go. It's history.* Water under the bridge, mud under the water.

Bodies under the mud.

He glanced at the briefcase on the sink beside him. *Jesus.* In the pocket of his leather jacket, in a series of plain envelopes, was almost $40,000 in small, nonsequential bills. That's what it all came down to, he thought: law school, career, marriage, the whole thing. Just a guy in a beat-up leather jacket, walking around the city, his pockets stuffed with cash.

He picked up the briefcase, walked across the narrow hall, pushed the door to the kitchen open a few inches. "Hey, where's my soup?"

Claude Raymond glanced up at him, scowled. "You gonna have to wait. I ain't killed the dog yet."

Danny smiled, pushed through the door. The kitchen was small and hot, a couple of woks steaming over high flames. A small television flickered silently on top of the refrigerator, and a newspaper lay spread out across one of the counters, below a rack of gleaming knives. Claude took a porcelain bowl down from a stack on a high shelf, went over to a large pot on the stove, ladled out some thick brown soup, and set it down on the counter in front of Danny. Then he reached over to a stack of silverware, grabbed a spoon and a paper napkin. "You want a beer?"

"You buying?"

Claude looked at him. "When was the last time you paid for anything in here?" He opened a metal cooler next to the refrigerator, took out a bottle of Asahi. "This here's from my private stash, so try to look grateful." He opened the bottle against the edge of the counter, passed it to Danny.

"I'm grateful." He took a spoonful of the soup, held it up to cool. "But that don't mean I'm not gonna steal your wife one 'a these days."

Claude laughed. "Then I'll come on back here every night, watch *you* do the cooking." He leaned back on the counter, took a toothpick from a box next to the stove, stuck it between his teeth. He was a large black man, some gray hair just starting to show up in his beard the last couple years. He lifted weights every morning, but you could see that he was fighting a losing battle. His apron stretched tight across his stomach, and he'd taken to wearing those loose cotton drawstring pants you see guys wear in the movies when they're relaxing at their beach house in Malibu. Where Phuong seemed to get smaller, her skin drawn taut across her bones, Claude only seemed to expand. Danny found it funny, but he never said a word. Claude kept all his knives in that rack on the counter, and they were *sharp*.

"You really know how to cook a dog?"

Claude shrugged. "How you want it?"

Claude and Phuong had met in Saigon when Claude was there with the 1st Marine Division in 1969. He'd walked into a restaurant back in the piled-up buildings along the river, a place with chickens hanging in the window, off an alley where dogs snapped at each other while kids sat on their heels and watched, and he'd taken one look at the teenage girl behind the counter and realized he wasn't going home without her. Her parents worked back in the kitchen, swearing violently at each other. It took him a week to get her to look at him. A month later, he got some more R&R, came back. When Claude walked in the door, she glanced up at him, and he could tell she'd remembered. He had four days, and by the end of it, he'd coaxed her into talking to him briefly. A week later, he was wounded in a firefight outside Da Nang. They shipped him home, and he spent three months in a VA hospital in San Diego, thinking of her. When they discharged him, he got a job unloading trucks at the vegetable market, stuck with it until he had enough saved up to pay for a ticket back to Saigon.

He got a job as a driver with USIA, escorting visiting journalists to the whorehouses back of Bring Cash Alley. He stayed three years. Every afternoon, before he went to work, he'd hang out on the steps of a bar across the alley from the restaurant where she worked. Her parents, when they realized why he'd returned, forbade her to speak to him. Only when they saw the Americans starting to leave, saw the nervous looks in the eyes of the South Vietnamese soldiers who'd begun to flood into the city, did her father come to the door one afternoon, wave him inside.

Claude married her at the Saigon records office, ignoring the stares of other couples as they filled out the papers. The next day, her father led him back into the filthy kitchen behind their restaurant, pointed at a pile of dead chickens, and said, "You learn cook."

And he did. Danny'd never tasted food like it, anywhere. Creole recipes that Claude's mama had learned from the group of old black women who raised her in Bayou Lafouche, mixed with the taste and smell of Saigon. Eating it was like watching a couple make love, fiercely, in some cheap hotel room in a border town. All great food is paid for in blood; men will conquer half the world for a new spice. When Saigon fell, Claude brought his bride home to New Orleans. For fifteen years they worked in other people's kitchens, grilling steaks, frying seafood, mashing potatoes. But at home they cooked food that tasted like a lost war, and when they'd saved enough, they opened a tiny restaurant, named it Lotus Flower for all that could not be forgotten.

Danny sipped at his beer, glanced up at the television on top of the refrigerator. It was tuned to the late news. Danny'd met the anchorwoman at one of Jimmy Boudrieux's parties a few months back; she was a young black woman, with cheekbones so sharp they looked carved into stone. Now she looked up at the camera and began speaking as a graphic came up beside her, showing a handgun overlaid on a school textbook. They cut away to thirty seconds of footage on a schoolyard shooting up near Shreveport, back in the spring. Danny'd seen the footage before: tense-looking cops holding back a crowd as emergency medical squads loaded small bodies into an ambulance, a shot of an empty playground, one bloody sneaker lying forgotten near the swings, then a brief glimpse of a twelve-year-old white boy being led away in handcuffs, his face only visible for a moment before he pulled the hood of his jacket up to hide his face. The image on the screen changed abruptly to a crowd of young black children lined up in front of a school gym for the cameras, watching as Jimmy Boudrieux spoke to reporters. Jimmy had pulled his tie loose under the TV lights, held his jacket folded loosely in one hand, like a man who wasn't comfortable wearing such clothes. Like the kids, he wore a yellow badge pinned to his shirt that read I DID MY PART! As he talked he gestured broadly, and Danny could see sweat stains under the arms of his shirt.

"Hey, Claude." Danny pointed up at the TV. "You mind turning that up a minute?"

Claude glanced up from his newspaper, the toothpick moving between his teeth. "Your boy Jimmy's puttin' on some weight, there."

Danny smiled. "He went out last week, got himself a StairMaster. Spends an hour every day on that thing, bouncing away. You get behind him, looks like a guy juggling a couple watermelons." He nodded at the television. "How 'bout some sound?"

Claude reached up, turned up the volume, and Danny heard Jimmy Boudrieux say, "These children are our future, and they have a right to live without fear!"

Claude shook his head. "Jesus." He went back to his newspaper.

Danny picked up his soup, leaned on the counter, watching Jimmy Boudrieux make a speech calling for legislation that would ban the sale of firearms within 250 yards of a school.

Danny had to hand it to him; he looked as if he meant every word.

"Now, the governor got his concealed weapons bill last year."

Jimmy rested one hand gently on the shoulder of a small boy who stood beside him. "He got the votes of the good people of this state, so he came up to Baton Rouge, told us, 'You boys pass this bill,' and we did it." He paused, smiled at the boy, squeezed his shoulder gently. "But I got a question for the governor. He likes to talk about how we got something in this country called the Second Amendment, gives us the right to bear arms. And he's right. It's right there in the Constitution, you can look it up." He looked up at the crowd of reporters, his face suddenly serious. "But, I ask you, what about this boy's rights? Doesn't he have the right to a quality education, free of the fear of violence?"

He glanced up at the sky briefly, and Danny figured he'd just felt the first drops of the hard rain that had started to fall as he finished his speech, making the kids scatter toward the school's doors the moment the TV lights were switched off. Earlier in the day, Danny had watched the whole thing happen from the edge of the playground, standing with Lucas Clay, Jimmy's chief legislative aide, against the chain-link fence back along Esplanade Avenue. He'd had his eye on the clouds piling up in the sky out over the Gulf of Mexico from the moment they got out of the car. When Jimmy stepped before the TV lights, Danny leaned over, whispered to Lucas, "Twenty bucks, he doesn't make it through his speech."

He watched Lucas glance up at the sky, the clouds so thick now they looked like you could strike a match to 'em, set the whole sky aflame. A few drops splattered on the pavement near their feet. Lucas seemed to consider the sky carefully, then he lowered his gaze to the crowd that stood under a circle of television lights at one end of the schoolyard. "He always makes it."

Danny followed his gaze. There was a rainbow painted over the school's front door, with the words MARTIN LUTHER KING JR. MIDDLE SCHOOL printed over it in bright colors and a mural that showed a black man pointing toward a distant mountaintop. But out here on the playground, there were weeds growing up through the cracks in the concrete, rusted basketball hoops with no nets, and Danny couldn't see any mountains from where he stood, just a storm blowing in off the Gulf. The playground had been swept clean in anticipation of their arrival, but chunks of glass from a broken beer bottle glittered in the weeds along the fence.

A bright slash of lightning split the sky. Danny saw several of the TV lighting guys glance up at the clouds, worried about their equipment, but Jimmy didn't seem to notice, just kept on with his speech. Danny felt a drop of rain against his face.

"You're so sure," he told Lucas, "take the bet."

"I don't bet." Lucas gave a thin smile. "I'm the guy who runs the game."

Danny stared at him for a moment, then shook his head. "Jesus. How long you been waiting to say that?"

Lucas didn't answer, just stood there, his eyes on the crowd of reporters listening to Jimmy's speech. The rain was starting to make spots on his silk tie, but he gave no sign that he noticed. *Guy'd watch us all drown,* Danny thought, *before he'd admit he was wrong.*

Lucas had spent five years up in Baton Rouge working with Jimmy, but it was hard not to think that he'd been there his whole life. Look closely, you might catch a glimpse of him at the back of a crowd in the official photographs. Jacket and silk tie in two shades of gray; buffed-leather loafers with tassels. His hair was the color of the red dust hills in north Louisiana where he'd grown up, but his face was a politician's, always just glancing away. His eyes made Danny think of a fast ride on a back-country gravel road, your tires throwing up a cloud, making the world vanish in your wake.

Danny'd heard somewhere that Lucas was the son of a hardshell Baptist preacher in some one-trough town up in Ouachita Parish. But a man can change. Now he kept an autographed picture of James

Carville on his desk, carried a cellular phone in one hand at all times, like a card player with a five-ace deck.

At that moment Lucas was keeping his eye on a man who stood a few yards away from Jimmy, just outside of the bright pool of the TV lights. He was a large man, tall and solidly built, with thick gray hair. He wore faded jeans, hiking boots, and a thick sweater, so he looked like he'd just come in from hunting, set his rifle down next to the door. *That's how you know a really rich man,* Danny thought, smiling. *He's the guy who looks like he shoots his supper.* Buddy Jeanrette kept an office behind his gun warehouse up in Chalmette, spent more time behind his desk than he did outdoors. Danny had been out there to see him more than once in recent weeks, and the place looked like he'd ordered the whole thing out of a *Rocky Mountain Design* catalog, had them ship a cabin down from Boulder, complete with Navajo rugs on the walls, a stone fireplace, and a glass-fronted gun case that took up most of one wall. Framed photographs hung on all the walls, Buddy with different guns, standing next to the animals he'd just shot. There was a fire crackling in the fireplace, but the room always felt crisp, like he kept the air conditioner running all night so he could come in first thing in the morning, light a fire, and pull on one of those big sweaters he liked to wear. He kept the shades drawn, a couple sun lamps up in the corner of the ceilings giving the room a soft glow. But Danny somehow felt sure that if you raised the shades, looked out the window, you'd see snow-capped mountains, not some empty lot next to the Mississippi River, a chain-link fence with weeds growing along it.

At Buddy's feet were several large boxes of sports equipment that he'd brought along as a donation to the city's after-school programs. He smiled broadly, applauded at each pause in Jimmy's speech. Besides his sporting goods stores, Buddy Jeanrette owned the state's largest chain of handgun ranges. Two months ago he'd testified before a legislative committee on the need for firearms education. At Lucas

Clay's suggestion, he'd used the opportunity to propose an industry standard, which the legislature promptly adopted. Now he was building a chain of gun schools, attached to his stores, to meet the anticipated demand. And, as it happened, his largest competitor operated a chain of small-town gun stores, over half of which were located within 250 yards of a public school. So he stood there with those boxes of basketballs at his feet and a look on his face like there was no God but good works.

Jimmy paused in his speech, rubbed a hand across the back of his neck, slowly. Danny saw Lucas glance at his watch. Jimmy always did that when he reached the last few paragraphs of a speech, threw that little pause in there, rubbed at his neck like some kind of backcountry farmer trying to think of the best way back to the highway before he gave you directions. Danny asked one of the staffers in Jimmy's office about the gesture once. The guy grinned, said, "You know, I *wrote* that damn speech, right down to the last word, and even I was impressed by how he was up there, talking from the heart."

Politics, Danny thought, gave a smile. *Just remember your lines, and try not to bump into the furniture.*

After a moment, Jimmy lifted his head, turned to wave a hand at the crowd of children behind him. "These children," he said, his voice rising, "they're on the firing line every day of their young lives. So I say to the governor, if you oppose this legislation, come on down here and explain to them why their schools aren't safe. Come on down here and help these children understand why the sound of gunfire is the first thing they learn, before Shakespeare, before Lincoln, before the Constitution on which their rights are based. Come tell them, and then I'll understand."

Lucas flipped his phone open, hit two buttons, said, "He's done." And just at that moment, Danny heard a sound like faint whispering, and the rain began to fall. It came down suddenly, the sky going very dark, as if somebody had just pulled a curtain. The children ran for the school building, and the TV crews rushed to shut off their lights. A long black car pulled up at the entrance to the playground, and Jimmy Boudrieux turned, walked away toward it. The rain pelted the pavement around him, but he didn't hurry, barely seemed to notice it.

Danny reached back, raised the collar of his leather jacket against the rain. "He got lucky."

Lucas slipped the phone into his pocket. "You surprised?"

As Jimmy passed them, he pulled the yellow badge out of his shirt, handed it to Danny. Danny glanced at it—I DID MY PART! Then he shoved it into his pocket, walked away.

Now, watching it play out on the TV news, Danny had to smile. *Lucas Clay, man.* Only guy he knew who'd take credit for the *weather.* But he'd been right: the rain held off, and the news crews got their footage. They'd probably run the clips dozens of times over the next few days, and within a week, Jimmy would be up at the Statehouse, meeting with the governor, cutting a deal on the gun bill that would be good for them both. Watch it on TV, you couldn't see the rain that was getting ready to come down, the bored looks on the faces of the reporters as Jimmy spoke to the cameras, or the man who stood off to one side with his hands shoved in the pockets of his expensive suit, watching it all unfold.

The TV cut away to an interview with a spokesman for the governor, who declared the governor's willingness to consider any measure that would ensure the safety of the state's schools. Claude glanced up at it, yawned. "You hear what you wanted?"

"Yeah, I'm good."

Claude reached up, turned it down. "We got to get you a life, son. It's bad enough you got to listen to that shit *once.*"

Danny smiled, picked up his beer. "You ever take one of those bayou cruises, down to Honey Island?"

Claude shrugged. "I took Phuong out there once when we first moved back here. She said it looked like where she grew up."

Danny rolled the beer bottle slightly between his palms, feeling the glass wet and cold on his skin. "You remember how they'd knock on the side of the boat, all those gators would come running down into the water, swim over to the boat?"

Claude laughed. "Yeah, sure. Scared the shit out of me."

"All the tourists screaming."

"Got to give 'em their money's worth."

Danny sipped at his beer, then set it down. It felt better just rolling the bottle between his hands. "You ever wonder how come those gators never figured it out?"

"What's to figure out? They ride out there every couple days, throw some chicken over the side, keeps 'em interested."

Danny nodded. "Yeah, but think about it. You're a gator, this boat goes past a couple times a day, full of people. They bang on the side, and you swim on out there. Got your taste up for chicken. But the boat just keeps going, right? Then every couple days, the boat comes back, but it's just the one guy, and he starts throwing chicken at you. After a while, you might figure it out."

Claude looked at him. "They're *gators,* Danny."

"Yeah, I guess." Danny smiled down at his beer. "Thing is, I'm starting to understand how they feel."

Claude sighed, shook his head. "I got to start putting more heat in that soup. Do something to wake your ass *up,* son."

Danny raised his beer bottle to his mouth, drained it. Phuong pushed the kitchen door open a crack and stuck her head through. "Did you ask him?" she said to Claude.

"Nah, not yet. He was eating."

"So? He done eating now." She went back into the dining room, the door swinging closed behind her.

Danny looked over at Claude. "What's up?"

"We got another problem with the landlord. Guy wants to start charging us for extra garbage pickup, claims it's in the lease." Claude looked down at his feet, frowned. "Phuong said I should ask you to take a look at it."

"Sure." Danny leaned over, tossed the beer bottle into the garbage can next to the stove. "You got it here?"

Claude pushed off the counter, went over to a file cabinet in the corner, dug through one of the drawers until he found a sheaf of papers, brought it back to Danny. "We got a letter yesterday. Says emptying our Dumpster twice a week comes under 'extraordinary charges,' on page three." He waved a hand at the stack of papers on top of the file cabinet. "I got the letter around here somewhere."

Danny flipped through the papers. Claude reached over, pointed to one of the sections, and Danny read through it carefully. "How long they been emptying your Dumpster, no charge?"

Claude shrugged. "Six, seven years."

"And nothing's changed?"

"Not till they sent us the letter."

Danny studied the lease. "The language isn't real clear. But the fact they've been doing it for years without charging you works in your favor." He tossed the papers on the counter. "You want me to send him a letter, challenge it?"

"Like our lawyer?"

Danny smiled. "I think I can still fake it."

Claude went over to the stove, stirred the soup with a wooden spoon. "So how come you don't open an office? Get some clients."

"I got a job."

Claude looked over at him. "Uh-huh. You in politics."

"Only game in town." Danny grinned. "Hey, you want, I can put your letter on Jimmy's stationery. That'll catch the guy's attention."

"Nah," Claude went back to stirring the soup. "I got enough problems."

They heard the bell on the restaurant's front door clatter.

"Sounds like you got some business." Danny glanced through the window in the kitchen door, saw two white men come in. One of them held the door open for two black teenagers in red sweatshirts, their hoods pulled up against the rain.

Claude turned to the stove, raised the flame under one of the woks. "Bout fuckin' time we got somebody *paid* for their food."

Danny saw that the white guys both had their hair cut very short, wore sport coats over jeans, cowboy boots. *Cops,* he thought. *Looking for a quiet place to have a talk, off the street.* The two black kids looked around nervously. One of the white men silently pointed them toward a table.

Danny turned, set his soup bowl in the sink full of dirty dishes, watched it float for a moment in the filthy water, then slowly fill and sink. "I better take off."

"Man's waitin' for his money, huh?"

"We're all waiting for something." Danny picked up the briefcase, pushed the screen door open, stepped out into the alley behind the kitchen. He stood there for a moment, eyes closed, his face raised into the falling rain. He felt tired, empty.

He walked down the alley, unlocked his car, tossed the briefcase on the passenger seat. Then he straightened up, glanced back at the restaurant. *Shit. He didn't give you the landlord's letter. You can't write to the guy, you don't have his address.*

He locked the car, walked back up the alley. A garbage truck turned in at the end of the street, and he had to step back into a doorway, wait for it to rumble slowly past. He paused, wincing as he watched it try to squeeze past his Mustang. He drove a '67 soft-top, pale blue, which he'd picked up a few years back at an auction down at the city seizure garage. Or rather, he'd gone down the day before the auction, had a talk with the guy who ran the garage, then showed up the next day to watch a pair of middle-aged doctors bid the car up over

$12,500 before he put in the winning bid. Then he walked over to the cashier's window, passed her the note that the garage manager had scribbled for him, and paid her the $7,900 they'd agreed upon the day before, in cash, small bills. The car spent as much time in the garage as on the road, but he loved it. Only problem was finding some place in New Orleans to park it without worrying that some kid would come along, run a key down the door, or just slit the top open, splice the wires under the dash, and drive it away. There were moments when Danny thought it might almost be a relief.

Now, watching the truck squeeze into the narrow gap between the car and the wall across from it, Danny was sure he was about to lose his side mirror. But the truck inched slowly forward, its brakes groaning loudly as the driver worked them so hard that the truck rocked on its springs. He backed off, found a couple extra inches on his right, swung clear of the car's rear fender. Danny watched as the truck squeezed through, rolled away down the alley, picking up speed. Then he turned, walked back toward the restaurant. The rain was coming down harder now; it ran down the back of his neck, getting under his jacket. *Nothing you can do, son. Just got to take it.*

Hell, you should be good at that by now.

He reached the kitchen door, glanced in through the screen. The kitchen was empty. Smoke rose from a wok that hissed and spit over a high flame, oil splattering the stove. Over in the sink, the water was running. The TV flickered on top of the refrigerator, silent.

Danny opened the door, stepped inside. "Claude?"

There was no answer, just the sound of oil popping, water running steadily in the sink. He went over to the swinging door that led into the dining room, glanced through the window. He could see a few empty tables, the cash register, and the front door beyond. Nothing moved; the whole scene was like a photograph somebody'd cut out of a magazine, pasted to the door. His hand came up, started to push the door open.

Then he froze.

At the lower corner of the window, something moved. Danny looked at it, the way a man might watch the wind moving in the trees. For a moment, it was no more than that.

And then, suddenly, it was.

A man's hand lay on the floor beneath one of the tables, palm up. The fingers were curled slightly, like a crab lying on the beach, its legs in the air. The fingers twitched once, as if grasping at something, and then lay still. Danny stared at it, uncomprehending.

Then he saw something moving beside it, like a worm making its slow way across the floor tiles. It took Danny a moment to realize what he was seeing.

Blood.

Danny felt the breath freeze in his lungs. He stood there, not moving. Behind him, the oil popped angrily in the wok.

Somewhere off in the distance, the rain began to come down hard.

2

"You ever eat in this place?" Detective Tom Acorsi swung the unmarked Ford up onto the sidewalk behind an ambulance, its lights flaring red across the wet street.

His partner, Maya Thomas, glanced up at the restaurant. It had bamboo shades in the windows, a flower painted on the glass, some kind of Vietnamese boat drifting down a river. "Not my neighborhood. You?"

Acorsi shook his head. "Drive past it all the time." He reached across the front seat to dig his notebook out of the glove box. "Don't look like we'll get much of a chance now."

Three patrol cars were pulled up in front of the entrance, doors open. A pair of uniformed cops was stringing crime scene tape across the empty sidewalk. An emergency medical crew lifted a metal gurney out of the back of the ambulance and carried it across the sidewalk. One of the cops grabbed the door for them, then let it swing slowly closed.

Acorsi sighed, shook his head. "Friday night."

"Everybody loves a party."

Acorsi glanced over at Maya. Her eyes were tired. They'd been partners for two years, and it never failed to amaze him how she moved through the city, working homicides in neighborhoods where you can buy crack on every corner but it takes a forty-minute bus ride to get groceries, where a teenager with a 9 mm semiautomatic pistol shoved in the waistband of his jeans carries more authority than the cop who cruises past in his squad car—and yet, when they pulled up next to the yellow tape at a crime scene and pushed through the crowd to get to the body, there'd be some kid who'd yell out, "Hey, *Maya*! Mama says when you gonna come by for that crab pot?"

And she'd turn to glare at him, hands on her hips, call out, "Yo, Jarr*att*! Can't you see I'm *workin'* here, boy?" Then, shaking her head, "You tell her I come by tomorrow. How that be?"

She had family scattered across the city, and her husband worked in the mayor's community development office. *She's more New Orleans than me,* Acorsi thought, though he'd grown up in Bucktown, played high school ball at Jesuit before joining the NOPD. Most of the old Italian families he'd known growing up had moved out to the suburbs, or up across the lake to Slidell. So if she'd had to fight to survive the academy, shut her ears to the silence that greeted her when she came into the squad room in those first few years, then the future was her reward. She'd made homicide the same year that New Orleans had secured its place at the top of the national murder statistics, and their jobs were nothing if not secure. All you had to do was not think too hard about what the job was all about: those young men staring out from the case folders that passed across your desk. For an Italian kid from Bucktown, it wasn't too bad. But in recent months, he'd begun to notice Maya sitting at her desk, staring hard at a photograph of some black kid in their files, as if *willing* herself not to recognize the face.

Maya felt his gaze, glanced over at him, and Acorsi quickly looked away.

"What?" she said.

He shook his head, stuffed his notebook in the pocket of his raincoat. "You ready?"

Maya got out and ran across the sidewalk to the restaurant's door through the falling rain. When they'd first become partners, he'd spent the first couple weeks sneaking looks at her in the car. She wore her hair long, pulled back into a braid. Her face was thin, with high cheekbones and skin that was the color of good bourbon whiskey.

He got out, followed her, holding his notebook over his head to keep the rain out of his eyes. A uniformed cop looked up at them from under the hood of his slicker. Maya flashed her badge at him, and the man stepped back, swung the door open for them.

Inside, another uniform glanced up at them from where he was kneeling beside an overturned table and called out "Watch the prints!"

Acorsi saw Maya glance down at her feet, then step carefully around a smear of blood on the floor. The floor near the entrance was already wet from where the cops had tracked in rain, but Acorsi could see that somebody had marked a bloody footprint near the front counter, put a chair over it to protect it. A flashlight stood a few feet away, marking another one. Nearby, somebody had vomited on the linoleum floor.

Acorsi let his eyes move across the room, taking it all in. A white man lay beside a table near the kitchen, shot in the face. He lay on his back, one hand flung out, like a center fielder stretching up for a long fly ball. A gun lay next to his hand. Not far away, two black teenagers lay among the tables, both shot in the chest. Acorsi saw two more guns on the floor near them. Shell casings lay scattered across the floor. The last two bodies—an Asian woman and a black man wearing an apron—lay side by side against a back wall, in the corridor leading back to the toilets. There was blood smeared across the wall above them, as if somebody had made them stand against the wall, then just started shooting.

"Sweet Jesus." Maya stripped off her raincoat, draped it over a table. Then she took out her notebook and walked back through the room slowly, past the bodies scattered across the floor. Acorsi pulled off his raincoat, tossed it on the corner table next to Maya's, went over to where an ambulance attendant knelt beside one of the black teenagers. As Acorsi came up to him, the man stood up, rubbed at his neck wearily.

"Any survivors?"

The attendant shook his head. "Nah, they're all meat."

Maya went back into the kitchen, then came out again, walked over to Acorsi, scribbling something in her notebook. "Okay, we got five dead. Gunshot wounds. I count three weapons." She turned, nodded to the black teenagers. "Two here, one back there by the white guy. By the iron on the floor, I'm guessing we got more than ten shots fired."

"Jesus." Acorsi shook his head. "Some party."

The floor around the bodies was covered with blood. The air smelled like faded roses. Behind that, there was the smell of whiskey. Some bottles on a shelf behind the cash register were broken, and a pool of pale liquor dripped slowly onto the floor below. A fly circled lazily above it, then settled briefly on the shattered bottle. After a few seconds, it flew away. The cash register stood open, the drawer empty.

Acorsi walked back to the kitchen. Smoke was rising from a blackened wok, a high flame under it. A screen door led out into an alley. Otherwise, there wasn't much to see. A television flickered on top of the refrigerator, Roger Clemens on the mound out in Anaheim. Acorsi watched it for a moment, but they didn't show the score.

He went back to where Maya was standing by the cashier's counter. She had her notebook open, drawing a crude sketch of the room. She scribbled a few words at the bottom of the page, then went back to her drawing, marking the position of each body carefully with an X.

When she looked up, he said, "You recognize anybody?"

She shook her head. "Those two boys are wearing Conti Street colors, but I've never seen them before."

"Pretty far out of their territory."

Maya glanced down at them, her face tight. "You could say that, yeah." She turned, nodded to the dead man lying by the kitchen door. "Guy back there looks familiar. Might help if they hadn't shot him in the face."

Acorsi glanced back at the guy. "Not much of a loss, by the look of him." He waved one of the uniformed cops over. "You the first one on the scene?"

"Uh-huh." The cop took out a handkerchief, sneezed loudly into it, twice. Then he wiped his nose. "Me and my partner. He's outside, hanging tape."

"What can you tell me?"

The cop shoved his handkerchief into his pocket, dug out a notebook. "Nine-one-one call came in at ten thirty-two from the phone out front. Somebody dialed the number, set the phone down." Acorsi glanced at the phone behind the counter, saw it was off the hook. "My partner and me, we'd just cleared on a B and E over on Napoleon, so we got the call. Just figured it was a routine thing, you know? You get these kids call up nine-one-one all the time, they don't know it brings up the address on the dispatcher's computer. But we got to roll on every call. Mostly it's nothing. Cat knocked the phone off the hook, stepped on the auto dial. Stupid shit like that. We show up, everything's okay." He waved a hand toward the bodies scattered around the room. "Anyway, you see what we found. They come in, emptied the cash register, shot up the place."

Acorsi didn't say anything for a moment. He stood there, hands on his hips, letting his eyes wander across the room. "Any idea who made the call?"

The cop shrugged. "Nine-one-one operator said she figured it must have been after all the shooting was over. She stayed on the line, didn't hear any shots."

Acorsi looked up at him, raised his eyebrows.

The cop looked embarrassed. "Just thought I'd check, you know? While we were waiting for you to get here."

"No, that's good. Nice to see somebody on the ball."

The cop flushed, glanced away. Behind him, Acorsi saw Maya give a faint smile. He nodded at the bloody shoe print near the entrance. "Who marked that?"

"Me." The cop paused, sneezed again, twice. "Goddamn rain." He took out his handkerchief, blew his nose loudly. "Saw that print first thing when I came through the door. Figured I better put something over it before we got too many people walking around in here."

Acorsi went over to the shoe print, moved away the chair that protected it. "So somebody walked out of here after the bodies hit the floor."

A man's shoe, he figured. Or a boot, maybe. Round toe, a little line of blood along the front of the heel. He put his own foot next to it, comparing, then glanced up at Maya. "You ever see somebody shoot five people, dial nine-one-one on his way out the door?"

She looked up from her notebook. "Be pretty surprising."

"Witness?"

"You think they'd shoot five people, let somebody walk out of here?"

He shrugged. "It happens. Maybe he was in the toilet." He glanced at the front door. "Or maybe somebody walked in after, found the place like this."

"So why didn't he stick around?"

"Didn't want his name in the papers, have to testify at trial. Shit, I wasn't a cop, I'd probably do the same thing."

She looked around the room. "Not much use speculating about it. Tech guys get here, we'll get 'em to dust the phone for prints, get some blues to canvass the neighborhood, see if anybody ordered takeout."

Acorsi went around behind the counter, found an order pad next to the register. He flipped through it, scribbled some phone numbers in his notebook, then tore out the page. He glanced up at the cop. "What's your name?"

"Foret. Ronnie Foret."

"Okay, Ronnie." Acorsi slid the page across the counter to him. "How 'bout you run out to your unit, get on the radio, see if you can get us some addresses to go with these."

The cop picked up the paper. "No problem. You want me to check 'em out, after?"

"That's the next step."

The cop nodded, walked out. Acorsi looked at Maya, saw her smiling. "You planning to run for mayor?" she asked.

He shrugged. "Never hurts to have friends on patrol."

The crime scene technicians came in and unpacked their equipment on a clean section of floor by the front window. Acorsi set one to work dusting the phone and cash register for fingerprints, sent the other into the kitchen to do the back door. After a moment, the technician poked his head through the kitchen door and called out, "You got any problem if I shut off the stove back here? Probably be a good idea, we don't burn down the building."

Acorsi was crouched down beside the Asian woman, examining the gunshot wounds in her chest and abdomen. He glanced up at the technician, surprised. "Yeah, no problem."

Two years on the job, that was something that still got to him— some guy would get shot down, bleed to death in the street, you'd go to his apartment, there'd be a pot of soup cooking on the stove, a half-eaten sandwich on the kitchen counter, a note stuck to the refrigerator saying *Went out. Back in a minute.*

Nobody saw it coming. Even a guy who'd made enemies, survived two shootings already, he'd run out to the corner store, leave his kid asleep on the couch. Two hours later, the cops would show up at the apartment, find the kid watching *Barney,* his thumb in his mouth.

"Daddy go out," he'd tell them, then go back to watching Barney and some kids dancing with purple umbrellas in a gentle rain. And so the cops would wander through the apartment, trying to figure out if there was a mother they could call, tell her the kid's father was lying on the sidewalk out in front of their building, with a sack of groceries beside him and most of his face blown away by a shotgun blast.

Acorsi straightened, went back to the register, stood there letting his eyes move slowly over the scene. Something about the whole thing felt wrong to him. Too many bodies, not enough motive. Who'd stick up a Vietnamese restaurant, slaughter everyone in the place, just to empty the cash register?

Maya came over next to him. "So how do you figure it?"

"Cash register's empty. *Looks* like a robbery. But there's a lot of blood on the floor for a couple hundred bucks."

She looked over at the two black boys. "Not if it's a gang thing. We've seen this kind of violence before with gang robberies. Those liquor store holdups last year over in Harahan. They bust in, hold the place up—only somebody pulls a gun, they end up painting the walls with blood."

"You think a gang would leave a couple of their guys lying here?"

She shrugged. "Could be they didn't expect a fight. They're kids. Once the bullets start flying, they panic, take off. Nobody thinks about counting heads until it's too late." She glanced at the bodies scattered around the room, shook her head. "Makes as much sense as anything."

Acorsi was silent. He could see what she was thinking. *More dead black kids.*

3

Danny sat in his car, staring at his hands resting on the wheel. The muscles in his fingers twitched slightly, like the flame of a candle, flickering out. He closed his eyes, felt the breath come sharp and tight in his throat.

Jesus. And suddenly, it all came flooding back. The blood on the floor, the silence. Phuong's eyes, staring up at him, empty.

He felt a wave of nausea sweep over him, swallowed back something that rose in his throat. He opened his eyes, looked out at the big houses along Audubon Place, their windows lit up like a promise. A row of cars was parked along the median strip, and a cop in a rain slicker sat on the hood of a patrol car, listening to a ball game on a small radio. Jimmy Boudrieux was throwing a party, and he needed somebody to keep an eye on his guests' cars. Danny watched the cop lazily wave the traffic past. Easy shift, and Jimmy gives a nice tip at the end. Not a bad way to spend a summer night.

Danny looked away, a metal taste in his mouth. His throat still felt raw, tight. He opened his mouth, taking deep breaths of the moist night air. Like he could drink it in, wash that smell from his throat. It was the smell that had gotten to him as he stood there, staring at the bodies. Sweet, like flowers. And it was that thought that had made him suddenly gag, made him bend over, throw up the soup he'd eaten onto the floor at his feet.

Danny looked down at his hands. He could remember reaching across the counter to pick up the phone, dialing 911, then pausing to wipe the fingerprints from the receiver with the end of his shirt before he set it down on the counter, turned to walk back through the kitchen, out the screen door to the alley beyond. He remembered the feeling of the rain on his face as he ran toward his car. Then driving, the rain smearing the taillights of the car in front of him across his windshield.

Like blood.

The rain had stopped now. The night air smelled fresh, as if the rain had washed it clean. From somewhere, faint music drifted on the air.

He glanced down at his hands again. Quieter now. He took them off the wheel, looked at them.

Like a pair of white crabs, washed up on an empty shore.

He pushed the thought away, looked over at the briefcase on the seat beside him. He sat there for a moment, staring at it, then he reached over, unsnapped the clasps, and lifted the lid. Inside were four handguns: two revolvers and a pair of semiautomatics. Under each of them was a slip of paper, folded once. Danny reached over, slid one out. He unfolded it, then leaned across the seat to read what was written there by the faint glow from a streetlight. It was a photocopy of an NOPD computer printout, entitled *Bulletproof,* which gave summaries of two recent homicide cases, one in Gretna back in June 1995, and one in St. Bernard Parish in February 1997, in which the ballistics evidence—right twist at 1/5 degrees, six lands, with a characteristic pattern of breech face and firing pin markings left on the test-fired cartridge—matched a single handgun, a Star Model BKM 9 mm locked breech semiautomatic pistol. Danny glanced over at the briefcase; the gun had some words engraved along the slide. He tipped the briefcase slightly until the metal barrel caught the faint light from the glove box: *STAR, B. Echeverria, Eibar, Espana, S.A. Cal. 9 m/m P.* The gun looked battered, like it had seen some use over the years. There was a deep scar across the side of the grip, near the screw head, like somebody had tried to unscrew it and slipped with the screw-

C o l d
S t e e l
R a i n

driver. He looked back at the paper. According to the printout, the gun had been recovered at the arrest of a suspect in the 1997 case—Samuel "Shorty" Generis—submitted for ballistics examination, then tagged and bagged in the evidence room of the St. Bernard sheriff's department. There was a mark on the photocopy next to the St. Bernard case, where a Post-it tag had been left on during copying. Somebody had scrawled a phone number on it, the last few numbers cut off by the edge of the page.

Danny slid the paper back under the gun, closed the briefcase, then rubbed at his eyes with the heels of both hands. Two murder cases. The gun had been used before, seized as evidence, and now it was back on the street.

He glanced up at the brightly lit house across the street. Music drifted toward him. *What could Lucas Clay want with a briefcase full of guns?*

Suddenly the taste of metal was back in his mouth. *Go,* he thought. *Just start the car and get out of here.* He could cruise around until morning, stop at the bank up on Veterans where he kept $15,000 in cash and his passport in a safe deposit box for emergencies, then just get on I-10, head west until he hit the Texas border, in Houston by lunchtime. Sell the car, stick the briefcase in a bus station locker for safekeeping, catch a flight out to Cancún. Call Lucas when he got there, tell him where to pick up the guns.

But even as he thought it, sitting there on Audubon Place, music drifting toward him across the moist air, he knew he wouldn't do it.

He reached over, opened the glove box. Inside, under a New Orleans street map, lay a compact 9 mm Beretta semiautomatic he'd bought a few years back when he started working for Jimmy Boudrieux, riding around New Orleans with thick wads of cash in his pockets. He'd shoved the gun in the glove box, just for security, and left it there. Now he stared at it for a long moment; the faint light gleamed on the metal frame. Then he reached over, slid the gun out, and stuffed it into the pocket of his leather jacket.

He got out of the car, took the briefcase with him. As he waited for a break in the traffic, he raised a hand to the cop, saw him nod, letting Danny know he'd keep an eye on the car. Danny crossed the street, walked up the driveway to Jimmy's house. He could hear the music more clearly now, light jazz, which meant that Lucas had gotten to the sound system again. You could tell the guy was born to be a politician, every time he put on Kenny G.

Jimmy Boudrieux, the Speaker of the Louisiana House of Representatives, liked to tell people that he was the third most powerful man in the state, after the governor and Jimmy Lee, the head football coach up at LSU. But that was a few years back, before the election of Governor Russell Fordet, a conservative Republican from Shreveport who won the Statehouse on a platform of moral renewal, school prayer, and reform of gun laws. Now, Boudrieux told his closest friends, he saw a chance to move up.

"We gave him the gun bill, up front. Let him have the headlines the first couple weeks. So now he sends me down this school prayer bill, tells me he wants it passed this session. I tell him, 'You want school prayer? Hey, no problem. Which one you want, bro? Baptist or Cat'lic?'" Boudrieux grinned. "Hell, I know a guy down at Temple Islam, he's all set to demand *Muslim* prayers during Ramadan." He drained his whiskey glass, caught a piece of ice between his teeth, cracked it loudly. "By the time the governor gets the shit off his face on that one, we got nothing to worry about."

Watching him, Danny always thought of the time—God, twenty years back, now—when he'd gone deer hunting with his father and Jimmy on some wild acreage Jimmy owned up by Ponchatoula. It was the evening before Danny had shot his first buck. They were sitting on the porch of the little cabin that Jimmy'd had the highway department put up for him a few years before, getting a friend in Baton Rouge to designate it a survey hut because of the two wheel tracks that ran through the pine trees three quarters of a mile in from the main road. They'd sat in the pale light of a propane lamp, his father and Jimmy sipping from their glasses, watching as Danny took his first taste of Jack Daniel's. He was fourteen, but tall for his age. He choked back the flame that seemed to ignite in his throat, fixed his eyes on the darkness among the trees until the tears subsided. Without a word, he raised the glass again, took another sip, and when his throat cleared, he managed to wheeze out, "Like drinking fire."

Jimmy burst out laughing, said, "Boy's a poet, Roy." But Danny could still see the look in his father's eye, feel the weight of the hand that settled on his shoulder.

Later, they extinguished the lamp and sat silent in the darkness, Jimmy holding a flashlight across his lap for almost forty minutes, until they heard a rustling in the bushes near the spot where they'd tossed the chicken bones from their dinner. Jimmy flicked on the flashlight, trapped a racoon in its beam. It sat hunched beside the trash pile, gazing up at them calmly with its black eyes. It held a chicken wing between its paws, and as they watched, the racoon slowly raised the chicken bone to its mouth, took one careful bite. It seemed to study them as it chewed, then turned slowly, grasped the bone in its teeth, and walked away into the darkness.

Jimmy laughed, shaking his head. "Man, you got to steal, that's how you do it. Look 'em in the eye, huh?"

And that, Danny thought, was what Jimmy Boudrieux had been doing for the last seventeen years. Stealing with both hands, and making everyone smile as he did it. He'd faced down three corruption probes during his rise to the Speaker's chair, and a fourth seemed imminent. But here he was, holding forth in the garden of his house a block off St. Charles, in one of the most expensive neighborhoods in

New Orleans, surrounded by an admiring crowd of politicians, journalists, and lobbyists, all of 'em laughing as he told stories about the
old days, when the Statehouse was secure in the hands of good, corrupt
Democrats, who got the vote out and sent the money home.

"You clean up Louisiana politics, you know what ev'body run on,
huh?" Jimmy swirled his whiskey glass, letting the soft evening light
fill it with gold. "Race. Or crime, and turns out that's the same damn
thing." He raised his glass, drained it. "Only a matter of time, one 'a
these clowns wants to run all the niggers out of New Orleans gets in
the Statehouse." He leaned toward a light-skinned black woman who
covered state politics for the *Times-Picayune,* smiled at her. "Margie,
you know what you get, you take the niggers out of New Orleans?"

The reporter held his gaze for a moment, then shook her head
slowly. "No, Jimmy. What?"

"Tulsa." Jimmy threw his head back, laughed. "I'm tellin' you. Me,
I like my whiskey straight, but you makin' a gumbo, you *might* want
to stir it." He glanced around at the crowd, gestured with his empty
glass. "We can get rich together, but we get poor, we come apart."

And the crowd around him nodded, sipped at their drinks in the
warm summer evening. Nobody questioned how Jimmy Boudrieux
could afford such a house—with its high ceilings, polished oak floors,
a swimming pool gleaming at the foot of the garden—on a state legislator's salary. As several of the journalists had discovered, it would
have been futile to inquire, since on the record the house was owned
by Jimmy's elderly aunt, who rarely left her tiny house in Amite, and
never to come into the city. No one asked why such a woman had felt
the need to purchase the house in her seventy-fifth year, to pay for it in
cash and expensively redecorate. Such questions were better left
unasked, especially on a warm summer evening when the oak trees
seemed to gather the fading light in their branches, and the ice in your
glass made a sound like coins falling. Even at a wedding, no one hur-
ries to lift the veil.

So no one glanced at Danny Chaisson as he stood beneath an oak tree strung with colored lights. He moved his eyes over the crowd, looking for Lucas Clay, feeling the weight of the gun in his pocket, the briefcase heavy in his hand. He knew many of the people who came to Jimmy's parties, had gone to school with them, hung out with them on the lakefront in the summers. Or he knew their kids, had stopped by their houses on Saturday nights to pick up their daughters, taking 'em out to Tipatina's or Mulate's. That's how it was, if you grew up in New Orleans. You knew everybody, and everybody knew you.

Until, like Danny, you stumbled.

"Don't let it fool you," Jimmy said, smiling at the woman from the *Times-Picayune.* "The governor, he's a sharp politician. He ran a smart campaign, that's why he won." He reached back, ran his glass along the base of his neck, like a man who'd been working hard in a strong sun. "You know how he got his name?"

"How?" The woman smiled, waiting.

"Used to pronounce it *For-day,* back when I knew his daddy. Good man, ran a pharmacy up in Morgan City. But Russell, when he got into politics, he changed it. He was runnin' for the Parish council, used to go 'round the little towns up there, talkin' to the voters. They'd say, 'Son, we need us a new firehouse up y'here. How you stand on dat?' And old Russ, he'd say, 'Yup, I'm for dat!'"

Danny watched the woman laugh, raising her glass so that it caught her smile. She met Jimmy's gaze as she tipped the glass back, let a piece of ice slide between her teeth.

"That on the record, Jimmy?"

"Damn right! You can quote me on dat one, yeah."

Danny glanced at his watch. Jimmy's parties often ran late into the night, the crowd shrinking to a tight knot of journalists gathered around him, waiting for the bourbon to take its toll and the stream of good ol' boy stories to give way to a sudden flurry of attacks, laced with obscenities, on the state's most prominent political figures. It was at this moment that Lucas Clay would appear at the kitchen door, push his way through the crowd to take Jimmy's arm gently, and say—

"Phone call, Jimmy."

And Jimmy, glancing over at him, would flush, drain his glass, and give an apologetic shrug. "Gotta take this call, folks." And with a worried glance at the bar, "Go easy on my booze, hear? I got the Daughters of the Confederacy comin' by tomorrow."

Then, with a conspiratorial wink for the evening's favored journalist, he'd make his way through the crowd, crook a finger at Danny, standing with his briefcase under an oak tree, and vanish into the house.

And Danny would follow him. Every time, like he was born to do it. And, in a sense, he was. Danny's father, Roy Chaisson, had spent his life in politics. *Louisiana* politics. Not, as the man said, the art of the possible, but a *mystery,* a craft whose secrets were closely held. Even as a boy, Danny had watched his father work the phones late into every night. Gossip, strategy, angry shouting that could blister the paint off the kitchen walls when he felt betrayed. Later, as he watched power shift from the oak-lined streets of the Garden District to men from small bayou towns, or districts in the red dust hills upstate that seethed with Baptist indignation, Roy Chaisson laid his money on a dark horse, then stepped back into the shadows. In twelve years, Jimmy Boudrieux rose from a freshman state legislator from a district in St. Tammany Parish to Speaker of the State House of Representatives, playing off family connections in the white-glove society of uptown New Orleans against his image as a backwoods Cajun operator, a man as comfortable throwing dice on the pine floor of a roadhouse back room as he was in the offices of the state's most powerful men.

Louisiana politics, for Jimmy Boudrieux, was the art of the *improbable,*
a chance to see just how far a man can go before the crowd starts to
shuffle its feet, mutter to itself, and you know it's time to get the car
running. But when that time came, man, you'd have to *drag* him
away, because Jimmy loved it, with all his heart.

And Roy Chaisson went with him each morning, leaving his big
house a block off St. Charles to work the county fairs, the back rooms,
the tide of undeclared money that flowed through the state's political
landscape like a bayou, making it fertile, draining its harvest away.
Roy Chaisson waded into that swamp with both feet, and in the end,
it drowned him. He died when Danny was still in high school, his car
found in a gravel parking lot off River Road, halfway back to New Orleans from a meeting at the Statehouse in Baton Rouge, a suitcase full
of cash on the seat beside him and a single bullet in his head. The
gun—a .38 revolver, one shot fired—lay beside his hand. Danny's
mother identified it as the gun he kept beneath the driver's seat of his
car, for safety. He left no note, but a secretary in Jimmy Boudrieux's
office said he'd seemed "thoughtful" when he'd left, and on the morning of his funeral, the newspapers reported that he'd been the subject
of an FBI investigation into political corruption at the highest levels
of the state's political machine. That afternoon, Jimmy Boudrieux
gave a moving eulogy at Roy Chaisson's funeral, reminding the crowd
of mourners about his lifetime of service to the state and attacking
those who would soil his reputation in death.

And the Feds quietly closed their books on the matter.

Damn right, Danny thought, smiling. *Might as well let the dead lie,
'cause the living sure as hell will.*

But that was the whole problem. The dead didn't stay dead; they
showed up in your mirror every morning, staring back at you with
tired eyes. *Asking you how you ended up right back here, after all that.* In
the years after his father's death, Danny had graduated from Tulane,

put in three years at law school, landed a job as an assistant district attorney. Got married, bought furniture, even thought he was happy for a while.

Until it all came apart in your hands.

Three years ago, Danny'd left the D.A.'s office, gone to work for Jimmy. He didn't talk about why, and nobody asked. Most nights, Danny's job was to stand beneath the ancient oak in the garden, briefcase in his hand. *Like a warning,* he thought, bitterly. *An object lesson.* Pray your luck holds out, while the evening still seems a piece of silk draped across the oak trees, and Jimmy still moves easily through the crowd, grasping hands, throwing his head back to give his deep laugh. *'Cause this is what it could all come to, son. All your waking dreams, those futures that collect in the bottom of your whiskey glass, waiting for you to spill them out.* All of it reduced to this—a man standing in a garden with his pockets full of cash.

He was used to it, even enjoyed it after his glass had come up empty a few times, like a man with an ugly dog who enjoys walking it in the best neighborhood in town, letting it shit on the sidewalk. At least that's what he told himself, until he heard someone come up behind him, and a woman's voice gently say—

"Hello, Danny."

Danny felt his face stiffen. Some voices are like the blister on a burn. Just when you think you've healed, somebody touches you there, and suddenly the pain comes rushing back, hot and sharp.

He turned to look at her, taking the weight of it on his chest in one quick rush. He brought up a smile from some hidden reserve. "Helen."

She'd pulled her blond hair back from her face, wound it in a thick braid. She wore a pale silk suit, so he knew she'd come straight from the office, left her briefcase in the car. Her eyes met his briefly, then moved away. "How's life?"

Danny looked away toward the swimming pool and the bar, the black waiter in his starched jacket bending to lift a sack of ice cubes from a cooler. "You tell me."

She smiled. It was the smile she gave to old men who touched her arm when they talked to her, men who'd known her father, Jack Whelan, back when he was the state's attorney general, and were eager to tell her so if only to stand next to her, touch her arm, and smell the faint scent of lilac that clung to her hair. When they'd been married, Danny had found it sweet, the way she gave these men that smile. He'd let her know it as they drove home, draped their clothes over the backs of chairs, slid into bed—

"You gave that old man another twenty years, you know that?" Feeling her slip into the crook of his arm, her head coming to rest on his shoulder.

And she'd yawn, shake her head. "Not me. It's Jack they all loved. They want to see him in me."

Her eyes would catch the moonlight from the open window as she turned to look up at him. And that was all it took, for Danny, ever. Not knowing, as the moment slipped past, that he'd look back at it someday and think *Yeah, that was it.* It just went past, as such moments do, leaving their faint trace on your heart.

Helen let her gaze wander over the crowd. "The usual suspects."

"Jimmy makes a list Monday. Lucas told me you can match it to the legislative calendar, work out what's coming to the floor."

Her eyes moved across the party, and she nodded. She'd seen it many times before. Every Sunday afternoon when Helen was a girl, her mother would open the doors of her house on Loyola Avenue, smile quietly as she led the guests out to the back garden where Jack Whelan sat, surrounded by a small group of political cronies, a sack of raw oysters or boiled shrimp on the grass beside them. They'd split the oysters open, their harsh laughs ringing out; a dull metal keg of beer sat on ice behind her father's chair; and every few minutes he'd reach around, take the nozzle on its coiled hose, and lean forward to put a fresh head on someone's cup.

When Jimmy first appeared one spring, three years out of law school up at LSU, he'd shown up at Jack Whelan's house on a Sunday afternoon, looking for his elder brother's support in a race he was getting ready to run for a state representative's seat up in St. Tammany Parish. Jack Whelan had introduced him around, then pulled a chair up beside him, and said, "Time you got a real taste of politics, Jimmy."

Jimmy and Jack hadn't been close. There were sixteen years between them, and Jimmy had barely known their father before he'd died. They'd lived with their mothers, grown up thinking of each other as some distant fact—*my brother*—that seemed as hard to imagine as a young girl's dreams. When Jimmy's mother remarried, he'd taken his stepfather's name, Boudrieux, and never thought of himself as a Whelan until a few weeks before his law school graduation, when he saw on the front page of the Baton Rouge *Morning Advocate* that the governor-elect had appointed his campaign manager, Jack Whelan, to serve as the state's attorney general. Jimmy called to congratulate him, told him he'd see him up at the capital in a few years.

"Take your time," Jack Whelan had told him. "I'll be here."

Danny smiled at the memory. His father had been part of that circle of chairs too. Roy had come home from Jack Whelan's house the day Jimmy had first joined them, and told his wife, "Jack's little brother is runnin' for a seat up in St. Tammany. Came to see us with a tie on, shoes all shined up. Thought for a minute he was gonna make a speech."

Not seeing it, Danny thought. *The moment that changed their lives.*

He was starting to think of it as a genetic flaw, like those families who can't see the color red. You could write it up in the medical journals, *Congenital atemporality,* a genetic predisposition to miss the fuckin' boat. Carried by male members of the Chaisson family.

Helen Whelan had grown up a few blocks from Danny, up in the

Garden District, stayed on with her mother in their big house on Loyola even after her father went up to Baton Rouge to take the attorney general's job. Helen and Danny had dated a little in high school, but couldn't get past the look in their parents' eyes, like they'd planned it all along. *Not seeing it,* Danny thought, smiling. *Everything you were looking for, right there, under your eyes.* At Tulane, they became friends again. A few years later, in law school, they were competitors for law review, class rank, judicial internships. To Danny's irritation, Helen beat him every time.

Then, one night in the fall of their final year, they suddenly became passionate lovers. Like a pair of wrestlers, both of them struggling to be on top. The night before graduation, the sheets flung across the floor of Helen's bedroom, her suitcases already lined up in the hall for the move to Atlanta—where she'd taken an internship with a federal judge—Danny found himself staring at her in the darkness, a taste like metal in his mouth. He shook her awake, whispered, "Come back, okay?"

And she smiled at him, closed her eyes, murmured, "All right."

Two days later, she was gone. Danny started work as an assistant district attorney, taking his place as a young prosecutor in the vast, grinding legal factory run by New Orleans District Attorney Randall Keaton. On his first day they assigned him to Jim Broussard, a senior prosecutor who shook his hand and said, "I knew your father. He wasn't a bad lawyer, when he wasn't talking politics." Then he shoved a stack of files across the desk at Danny, said, "Now let's see what you can do."

For eighteen months, Danny barely left the tiny office they'd assigned him, except to go to court. He'd run home to grab a few hours' sleep, take a shower, and change his clothes before heading back to the office. He worked sixteen-hour days, bought lunch for his secretary when he saw her start to glare at him as he'd drop each new batch of files on her desk. It was an impossible job, prosecuting drug dealers, hookers, petty thieves. Like ferrying the dead. As soon as you shoved one batch out of your boat on that bleak, distant shore, you looked back, found the landing crowded with more bodies, stacked up like cordwood, waiting for you. No rest, no end. A job for a shovel and a strong stomach.

And he loved every minute of it. While his law school classmates were locked away in tiny offices, sweating over lease agreements and third-party trusts, he was in court, arguing cases before juries of car mechanics, secretaries, grocery store clerks. Making sense of it for them, showing them what the law meant, getting them to speak for the community, for justice. He never lost faith in that idea, even at the worst moments.

On weekends, he'd drive up to Atlanta to visit Helen, or she'd come down to him. They'd go out for dinner at Tujaque's or Café Degas, then go home to make love under a slowly whirling ceiling fan in the third-floor apartment he'd rented in an old house on Calhoun Street, a block from Audubon Park. At the end of the year she moved back to New Orleans, took the job as an associate with Morgan, Field, and Stratton. That summer they got married.

It was a life. Danny felt like he'd put his father's world behind him, pulled the shade against that hard light.

Until one day, when he came back from court to find a message slip on his desk that said *Call Lucas Clay.* No number. But none was necessary. After his father died, Danny'd felt Jimmy's eyes on him from a distance. When his high school baseball team made the play-offs, Danny spotted Jimmy in the stands, next to Danny's mother. A year later, when he graduated, Jimmy showed up at the ceremony, slipped Danny a check for his first year's tuition at Tulane. Danny thanked him, clenching his teeth as Jimmy slipped an arm around his shoulder and said, "Just keeping a promise I made to your father, son. A man's only as good as his promises, remember that."

The next year, when Danny's mother died just before Christmas,

Jimmy gave the eulogy at her funeral, arranged for the sale of the big house on Octavia Street, had the money put into trust to pay for Danny's education so he could come out of law school without a burden of loans to pay off.

"That way, you got a choice," he told Danny. "You want to go work for a fancy firm, that's fine. But you want to go save the world, won't nobody stop you."

And when that time came, Danny was grateful to Jimmy for his help. While his classmates staggered out of law school beneath the weight of their debts, took corporate jobs they hated simply to ease the burden, Danny found a place waiting for him in the district attorney's office, where every day he felt like somebody'd shuffled the cards, dealt him another winning hand.

He had done some campaign work for Jimmy during the last election: hung posters, helped turn out the vote in his district on election day. That was when he'd first met Lucas Clay, a man who reminded him of dust settling on curtains in an empty room. It quickly became clear to him that it was Lucas who ran the campaign, kept Jimmy on message, saw to it that the right people got threatened or praised. One day Lucas stopped by the desk in Jimmy's campaign headquarters where Danny was working the phones, and said, "I understand you're with the district attorney's office."

Danny sat back, grinned. "Yeah, I'm one of the bad guys."

Lucas had simply smiled and walked away. Like he'd filed the information away, slid the drawer closed.

So when Danny saw that name on a message slip, he felt something cold across the back of his neck, like somebody had drawn the tip of a needle lightly over the skin. No pressure, but a point there. He picked up the phone, dialed Jimmy's office at the Statehouse up in Baton Rouge, asked for Lucas Clay.

"Let me give you his mobile number," the secretary told him. "He's down in New Orleans today."

As it happened, he was two blocks from Danny's office, having lunch with a lawyer representing a building contractor who was about to go to trial for an unpleasant incident at a motel over on the West Bank involving cocaine, pornographic videos, and a thirteen-year-old boy. Danny left his office, walked the two blocks, joined them for coffee, feeling as if he was being carried out to sea by a powerful tide.

"You see," the lawyer told him, "my client is concerned at the thought of a prison sentence. We don't stand a chance at trial, so we're left with no option but to consider other alternatives." He paused, glanced over at Lucas. "Mr. Clay thought it might be a good idea for us to talk to you before my client makes the decision to enter into a co-operation agreement with any other parties."

Danny looked at Lucas, who sat without moving, gazing down at his hand resting on the tablecloth. "They got something on Jimmy?"

Lucas's eyes were impassive. "Jimmy likes to help his friends, Danny. You know that." He returned his gaze to the tablecloth, gently rubbed at a stain with one finger. "Let's say that it might be best for everybody if this case went no further."

"So why call me? I don't work sex crimes."

"But you have access to case files, right?" The lawyer reached into his briefcase, took out a manila envelope, laid it on the table. His hand rested on the envelope, like he was protecting it from Danny's gaze. "We would be grateful if you could see that this gets into the file. That's all."

Danny glanced down at the envelope. "What is it?"

The lawyer hesitated, glanced at Lucas, who nodded, then looked away. "It's a transcript of a conversation in my client's office last year. With me. He admitted he's got a problem with little boys."

For a moment, Danny stared at him. "A surveillance transcript?"

"You got it."

"And it's real?"

The lawyer grinned. "FBI ran a surveillance on my client last

February. Seems they thought he might be a useful witness if they ever put together a case against Jimmy. Lucas talked to some friends over in the federal building last week, got us a copy by midnight express."

Danny sat back, slowly. "So you're corrupting the case. Slip a privileged conversation into the prosecutor's file, you can claim the whole case is fruit of the poisoned tree. Get the conviction over-turned."

The lawyer smiled. "Actually, we thought we'd move for a mistrial. Charge prosecutorial misconduct and avoid the conviction altogether. If they try to bring new charges, we argue that the case was corrupted at the source. So there's no way they can go to trial after that without running up against the same problem."

Danny looked off across the restaurant, watching the lunch crowd start to break up. After a while he shook his head. "It won't work."

"Yeah? Why not?"

"First off, you'd have to get the prosecutor to admit that the file was corrupted, so you'll need some way to prove that this transcript was in their files. That means getting somebody inside their office to testify that it appeared in the file prior to the indictment."

The lawyer leaned forward. "The court won't demand that standard. They come down hard on violations of attorney-client privilege. That's what holds the whole system together."

Danny leaned forward, picked up his coffee cup, swirled it slightly between his hands. "Okay, then that brings us to the second problem, which is that I won't do it. You're asking me to give up my career for a guy who fucks little boys." He drained his coffee cup, set it down on the table, and stood up. "I won't tell anybody about this conversation, but that's as far as I'll go. Find someone else."

The lawyer raised his eyebrows at Lucas. Lucas gave a sigh and said, "Would you mind excusing us for a moment?"

The lawyer shrugged, stood up, went off to find the men's room. Lucas glanced up at Danny, wearily. "Sit down, Danny."

Danny hesitated, then sat down. "I can't do this, Lucas."

Lucas picked up a knife, ran his thumb lightly across the edge. "This guy is very scared. He doesn't want to get sent up to Angola with a child-molesting jacket."

"I don't blame him. But he should have thought of that before he messed up that kid."

Lucas nodded. "No argument. But that doesn't solve my problem. See, he's made it clear he'll go to the Feds if he has to, cut a deal for his testimony. And he knows enough to put Jimmy in prison."

Danny was silent.

"We really need your help on this one, Danny. Jimmy's been good to you."

"And I'm grateful. But think about what you're asking me to do. I'm a *prosecutor,* Lucas. It's my job to put guys like that in prison."

Lucas glanced up at him, smiled. "How do you think you *got* that job, Danny?"

Danny sat back, slowly. He felt like somebody had punched him in the chest, a short, sharp jab. He watched Lucas set the knife down on the table, reach across and pick up the envelope. He laid it beside Danny's hand.

"We all got our part to play, Danny. That's how it works."

Danny had no memory of walking back to his office, knew only that when he got there and sat down at his desk, the envelope was in his hand. He shoved it into a drawer, under a stack of files.

That night he worked late. Sometime after midnight, he gathered up his papers, packed them into his briefcase, slid his jacket off the back of the chair, shut off his desk lamp. Then, without thinking about it, he opened the drawer, slid the envelope out, tossed it into his briefcase on top of his other papers. On his way out of the office, he stopped in sex crimes, found the file on the lead prosecutor's desk. He stood there for a few moments, reading over the boy's testimony, until his stomach felt as if it would bring up everything he'd eaten that day.

Then he laid his briefcase on the desk, took out the envelope, tore it open, and slid the transcript into the back of the file.

The next morning, he submitted his resignation.

"Couldn't live with it, huh?" Jimmy Boudrieux leaned back in his chair, fixed Danny with his gaze. "Takes a strong stomach sometimes."

Danny kept silent.

"You tell Helen yet?"

"No."

Jimmy nodded, slowly. "I guess you're puttin' that off." He folded his fingers together behind his head and tipped his chair back, let it rock slightly. "It's a small town. You think maybe she's heard already?"

"I thought I should talk to you first."

Jimmy nodded. He let his gaze travel off across the room, as if considering the rows of bookshelves, the glass-fronted gun cabinet with its pair of antique shotguns, the framed photographs of Jimmy with national politicians who'd come through town looking for votes. "So what you gonna do now?"

"I was hoping you might have a suggestion." Danny looked out the window. An old black man was trimming the rose bushes next to the pool. "Might be some trouble with the Bar Association, this stuff gets out."

Jimmy grinned. "Yeah? You worried somebody's gonna take away your Dictaphone, make you work for a living?"

Danny shrugged. "I put in three years at law school, Jimmy."

"You like being a lawyer?"

"It's got its moments."

"You any good at it?"

"Yeah."

Jimmy leaned forward, took a cigar from a carved walnut box on the desk, slid the paper band off. He rolled it between two fingers absently. "You know what my daddy used to say? He'd tell me, 'Boy, it don't matter if you shit downhill, 'cause it all comes home in the end.'" Jimmy looked up at Danny, smiled. "Ask me what that means." He shrugged. "Me? I say, 'Never let the past catch up with you. Keep moving.'" He looked down at the cigar in his hand and sighed. "I used to love these things. Now everybody smokes 'em, even women. Takes all the pleasure out of it."

Danny nodded, feeling Jimmy's eyes studying him.

"Okay," Jimmy said, leaning forward so his arms came to rest on the desk. "You're waiting for me to say I owe you one. Well, you'll get no argument from me there. So don't worry, I'm gonna make sure everything comes out right for you." He reached for his Rolodex, slid it toward him across the desk. "I got some friends at a couple of the big firms downtown. Want me to make a few calls?"

"No, I guess not."

Jimmy looked up at him, surprised. "You want to open your own shop?"

Danny shrugged. "Lotsa guys do it."

"Yeah, right. Little office out on Airline Highway. You spend your life bailing out pimps, maybe sell a little insurance on the side." Jimmy shook his head, raised the cigar to his mouth. "Not much of a life, Danny."

"Do I have a choice?"

Jimmy glanced down at the cigar, frowned. He laid it on the desk, settled back in his chair. "Tell you what. You come work for me. We'll get you set up in an office, someplace you don't have to get a police escort, you go out for lunch. When you get your practice on its feet, terrific." He smiled. "Until then, I always got something needs doing."

Danny gazed out across the party, thinking, *Yeah, Jimmy, he always had something.* But at the time there'd been only the tight feeling in Danny's jaw, the way he stiffened every time Helen looked at him, waiting for the argument that never came. After he went to work for Jimmy, he'd started coming home late every night. At first Helen kept a plate warm for him, sat at the kitchen table, watching him eat in silence. Soon there was nothing left but the silence. Helen gave up leaving the light on for him, so he sat in the darkness, watching the lights move slowly across the walls when cars passed. When he finally came to bed, just before dawn, Helen turned on her side, away from him.

He couldn't explain it. He still loved her as much as ever, *wanted* her even more, now that they'd drifted into their separate, silent despairs. Even now, he still woke up at night, aching for her body, for her smile. The curve of her neck as she sat reading in the lamplight. The way she'd curl up against him at night, one hand resting on his chest.

Danny swallowed hard, looked away across the party.

During the divorce, they'd sat across a conference table from each other in her lawyer's office, Helen looking at him sadly, like she was giving him what *he* wanted. They put the papers in front of him, and he signed them. He looked up at her, smiled. As she got up to leave the room, she leaned over, laid a hand on his shoulder, said, "Do something about your anger, Danny."

Then she was gone. He'd stared after her. *Anger?*

It all seemed like a long time ago now. Like watching ghosts caught in your headlights, vanishing as you pass.

Danny and Helen stood in silence, looking out across the crowd. Danny saw a man come toward them, carrying two glasses of wine. He was dark-haired, slim, and handsome, and Danny felt something in his chest tighten as Helen smiled at the man, reached out to take a wineglass from his hand.

"Danny, have you met Richard?"

Danny watched the man wipe his hand on his trousers briefly, then offer it to him, smiling. "Richard Brooks."

Danny shook hands, watching the man's eyes narrow slightly as he said, "Danny Chaisson." He'd seen that response in many people's eyes over the last few years, even come to enjoy it. *Like they've heard something about you, gives 'em a little thrill.* When he saw that slight flicker in their eye, Danny always knew exactly where he stood.

But as Brooks released his hand, he raised one finger to touch his own face, near the eye. "You've got something there, on your cheek."

Danny reached up, felt something hard and dry. He scraped at it, felt it come away under his fingernail. He took his hand away, glanced at it for a moment, then flicked it away into the grass.

Blood.

"Richard's over at the U.S. Attorney's office," Helen said. "I've brought him to meet Jimmy."

"That should be interesting."

Helen turned to Brooks. "Danny used to be an assistant district attorney."

Danny watched Brooks raise his eyebrows slightly, like a man cornered by an elderly uncle at a family reunion, trying to show interest. Danny looked over at Helen, gave a thin smile. "I get the feeling Richard knows most of this already."

Helen glanced over to where Jimmy Boudrieux stood talking to several members of the state legislature. Then she turned back, gave him her party smile, like she was holding a small chunk of ice in her mouth, keeping it safe there. "We should go talk to Jimmy."

Danny smiled. "Got to do your job."

She looked at him, and he caught a brief flash of anger in her eyes. "That's right, Danny. I do. Not all of us can cut and run."

He shrugged, watched her turn away.

Brooks held out his hand again, smoothly and said, "Good to meet you, Danny."

Danny looked up at him, met his gaze, and for a moment, he had the strange sensation that he was looking into a mirror. Young lawyer, proud of his work, stopping by Jimmy's party with Helen. Brooks wore a tight, ironic smile, as if what he'd just watched happen had confirmed his expectations.

It was the same look Danny always caught himself wearing when he passed a mirror.

He watched them cross the lawn, saw Jimmy take Helen's hand, kiss her, then turn to shake hands with Brooks. Within a few moments they were deep in conversation, and Helen turned her attention to the newly appointed head of the State Gaming Commission. As Danny watched, she laughed at something he'd said, laying a hand lightly on his arm. The man beamed.

Danny felt his chest tighten. *Let it go.*

But even as he turned away, he knew it wasn't possible. Nothing dies without a fight. *Especially love.*

4

Special Agent Mickie Vega of the Bureau of Alcohol, Tobacco and Firearms sat in her battered Chevy Nova in a loading zone near the corner of Claiborne Avenue, watching a pair of crime scene technicians unload several metal cases from the trunk of their car. A uniformed cop in a dark blue rain slicker lifted the yellow crime scene tape strung across the entrance, held it for them as they dragged their equipment inside.

She leaned forward, used her sleeve to wipe the fog from the inside of her windshield. A heavy rain was falling, and her wipers smeared the ambulance's red lights across the glass. Just beyond, three police cruisers blocked the street. The rain glittered against their flaring lights. Between them, the wet street looked like a child's painting.

Beautiful, she thought, gazing out at it. *Like something in a dream.*

A pair of headlights came up behind her, and she turned, watched a car pull to a stop on her rear bumper. The headlights flashed once, then went out.

Mickie reached down, gave a quick tug at the knee brace she wore on her left leg, then got out and walked back through the rain to the car behind her. The man in the driver's seat reached back to unlock the rear door for her, and she got in.

Her boss, Jim Dubrow, special agent in charge of the New Orleans district office of the ATF, reached down, lowered the volume on the police scanner beneath the dashboard, then turned to look back at her. "So? What's the story?"

"Not clear." Mickie wiped the rain off her face with one hand.

"First radio calls said they've got five bodies on the floor. They've got the EMT guys in there, so it's possible there were survivors, but they haven't brought anybody out yet. Homicide team went in about twenty minutes ago. They've got some uniforms sealing off the scene, a couple more knocking on doors up the block." She looked up at Dubrow. "Looks pretty bad."

Dubrow turned to look out the window at the front of the restaurant. He took a deep breath, let it out slowly. He glanced at the man next to him. "Anything new on the radio?"

The man shook his head, and Mickie saw that he was wearing a radio headset. A thin cord ran down one side of his neck. She leaned forward, saw that he had a small radio unit in his lap. A tiny red light flashed slowly.

Mickie reached down, rubbed at her swollen knee in the darkness. It felt stiff from sitting in her car for so long. And the rain didn't help. Like somebody had wrapped her knee in wet cotton, then slowly pulled it tight, until the bones scraped against each other as she walked. Some nights she'd limp up the stairs to her tiny apartment, thinking of her grandmother back in Phoenix, who'd come home from a day spent washing dishes at Taqueria Loco, stretch out on the couch with a heating pad under each knee. After half an hour she'd get up, shuffle into the kitchen to make dinner while the kids raced around her, shouting. Sixty-eight and worn out, thin as a wisp of smoke. Standing beside the bathtub, waiting for it to fill so she could soak her knee, Mickie would smile at the memory. *And you're only twenty-seven.*

She'd twisted the knee during a training exercise at the Federal Law Enforcement Training Center in Glynco, Georgia. "Dynamic entry" they called it, which meant crashing through a suspect's door in body armor, scanning a badly lit room over the sights of a Heckler & Koch assault rifle. Two weeks of climbing over roofs, using tension hooks to jerk the frame out of windows, then diving through the hole onto a carpet of broken glass. Then up on one knee, rifle at your shoulder. Their instructors videotaped every move, spent hours going over it with her each evening. Longer, she realized quickly, than with any of the men in her training unit. One of the instructors liked to freeze the video on a close-up of her face, serious, listening to instructions. "Now how'd that pretty girl get in there?"

She'd smile back at him, carefully, then ask a question about proper search and seizure procedures. After a while she got used to it. Men, she'd found, need to wave their cocks at you at least once in every conversation. Like they were scared you wouldn't notice it. And that's the *nice* ones. There were some who still just grabbed at you, even after Anita Hill, Packwood, Clinton. But she'd become good at slipping their grasp. She'd had a lot of practice. Men looked at her in the street, on buses, in the supermarket. Sometimes, standing in front of her bathroom mirror, she caught a glimpse of herself through their eyes: a pretty girl, dark hair pulled back, eyes sharp and watchful. Pretty enough, it seemed, to cause a man's eye to pause in its wandering, make him spend a moment considering his future.

She'd turn away from the mirror, shake her head. *Weird.* Like they thought you really were the woman they stared at. Not some scared seven-year-old on her first day of school, hair cut straight across her forehead. That's how she'd always pictured herself.

Until they handed her the assault rifle. Then things began to change.

Not that the instructors weren't tough on her, always. They'd smile at her in that lazy way that told you they were comfortable with attractive women, then spend the rest of the hour running the videotapes back and forth, criticizing her decisions, her tactics, everything—it seemed to her—except the running shot that took down an instructor posing as a sniper crouched behind a metal fence of the "Armed Resistance Compound" on the final day of combat training. They'd spent the morning screening videotapes of the shoot-out at Waco, watching an agent climb up onto the roof, then wincing as the

.50-caliber machine gun the Davidians had set up inside methodically punched holes in the wall beside him, until the agent rolled over—too slowly, it seemed to Mickie—and slid from the roof. A "sobriety check," the instructors called it, one of them holding up a piece of body armor with three neat holes stitched across the chest.

"Nothing can protect you from poor leadership," the instructor told them. "These people have the firepower to take you out. If they didn't, we wouldn't be there."

But Mickie came from a cop family; they didn't have to remind her of the risks. Anyway, she'd just spent three months sweating classes like Psychology and Physical Combat, Arson for Profit, and Advanced Conspiracy, all of it leading up to The Big Case, a complete investigation, from its earliest clues through testimony at trial. After all that, no *way* was she going to let them spook her, now that they'd finally gotten to the fun stuff.

That afternoon her trainee unit had come under heavy fire while trying to serve an arrest warrant on the leader of an armed religious cult. As their carefully laid operational plan fell to pieces around them and she watched the entry team go down under a hail of bullets, Mickie felt a surge of adrenaline rush through her. She moved forward, as she'd been taught, using the blind corner of the building as cover, and managed to drag three "wounded" trainees out of the firing line. One of them reached up, caught her hand as she finished pulling him to shelter. He grinned at her, whispered, "Kiss me, I'm dying."

"Too late," she'd told him. "Head wound." Then she'd leaned across him, grabbed the AR-15 out of his hand, jumped up and ran a few yards to her left, laying down the suppressing fire that took out the sniper. After that, the remains of her team regrouped, completed their entry, secured the heavy weapons, and brought their "suspect" out alive. Only after it was all over, as they gathered around the instructors for debriefing, did Mickie realize that she was limping. That night, they all went out to a bar just off the base. As the members of her trainee unit bought her round after round of Dos Equis, the guys all talking about the gunfight excitedly, Mickie sat in silence, feeling her knee slowly begin to swell.

At the "trial" that followed over the next few days, she listened as one of the instructors playing the part of a defense attorney charged her with violating the sniper's constitutional rights by her use of deadly force. She'd stayed cool, testified that she'd "returned fire according to the Bureau's rules of engagement after three agents were wounded." But all she could think about was getting up to the witness stand and back without limping; if the instructors saw that she was injured, she knew they'd wash her out. Then it would be three months of waiting—and a doctor's certification of her fitness for duty—before she could return to start the long process of training all over again. That evening, she slipped off the base after dinner, drove into town, and bought a runner's knee brace at a drugstore. She figured she'd wear it for a few days, until the swelling went down. It had been with her ever since.

After dynamic entry came three weeks of Advanced Undercover exercises, constructing false identities, police records, and employment histories. When she'd finished, the Bureau sent her back to Phoenix for three years of field training. Her first night home, her older brother, a narcotics detective with the Albuquerque Police Department, sat on their father's couch, listening to her talk excitedly about her training. When she finished, he got up, went into the kitchen, and poured himself a Scotch. "Try social work," he told her. "You might do some good."

She'd stared at him, his face expressionless as he carried his drink out onto the back patio, sat down on the picnic bench, leaned back wearily to look up at the night sky.

Anything but this, she thought. *Anywhere but here.*

She started work the next day. They assigned her to license fraud, sorting through federal gun dealer license applications, checking for irregularities, running the applicants' names against a computer registry of convicted felons.

Two hours into her first morning, the acting special agent in charge of the Phoenix office stopped by her desk, and said, "Vega, right?"

"That's right." She stood up, shook hands with him.

"I'm Jim Wright, the ASAC. Your father's an old friend of mine. Promised I'd watch out for you." Smiling at her that way older men do, she expected him to reach out, ruffle her hair.

She applied for the Bureau's Tactical Squad at the first opportunity, returned to Glynco—the only woman this time—and managed to limp through the test exercises on the combat course with good scores, only to be rejected for lack of experience. *Okay,* she thought when she read the letter. *Live with it.*

Back in Phoenix, she'd started to feel like she was suffocating. It was eighteen months after Waco, six months before Oklahoma City. Morale was low, and older agents had begun retiring in large numbers. *Fine,* Mickie thought. That meant opportunities for younger agents, even women, a chance to do something more interesting than sorting through papers, shuffling them into files. She was starting to wake up each morning with the taste of dust in her mouth; for the first time in her life, she began to hate the endless bone-dry horizons of Arizona. After four months, she applied for a transfer to New Orleans, a city where water fell from the sky.

To celebrate her transfer, her brothers put some money together, got her a lifetime membership in the NRA and a pair of jackboots. Her father went out and bought her a Kevlar vest, a Colt Pony .380 semiautomatic pistol, and a Mitch Rosen burnished leather concealment holster and gunbelt. *Terrific,* she thought. *Like I'm heading off to my first day of school, new lunch box, pencils, .380 semiautomatic . . .*

In New Orleans, Jim Dubrow assigned her to license fraud. And it rained every day for four months. Sitting at her desk, behind a pile of forms, she could look out the window, see the rain falling across the city's skyline. But after that first four months passed, Dubrow called her into his office and gave her a new assignment, tracking illegal gun sales to juveniles through the justice system, posing as a juvenile officer to try to coax testimony from teenage boys arrested on gun charges. She worked out of the tiny office of the Orleans Indigent Defendants Program at the juvenile court building on Loyola Avenue. Six exhausted public defenders, sharing an office the size of a closet, with a single desk, two metal chairs, and an ancient computer. Still, it gave her a place to hang her coat. One of the secretaries in the D.A.'s office across the hall agreed to take phone messages for her, left them in a cardboard box on the edge of her cluttered desk. The lawyers mostly ignored her, smiling slightly to themselves when anyone mentioned *the new juvenile officer.* There were no juvenile officers in Orleans Parish. The sullen teenagers arrested on weapons charges didn't know that, and the prosecutors and public defenders who handled their cases quickly realized that it didn't hurt to leave them in the dark. Mickie got a copy of the booking sheet on every juvenile arrested by the NOPD Gangs Unit on weapons charges. She'd talk to the boys, then cut deals with the lawyers, offering to have charges dropped in return for cooperation. If a kid seemed talkative, she'd pass him on to a more senior agent for questioning. It felt like swinging a tennis racket at a swarm of flies, but at least it got her out of the office.

And the rain kept falling. It made her thirsty, as if she could just walk out into that rain, stand with her mouth open, feeling it splash against her tongue, her eyelids, her neck. But when she got home at the end of the day, her knee felt like a piece of broken glass was caught between the bones. She dug out her knee brace, got used to pulling it on every morning when she got dressed, along with her gun.

Some nights, when the streetlights ran like melting butter on the wet pavement, it was no help at all. She shifted her weight, tried to stretch her leg out across the backseat of Dubrow's car without being noticed, her fingers working at the knee roughly. She'd found she couldn't treat it gently, not if she wanted it to work when she needed it. Better just to dig your fingers into the flesh, like scraping paint from a stuck window. Don't limp, don't wince, and don't complain. Just do your job, girl. Stay sharp. 'Cause it's just like they told you on the firing range back at Glynco: you might only get one shot.

And this, she had a feeling, was going to be hers.

Dubrow turned on the wipers for a moment to clear the windshield, and they got a good look at the cop in his rain slicker, doing his best to stay dry.

"They get a positive ID on the victims?" Mickie asked. "Are we sure it's Foley?"

Dubrow shook his head. "Not yet. Sounds like somebody walked away from it. They got a nine-one-one call from inside the restaurant. Whoever it was didn't say anything, just set the phone down, walked away."

"Witness?"

"Locals seem to think so. Could be wishful thinking."

They were silent, watching the cop shake the rain off his slicker. He kept looking up at the sky, then shaking his head. In the car, they sat in silence. Mickie gazed out at the rain, watching it spill into the gutters, then flow slowly toward the corner, where it ran into a storm drain. Months of work, gone. She'd passed six cases on to the senior agents since she began working down at the juvenile courts, and four teenage boys had agreed to testify that they'd bought handguns from a guy who hung out in a coffee shop on upper Canal Street, a small-time gun dealer named Dewitt Foley. When the case looked rock-solid, they brought Foley in, showed him the affidavits, let him know that he was looking at fifteen years in a federal penitentiary. Unless, of course, he wanted to help them by naming his suppliers . . .

Now it looked like Foley was dead. Shot in an armed robbery. What were the chances? Mickie sat watching the rain come down. A miracle. Water from the skies.

"All right," Dubrow said, wearily. He looked back at Mickie. "I guess we better get somebody in there, find out what's happening."

Mickie nodded, got out of the car. She pulled her raincoat tighter, ran across the street toward the police tape. There was a bright flash in one of the windows. *Camera,* she thought, but she felt her skin go cold.

The cop standing next to the tape raised a hand to stop her as she came toward him. Rain dripped off the hood of his slicker, and he kept lifting one damp shoe, miserably. "Sorry, ma'am. Private party tonight."

She reached back, pulled her badge from her back pocket, flipped it open for him. He raised his eyebrows, then reached out for it, held it up to the light.

"ATF, huh?" He gave a laugh, passed it back to her. "You a little late, honey." He lifted the tape, held it for her as she ducked under. She crossed the sidewalk, pushed the door to the restaurant open, and stepped inside.

Later, what she would remember was the blood smeared on the walls. It looked, she thought in that brief moment when her eyes came to rest on it, like rose petals scattered on a field covered by snow. Then she saw the body below it, and realized what she was seeing. There were others scattered across the room. Two plainclothes detectives were squatting among the bodies. They looked up at her.

"Watch the prints," somebody yelled. She glanced down, saw a smear of blood on the floor.

It was then that the smell hit her, like rotten flowers. She felt something rise in her throat, turned, pushed out through the door. She stood there for a moment on the sidewalk, hands on her knees, breathing. When she straightened, she saw the cop watching her.

"You okay?"

She took a deep breath, nodded. Across the street, she saw the headlights of Dubrow's car go on. It started up, swung out from the curb and made a left at the corner, its red taillights flaring for a moment, then fading along the wet pavement.

"It gets easier," the cop told her. "After a while, you don't hardly notice it."

Mickie raised her face, looked up at the rain falling out of the dark sky, feeling it splash on her face for a moment. *God.*

Then she turned, went back inside.

5

It was close to eleven, and Danny stood at the long table that Jimmy'd had set up as a bar, looking at the row of whiskey bottles gleaming in the red light. *Roses. A slow, circling fly.*

He pushed the thought away, looked up at the black waiter who came down the bar toward him. "What's up, George?"

"Not much." The waiter nodded to the row of liquor bottles on the table. "Fix you up, there?"

Danny shook his head. "Later, maybe. You seen Lucas? I really need to talk to him."

The waiter looked out across the crowd. "I guess he's around here somewhere."

"You see him, tell him I'm lookin' for him, okay?"

The waiter shrugged. "You probably see the man first. Me, I'm stuck behind this table."

Danny glanced down at his hand. No trembling, but the muscles in his fingers looked tensed, like they were holding on to something tightly, refusing to let go. He closed his eyes, and there it was, in a flash—the bodies scattered across the floor, that smell, like flowers crushed under your foot.

He turned back to the waiter, nodded at the bottles on the table. "You better slice me off a chunk of that. Looks like we're gonna be here a while."

The waiter smiled, took a bottle of Jack Daniel's from the table behind him, and poured a couple fingers into Danny's glass. "Ice?"

"Do I look like I want ice?"

The waiter stared at him for a moment, then slid the glass across the table. "You really want me to answer that?"

"That bad?"

"You want the truth?"

Danny shrugged.

"You look like a guy watching his own piss boil."

He saw the waiter's eyes shift slightly to his left, felt a hand close on his shoulder. "Well, look't here. It's our boy Danny."

He turned, and Buddy Jeanrette grinned at him. "How's it goin', son? Easing back after a hard day's work?"

Danny shook hands with him. Buddy held on to Danny's hand, turned it palm up, as if examining it. "Man, look at this. I've put so much money in this hand, last couple months, I'm surprised it ain't green." He shook his head. "You know what this hand is? That's the beast I got to feed." He folded up Danny's palm, tight, let it drop. "One 'a these days, that hand gonna eat me *alive.*"

Danny glanced out at the party, smiled. "Looks like you're doin' all right. Got the world at your feet."

Buddy followed his gaze, looking out at the crowd of journalists and politicians. "Shit on my shoes, more like." Then he grinned. "But that's how it is. You got to spread some shit around, you want to make something grow." He shoved his hands in his pockets and stood there, rocking slightly on his knees, gazing across the party like a man pacing off his lands. "Hey, you see the news?"

Danny looked at him. "What news?"

"They gave three minutes to Jimmy's speech. Channel Four. Made it sound like the flood waters were rising, he's the man with the oars."

"That surprise you?"

"Hell, yes, it surprises me. Every time I hear those guys say something doesn't make me want to throw up, I'm surprised." Buddy looked in the direction of the journalists gathered around Jimmy. "You know how they usually talk about people like me? Two years ago, we used to hold meetings of the Second Amendment Action Group out at a place on West End Boulevard. Talk about the concealed weapons bill, get ready for the election. We had everybody out there: grandmothers, Miss Louisiana, everybody. But these reporters would come out there, all they'd want to talk about was militias. Like we were all just a buncha lunatics, want to go blow up the federal building." He smiled, shook his head. "Like all those people come out there on a Monday night, not because they're worried about crime, or 'cause they actually *believe* that stuff in the Constitution about the right to bear arms, but because they *need* guns, got some character flaw makes 'em feel inadequate unless they're carrying a thirty-eight on their hip. Got a castration anxiety, makes 'em want to feel their hands on a gun. Hell, I had a reporter come into my store once, nice-lookin' woman, tried to convince me I liked guns 'cause forty years ago I saw my dad pissing on a tree. Left me with 'unresolved feelings of inadequacy.' I was real polite. I heard her out. Then I unzipped my pants, asked her, 'Do I *look* like I got unresolved feelings of inadequacy?'"

"What'd she say?"

Buddy smiled. "She said, 'Damn, that thing loaded?'" He gave a laugh. "Nice lady. Good sense of humor, you get past all the bullshit."

Danny watched Helen move away from one group of people, join another. Working the crowd. She stood with a wineglass in her hand, the pale light from the pool lamps draped around her, looking like a woman gazing out to sea.

"You two used to be married, huh?"

Danny glanced over at Buddy, saw that he'd followed Danny's gaze, was looking over at Helen. "Once upon a time."

"She's quite a gal." Buddy smiled. "Good lawyer, too. I got her on retainer, handling my public offering. You heard we were going public, right? I'm selling seventy percent of my shares. Give the people a stake in the business, raise some capital for new projects. Jimmy's idea. Helen also got me the site approval on this real estate

deal I got in development, down at English Turn. I got my whole future in her hands."

Danny looked at him, said nothing. Buddy slid a cigar from the
inner pocket of his jacket and took a moment getting it lit.

"We're gonna be big, Danny. I could sell all my shares twice over.
Got investors lining up to buy in. You know why? It's a growth industry. This state, we could be like McDonald's. Have a gun range in every
town. Up till now, it's been a single-sale business. You sell a guy a hunting rifle, maybe a handgun, and that's it. Could be ten years before you
see that guy again. He's out in the woods, shooting at bottles. What's he
need a gun range for? But with this new law, he's got to show he's done
safety training to get a concealed weapons permit. That's the future,
Danny. Every guy wants to feel like James Bond, carry a gun in a shoulder rig under his coat. And we can give it to 'em. Return business, that's
the key. Hell, car dealerships make over half their profits on service. We
move beyond a onetime sale, get into gun courses, permit certification,
after-school clubs. Get 'em on the range for the safety course, you can
give 'em a taste of combat training, multi-target rooms, street scenes.
We got interactive video coming, just like the SWAT teams use. Feels
like you're in a movie. You gonna go pay seven bucks to watch Mel Gib-
son blast the bad guys, you can do it yourself? We'll do paint ball, that's
not real enough. It'll be family entertainment. Friday night dates. Get
'em coming back, make sure they got to walk through the store on the
way out, see all the shiny new stuff." He considered the tip of his cigar,
flicked ashes onto the grass. "It's in the blood, Danny. Buried in our cul-
ture like a dream. Every boy wants a car and a gun."

Danny stared off at Helen. "So why sell your shares?"

Buddy looked over at him, then he grinned. "Hey, call me stupid, but I *believe* in all that stuff about the free market. People buy into
your business, it's a vote of confidence. People up in Baton Rouge,
Washington, they got to hear that. We're the future of this country."

Danny smiled. *Yeah, and then there's the lawsuits.* A couple of local product liability lawyers who'd won suits against the tobacco companies had just filed a writ against the gun manufacturers, seeking compensation for the city's costs in police overtime, emergency services, and medical care. They had the mayor's support, and several other cities had recently joined in as co-plaintiffs. So Buddy was hedging his bets. Selling his shares now, putting the money in other ventures. That way, if the whole industry suddenly went under in a rising tide of lawsuits, he'd be out clean with a bucket of cash, leaving the new shareholders to pay off the judgments.

Buy the future by selling the past. Danny looked away. *Just watch out for those ghosts.*

"Jesus, look't you," Buddy said. "You ain't blinked the whole time I been talking to you. Look like somebody wired your eyes open." He grinned, shook his head. "Don't be so fuckin' serious, Danny. It's a short life, then they put you in the ground. And you won't get too many laughs there."

"I don't know," Danny said, draining his drink. "Could be that's when the laughing starts."

He walked away, crossed the grass toward the trees at the back of the house. He could hear wind rustle the leaves over his head, the red lights flickering slightly on the grass.

"Making some nice new friends?"

Danny turned, saw Maura Boudrieux sitting on a wooden swing in the shadows of an oak tree a few feet away, watching him. She had her shoes off, her legs curled up on the seat beside her and a glass of whiskey tucked away behind a ficus plant, within easy reach.

"You know your problem, Danny?" She smiled, uncurled her legs to make a space on the swing. "You never give up." She patted the seat next to her. "Always a place for you among the pariahs."

Danny glanced over at Jimmy, sitting at a table on the far side of the pool, deep in conversation with a state senator from a conservative district near Shreveport. Helen stood at the edge of the pool a few feet away, looking down at the bright water, her silk suit catching the yellow glow from the underwater lights so it seemed almost liquid.

Maura followed his gaze. "Don't worry. She won't see you."

He turned, walked over to the swing, sat down. "I just wondered where Jimmy was."

"Yeah?" She smiled, reached for her whiskey glass. "You worried the boss will catch on you're fucking his daughter?"

"Not really." He set the briefcase on the ground between his feet, shrugged off his jacket, draped it over the arm of the swing. "Just doing my job."

Maura smiled, stretched out one bare foot, set the swing moving slowly. She nodded at the briefcase between his feet. "You got to lay your burden down, son."

He looked out across the party, smiled. "I'm used to it."

"Yeah, I can see that." She took a sip from her glass, hid it back behind the planter. "Ain't we all."

Three weeks after he'd quit his job at the D.A.'s office, Danny started working for Jimmy, making his collections around the city. A few months later, Helen was gone. Danny started showing up early at the restaurants and nightclubs where he made most of his pickups, sitting at the bar, nursing a beer. While he waited for the owner to come out of the back, slip him an envelope stuffed with cash. He was sitting in a bar on Poydras when he noticed a woman staring at him. Danny glanced over at her once, looked away. Then his eyes came back to her face, and he saw her give a slow, ironic smile. Her lips formed the word *Hello*. Silently.

Maura Boudrieux.

He hadn't seen her since high school. She'd gone off to school out west, a women's college out in Oakland, stayed away from New Orleans for ten years, as if afraid it might drag her down, like a tide. But now she was back, sitting at a table across the room from him with three guys who looked like they'd rode in on Harleys, staring at him with those dark, angry eyes. Her black hair was cut short, razored up the back of her neck to the base of her skull. She'd become very thin, like she'd given up on food, started feeding on darkness.

He smiled at her uneasily, raised a hand. One of the guys she was with turned to see what she was looking at, and Danny shifted his eyes away. When he glanced back, a moment later, she was still staring at him, a slight smile on her face, like she was waiting for something. Jesus, all his life, people had been looking at him like that, the whole city, watching to see how long it took until he went down in flames.

He was relieved when the owner appeared behind the bar, laid an envelope in front of him. "Tell Jimmy we're still waiting on that license."

Danny slipped the envelope into his jacket pocket, smiled. "Yeah, well, these things take time."

As he stepped outside, he felt somebody come up beside him on the sidewalk, catch his arm.

"Hi." Maura gave him her dark smile. "I heard you and Helen split up. Looks like we're traveling the same road."

Danny winced at the memory. They'd grown up two blocks away from each other, gone to the same schools. But they'd never been close. She was Helen's cousin, Jimmy Boudrieux's daughter. In high school, she'd been the girl who wore black eyeshadow, wrote poems about her suicide attempts. Two weeks after her father won election as Speaker of the state legislature, she ran away to Vegas with an auto mechanic she'd met in group therapy. Jimmy, enraged, had sent Lucas Clay to bring her back. They'd spread some money around, gotten the marriage annulled, paid off the guy to stay out of New Orleans.

"You want to throw your life away," Jimmy had shouted at her in the big house on Audubon Place he'd bought a few years earlier, "at least pick a guy who can give a decent tuneup. You know why they fired him from Milla's? They got a whole file of complaints over there. The guy's manic depressive. He works on a car, one day it's revving too high, the next it won't fucking start."

Maura just stared at the floor, her eyes angry. "You don't know anything about him."

"I know he took thirty thousand dollars off me to get lost." Jimmy shook his head. "I'll have to put him down as a political consultant." He looked over at Lucas, standing next to the window, grinned. "Hell, we never thought of that. Probably call the vote better than a pollster, way this state goes."

Lucas smiled, silent.

"We could put him on the platform committee, help us run the state," Jimmy went on, laughing. "Put this place on lithium, you *might* be able to govern it."

Maura got up, stomped away. At the door, she paused, screamed back at her father, "This *isn't* about politics!"

Jimmy had let her slam the door before calling after her, "Honey, what you think politics *is?*"

Too much history, Danny thought. He'd heard the story from Lucas Clay around the same time he'd started working for Jimmy Boudrieux. *Moving forward by going back. Like walking through a swamp. Every step, you got to jerk your feet out of the mud, keep it from pulling you down.*

Before long, he'd started running into her all over town. One night, he saw her in a liquor store on St. Charles, loading her cart with bottles of discount vodka. "What?" she said, when she saw him looking at her cart. "I'm into sedation."

He smiled. "Looks like you might need some help."

She rolled her eyes. "Jesus, don't you start that shit, Danny. I hear it enough from my father . . ."

"I meant getting it out to your car."

She looked at him. "You always were a gentleman, Danny. Under all the bullshit."

They went out for coffee, not saying much. It felt strangely comfortable, like a married couple who wake up one day to discover they've grown old together.

"Everybody needs somebody to be miserable with," she told him, smiling. "I always knew we could be unhappy together, if we just gave it half a chance."

So they sat staring down at the steam rising from their cups, watching it drift between them. Then, as he watched her drain her cup, her eyelids fluttering slightly as she tipped her head back, he discovered that he was staring at her with an empty feeling in his chest and a fierce erection. The empty feeling he was used to, but the erection surprised him. One day, nothing; the next, it's there like an angry ghost, back from the dead to take over your life.

"Something wrong?" Maura asked him.

He looked away quickly, shook his head.

For a moment, she stared at him. Then she gave a slow smile. "Why don't you take me home."

He drove her back to his apartment, watched her glance around at the stack of newspapers on his dining room table, the photographs of Helen with her family. "Pretty grim," she said, then walked down the hall to the bedroom. He followed, caught a glimpse of her stepping out of her underpants, slipping under the sheets, naked. He stood there in the doorway, looking at her.

"This feels too quick."

She laughed. "That's my line." Then she reached out, patted the bed beside her. "Just don't make me use it."

Danny had a mirror on top of his dresser, and halfway through, Maura got up, adjusted it so that she could see them in it when she glanced over. She made love with her head turned to one side, as if their image in the glass were more real to her than the tremors that shook her body. Danny felt tentative at first, his hands clumsy, unfamiliar with her body, its sharp angles and barely concealed bones, the pale scars he found on her upper thigh and belly, her wrists. But she guided his hands with her own, drew him on with her rage.

"Don't worry. You can't hurt me," she whispered to him, then turned her head to gaze at them in the mirror, her hands gripping his back.

When they'd finished, she lay there for a few moments, staring up at the ceiling, then got up, went over to the mirror, and turned it to the wall. She picked up a photograph of Helen from Danny's dresser, studied it for a long time.

"Jesus. Why couldn't I look like this?"

Danny didn't answer. He watched her replace the picture on the dresser. Then she smiled. "I guess you married the wrong girl."

"No, she married the wrong guy."

She came back to the bed, lay down beside him, one hand reaching down to squeeze the muscle of his thigh, gently. "I've fucked most of the guys who work for my father. My therapist says it's a revenge thing."

Danny winced. "Tell me you didn't fuck Lucas."

"No." She smiled. "Not Lucas."

"So I was next on your list?"

She laughed. "It's an old joke, you know? 'I gave up sex to be a drug addict, then I gave up drugs to be a sex addict.'" She lay back, ran a hand across her own body. "But sex is just a consolation prize. It's the only good thing about giving up drugs: it gives you a good excuse to fuck like a rabbit."

"Seems like a tough way to score."

She sighed. "Don't use that word, okay? It's too painful."

He reached down, pulled up the sheet, and hit the switch on the wall next to the bed to turn off the ceiling fan. "Cooling off. Must be getting late."

"Okay, I get the message." She sat up, felt around on the floor for her clothes. As she got dressed, she gazed down at him and smiled. "Don't ever change, Danny. Everybody loves a good car wreck."

A few weeks later, he'd heard from an old friend that Helen had started seeing a lawyer he knew named Richard Trice, a partner at her firm. For a moment, he'd felt a pure shot of pain through his chest. He went to a pay phone and started to dial her number, but instead, he found himself calling Maura. Danny leaned his head against the cool glass of the phone booth, waiting. When she answered, he said, "It's bad today."

"Danny?" There was a pause, and he heard her lighting a cigarette. "What's up?"

"Helen. She's with somebody."

There was a pause, then Maura said, "Had to happen sometime."

"Yeah, I know. It's just—*this* guy?"

"You know him?"

"He's a lawyer in her firm, a real prick."

Maura laughed. "Hey, she married you, right?"

And suddenly Danny had found himself laughing, the phone pressed to his ear, until the tears rolled down his cheeks. That's what saved him, every time. You laugh, you live.

"So invite me over," Maura told him. "We'll celebrate your freedom."

She made love with unsuppressed anger and self-loathing, like she was tearing at her own flesh, or setting it aflame. Later, they'd lie there with the sweat dripping from them, not touching. After a time, she'd raise her head, gaze down at her own body, then let her head drop back to the pillow, disgusted.

"Jesus," she'd say. "How can you want me? I'm a sack of bones."

And though he'd smile at those moments, reach out to stroke her belly gently, deep down he wondered the same thing. She was like one of those famine children you see on the TV news, her eyes hungry, as if she thought he could fill some empty place inside her, save her from the dry sound she heard in her voice when she spoke, the harsh whisper of her anger, her despair.

Now, sitting in the faint red light from the oak trees, she looked off across the party, shook her head in disgust.

"You know who these people remind me of?" she asked him. "Go down to the aquarium, look in the shark tank." Her eyes moved across the crowd. "These people, they're the fish they put in there for the sharks to feed on."

"What's that make us?"

"You and me?" She smiled. "We're what they scrape off the bottom of the tank."

Danny sipped at his whiskey, felt the fire catch inside him with relief. "That's what I like about you, Maura. You always look on the bright side."

"Yeah, my therapist says I got to work on my *belief system.*" She gave the swing another push, looked out at the crowd. "It's funny, isn't it? Most of these people don't believe in shit, except for what you got in that briefcase."

Danny stared at her, then realized, *Money. She thinks it's money.* "Everybody's got to believe in something," he said.

Maura looked at him, then shook her head sadly, reached back for her glass. "Danny, what you got in that briefcase, it's just bets on an old horse." She looked down at her drink, swirled it so it caught the faint light. "Trust me on that, okay?"

Trust me. Everybody trying to tell you how it is, some secret only they know. Danny looked over at Jimmy, his head close to the state senator's ear, whispering. *Trust me,* he was probably saying. *I know the score.*

But sometimes, Danny thought, *you've got no choice.*

A little before midnight, Danny was back under his oak tree when Lucas Clay appeared at Jimmy's side, caught his arm just above the elbow, whispered—"Phone call, Jimmy."

Danny tossed the remains of his drink into the grass, left the glass on a wrought iron table next to the pool. He followed the narrow gravel path through the bushes at the side of the house and let himself into Jimmy's study. He took a seat on the leather couch with the brief-case between his feet, leaned his head back against the top of the couch and closed his eyes, and there was Phuong curled on the floor of the dining room, staring up at him with empty eyes . . .

He sat up, opened his eyes. But it was all still there, inside him. Like a movie, flickering in the darkness, and no end to it, ever.

So he leaned forward, rested his elbows on his knees, and rubbed at his face with both hands, waiting.

Over the years, what Danny had learned about politics was that it's what a man *doesn't* say that counts. Not the stuff the guy tells you to your face, but the thing he doesn't have to say, just letting it hang there, like a fruit you have to pluck off the branch. That's power, man. The more power, the less gets said, things getting quieter and quieter as you move on up the line. God, Danny figured, must have taken a vow of silence.

With Jimmy Boudrieux, you could see it all in the little laugh he gave, halfway through a sentence. Just a chuckle, really, his eyebrows going up slightly so you wanted to nod, *uh-huh.* Then he'd look off into the distance, like he'd come to a wall, wasn't going any farther. But, hey, you want to climb on over, bring me back some of them apples . . . ?

Jimmy never touched the money, never even glanced at it, like it didn't interest him. Just a fact of life, part of the job. You got a brief-case? Give it to Lucas. We'll sit down, crack open some oysters. Politics, for Jimmy Boudrieux, was the only job you could do with just a six-pack of Dixie and a sack of Gulf oysters. Tell some jokes, some stories, a couple hours later, you head over to the Statehouse, watch the guy cast his vote. You don't have to *tell* him how to vote. You just stand back and watch him. If you got the power, that's all it takes.

And so, when Jimmy came in, glanced over at Danny for a moment, then slowly lowered himself into his chair, Danny knew better than to say a word. Lucas came over to the couch, picked up the briefcase from the floor beside Danny, and carried it away somewhere. Danny sat there in silence, watching Jimmy lean back in his chair, hands folded behind his head, gazing up at the ceiling. Only when Lucas came back and took a seat beside Danny on the couch did Jimmy glance over and say, "So what's up, son? You got something on your mind?"

Danny sat forward on the soft leather couch, felt it sigh with the weight that he laid on it, and suddenly he realized that he was tired.

"I ran into a little problem," he said quietly.

6

Danny kept an office on the third floor of a building on St. Charles, two doors down from the Pearl Oyster Bar. One room, a beat-up metal desk that he'd found under a plastic sheet in his mother's garage, a brown leather couch from his father's office in the old house on Octavia Street, a filing cabinet with three empty drawers, a window air conditioner that dripped into a small plastic bucket, and a squat Mosler safe, in which he kept, on average, between $150,000 and $200,000 in small, nonsequential bills.

There were three other lawyers on his floor, each scraping a living from low-end criminal work, the occasional auto claim. After four years, they still eyed him with suspicion when they passed on the stairs. When he'd moved in, the building manager had sent a man around to paint his name on the glass door—DANIEL CHAISSON, AT-TORNEY AT LAW. He'd hung his law degree on the wall over his desk, the same spot where it had hung during his eighteen months as an assistant district attorney, prosecuting drug dealers and auto thieves. After two weeks he took it down, shoved it into a bottom drawer of his desk.

In four years, he'd seen exactly seven "clients." Two had picked his name at random from a directory supplied by the Louisiana Bar Association, and the rest had wandered in off the street. In each case, he was polite but firm, telling them that, unfortunately, his caseload was full at the moment, but had they tried one of the other firms in the building?

Saturday afternoons, the building was deserted. But Danny sat at his beat-up desk, listening to the air conditioner groaning in the window behind him. There was a newspaper open in his hands, and its front page told of an armed robbery in a Vietnamese restaurant on Claiborne Avenue that left five dead. Gang links were suspected. Danny sat there, motionless, for almost twenty minutes, staring at the photographs of the victims. The newspaper had found a copy of Claude and Phuong's wedding photograph, showing them very young, smiling in front of a tattered curtain inscribed in Vietnamese. LONG LIFE AND HAPPINESS, the caption below the photograph read. Dewitt Foley grinned out at him from a picnic table, a can of Bud in his hand. A woman's hand rested on his shoulder, and he looked happy. *Jesus,* Danny thought. *Even Foley had friends.*

Below, two black teenagers stared out at the camera, sullen, in police photographs taken at the time of a previous arrest. *Like that's all you need to know,* Danny thought. *A couple black kids with guns.*

The American dream.

Only, Danny knew differently. Two white men had brought those boys into the restaurant, two men who dressed and acted like plainclothes cops. And when those two men had walked out of there, everybody in the place was dead.

So maybe you were wrong, he thought. *Maybe they weren't cops, just a couple of white guys on the muscle. Going for that cop look, 'cause it makes people do what they say.*

Made more sense, you think about it. After all, who'd believe two cops could walk into a restaurant, slaughter everybody in the place just to empty the cash register?

Danny smiled, shook his head. *Anybody in New Orleans.* A couple of years before, a policewoman had walked into a restaurant over on the West Bank, shot everybody in the place, and walked away with the cash out of the register. Turned out she'd worked security there when she was off duty, so everybody knew her. Easier to kill everybody than take the time to case another place. A couple weeks later, another cop had been caught on tape using the radio in his squad car to set up a hit on a woman who'd filed a civil rights complaint against him. The gunman had found the woman standing on a street corner and shot her dead. Both cops were up on death row now.

Danny gazed down at the photographs in the newspaper. These two guys had shot five people, and he'd put money down that it wasn't to empty the register. They'd walked in there planning to leave blood on the floor, brought the two boys along to make it look like a robbery.

Doesn't take much to figure it out, Danny thought. They'd come for Foley. He'd been nervous, almost begging Danny to carry the briefcase back to Lucas. He needed protection, somebody to cut a deal for him to take the heat off. Looking back at it, Danny could see that what he'd taken for nervous energy was *fear.* Foley was scared, searching for a way out. Only they found him before he could play out his cards, shot him in the face, left him lying on the restaurant floor while they calmly slaughtered everybody in the place.

And you brought him there, Danny told himself, rubbing at his eyes. *You told him to meet you there. So now Claude and Phuong are dead.*

"Go easy on yourself," Jimmy had told him when he finished telling his story. "No way you could have known what was gonna happen."

Danny'd looked out the window at the lights in the garden, watched them flicker off, one by one. He watched the trees vanish into the darkness abruptly, leaving only the faint glimmer from the pool. A moment later, that went out too.

"Tell me what this is about," he said quietly.

Lucas glanced over at Jimmy. Jimmy met his eyes, then looked down at his desk, silent. "It's like you figured," Lucas told Danny. "Foley got in touch with us, wanted Jimmy's help. He said he had something we'd be interested in." Lucas sat forward, spread his hands. "Danny, we didn't know what was in that briefcase any more than you did. It's important that you understand that."

Danny looked at him for a moment, then over at Jimmy. "So what do we do now?"

Lucas sat back, was silent for a moment. "That could get complicated. First, we'd better work out exactly what's going on here." He glanced over at Jimmy, who said nothing. "In the meantime, I think it would probably be best if you just carry on as usual. Like nothing's happened."

"You think that's a good idea? Going on as usual?" Danny glanced over at Jimmy, who seemed to have vanished into an inner distance, like a match burning out. "I'm a material witness in a homicide. Eventually, the cops are gonna figure that out. And if I'm working when they show up . . ." He shrugged, left the sentence unfinished.

Lucas was silent for a moment. "How much you got at the office?"

"About one-eighty. After my expenses."

Lucas nodded. "I'll make some calls," he said. "Work out another arrangement for the collections. You got Keyes coming by tomorrow, right?"

Danny nodded.

"Just give him the usual payment. I've got some meetings in the morning, but I'll come by later and empty out your safe." He paused, glanced over at Jimmy, who hadn't moved, his eyes still fixed on the window. Lucas brought his gaze back to Danny. "In the meantime, try not to worry about it too much. We'll take care of you, okay?"

Now, looking back at it, Danny had to smile. *Don't worry about it.* That was perfect Lucas, man. Like he had everything under control.

Danny looked down at the photographs in the newspaper, the dead staring back at him. Five people were dead already, Claude and Phuong simply because they'd gotten in the way. These were men who didn't leave witnesses. And he'd seen their faces, could ID them in a lineup if it ever came to that. If he was right, and they *were* cops . . .

He reached over and picked up the phone on his desk, dialed a number over at the federal building. A woman's voice answered, "Federal Bureau of Investigation. Special Agent Seagraves's office."

"Is he in?"

"I'm sorry, he's out in the field today. Can I take a message?"

Danny hesitated, looked down at the photographs in the newspaper spread across his desk. "No message."

Danny hung up the phone, sat back. He heard footsteps pass in the corridor outside his office, then the door to the shared ladies' room next door swung closed. After a moment, he heard a toilet flush, then water running in the sink. The footsteps came out and passed back along the corridor toward one of the other lawyers' offices at the end of the hall. Danny sat there, motionless, following them with his eyes as they went past his door.

His leather jacket hung on a hook by the door. The Beretta was still in the pocket, making it hang low on one side. He got up, went over and took the jacket down, carried it back to his desk, and draped it over the back of his chair. Then he sat down, let his hand slide over the gun's weight.

Twenty minutes later he heard steps in the hall, then Wendell Keyes tapped on the glass, *tick-tick* with his wedding ring. Danny could hear him catching his breath after the stairs. He glanced at his watch, then got up, went over to the safe, took out an envelope, and tossed it onto the desktop. He sat down and called out, "It's open."

Wendell Keyes came in, his face red and dripping from the heat. He raised a hand at Danny, crossed to the window, and squatted down with his face in front of the air conditioner.

"Jesus, it's fuckin' hot." Keyes dug a handkerchief out of his pocket, wiped his forehead, then turned his face slowly from side to side in the cool air. He was a small man, thin as a snapped whip, but he wore suits cut two sizes too large, from when he'd lost almost forty pounds after his cancer surgery. For a long time, Danny had thought he was just too cheap to buy a new suit, but then a guy he knew had told him Keyes owned commercial property up along Veterans Boulevard, had been stashing away money for years.

"So why's he wear those old suits?" Danny asked.

The guy had smiled, like they'd arrived at an important truth. "He wants everybody to know he beat the cancer. Like that guy owns the liquor store down on Magazine, wears the bullet on a chain around his neck from when the guy shot him in a holdup. Six years, nobody's tried to rob him once. Only store on the street hasn't been held up."

To Danny, Keyes looked like one of those guys you see hanging around the racetrack in old movies. The guy who always gets shot in the back just when he's about to tell the detective the real story, dies in his arms, saying, *Take care 'a my girl, Marlowe.*

Keyes had his eyes closed, his forehead leaned against the vent. "How you been, Danny?"

"Okay. You?"

"Not bad." Keyes straightened up, wiped his face with the handkerchief. He had six red lines running across his forehead from the vent. He glanced at the newspaper open on Danny's desk. "Jesus, that's something, huh? All those people got shot up?" He came over, lowered himself into a chair opposite Danny. "I just heard on the radio the cops spent the whole night rounding up niggers down on Conti Street. They figure it's a gang thing." He glanced at his watch. "Listen, I got to be up in Baton Rouge by five. You got it ready?"

Danny reached out, slid the envelope across the desk to Keyes. Keyes opened it, slid out five thick packs of bills, then counted through it quickly, his fingers walking over the packs of bills. Danny watched him, silent. It took only a few moments, Keyes starting to nod even before he finished thumbing through the last pack. "Okay, twenty-four thousand." He dug out his handkerchief, wiped his fingertips carefully. "We're doing the casino bill, right?"

"And the gun bill." Danny nodded at the envelope. "That's why you got a double count in there."

Keyes glanced at his watch. "That's a lot of stops. I got to be back from Baton Rouge by seven. I'm taking the family out to Mandina's."

Danny shrugged. "There's floor votes scheduled on both bills next week. I been out shakin' the trees all week."

Keyes looked down at the money, gave a sigh. "I better call my wife."

Danny shoved the phone across the desk, then sat back and rubbed at his eyes as Keyes made the call. According to his tax returns, Keyes worked as a messenger for Legislative Services, Inc., a document service that had a contract with the state legislature. Twice a week, he made his rounds in the capitol building, dropping off thick manila envelopes containing draft bills, amendments to the legislative calendar, Speaker's notices. Depending on the legislative schedule, some of the envelopes were a bit thicker each week, based on verbal instructions from Lucas Clay. And Keyes kept it all in his head, knew which envelopes could go to secretaries or aides, which had to be delivered directly into the hands of an upstate representative with a reform agenda and a staff drawn from the Christian Coalition.

Now Danny listened to him saying into the phone, "Yeah, sure. If I'd *known,* I'd have got an earlier start. But I *didn't* know, did I?" He winced, took the phone away from his ear to wipe the sweat off his forehead with his sleeve. Danny'd met his wife once, a huge woman with a face that looked like she'd stepped on a rake. She had a voice like two forks tangled up in a drawer. Whenever he spoke to her on the phone, Keyes's voice took on a whining sound, like a child pleading not to be whipped.

Danny reached behind him, turned the air-conditioning up a notch. He heard Keyes say, "Yeah. Yeah, okay, baby. I'll be there." Then he hung up the phone, looked over at Danny. "So you goin' by Jimmy's tonight?"

"I don't think so. Why?"

"You see Lucas, tell him I got to have more warning, next time he changes the distribution."

"You can tell him yourself. He's gonna call you later. I'm taking some time off, so he wants you to make the pickups for a while."

Keyes stared at him. "That makes me nervous, Danny. Leaves me holding both ends of the rope."

"Shouldn't be too long. Couple weeks, maybe." Danny shrugged. "You got a problem with it, talk to Lucas."

"Yeah, I'll do that." Keyes stood up, took the manila envelope from the desk and held it by the edge, swept the packs of cash into it with his other hand.

He grinned at Danny as the money disappeared into the envelope. "One day I'm gonna miss, get some 'a this on my shoes."

It was evening when Lucas finally showed up. Danny, staring out the window at the sky melting in the late afternoon heat, recognized his careful step as he crossed the hall, knocked at the door to Danny's office.

"It's open."

In the four years that they'd worked together, Danny could remember Lucas coming to his office twice. The first time had been three days after he'd moved in, on the afternoon when he took delivery of the safe: they'd sat in silence, watching as two black delivery men wrestled it up the stairs on a hand truck, then wheeled it into the office, slid it into the corner where it now stood. Danny signed for the delivery, tore open the envelope that contained the combination, and handed the extra copy across the desk to Lucas. Lucas glanced at it, then crumpled the paper up, laid it in an ashtray on Danny's desk, and set a match to it.

"Shouldn't you save that?"

Lucas shook his head. "I'll remember."

The only other time Lucas came to Danny's office had been eighteen months back, during a federal criminal investigation into Jimmy's role in the awarding of a state contract for computers in public schools. Lucas had taken a seat, handed Danny a stapled sheaf of papers, and they'd spent forty minutes reading out a carefully drafted conversation—for the benefit of any microphones that might have been planted in Danny's office—making clear that Danny was operating as Jimmy's attorney of record in certain matters relating to the investigation, and was therefore covered by attorney-client privilege. Danny wasn't convinced the conversation would have stood up in court, but two plumbers had shown up the next morning to fix a toilet in the ladies' room next door. Danny'd left while they were drilling into the wall that adjoined his office. When he came back that evening, they were gone, but a secretary down the hall told him that the toilet still ran constantly. Six weeks later, the investigation was closed for lack of evidence.

Now Lucas swung the door closed behind him, glanced around Danny's office with a slight smile on his face. "Nice to see that some things in this world don't change."

Danny sat back, heard his chair creak under him. "Some things are perfect just the way they are."

Lucas nodded. He glanced over at the open safe. The money was stacked neatly, wrapped in rubber bands. "Keyes come by?"

"Yeah. I told him you wanted him to make the pickups for a couple weeks. He didn't seem too happy about it.

Lucas shrugged. "He'll live." He went over, laid his briefcase on the couch, unsnapped the clasps. "Anyway, it shouldn't be but a couple weeks," he said, shoving some papers aside in his briefcase to make room for the money. "I made some calls. The problem's taken care of."

"Anything I should know?"

Lucas shook his head. "Best just to consider it closed." He knelt in front of the safe, began loading the stacks of cash into his briefcase. "We got one more pickup we'll need you to make. Tomorrow night, out in St. Bernard. After that, you can take a little break until this thing's resolved." He laid the cash in neat rows in the briefcase.

"Where in St. Bernard?"

"You know the Belle Chasse ferry? There's a gas station on the St. Bernard side. He'll meet you out there at eleven."

Danny was silent for a moment. "He's been watching too many movies."

Lucas glanced up at him, smiled. "Everybody's scared their first time. You should know that, Danny." He cleared the last few stacks of bills out of the back of the safe, shoved them into the briefcase, then straightened up. "Give me a call when you're done. We'll work out a place to meet. Jimmy figures it might be better if you stayed away from the house, next couple weeks. Take yourself a vacation. Go lie on a beach someplace, get a tan." Lucas took a packet of bills off one of the stacks, ran his thumb over it quickly, then turned, tossed it on Danny's desk. "That should cover your expenses until you come back to work. Let me know if you need more."

Danny looked at the money, not moving. "That's plenty."

After that, they were silent. When he was done, Lucas stood up, closed the briefcase, and snapped the locks closed. He glanced over at Danny. "Anything you want me to tell Jimmy?"

Danny shrugged. "He knows how to reach me."

Lucas smiled. "Always has."

Danny listened to Lucas's footsteps as he crossed the empty hall, disappeared down the stairs. When he couldn't hear them anymore, he sat listening to the silence. Saturday night. The traffic on Canal was heavy with tourists heading down to the Quarter, but around him, the building was empty. Danny'd spent a lot of time there on the weekends over the last few years, and he liked it that way. Like when you had to stay after school as a kid, you came out into the hall, felt that emptiness like a hollow sound in your bones.

He glanced over at the safe. It stood open, empty. He looked at the small packet of money on the desk, then picked it up, tossed it into the safe, used his foot to shove the door closed.

The light was flashing on his answering machine when he got home, and he hit the button as he went into the kitchen. He got a beer from the refrigerator, opened it, then went back into the living room to open the front windows as the machine finished rewinding.

"Hi, Danny. It's Maura. Guess you're out. You're always out. Except when you're in. I'm out, too. Even when I'm in. Actually, I'm inside out. So I thought maybe we could be out together. Or in. Or both. But you're out. So . . . whatever."

The machine clicked, shut itself off. Danny smiled, took a sip of his beer. *Whatever.* You got no choice, so just enjoy the ride. Maura, she'd lived with her father long enough to figure that much out. Sitting in her room, listening to the murmur of voices from her father's office below. Where things got decided.

And everybody lets them.

He stood at the open window, watching a few drops of rain start to fleck the sidewalk under the streetlight. *What's Lucas want with a briefcase full of guns?* The night smelled like a wet animal, something quick and brutal. Then he heard a sound like a faint whispering among the leaves of the oak tree at the street's edge, and the rain started coming down in sheets.

7

Bayou Seafood on Paris Road out in St. Bernard Parish was a tin-roofed shed with old cable spools for picnic tables and a parking lot filled with oyster shells that made a low crunching sound as the pickup trucks pulled in on a Saturday afternoon. It was the kind of place where they'd spread newspaper on your table, dump a bucket of steaming boiled shrimp in a pile in the middle, hand you a roll of paper towels so you could wipe your hands when you finished eating. The beer was cold, and you drank it out of the bottle, bought your kid a Coke that came in a red plastic glass like they used to give away at gas stations. If the weather was good, you could sit out on the deck, put your feet up on the rail, watch the boats in the marina.

It was raining when Ray Morrisey pulled into the parking lot. He was a heavyset man, with bright red hair, which he wore razored tight against his skull like a Parris Island drill sergeant. His skin was as pale as a newborn pig's. Not that anybody would have said that aloud. Morrisey was a St. Bernard Parish sheriff's deputy, famous for riding up and down West Judge Perez Drive in his squad car, watching for black kids crossing the parish line from New Orleans. When he'd spot one, he'd use the spotlight mounted on the door of his cruiser to blind the driver. If the other car swerved, he'd pull a U-turn across the traffic lanes, flip on his lights, and pull the car over for a reasonable cause search. Last year, Morrisey had been the subject of a civil rights lawsuit brought by a group of black Tulane students after he'd pulled them over on a traffic violation, searched the car, and found the dried-up remains of an ancient roach under the passenger's seat. When

Morrisey reached for the handcuffs, the driver protested, arguing that he'd only bought the car from a used-car lot over in Abbeville three weeks before. His mistake was to reach over to the glove compartment for the bill of sale. Before he could bring out the papers to prove his claim, Morrisey had drawn his service revolver and shot the kid three times. By some miracle, the boy survived, and came out of the hospital four months later to be greeted by a crowd of protestors chanting in support of his demand for a federal civil rights investigation into the St. Bernard Sheriff's Department.

But the investigation never came. And a week later, somebody fired sixteen shots through the windows of the boy's family home in New Iberia. Then his father's dental office burned to the ground. Within a few days, the boy quietly accepted an out-of-court settlement to his civil suit, and all four students involved transferred to Morehouse College in Atlanta. But Morrisey stayed on active duty. Two days after the settlement, he confronted two black teenagers breaking into a video shop in Arabi. When one reached for a gun, he shot them both to death. An internal investigation launched by the sheriff's office lasted three days, clearing him of any wrongdoing, and he went back on patrol the same evening. Ray Morrisey was a man who enjoyed his work.

He got out of his cruiser, ran over to the restaurant's door, pausing just inside the entrance to wipe the rain off the back of his neck. The place was packed, the windows steamed by the heat of the crowd. He scanned the room, spotted a pair of deputies who worked his shift, Russ Sadler and Joe Bartolo, wearing street clothes, sitting at the bar, drinking beer and watching a stock-car race on the TV mounted over the register. He walked over, dug a five-dollar bill out of his pocket, and tossed it on the bar in front of them.

"Drink up. We gotta talk."

He watched the two men glance over at him, surprised. Without a word, they drained their beers, then followed him back out to the cruiser. Morrisey got behind the wheel, waited while the two men climbed into the backseat. He watched them in the rearview and waited until they felt his silence and glanced up at his eyes in the mirror, then said—

"You two fucked up. There's a witness."

They looked up at his eyes in the mirror, Jesus, like a couple kids just got sent to the principal's office for throwing spitballs. Both men spent a lot of time lifting weights; you could see it in the way they sat, shoulders hunched forward slightly, their sports jackets stetched tight across their backs. Sadler's hair was so blond it looked almost white, while Bartolo had tight black curls, like he'd stuck his head in a bucket of 4-in-1 oil. But Morrisey had trouble not thinking of them as twins. Like fucking boys, playing cops.

Russ Sadler leaned forward, rested an arm on the front seat and said, "No fuckin' way, Ray. It's a small place. Joe checked the toilets, twice. We got everybody."

Morrisey sighed, looked out at the rain. "The guy Foley was meeting saw you come in. He went out the back before you started rounding everybody up."

"Shit, he was supposed to be gone. We checked before we went in. Only guy in the place was Foley."

"He was back in the kitchen, talkin' to the cook."

Sadler sat back, disgusted. "C'mon, Ray. How could we know that?"

"Hey, I don't give a shit *how* it happened. It happened." Morrisey turned, looked back at them. "Point is, there's a guy who can put you two at the scene."

"That don't prove shit," Bartolo said. "So we were there. Anybody asks, we got some takeout, left before the niggers showed up."

Morrisey sighed, ran a hand over his wet hair wearily. "Joe, he saw you bring 'em in. He made you two the minute you walked in the door, figured he'd take off before you connected him with Foley."

They were both silent for a moment; the only sound was the rain beating on the car's roof.

"Cops know about this guy?"

"Not yet."

"You know where we can find him?"

Morrisey smiled. "He's supposed to meet somebody at the Belle Chasse ferry tomorrow night. He'll be waiting at a gas station on our side of the river. We got it fixed so he'll miss the last ferry back to the city, so you can take him on the highway, out by the canal."

Sadler wiped the fog from his window, looked out at the marina. "You set that up, Ray?"

"Anything's possible, you know the right people."

Sadler grinned. "And you know the right people, huh?"

"Damn right."

"What about the gun?"

Morrisey reached into the breast pocket of his uniform, came out with a folded sheet of paper. "They picked up a kid down by the Saint Thomas projects this morning, had the gun in a paper bag, like he was bringing home the groceries." He unfolded the paper, passed it back to Sadler. Scrawled on it was a name, *James Collette,* and an NOPD booking number. "He's in on simple possession. Probably take 'em a couple days to run the ballistics, connect the gun with the shootings. They put that together, they'll be busy chasing niggers."

"Then we got no problem."

Morrisey glanced up at them in the mirror. "Not unless you two fuck up again."

"Looks like we got company."

Acorsi glanced up from the booking forms on his desk, saw Maya gazing over at the door to the homicide squad room, where Mickie Vega stood studying the duty board. Acorsi got up, walked over to her. "Agent Vega?"

She turned, looked up at him. Her eyes were clear and hard. For a moment, Acorsi felt like somebody had flashed a bright light in his eyes. "Sorry to bother you, Detective," she said. "You have a few minutes?"

He nodded, waved her back toward his desk. Maya sat back, watched them cross the room toward her.

"Your partner doesn't look happy to see me," Mickie said.

Acorsi shrugged. "She thinks you're holding back information from us."

"You agree?"

"Depends what you've got to say today."

She'd shown up at the murder scene twenty minutes after Maya and Acorsi had called in a preliminary identification of a white male gunshot victim as Dewitt Foley, a Canal Street grifter with two previous federal felony convictions for the unlicensed sale of firearms. Acorsi had watched her take quick glances over at the bodies on the floor as she showed him her ID, then she walked over to have a closer look at Foley.

"Yeah, that's him." She looked away quickly. "Jesus."

"You okay?" Acorsi pulled out a chair from one of the tables nearby and offered it to her, but she waved him away. He watched her give a quick glance over at Foley again, her face pale. "Not much like you imagined it, huh?"

She shook her head. "You do this every day?"

"Just about." He took her arm, led her back into the kitchen. He took a glass down off one of the shelves, ran some water into it at the sink, handed it to her. "You work homicide in New Orleans, there's not much left to the imagination."

She drank the water down, set the glass next to the sink. "Thanks. I'm okay now."

Acorsi nodded. "So what's the ATF's interest here? You know any reason somebody'd want to kill this guy Foley?"

She looked at him, hesitated. "You have anything to suggest this wasn't just a robbery?"

"That's what I'm asking you." He studied her face for a moment, but she said nothing. He sighed, waved a hand toward the dining room. "You know what I've got out there, Agent Vega? Five dead bodies and an empty cash register. A few minutes ago, that's *all* I had. Then you walk in here, and now I've got an ATF agent who's interested enough to come out in the rain to look at a dead guy." He gave a slight smile. "You're starting to look like one of my best leads."

Mickie turned, walked over to the screen door at the back of the kitchen. "Where's this go?"

"Alley that runs the length of the block. Lots of garbage cans."

Mickie nodded. She turned, went over to the swinging door that led into the dining room, looked through the window. From there, she couldn't see the bodies, just Foley's outstretched hand, motionless in a spreading pool of blood.

"I'll have to talk to my C.O.," she told Acorsi. "Get his authorization to fill you in on Foley." She faced him. "If you've got anything that could suggest this is more than an armed robbery, it might help us to know that."

Acorsi stared at her. "It might help *you?*" He shook his head. "Lady, I just *got* here. Everything I know, you've just seen in there on the floor. Sounds to me like you're the one with the information, here."

Mickie met his gaze. "I'll see what I can do. You got a number, I can reach you?"

Acorsi dug out his wallet, gave her a card. "That's my pager number at the bottom. You call me when you make up your mind."

Later, when he got back to his office, he made a note of the conversation in the case file, scribbled a reminder on his calendar to call her over at the ATF if she didn't get in touch within three days. Then he put the questions she'd raised about Foley aside, rode down to Conti Street with Maya, and watched as the patrol cars swept along the street, picking up every kid they saw in a red sweatshirt—Conti

Street colors. At the station, they sorted them out, half the boys they'd picked up just scared children, trying to look like they were down with the bad boys. Acorsi and Maya split them up, spent hours asking them the same set of questions over and over: *Where were you last night? Did anybody see you there? Did you know the two boys who were killed? When did you last see them?*

They got nowhere. The boys sat there, silent, or shrugged off the questions, gave alibis that checked out within an hour—a party down on Conti Street, over forty people saw them there together. Yeah, the two boys were down with them, but they never showed that night. Went out to score some smoke, never came back. Same story, over and over.

Two of the boys had been carrying guns when they were picked up. Saturday morning, Acorsi sent the guns down to ballistics, put a rush on the tests. They came back clean. One of the guns jammed every time they tried to fire it. "Stupid fucker bought himself a bad gun," the technician told Acorsi on the phone, laughing. "You might could use it to beat somebody to death, but that's the only way it'll ever be a weapon."

"Okay, thanks," Acorsi said, disappointed. He rubbed his eyes, exhausted. "You get any more guns so far this weekend?"

"Yeah, a couple."

"How 'bout testing 'em for me, just so we know."

The technician sighed. "Tom, I got over twenty guns on my desk here, every one of 'em has 'Rush' marked on the tag."

"And I got reporters calling me every twenty minutes, this thing. You want me to tell 'em you're too busy to run the tests?"

"Okay. I hear you." The technician paused. "Listen, Tom? I got a call from a woman named Vega over at ATF a little while ago, requesting that I copy her on any ballistics reports related to this case. That okay with you?"

"We got a choice?"

"Could kick it upstairs, let the brass argue about it."

"Nah, send it to her. Maybe they'll come up with something useful."

The technician laughed. "ATF? Don't hold your breath."

Acorsi hung up, went back to his case notes. They'd spent the night sorting the real gang members from the wannabes, which left them with fourteen potential suspects, every one of them with a verifiable alibi. Beyond that, they had a pair of negative ballistics sheets and a thick file of useless canvass reports from the officers who'd spent the night knocking on doors. All of it adding up to nothing. Acorsi had started to wonder if maybe the two dead boys had tried to rob the place on their own, executed the restaurant's owners, then were caught by surprise when Foley pulled out a gun and started shooting. As a solution, it seemed too neat. They'd have to wait for the lab to finish running ballistics on the guns found by the bodies, see if all the bullets taken from the victims matched up to one of the guns recovered. Until then, they were only guessing.

Now, as he led Mickie back to his desk, Acorsi tried not to get his hopes up. Whatever background information she gave him on Foley, the chances that it would tell them what happened in that restaurant were small. At best, she might give them some new leads to run down, a couple new names to add to their list of suspects, but even that seemed like wishful thinking. Without a witness or some hard physical evidence, they were flying blind.

He waved her toward a plastic chair beside his desk. Then he sat down behind the desk, tipped his chair back, and folded his hands behind his head. "So?" he said. "What's the story? Your boss say you could talk to us?"

She glanced at the case file spread out on his desk. "Looks like you're doing pretty well without me."

"Paper don't mean progress. Paper just means you're covering your ass."

She smiled, reached into the leather briefcase that she'd set down beside her chair, came out with a case binder stuffed with papers. She laid it on the desk. "It works the same way over at ATF."

Acorsi looked at the binder, then over at Maya. She raised her eyebrows.

"Here's the deal," Mickie said. "I can't let you keep this, and I've got to keep any operational details confidential. But my C.O. figures any case we could've made died with Foley, so he's authorized me to show you his file."

Acorsi was silent for a moment. He looked at the folder, then at his watch. It was almost six. If they got started on the file now, no way they'd be home before ten. He sighed, leaned forward, and slid the folder across the desk toward him.

"Okay," he said to Mickie. "Let's get at it."

Sunday morning, Danny got up early, put on his best suit, then drove out Canal Street to the cemetery, where a small crowd gathered around a gravesite to watch two coffins lowered into the ground. The crowd was split into two groups, one black, the other Vietnamese. They stared at each other over the graves, uneasily. Danny stood at the back of the crowd, out of the way. When the service was over, they filed back to the road, got into separate cars. Danny waited until the rest had left, then started his car and drove home slowly.

He made a pot of coffee, carried a cup over to his front window, set it down on the ledge next to his chair. He opened the window, feeling the damp air against his face. A slight breeze was blowing the rain around, and he sat there watching it. Some time later, he realized that the coffee was cold and he couldn't see the rain anymore against a sky grown heavy with dusk. Surprised, he glanced at his watch, found that the whole day had vanished, like something swept away on a steady tide. He got up, stretched, then grabbed his jacket off the back of the couch, picked up his keys off the table next to the door and paused to brush his hand over the gun in his pocket before he headed out. Still a couple hours to kill before heading out to St. Bernard. No point just hanging around, drilling holes in the wall with your eyes.

He rode over to St. Charles and got a burger at the Hummingbird Café, then found an empty bar where he could sit by the window, drink a beer, watch the rain come down. Behind him, two drunks were arguing loudly about which president's face was on the hundred-dollar bill. Then one of them shoved the other, and the bartender told them to take it outside. Danny watched them walk out the door and head for a bar across the street, the whole thing forgotten. He sipped at his beer, finding the soft murmur of voices in the room behind him soothing. After a while, the place started to get crowded, and the bartender turned the music up. Danny finished his beer and left.

It was almost nine. He drove up to City Park, rode around the art museum for a while, then got on Wisner Boulevard and followed it up to the lakefront. He found a place to park along Lakeshore Drive, got out, and sat on a picnic bench under a tree, looking out across the water, the rain falling gently around him.

Killing time. That's what people in New Orleans did best. You want to live fast, move up to New York. Or, shit, even *Atlanta.* You live here, it's 'cause you like the way the afternoons wear slowly away, people sitting out on their porches, watching the night settle in. No hurry, no stress. No place in the world you'd rather be.

The thought made Danny impatient. He glanced at his watch. A few minutes past ten, still too early to head over to Paris Road. He shoved his hands into the pocket of his leather jacket so he wouldn't keep looking at his watch every five minutes, and his fingers instinctively closed around the grip of the Beretta. It was something to hold on to while he waited for the time to pass.

Maybe that's all any of it is, he thought. *Family, career, politics, all that shit. Just something to hang on to while your life goes past.* That's what he'd told himself over the last couple years. It made it easier to be what he'd become—just a guy sitting in the rain, staring out at a black lake that stretched all the way to the horizon.

Danny smiled to himself, shook his head. *At least that's how it looks. And that's what counts.*

He sat there for another twenty minutes until he couldn't take it anymore, then got in his car, hunted around on the radio until he found Nina Simone doing "My Baby Just Cares for Me." The rain was coming down harder now; he listened to a couple more songs he didn't recognize before starting the Mustang up and heading back to the highway.

He headed down I-10, crossed the river into Gretna, then took the Belle Chasse Highway out past the Intracoastal Waterway into Plaquemines Parish. He got to the ferry landing just before eleven, crossed the river, and pulled into the gravel lot of a Chevron station across the highway from the landing. A single street lamp lit up two pay phones and a Dumpster. Danny pulled up next to the pay phones, shut the Mustang off, and rolled down his window. He could smell the river. A light drizzle made the air feel cool.

He waited forty minutes before he finally got out of the car, went over to the pay phone, and called Lucas. When Lucas answered, Danny could hear the faint sound of music in the background, a woman laughing.

"Lucas, it's Danny. I'm out at Belle Chasse. Your guy didn't show."

"Yeah? Give him another half hour. He's probably running late."

"The last ferry leaves at midnight." Danny leaned against the glass, looked out at the darkness. "You really want me to wait?"

"I told the guy you'd be there. He doesn't show, I'll get Keyes to handle it later this week. Sorry to make you go all the way out there."

Danny was silent for a moment, surprised. Lucas had never apologized to him before, for anything. Everything was strictly business with him. If Danny got stood up, Lucas figured that was part of his job.

"No problem," Danny said. "You want me to call you tomorrow, let you know if he showed?"

"Only if you got something for me. I'll give you a call in a couple weeks, let you know what's happening."

Danny hung up, got back in the Mustang, turned the radio on, hunted through the dial without finding anything. He shut it off, sat looking off into the darkness for a while, then started up the Mustang, made a left out of the gas station, headed back up the highway toward Chalmette.

"Where you going?"

Bartolo paused with the passenger door to the squad car halfway open, glanced back at Sadler. "I gotta take a leak." He crumpled the Styrofoam takeout cup in his hand, then pitched it into the weeds. "All that fucking coffee."

"Well, hurry it up." Sadler glanced up at the empty highway, watching for headlights. They were parked in the entrance to a boat launch along the Caernarvon Canal, the squad car pulled up tight against the wire gate. Sadler dug through his pockets. "Hey," he called out the window to Bartolo. "You see where I put that paper Ray gave us?"

Bartolo turned slightly to glance back at him, his hands still busy in front of him. Sadler heard him pissing on some leaves. "Your wallet."

Sadler sighed and grabbed the steering wheel, raising up on one side to slide his wallet out. He dug through it until he found the folded sheet of paper, pulled it out. "I must be losing my fucking mind." He unfolded the paper and switched on the overhead light to look at it. "You believe this shit? This kid they picked up with the gun? He's *fourteen*." He shook his head, disgusted. "You know what that means? Even if they get him on the shooting, he's gonna do juvenile time. Most he could serve is four years."

Bartolo finished pissing, and Sadler heard him zip up. He got in, left his door open for some air. "What the fuck you care? Just so he takes the fall."

"You picture this kid in front of a jury? *New Orleans* jury? No way they'll buy he did the shooting." He sighed, tossed the paper on the seat between them. "You ask me, this whole thing's fucked up. We take all the fuckin' chances, and somebody else gets the money."

"You're getting paid."

"Yeah, sure. I'll pay off my car note. But you think that's enough, what we're doing?" He shook his head. "We clear this up, I'm gonna have a talk with Ray, tell him it's time we saw more out of this deal."

Bartolo glanced over at him. "Ray ain't gonna like that."

"Fuck Ray. I'm sick 'a his shit anyway."

Bartolo raised his eyebrows, said nothing for a moment. Then he shrugged, "Yeah, okay. We'll talk to him together." A pair of head-lights appeared along the bend in the highway, heading back from the ferry landing. "Looks like our boy's comin'."

Sadler started the car. " 'Bout fuckin' time."

It was almost midnight when Danny turned north on the St. Bernard Highway, headed back into the city. He switched the radio on, playing with the dial until he picked up a late-night blues show out of Memphis. The road was empty of traffic, just one car pulling out of a boat launch behind him as he went past. Everybody home in bed, the weekend over.

He was passing a thick stretch of trees when he saw the lights flashing behind him, glanced up at the rearview. "Shit!"

Only car on the road, they fucking pull him over. He glanced down at the dashboard, saw he was only going forty-five. So what's the deal?

Guy was probably falling asleep, Danny thought, easing the Mustang over onto the narrow shoulder. *Decided to pull me over just to wake himself up.*

He cranked his window down, then rested his hands on the wheel and watched in the rearview as the cop car pulled up behind him, two wheels still on the road because of the narrow shoulder, the guy taking care to stay out of the steep ditch next to the road. Danny saw ST. BERNARD PARISH SHERIFF'S DEPARTMENT on the car's hood,

the words curving around a silver badge. Two deputies got out, the
guy on the passenger side standing in the door and resting his gun on
the roof to cover his partner, standard procedure in New Orleans these
days, when a late-night traffic stop could turn deadly. Danny'd read
somewhere that more cops were killed doing routine traffic stops than
anything else. In New Orleans, if you were pulled over, the most important rule was, Don't be black. After that, your best chance of sur-
vival was to sit up straight and keep your hands on the wheel, 'cause
you knew the guy walking up to your window had his gun drawn and
his nerves wound up tight.

Danny watched the driver slip his gun out of a holster on his hip,
ease up to the window with the gun held in both hands, pointed at the
ground a few feet in front of him. Danny let him get up close enough to
see his hands clearly, then squinted up at him, the headlights from the
car behind shining in his eyes, and said, "What's the problem, officer?"

The deputy hung back a few feet behind him, his back to the
bright lights from the car behind them, his face hidden in shadow. He
looked like a big guy, a weight lifter maybe. Blond hair, cut very
short. The raindrops in his hair caught the light, and Danny saw the
handcuffs clipped to his gunbelt shining. The cop wore a heavy diver's
watch on his left wrist, no wedding ring. The gun in his hand was a
black semiautomatic.

"May I see your license and registration, please?"

Danny nodded, reached back for his wallet slowly. He slid the license out of its plastic compartment, handed it to the deputy, then
said, "Registration's in the glove compartment."

"That's fine. Nice and slow."

Danny leaned over, opened the glove box, and slid the car's hand-
book out. He flipped it open on the seat beside him, found the registration, and handed it to the cop, who took it in the same hand with
the license, then stepped back without a glance at either of them and
swung his gun up.

"Now, step out of the car, please."

"What's this about?"

"Just step out of the car, sir."

Danny shrugged, opened the door and got out. "Do I have a tail-light out?"

"Step back to the patrol car, please." The deputy moved back into the empty road keeping his gun between them as Danny went past. He held Danny's license and registration in one hand, the gun in the other, as if each step in the process had been carefully choreographed. The other deputy stayed behind the door of the squad car, following Danny with his gun as he moved to stand beside the car's hood.

"Now place your hands on the hood and move your feet apart."

Danny did as he was told. He felt the deputy move in close behind him and run a hand under his arms. "There's a gun in the right pocket of my jacket," Danny told him. "I've got a permit for it in my wallet."

The deputy paused, then reached down to feel Danny's pocket. He slid his hand into the pocket carefully, drew the Beretta out, then leaned over and tossed it on the driver's seat of the squad car. Then he slid Danny's wallet out of the back pocket of his jeans and tossed it on the hood. "Take your permit out, please."

Danny reached over with one hand, flipped the wallet open, dug through it with two fingers until he found the concealed weapons permit, slid it out. He laid it on the hood next to the wallet. "I work for Representative Boudrieux," he told them. "I'm his legislative assistant." He slid his Statehouse pass out of his wallet, laid it next to the permit.

The deputy reached over, picked up his Statehouse pass, looked at it in the light from the squad car's interior. "Jesus, I guess we really got the wrong guy this time, Joe."

The guy on the other side of the car lowered his gun, leaned against the car's roof. "Yeah?"

"Sure looks like it."

The deputy dropped the pass on the hood beside Danny's wallet and stepped back.

"Sorry about that," the deputy said. "We've had some burglaries out at the boat slips the last few weeks. We got it staked out a couple nights a week. Looked like you were slowing down to turn in there until you spotted us, so we had to check you out."

"Hey, no problem. You guys are just doing your job." Danny straightened up, reached back to rub at the muscles in his neck. Then he turned to grin at the deputy, but what he saw made his smile suddenly vanish.

The deputy had his gun pointed at Danny's head. He gave a laugh, said, "I guess a guy like you figures he can walk away from just about anything, huh?"

Danny, seeing the man's face in the light from the squad car, felt his chest go very tight. A taste like metal rose in his throat, and suddenly he could smell whiskey and rotting flowers.

He heard the other deputy laugh. "He just recognized you."

Danny stood very still, waiting. There was nothing he could do. They were going to kill him, just like they'd killed everybody in the restaurant. And there was no way he could stop them.

Then another thought made his body go tight with anger. *They knew right where to find you.*

"You're being set up," he said, quietly. "The guys you work for, they'll bury you. They'll have to kill you to cover their asses."

The driver grinned, pressed his gun gently against Danny's forehead. "Yeah? You think everybody's as stupid as you?"

"Car," said the other deputy. A faint pair of headlights had appeared down the road, glittering on the wet pavement.

"Shit." The driver lowered his gun. He stepped around behind the squad car's door, reached into the car, and grabbed the radio handset. He leaned one elbow on the car's roof, grinned at Danny, keeping his gun hidden just below the edge of the door. "You smell the rain?"

He took a deep breath, let it out slowly. "I love that smell, since I was a kid. You're a lucky guy. You got about a minute here, you can enjoy it. My time comes, I want that to be the last thing I smell."

Danny saw that the other deputy had lowered his gun, out of sight below the car's roof. From a passing car, it would look like a routine traffic stop on an empty road, the cops relaxed, just taking a minute to run a radio check for outstanding warrants. Danny glanced at the approaching car. The driver would give them a brief glance as he went past, then go on home to bed. Maybe he'd read about the shooting in the paper the next day, self-defense, two cops killing a man who'd suddenly pulled a weapon. He'd shake his head, turn back to the sports section, never realizing what he'd seen.

The headlights were closer now, the guy slowing down slightly for the flashing lights. His headlights flashed among the trees on both sides of the road, making the woods appear ghostly, like something awoken from a deep sleep. Danny looked at the trees and thought, *Too far. No chance.* But the lights caught at the branches, making the rain glitter as it fell, and he knew suddenly that he had no choice.

He looked down at the hood of the squad car, hearing the sound of the tires on the wet pavement, coming toward him. And then, as the headlights flared bright across his face, making the deputies squint against the glare, he suddenly pushed himself back off the hood, spun, and ran across the road, directly into the path of the oncoming car.

Virgil Sinfield, heading home from his four-to-midnight shift as a machinist at the Metals Recovery Plant in Braithwaite, saw the flashing lights up ahead of him as he passed the marina entrance. He glanced down at his speedometer, eased up on the gas until he was under the speed limit. His wipers were bad, smearing the rain across the windshield of his Taurus, but he could see that two deputies had a guy out of his car, spread out on the hood of the squad car.

He slowed, swung out wide around them, seeing the guy glance up at his headlights, his face pale, his dark hair wet with rain. *Bad luck, buddy,* Virgil thought, then reached down to shake a cigarette out of the pack on the seat beside him. Suddenly, from the corner of his eye, he saw something flash across his path, bright in his headlights. "Jesus!" He swerved and hit the brakes hard, felt a thud as it went over his hood, then the Taurus started to slide. He swung the wheel hard to the left, but the sheriff's cruiser was straight ahead, and the Taurus slid straight toward it on the wet road. He saw the deputy standing in the driver's door, eyes wide, drop the radio handset and start to run only seconds before the Taurus slammed into the cruiser's side.

Danny lay in the gravel by the side of the road, staring up at the falling rain. Everything was very quiet, as if a storm had recently swept through and left only this gentle rain landing on his face. His mouth was open, gasping at the moist air like a swimmer who'd just broken the surface. He could feel the rain in his throat.

It took a moment for him to realize that he could breathe again. He became aware of the smell of the wet pines, the damp gravel under his head. But there was something else, another smell behind it now. A sharp, acrid smell, like burnt rubber.

I love that smell, since I was a kid.

He sat up slowly. For a moment, everything spun. He closed his eyes, waited until it passed. He got to his knees, wincing as he came up off the gravel. There was dirt and blood on the palms of both hands where he'd torn the flesh away as he landed on the road. His hip felt like he'd been kicked down a flight of stairs, but nothing felt broken.

He looked over at the other side of the road. The squad car was gone. His Mustang was right where he'd left it, the driver's door open. Behind it, a small car's rear wheels stuck straight up out of the ditch, the right one turning slowly. As he stood there, watching, it came to a stop. He looked up the road, both ways. No lights; it was empty.

He crossed the road to the wrecked car. Bits of glass crunched under his feet. When he got to the edge of the ditch, he saw the squad car lying on its side in the long weeds, one side crushed by the impact, the other car resting on it where the driver's door had once been. Danny stood there for a moment, looking down at it, then slid down into the ditch to where the smaller car's door hung partly open. He braced his shoulder against it, shoved it open wider, and looked inside. The driver lay sprawled across the floor of the front seat as if he'd been lifted out of his seat, flung forward against the dashboard, then dropped. His face was covered with blood, and Danny saw blood smeared on the shattered windshield. The man's eyes were open, fixed.

Danny eased out, slid down to where the squad car lay. His feet struck against something in the weeds. Danny looked down, saw it was a man's body in a blood-spattered deputy's uniform. There was no head. He felt something rise in his throat, scrambled away. And then, faintly, he heard moaning below him. He slid down to the bottom of the ditch and splashed through the shallow water to the other side of the squad car. The dark-haired deputy lay crushed under the car's front end. His eyes were open, staring up at the night sky, and he gasped for breath. His hands clutched at the weeds beside him, as if he was hanging on to keep from falling.

"Ah, Christ." Danny squeezed past the car's bumper and along the opposite slope until he reached the man, who looked up at him, eyes wide. His dark hair was caked with mud and blood. One hand let go of its hold on the weeds, grabbed Danny's shirt.

"Get this off me," he gasped.

Danny tried to get up, but the hand clung to him, pulling him down. He tried to pull it away, gently, but it tightened its grip. The man's eyes were closed now, and he seemed to be concentrating on a distant sound. "Let go," Danny said. "I'll try to lift it."

He didn't seem to hear. Danny dug his thumb into the man's wrist until the fingers slowly opened, then he slipped out of his reach, moved over to where the car's right front fender lay across the man's hips. He caught hold of the bumper, planted his feet in the thick mud, and heaved.

Nothing happened. He lost his footing, the mud shifting under him. He let go, shifted his stance, then bent over the bumper and tried again. After a moment, he gasped, let go. He looked over at the man's face. His eyes were open again, watching him. His lips moved, but no sound came out.

"I can't move it," Danny said. "I've got to leave you for a minute to use the radio."

The man swallowed. "Hurry," he whispered.

Danny edged past him, down the car's hood to where the windshield had been. The roof had collapsed flat against the dashboard. The car lay on one of its doors; the other was blocked by the front bumper of the Taurus, balanced on top of it. Danny moved back to where the rear windshield hung in its frame, a web of shattered safety glass. He braced himself against the side of the ditch and kicked at it. A large section broke away, fell into the backseat. Danny climbed up the side of the ditch, trying to find some firm footing from which he could kick the rest away, but he kept sliding down. After several tries, he gave up and went looking for something he could swing at it. He splashed back behind the car, saw a chunk of the rear bumper hanging loose, grabbed it with both hands, and wrenched it free. As he stepped back, he saw something lying in the mud near his feet.

It was the blond man's head.

He turned back to the rear windshield, swung the chunk of bumper at it, and saw it burst like a sheet of ice raining down. He tossed the bumper aside and got down on his knees to crawl into the car when he heard the injured man give a sound like he had something caught in his throat. Danny looked over to see him raise up slightly and give a violent cough. Blood spilled from his mouth. Then he lay back, looked up at the sky, and stopped breathing.

For a moment Danny didn't move. Then he stood up slowly. He looked down at the window he'd broken. Something silver lay among the shards of broken glass on the backseat. He reached in, lifted it out. It was his Beretta.

And suddenly, he realized that he had to get out of there. He shoved the gun into his pocket, scrambled back up the side of the ditch to the road. He went over to the open door of his Mustang, tossed the gun on the passenger seat, then reached under the driver's seat, felt around until he found a flashlight. The light was faint, but it worked. He walked back along the side of the road, searching the gravel. He found his wallet lying in the weeds at the edge of the ditch, his driver's license up on the road. It took him several minutes of searching, but he finally found the handgun permit and his Statehouse pass in the ditch, near the deputy's body. As he splashed back past the overturned squad car, his flashlight picked up a scrap of paper floating on the surface of the water. He bent to pick it up. Scribbled on it was a name, *James Collette,* and a number that he recognized as an NOPD booking record. But what made him pause in the act of crumpling it was the handwriting; he held it up to the flashlight, looked at it closely. Over the last three years, he'd been handed hundreds of scraps of paper like this: a name and a number. No dollar sign, just a figure scribbled under the name. Danny would nod, crumple up the note, and set fire to it in an ashtray. And the man who wrote it would walk away without a word.

Lucas Clay.

Danny folded the paper carefully, shoved it into the pocket of his leather jacket with the gun. Then he climbed back out of the ditch, tossed everything else on the front seat of the Mustang, and got in. The keys hung in the ignition where he'd left them. The roar of the engine starting up surprised him, like a bright sky after a violent storm.

9

Mickie Vega slid into the back row of a second-floor courtroom in the juvenile court building on Loyola Avenue, watched as a black bailiff called the court back into session—"Section C of the Orleans Parish District Courts, juvenile division, Judge Macon Rollins presiding. All *rise.*"

She picked up the slender file with her case notes, got to her feet as the judge came out a door behind the bench, climbed two steps up to his chair, and settled into it, leaning to his right to talk something over with his clerk. Mickie sat down, glanced around the room. A young Asian woman had her briefcase open at the prosecution table, sorting through a thick sheaf of papers. Across the aisle, Gregory Nowles, the public defender assigned to this session, had his own briefcase open, scribbling some quick notes on a legal pad. The only other people in the courtroom were five middle-aged black women sitting stiffly in the second row, waiting.

The judge glanced over at the bailiff, nodded. The bailiff disappeared behind the bench, and appeared again a moment later, leading five black teenagers on a wrist chain. They wore orange jumpsuits with the letters *OPP* printed on the back. The jumpsuits were too big for them, but they gave no sign of noticing, all of them walking with a slow roll at the hip and shoulder, glancing around at the courtroom with bored expressions. A couple of them glanced over at Mickie, giving her a long appraising look, as if the fact that they were chained together, shuffling into court to be arraigned by a judicial system that could lock them away for years was no reason not to take a moment to check her out, flash her a look, like, *Uh-huh, I see you, baby.* Three of the prisoners had gang emblems shaved into their hair over the ear. None of them looked over at the row of women, who sat in silence as the deputy led the boys to the first row of benches, unlocked the chain, and told them to sit. There was a brief shuffle as the women switched places, then they leaned in behind the prisoners, whispering. The young men sat facing straight ahead, stiffly, as if the women were asking for something they refused to give.

Mickie smiled. *Tough to be a bad motherfucker when your mama's sitting there, whispering, "Did you get enough to eat, baby?"*

As she watched, Nowles folded his arms and leaned against the defense table, listening with a blank expression as one of the prisoners tried to explain something with lots of hand gestures, two fingers jabbing forward, the rest folded like a gun.

Mickie glanced down at the file in her hands, the name typed across the top of the case sheet: *Collette, James.*

Another kid with a gun.

She'd spent six hours talking to the cops over the weekend, going over the problem of Dewitt Foley. Foley selling guns to street gangs. Foley, confronted with evidence, pressured to testify. And now, Foley dead. His presence at the murder scene, a ragged bullet hole in his face, was like a knot in a piece of string. Was he the target? Or was it just an armed robbery that went bad? Maybe Foley just happened to be eating dinner there at the time. Bad luck for everybody.

No way to know, the cops told her. *Not till we finish digging all the bullets out, figure out who shot who.*

And so, Monday morning, early, she'd stood in the corridor outside the conference room in the ATF district office on Veterans Boulevard, nodding as Dubrow said, "Looks like we're back to square one. Go find us a kid who'll give up his supplier." She flipped through the file, saw it contained little more than an arrest record and a sheet showing that the kid had no priors.

Mickie watched Nowles lean back against the defense table, listening to what his client said with an expression like ice melting on a stove. He was a black man in his mid-fifties, the oldest attorney in the New Orleans public defender's office by a good twenty years. Most of them burned out after a few years, went into private practice. But Nowles kept at it, his face growing more deeply lined each year, his close-cropped hair now running to gray. He'd come out of the civil rights movement in the early seventies, the last of that generation, still fighting the good fight. His face looked tired to Mickie. *Like a man trying to fix a seawall,* she thought, *after the storm has washed it away.*

Nowles's eyes wandered across the empty courtroom and met her gaze, expressionless. Then he glanced down at the file in her lap before his eyes came back up to her face. She watched him ease up off the desk, stretch his shoulders, his eyes moving off across the courtroom.

Mickie glanced down at the file in her lap. James Collette. She flipped through the forms. The booking sheet gave the kid's age as fourteen, arrested two blocks from his home, carrying a 9 mm Heckler & Koch semiautomatic pistol. *Jesus. That's a lot of gun for a fourteen-year-old kid.*

She leaned forward and tried to peer down the row of prisoners, but they were all facing straight ahead. The kid at the far end of the row looked small enough, but that didn't mean much. None of them looked more than about sixteen.

The judge was frowning at a paper his clerk had just handed him, looking like he was in no hurry to get the proceedings started. Mickie sighed, shut the file, and stood up.

Time to talk to the lawyer.

"Collette, right? Weapons possession?"

"That's right." Mickie opened the file in her hands, glanced down at it. "I just got the paper on him this morning."

Greg Nowles considered the row of prisoners. They looked up at him, and for a moment he felt like a coach, getting ready to give a halftime fire-'em-up to a basketball squad. Then he sighed, shook his head. "Which one of you is James Collette?"

At the far end of the bench, a boy raised his hand. "Here."

Like he's in school, Mickie thought. *Teacher calls the roll.*

She was surprised how young the kid looked. He kept glancing down the row at the other boys, trying to imitate their scowls, giving it his best death row, don't-give-a-shit stare. But he had the kind of face they used to call *Say Hey,* like one of those kids who hung out at the ball field, lined up along the outfield wall, their faces bright with sunlight and dreams.

Mickie turned, walked down the front row, ignoring the stares she got from the prisoners. At the end, she squeezed between the bench and the wall to slip into the second row. A young black woman sat behind the boy, whispering to him. She was wearing the uniform of a nurse's aide over at City Hospital. Late twenties, Mickie guessed. *Could be a sister.* Then she realized, with a recognition that startled her, *Christ, that's old enough to be his mother, these days.* The woman's face looked tired, anxious. "Mrs. Collette?"

The woman looked up at her, surprised. Her eyes moved over Mickie's face, then down to the file in her hands, and her eyes narrowed. "Yeah?"

"I'm Mickie Vega. I've been assigned as your son's juvenile officer. There's a few matters I'd like to discuss with you."

It took forty minutes for the judge to move through the first three cases on the docket, listening with a blank expression as the prosecutor conducted the arraignments, glancing down at his papers from time to time as if he had no real interest in the matter. His voice was calm, matter-of-fact, and for a moment, Mickie could see the young boys in the front row relax, as if they'd decided it wasn't like the movies, some guy in a fancy suit wants your ass for breakfast. No, watching it, they saw that the whole thing was about *papers*—the prosecutor had them, the judge had a stack, even Nowles kept glancing down at a set, like it was a card game, everybody just playing out the hand they were dealt. One of those games, you had to get rid of all your cards. Somebody hands you a sheet of paper, you pass it on down the line.

Watching, Mickie thought, *Only nobody ever wins.*

Nowles entered a plea on two of the defendants, noted the trial date issued by the judge, and turned to whisper briefly to the next defendant as the previous one was led away. The fourth case called was James Collette, charged with possession of an unregistered firearm. As the boy stood up, Mickie leaned forward to get a good look at him. He was small, even for his age, and he looked scared. *Good,* Mickie thought. *Maybe he'll listen, somebody tries to cut him a deal.*

"Your honor, it's my understanding that the defendant is prepared to plead to these charges," Nowles said. "But I've just received the details on this case this morning. If you have no objection, I'd like to move for a continuation until I've had time to speak to my client."

The judge peered at Nowles over the rim of his glasses. "How long?"

"Two days should be fine."

The judge took a moment to think about it, then glanced over at the defendant, who seemed to have become smaller since he'd stood up, the OPP jumpsuit baggy around his ankles. "But you want bail, right?"

"We ask for reasonable bond, yes."

The judge sighed and looked over at the prosecutor. "You got any problem with that?"

The woman studied her papers. "Your honor, defendant was charged with possession of a loaded weapon."

"It's my understanding that this was a stop and frisk, your honor," Nowles said. "No crime was committed."

The judge frowned. "He had the gun, didn't he? That's a crime."

"Yes, sir. I meant there's no evidence that he used the weapon in the commission of a crime."

The judge slipped his glasses off, looked over at the kid. "Where do you live, son?"

The boy hesitated, wet his lips. "Saint Thomas," he murmured, his voice barely audible.

"That's a rough neighborhood, huh?"

The boy shrugged. "It's okay."

The judge paused for a moment, then nodded slowly. "You go to school?"

"Yes sir."

"Where?"

"Saint Matthews."

The judge raised an eyebrow. "Over on Loyola?"

"Yes sir."

"Isn't that a bit out of your neighborhood?"

The boy mumbled something. The judge leaned forward and cupped one hand behind his ear. "What's that?"

"Yeah," the boy murmured.

The judge folded his hands, rested his chin on them. He smiled. "If memory serves, they run a program for gifted students over there. You go to that?"

The boy was silent for a moment, then nodded.

"What's your best subject?"

The boy shrugged. "Math, I guess."

The judge nodded slowly. He studied the boy for a moment,

then glanced over at his clerk. "Ruth, you carry a calculator in your handbag, don't you?"

The clerk looked up from her papers, surprised. "I'm sorry?"

"Pass it up here."

She glanced around the courtroom for a moment, as if that might explain it, then took her purse out from under the desk, dug around in it for a moment, and stood up to pass a pocket calculator up to the judge. He leaned over the bench to take it, then sat back and hit a button to switch it on. He adjusted his glasses, tapped a few keys, and glanced up at the kid.

"Tell you what. I'm gonna throw some numbers at you, see if you can keep a running total. You do that for me?"

The boy shrugged. "Yeah, okay."

"Three hundred fifty-seven and six hundred ninety-two." The judge squinted at the calculator, then up at the kid. "You with me?"

"Uh-huh. Thousand forty-nine."

"Times forty-two."

Mickie saw the kid go away somewhere, his eyes focused on a spot in the distance, beyond the back wall of the courtroom.

"Forty-four thousand fifty-eight."

"Divided by three hundred seventy-two."

"One hundred eighteen point forty-three."

The judge smiled. "Times seven point five three."

"Eight hundred ninety-one point eighty-one."

"Okay, now give me thirty-eight percent of that."

"Three hundred thirty-eight point eight nine."

The judge sighed, switched off the calculator, passed it back to the clerk. "So how come you carryin' a gun?"

Mickie saw the kid take a moment to come back. He glanced around the courtroom, as if surprised to find himself there, then fixed his eyes on the floor. His shoulders seemed to draw up, and he gave a shrug. "Found it."

"You *found* it?"

"Uh-huh."

The judge settled back in his chair and folded his arms across his chest. He looked over at Nowles, wearily. "Have your client back here in two days, counselor. Bail is set at five thousand dollars."

10

Martelle Collette stood in the narrow corridor outside the courtroom, staring at the paper in her hand. *Five thousand dollars. Go 'cross the street, like the lawyer tell you, the bail bond place take five hundred, and your boy be out this afternoon.*

The only problem, she wanted to tell him, was she didn't have no $500 to pay the man, get her boy out of jail. But the lawyer turned away, started talking to one of the other boys about *his* case, and she had to sit there, watch them lead James out through that door behind the curtain, the deputy holding that chain around his wrists. She saw him glance back quickly before he disappeared through the door, his eyes scared. But what could she do? Five hundred dollars, she wanted to tell him. Who could she ask for money like that?

Now the juvenile officer, Mexican woman, was standing at her elbow, talkin' to her all about *sentencing guidelines, probationary requirements,* all manner of shit she couldn't no way listen to just now, lookin' down at that paper in her hand. *Five hundred dollars.*

The Mexican woman took her arm, led her over to a corner, saying now maybe James didn't have to go to jail. Her voice quiet now, almost a whisper, like she was telling Martelle a secret, just for her. How the woman knew some people who'd like to help them. How all they wanted was to talk to James, ask him a couple questions.

Martelle stared at her blankly.

"Naturally," the woman told her quickly, "we could arrange for his bail."

Mickie kept up a steady chatter as she led the boy's mother down the hall to the clerk's office, telling her how they could clear the boy's record if he cooperated, arrange with the district attorney's office to have the charges withdrawn, his arrest expunged from the official record. Keeping her moving toward the moment when she saw her boy released, not letting her stop to think about what she'd agreed to.

At the counter, Mickie took the paper that the lawyer had given her and passed it to the clerk, saying, "We'd like to post bail for James Collette, juvenile court, section C."

The clerk took the paper and went away. Mickie turned back to the boy's mother, smiled and said, "Won't be long now."

Martelle looked at Mickie, seeming lost now without the paper in her hand. "I just want to take my boy home."

Mickie nodded, gave her an encouraging smile. "Just a few quick questions. You'll have him home for dinner."

The clerk came back, slid the paper back through the window. "Somebody already paid it," he told Mickie. "'Bout ten minutes ago."

Mickie frowned. "Are you sure?"

"That's what it says in the file. We put the papers through on him already. Kid's being processed right now."

Mickie turned to the boy's mother. "Is there anybody else who might have bailed your son?"

The woman shook her head. "I'm his mama. There ain't nobody else."

"What about the boy's father?"

"He ain't around."

Mickie could feel the people in the line behind them start to shuffle their feet impatiently. She took Martelle's arm, drew her aside. "And you can't think of anybody else who might have a reason to post your son's bond?"

She saw the woman's face stiffen, her eyes getting hard. "You got a question. Ask him."

They sat on a bench outside the clerk's office, the boy leaning against a wall, casually. He looked around, his face bored. Martelle grabbed him by the wrist and jerked him onto the bench beside her. He scowled, pushed her hand away.

Mickie leaned forward, smiled. "James, I'd like to ask you a few questions, okay?" He shrugged, looked down at his Jordans, the laces still in his back pocket from when the police gave 'em back to him. His mother glared at him, said, "You answer the lady, you hear?"

James nodded, once, his eyes not moving from his shoes.

"And when she done, you *better* have some answers for me."

Mickie sat back. She waited until James looked up at her, warily, then smiled at him. "How 'bout we start by you tellin' me what happened. How'd that be?"

James shrugged, went back to looking at his shoes.

Martelle reached over, took his chin in her hand, and raised it up so he was looking her in the eye. "The lady *talkin'* to you."

James jerked his head free, gave her a look that showed her, for a brief moment, what he'd look like as a grown man. Then his hand came up to rub at his jaw, like he could rub away the spot where she'd touched him, and suddenly he was a little boy again. Watching it happen, Martelle felt tears fill her eyes, turned away to dig in her pocketbook for a tissue.

"Like I said, I found it."

Mickie nodded. "Where?"

"In a trash can, over behind the hospital."

Mickie was silent for a moment, then said, "That the whole story?"

"Uh-huh."

She sat back wearily. It was a waste of time. She'd send the kid home with his mother and forget about him. He'd be back in court in a few days, draw probation or a brief custodial sentence, youth center, maybe, or one of the state's boot camps for juvenile offenders. Come out flat-eyed and angry, looking for trouble. When he was seventeen, they'd pick him up for something serious, ship him off to Angola State Penitentiary. It all lay before him, like the view from the top of the playground slide. No way to go but down.

She glanced over at him, remembered his answers to the judge's questions, his voice quiet, shy. "Mrs. Collette," she said, turning to his mother. "Do you think I could talk to your son alone for a few minutes?"

Martelle shifted slightly on the bench. She looked over at James, who was studying his shoes, like there was some private little movie playing there, just for him.

"I'm his mama," she told Mickie. "There ain't nothing he's gonna say to you he can't say it in front of me."

Mickie sighed. *Yeah, right.* She looked past Martelle at the boy. "See, here's the thing, James . . ."

"Everybody call me Sugar Bear."

Martelle looked over at him, surprised. "Everybody *who?* You hear me call you that?"

James seemed to shrink, bending over his knees like somebody'd folded him in half. But he shook his head slowly. "My *friends.*"

"Your *friends* a buncha low-life niggers, don't got the sense to stop hangin' 'round with those *drug* dealers." Martelle hearing her mama's voice even as she said it. But she couldn't stop now, had to say the whole thing, like some kind of magic spell. "Did I bring you up to be like that? *Huh?*"

"No, ma'am," James murmured, folding himself even smaller, like maybe they'd forget he was there.

"And your name is *James*."

Mickie ran one hand up over her hair, then left it there, feeling like if she took it away, the top of her head might fly off. "Uh, well, see, here's the thing. They seize a gun, like in this case, they got to run a ballistics test on it. You know what that is?"

Martelle looked at her. "Uh-*huh*."

Mickie held up both hands. "Okay, sorry. Just wanted to make sure you're clear on the issues."

Martelle folded her arms, waiting.

"Anyway, they run a ballistics test, they got to test-fire the gun, see if they get a match with any bullets recovered at crime scenes." She looked over at James. "If you found the gun, like you say, not only is there nothing your lawyer can do but plead you on the possession charge, but they can also try to link you to any other crimes they think the gun might have been used in. You see the problem?"

James looked up at her, nodded. "I still found it."

Mickie flinched as Martelle leaned over, slapped him upside the head, hard. "You gonna tell this lady the truth, boy?"

But then he surprised Martelle by straightening up, giving her a contemptuous look, telling her, "She don't *want* the truth, Mama."

Martelle looked up at Mickie, then around her at the narrow hallway, policemen standing around, thinking, *Ah, Jesus.* Then she stood up abruptly, grabbed James's arm, and yanked him to his feet. She turned to face Mickie, her face hot, and said, "You got any more *questions* for my boy, you talk to his *lawyer.* You hear?"

Then she turned on her heel and headed for the stairs.

Mickie sat there, watching them disappear down the stairs. *Jesus.* Like somebody'd flicked a switch, turned on a bright light that blinded them all. She thought about the way the boy had looked over at his mama, his face angry. But also the way he'd tried to fold himself up, get out of her sight. *Like a kid who's broken a window in the neighbor's house, now he's got to sit there and listen to her tell him what a bad boy he's been.* Mickie tried to picture him in a cell at the Youth Study Center over on Milton Street, in there with all the walking dead, but she couldn't see it. From what she'd heard, they didn't do much *studying* in there. Way that boy looked, it was surprising they didn't eat him alive.

She glanced down at the release forms in front of her. *So who put up his bail?* She thought about that baby-faced kid walking out of YSC, not a mark on him. Seeing the line of prisoners led into the courtroom on the wrist chain, the way none of them glanced down the row at James Collette, even when the judge had him do the number tricks. The other prisoners sitting there like it was normal, eyes half closed, staring at the floor. Like they'd seen it all before. Or like they knew enough, growing up in New Orleans, to stay out of something that don't no *way* concern them.

She opened the file on her lap, wrote *Possible* at the top of the first page.

11

Rodney Collette was only twelve, but almost as tall as his brother. When he was little, his uncle Andre used to grab him up off the floor of the kitchen, lift him up to his shoulder, let him sit there so the world seemed to jump back—table, chairs, wide scrubbed floor, his mama's face glancing up at him from where she stood by the stove, sayin', "Boy, you got big, huh?"

"That's my *tall* man," Uncle Andre would say. "Got to get this boy some basketball shoes."

And he'd see James look up from his homework, screw up his face like it was some baby thing, this flying, this joy.

"Tha's all right," Uncle Andre would tell him. "You get to the NBA, you let James here keep track of all your money, huh?"

And Rodney would grin down at James, even though he was no good at basketball, and even though he knew Uncle Andre was only sayin' it to make up for how he'd always sit down with James after dinner, talk about some math problem he was working on. Andre was their mama's half brother. He taught seventh grade over at Redemptorist, commuted in from Slidell. Once a week, he'd stay for dinner, "spend some time with his boys." Mostly that meant helping James with his homework, but he always made time for Rodney too.

And he was *real* tall.

Later on, when Rodney got too big to lift onto his shoulder, Andre started taking him out for a walk before dinner, which meant they'd go downstairs, walk up a couple blocks to the high school, sit on the bleachers next to the track, have a talk.

And that's where they were, evening coming down warm and thick, Andre leaning back with his elbows on the seat behind him, looking up at the sky.

"So James got arrested, huh?"

"Yeah."

"Your mama have to go bail him out?"

"Uh-huh." Rodney peered down between the bleachers, wondering if money ever fell out of people's pockets. Maybe other stuff, too, lying down there in the weeds.

"How you feel 'bout that?"

Rodney looked up. "What?"

"James."

Rodney shrugged. "Okay, I guess." He felt Andre look over at him, tried to think of something else to say so he wouldn't be disappointed, get all silent like he did, but the truth was he didn't feel much of anything about it, really. So when a kid Rodney didn't recognize came up to the fence, yelled out, "Hey, James!" Rodney glanced over, relieved.

He felt Andre stiffen next to him, the way he did when some kid from the project came up to them on the street, started talkin' to him. Andre was a cool guy, in his own way, but sometimes he was, like, *white*. Rodney jumped down off the side of the bleachers, walked over to the fence to tell the guy how James was up at the house, and the way their mama was yelling, man, forget it, he wasn't *never* getting out.

The kid was standing by a streetlight, waving his hand in front of his face to chase off the bugs. Rodney could see them swirling around the light, crashing against the glass. It made him feel slightly sick, watching them, like the time he rode his bike right into a thick cloud of gnats, felt 'em in his eyes, his nose, down his throat.

"What's up?" the kid said, then looked at him real close. "Man, I thought you was James."

"James got busted. He's up at the house, waitin' to see if Mama's gonna take his hide off."

The kid pursed his lips, made a whistling sound. "Yeah? He got busted, for real?"

"Uh-huh. Had him a gun."

The kid shook his head, slowly. "Man, I heard that, but I thought, like, *James?* No way, you know?"

Rodney leaned on the fence, glanced back at Andre. He was standing at the edge of the bleachers, watching them.

The kid kicked at the bottom of the fence a couple times with his sneaker; Rodney felt it shake under his hand.

"You see James," the kid said, "tell him there's some guys come by Saint Andrew lookin' for him, okay?"

"Yeah? What guys?"

"L'Dog and them." The kid pushed off the fence, walked a few steps away, then turned so he was walking backwards. He raised one hand to point at Rodney with his fingers folded like a gun. "Yo, man. Don't tell no one I told you, right?"

Rodney shrugged, and the kid walked off into the darkness. Rodney glanced up at the streetlight. There were bugs crawling all over the glass, flailing through the cone of yellow light below it.

That's what it's like to be dead, he thought. *Bugs all up in your nose, your ears.*

Then he turned, walked back to where Andre stood, waiting for him with that look on his face told you he still wanted to have a serious *talk.* Like he wanted to pick you up, show you how the world looked from where he stood.

Still thinkin' I'm just a kid, Rodney thought. *But, like James say, it just ain't that easy anymore.*

"You know your problem?"

Maura sat up in Danny's bed with her knees drawn up under the sheet and her chin resting on her folded arms, watching him in the darkness. He lay stretched out across the foot of the bed, naked, one arm draped across his eyes.

"What's my problem?"

"You're good-looking." Maura smiled. "I've been doing a study of attractive men over the last few years, and I've come to the conclusion that you're all deeply fucked up."

Danny lay there, not moving.

"Not as bad as beautiful women, of course. They're *really* fucked up. But it's the same problem, basically. Everybody wants you. Things come too easy."

"That so?"

"Uh-huh. Look at Helen. She's a mess. I mean, her marriage? She married a prince, and he turns into a frog. That'd fuck anybody up."

Danny smiled.

She leaned over, felt around on the bedside table for her cigarettes. "We all got one story we live by, Danny. But I gotta tell you, you been playing this frog-prince gig too long."

Danny sat up wearily and rubbed at his face with both hands. "So what's your story?"

"Me?" She smiled. "The Emperor's New Clothes." Then she reached over to run her hand through his hair. "Hey, don't let it get you down. I like you better as a frog. It works for you."

Danny said nothing. He lay there, gazing up at the ceiling somewhere above him in the darkness. If he stared hard enough, he could almost believe that he saw it up there above him. It was something to believe in. Something to contain the darkness that surrounded him.

He'd lain awake most of the previous night, staring at the ceiling as his mind replayed what had happened out on that empty highway, seeing it over and over like a broken projector that he couldn't figure out how to shut off. It was almost dawn when sleep finally came, and he dreamed that he was struggling to dig a deep hole in a mudflat, the sides collapsing on him whenever he got it deep enough to hide in. He woke around noon, his body bruised and stiff. It took him ten minutes just to get out of bed, the room starting to spin whenever he tried to sit up. Finally he got to his feet and dragged himself into the bathroom, where he stood under a steaming shower for almost twenty minutes, until the tank emptied and the water ran cold. He eased his clothes on gingerly, wincing as he slid his jeans over his bruised hip. Then he went out into the kitchen, made a pot of strong coffee, and sat down to think.

Mostly he thought about his father. Roy Chaisson, slumped over the wheel of his car on an empty roadside, a gun lying on the seat beside him. Had he also been sent out to a meeting with a guy who didn't show? Danny closed his eyes, feeling the anger rise like a flame within him. He got up and went into the living room, where his jacket hung on a chair next to the door. He dug the scrap of paper out of the pocket, carried it back into the kitchen.

James Collette, DOB 9/7/85, arrested for weapons possession. Why was Lucas Clay interested in a fourteen-year-old boy? What could make a kid like that interesting enough for Lucas to pass his name on to a couple of cops who didn't mind using their guns to solve a problem? Danny stared at the name on the paper, thought, *Looks like we got something in common, kid.*

He made himself eat a cup of yogurt and a couple slices of bread, then grabbed his jacket off the chair by the door and went out. In the car, he switched on the twenty-four-hour news radio station, had to wait until twenty past the hour before the first report came up on the dead sheriff's deputies out in St. Bernard Parish. Investigators were treating it as an accident, the newscaster said, but there was evidence that a driver uninvolved in the accident had left the scene. Dan Furman, the St. Bernard sheriff, made a statement asking for witnesses to the crash to come forward.

Yeah, right, Danny thought. He wondered briefly what evidence they might have been talking about, then it hit him. *Tire tracks.* They'd pulled him over on a wet gravel shoulder, so his tires had probably left tread marks behind. He'd been headed up Broadway to the juvenile court building over on Loyola Avenue, but now he made a quick right on Claiborne, found a Quick-E Tire Service, got the guy behind the counter to ring him up a complete set of new tires. The guy walked out to the Mustang with his clipboard to take a look at the tires he had on it.

"Not much wear on these," he told Danny, pointing to one of the rear tires with his pen. "You could probably get another couple months out of this set, no problem."

Danny shrugged. "No point taking chances."

While he waited, he walked down to the K&B Drugs at the corner, bought a *Times-Picayune,* and flipped through it. There was nothing on the two deputies. They must have found them too late for the morning edition, he figured.

When the car was finished, he drove up to the courthouse, parked in the lot across the street. He went into the courthouse and took the stairs to the clerk's office. When his turn came, he dug the scrap of paper out of his pocket, laid it on the counter. "Can you give me the status on this case?"

The woman checked the number on the paper, then went away. When she came back, she was carrying a juvenile court case disposition form. "Went through morning arraignment," she told Danny. "Defendant posted early this afternoon."

"They cut him loose yet?"

"Probably. You'd have to ask over at the sheriff's office."

Danny nodded, dug a pen out of his pocket. "You got an address on the defendant?"

The woman looked up at him, raised her eyebrows. "I can't give out that information. Not unless you're a parent or legal guardian."

Danny stared at her. "If I was a parent or legal guardian, why would I need it?" The woman's eyes narrowed, and she started to turn away. Danny raised both hands quickly and said, "Okay, look, I'm sorry. I just need to get in touch with the kid's parents, that's all." He thought for a moment. "Who's the kid's counsel?"

She looked at the form. "Nowles."

Danny smiled. "Okay, thanks. That's all I need to know."

Downstairs, Danny stopped in the public defender's office, left a message asking for Greg Nowles to call him at home. After he hung up, he glanced at his watch, thought about what he should do next. For a moment, he considered riding over to Audubon Place, sitting in his car outside Jimmy's house until Lucas came out, then slamming his head against the sidewalk until Lucas told him what was going on. It was a tempting idea, but then he thought, *No, wait until you've got more to use on him.* Then he smiled. *Let him worry about what happened to the deputies for a couple days, then go see him.*

He found Maura sitting on the steps of his house when he got home. Without a word, she stood up, waited for him to unlock the door, then followed him up the stairs to his apartment on the second floor. Inside, she let her bag drop to the floor, walked straight into the bedroom. He stayed in the living room for a while, looking out the window at the late-afternoon shadows cast by the oak tree on the street, then he followed her. As he got undressed in the half-light of the bedroom, he heard her say, "You sure know how to keep a girl waiting."

"Sorry."

"Don't apologize. That way I can think you do it on purpose, like you're one of those guys who think women want to be treated like shit." He saw her smile in the near-darkness. "Makes it easier for me to leave in the morning."

He dropped his clothes on the floor, got into bed, felt her slide into the curl of his arm. "Is that what women want?"

She drew back, looked at him. "You're kidding, right?"

He shrugged. "So what do you want?"

She settled back, her head resting against his shoulder. "Big mystery. Women want it all. Just like you. But we'd settle for the things we had when we were little girls. Dance lessons. Love. *Food.*" She smiled. "After that, we'll figure it out as we go along."

"That simple, huh?"

She looked up at him, serious. "It's not simple at all, Danny."

After they made love, she was always full of nervous energy, getting up, moving around the room, looking at whatever came to hand. He lay across the foot of the bed, one arm draped across his eyes, waiting. At last she came back to bed, sat with her knees drawn up, looking down at him. Studying him, like he was a problem she intended to solve. When she finally spoke, her voice was cool, detached, as if they'd never made love, never even touched. "You got a lot of problems, Danny. You know that?"

Later, she slept. Danny lay beside her, staring up at the ceiling, thinking. After a while, he got up, went into the living room, where he opened the French doors onto the small front porch, dragged a chair over, and sat there, staring out into the darkness. In his mind, he kept seeing headlights rushing toward him, only the man behind the wheel was his father.

Jesus, he thought, rubbing at his eyes. *What's that about?*

But maybe it wasn't so hard to figure out. His father was a man who loved Louisiana politics so much that he gave his life to it.

Not me, Danny thought, angrily. *No fucking way.*

"This a guy thing?"

Danny turned to see Maura standing in the bedroom door, naked, watching him.

"You like to sit there, huh? Stare out into the darkness, think deep thoughts. Like the movie's about you, right?"

He smiled. "I just realized something."

"Yeah? What's that?"

"I'm not my father."

"Jesus, it took you this long to figure that out?" Maura perched on the arm of the leather couch, folded her arms tightly across her small breasts. "I could've told you that years ago, Danny."

Danny looked off into the darkness. "Yeah, I guess I had to figure it out for myself."

She studied her feet like they were part of some other body. "They've been talking about you, Danny. My father and Lucas."

He looked over at her. "You hear what they said?"

"Just the way they say your name. Like you're a situation that's come up."

He smiled. "That sounds about right."

She stared at him. "I worry about you, Danny. Which is funny, since you don't give a shit about me. But I watch you, and it breaks my heart. You're like a kid trying to step on his own shadow." She shook her head sadly. "Tell me something, you think Lucas and my father are your friends?"

Danny smiled. "Guys like that don't have friends. I'm useful to them sometimes."

Maura looked at him, and he saw anger flash in her eyes. "And you can live with that?"

Danny looked away. She stood up suddenly, looked around the room like she expected the walls to crack open and let the darkness come rushing in. When her eyes came to him, they paused, examining his expression. Then, without warning, she smiled, reached out a hand to him.

"Come to bed, okay? I need someone to turn my back on."

12

According to a neighbor, James Collette left his mother's apartment on the third floor of a building in the St. Thomas housing project just after 11:30 P.M. She knew because she'd been watching Leno, then decided to take out the garbage before going to bed.

Tom Acorsi glanced up from his notebook. "You know *anybody* in Saint Thomas would take out the garbage that time of night?"

"Probably went out to score."

St. Thomas was a homicide cop's nightmare, a complex of low-rise brick buildings spread over several city blocks, where people sat out on their front stoops late into the evenings, talking, cooking barbecue, drinking beer out of long-necked bottles, until something happened. Then they vanished. No witnesses, no memory. A city of the blind. You couldn't blame 'em, really. Most of the residents were working poor, women struggling to raise a family on one salary, going off to work in the city's hospitals, its hotels, the fast-food restaurants down along Canal Street. Stay clean, stay out of trouble, you can work for $4.85 an hour, sweeping up the french fries that fall off people's trays. The kids saw the drug dealers, teenage boys, riding around in their cars, they said, *Yeah, I'll take that.* So now there were too many dealers, and the turf was getting squeezed. You got drive-by shootings, snipers firing off rooftops, even a kid who used to ride by on his ten-speed, open up with his daddy's old service revolver. And the people sitting on their stoops, they saw it all, went back inside until the shooting stopped, then came back out to watch the ambulance arrive to pick up the body. They'd listen to the cops ask their questions, then look down at their shoes, shake their heads slowly. *Nah, didn't see nothin'*.

Acorsi and Maya sat in an unmarked a half block from the benches on St. Andrew Street, where three teenage boys perched on the back of the bench, eyeing them, trying to prove something to themselves by sticking it out. A couple cars had come past while they sat there, slowing by the benches until the drivers saw that the boys weren't moving to come over; one of them flicked his eyes over to where the two cops sat in the brown Ford, its interior light switched on so you could see them just sitting there, talking.

Now Acorsi watched one of them glance over, meet his eyes. The kid turned to say something to his buddies, then leaned over and spit onto the ground in front of the bench.

"What about these guys? Could ask them where he went," Acorsi said.

Maya glanced up at the boys on the bench, shook her head. "I know one of those boys. My husband's cousin lives here, works up at Charity Hospital. That's her kid on the end."

Acorsi looked over. The kid looked sixteen, seventeen. He wore baggy jeans, high-top BK Knights, and an old, worn-out New Orleans Jazz T-shirt that looked like it had seen a lot of summer nights since the team gave up on the city, took off for Salt Lake.

"He recognize you?"

"Yeah, he keeps lookin' over here, like he's waiting for me to say something to him." She shook her head sadly, went back to scribbling something in her notebook.

Acorsi looked down at his notebook. "So we got anything real here?"

"The boy's mother spends most of the night yelling at him, sends him off to bed about ten." Maya's voice was tired, and she rubbed at her eyes as she spoke. "He waits until she's asleep, sneaks out. This neighbor woman goes to put out the trash about eleven-thirty, sees him coming out of his apartment. He meets some other kid who's waiting in the stairs, and they leave together. This other kid looks a couple years older, he's wearing some kind of hooded sweatshirt, but it's dark and he's got the hood up, so she doesn't know if he's from around here."

"Pretty hot night for a hooded sweatshirt."

"You think she's full of shit?"

"I think she recognized the kid, but she doesn't want to say."

"No, I guess not." Maya looked up at the boys on the bench. "Not if she's a buyer."

He shook his head, flipped a page in his notes. "C'mon, she was just takin' out the *garbage.*"

Maya glanced over at him but let it pass. They were tired, hungry. When the call first came in from the ballistics lab, connecting the gun recovered from a juvenile named James Collette with the Claiborne Avenue shootings, they'd felt that rush that comes when you see it all snap together, when you catch a break that drops the whole case in your lap. Excited, Acorsi had jammed a finger down on the phone, dialed up the juvenile section of Orleans Parish Prison, asked if they were still holding the kid. The clerk put the phone down, went away to check his records. When he came back, he said, "Sorry. The kid posted bail at morning arraignment."

Maya, watching, saw Acorsi close his eyes, wearily. "You got an address?"

He'd been released to his mother, who lived down in the St. Thomas housing project, less than a mile from the scene of the shootings on Claiborne Avenue. Acorsi asked the clerk to pull the file, run a copy of the kid's booking sheet and release papers. Then he hung up, called over to the night duty clerk at the courthouse, and arranged for a judge to sign off on a warrant for the kid's arrest on five charges of homicide.

It took them two hours to get the paperwork done, then run it over to the courthouse for the judge's signature. When they finally headed down to St. Thomas, Maya driving, she could feel the tiredness in her eyes.

No surprise when they got there. The kid had vanished. *Probably halfway to Detroit by now,* Maya thought. *If he's got any sense.*

She watched Acorsi close his notebook, lean his head against the back of the seat, and close his eyes. He looked pale, like a man who'd spent the last few days allowing the blood to be slowly drained from his body, until nothing was left but the sound of his breathing.

She opened the file on her lap, looked at the sheet on James Collette. Fourteen years old, no priors. According to the arresting officer's report, he'd been picked up with a stolen 9 mm Beretta pistol early Saturday morning, during a routine stop and frisk by undercover narcotics detectives at a *known drug location.* What that probably meant, she knew, was the kid had been walking past a dealer's corner, caught the eye of one of the narco guys, who decided he looked jumpy. Walking funny, maybe. Nervous, seeing these white guys sitting in an unmarked on an empty street, wearing *Surf Bum!* T-shirts over their muscles. So they put him against the wall, looked in his bag, saying, "Well, well, well. What we got here?" Taking the gun out with two fingers, holding it up so the kid could see it, grinning at him. *Uh-oh! Wipeout!*

It was just a game to those guys. Street hockey. Find the guy with the puck, slam him against the boards. They loved the pure muscle of it, getting in some black kid's face, make him sweat while they dug through his pockets, shoved their hands down his pants. "Got anything for me today? Little piece of the rock?" They came up with drugs, guns, knives, and once a crudely scrawled note on a scrap of brown paper from a shopping bag: *I have a gun. Giv me all your monny.* The narco guys had laughed so hard at that one, they almost pissed themselves. Down on their knees, laughing, right there on the sidewalk.

But this one had turned serious. Ballistics tests run on the kid's gun had produced a match, and so James Collette, age fourteen, was now their best suspect in a multiple homicide.

"This is interesting."

Acorsi opened his eyes, looked over at Maya. She had the case file open on her lap, the pages folded back over the metal clip to the kid's release form.

"You want to speculate on where the mother got five thousand *cash* to make the kid's bail?" She flipped the page, glanced at the next sheet, then flipped back to the release sheet. "Kid walked an hour after his arraignment. Looks like somebody was in a hurry to get him back on the street."

Acorsi opened his eyes and leaned over to look at the form on her lap. Then he sat back, closed his eyes again. "It strike you that we're an awful long way from Conti Street, here?"

"Yeah, I was thinking that on the way over."

"What are the chances this kid's down with those boys who got shot?"

Maya shrugged. "I've got cousins across town. Could be something like that."

"You pull armed robberies with your cousins?"

She smiled. "I'm a big girl now."

Acorsi opened his eyes, looked over at her. "No, really. This kid's, what? Fourteen? You really see him as the gunman, a deal like this? Goes in there, blows five people away, then gets himself arrested walking home."

"You figure he's a short?"

"Makes sense." He looked over at the boys on the bench. "These guys, they all got some kid to hold their dope, guns. Kid gets picked up with it, it's six months in a juvie hall. You're a couple years older, you take the long ride." He shook his head. "Jesus, I just shot five people, I wouldn't *walk* home, the gun in my pocket."

"You'd hand it off to some kid."

"Maybe. Of course, then the kid's a witness."

"In which case, you'd want him back on the street." Maya looked over at him. "Where you could get at him."

He nodded. "You just killed five people, what's one more?"

They were silent for a while, looking out at the night. Then Acorsi said, "Jesus, I used to love this city. Now all I see is bodies on the sidewalk."

"You figure this kid's next?"

"That's how it looks." Acorsi yawned and let his head sink back against the seat. "He's not in the morgue by morning, we can start asking who he hangs with. See what we get that way."

Maya nodded. She reached down, started the car. "Seems like we spend half our time waiting for the next kid to die."

"Closest we ever get to justice, this town."

She looked over at him. "Get some sleep, Tom."

Ray Morrisey sat in the darkness of his unmarked Chevy, watching as the homicide cops drove away. He had a paper sack spread out on the seat beside him, reaching over to grab french fries out of a cardboard take-out box. He held a large paper cup of Diet Coke between his legs, felt the straw poke into his stomach when he leaned forward to grab his binoculars off the dashboard, check the number painted on the side of the building he'd watched the cops come out of a few minutes earlier. *Well, shit.* They'd connected the gun to the Collette kid already. Morrisey'd figured it would take a couple days, at least. Enough time for Sadler and Bartolo to put the last touch on the whole deal by setting up a little drive-by to take out the kid. *Hell,* he'd told them when he explained the plan, *you give the NOPD a dead nigger kid with a gun, they'll write the whole thing off as a gang thing, close the case.* Only Sadler and Bartolo had fucked everything up again, ended up dead in some ditch out on the St. Bernard Highway when they were supposed to be down here taking care of the kid.

He tossed the binoculars back on the dash, picked up his hamburger, took a bite. *Same old story. You want something done right, you got to do it yourself.*

The only good thing, it looked like the two cops had struck out. Kid had any brains, he'd skipped town. Sorry 'bout the bail, Ma, but your boy can't do no jail. Hell, he stayed gone, might be almost as good as dead. Only problem was, you couldn't count on a kid to stay gone. They always come back. Got to sneak back home, see their mamas, show off all that gold jewelry they bought out in L.A. All the cops have to do is wait.

Morrisey glanced down at the burger in his hand, chewing slowly. Not a bad burger, for a nigger joint. But, hell, you let that stuff get to you, can't eat no place in New Orleans these days. Still, he'd watched the girl behind the counter closely as she rang up his order, went in the back to get the food. When she came out, he grinned at her and said, "You wouldn't spit in my burger, now, would you?"

The girl stared at him, her eyes wide. "No, sir."

He reached over, took the bag from her hands. "That's fine, darling. 'Cause I'd hate to have to come back here and shove it down your throat."

Now he watched the boys sitting on the bench as he finished off the burger, wiped his fingers on a paper napkin. The boys had loosened up when the two cops drove away: one of them got down off the bench and walked out to the curb stiffly, a white cop's walk, like somebody'd just shoved his badge up his ass, used his gun to push it up in there a couple more inches. That broke the tension, got the rest of 'em laughing. Stupid fuckers hadn't spotted him yet, sitting in the darkness at the far end of the block, watching.

Not that he gave a shit. They were up in his part of town, he'd have to pay them a visit, right quick. Tell 'em the rules, they got to pay up or shut down, their choice. But right now he was only interested in the kid. No point getting involved in shit that don't concern you. No percentage in that.

Morrisey finished off his french fries and reached across to the glove compartment, took out a pint bottle of Wild Turkey, poured some into his Diet Coke. Then he sat back, sipped at it through the straw, thinking.

The whole thing was fucked up. Okay, Sadler and Bartolo were dead, so that was one problem solved. Both men had been nominated for posthumous service medals, to be awarded to their widows at a special ceremony at the City Hall in Chalmette, and the sheriff went on TV, called 'em "real heroes, our city's finest sons." Morrisey grinned, shook his head at the thought.

Pretty damn funny, you think about it.

But that meant the witness, this guy Chaisson, was still out there, another problem waiting to be solved.

Morrisey sipped at his Diet Coke, gazing off across the concrete playground at the kid's building. Two bullets, the whole mess is cleaned up. The cops find the kid, figure it's a gang payback, and the witness just disappears. Easy to get rid of a body in New Orleans. Twenty minutes in any direction, you're out in the swamps. Take a miracle for anybody to find him out there. And that's if they're looking. From what he'd heard about this guy, it sounded like nobody would much notice he was gone, except the people who wanted him to disappear. Morrisey smiled, imagining the expression on the guy's face when he told him that. *Hey, tough break, pal. Looks like you're the shit on everybody's shoe.*

He leaned forward, staring at the entrance to the building. A shadow appeared in the open door, somebody hanging back in the darkness for a moment as he scanned the street out front. When he was sure the street was empty, a boy slid out of the shadows, ran across the concrete playground to the street. Morrisey trailed him with his eyes, a black kid, looked about the right age, moving fast. The kid made a right at the street, vanished into the darkness beyond the streetlights at the end of the block.

Morrisey grinned, leaned forward, started the car. *Looks like somebody lit a fire under that boy's ass.* He put the car in gear, pulled away from the curb.

Hell, sometimes you catch a break.

Sugar Bear hadn't realized you could make up your own name, just, like, pick something 'cause you like the sound of it, tell people, *That's my name, right?* Shit, he'd known that, you think he wouldn't have come up with something a whole lot better than *Sugar Bear?* Everybody on the street calling him that now, ever since that first time they took him to meet Jabril, the man sittin' there on his couch, watchin' that white preacher on the TV, glancin' up at him.

"What's your name, boy?"

"James."

Jabril sighed, rubbed at his face with one hand, like he was tired. "James, huh? Boy, you don't look like no fuckin' *James* to me. You know who you look like? That little bear used to come on TV Saturday mornings, always gettin' in trouble 'cause he loved that cereal so much?" Turning to ask L'Dog, "You know who I mean, right? What's that fuckin' bear called?"

"Sugar Bear."

Jabril turning back to him, grinning. "Yeah, Sugar Bear. Always got that little smile on his face. Real sweet."

And that was it. His mama, she didn't see how it was on the street. No *way* was anybody gonna call him no fuckin' *James,* you know?

Still, he figured L'Dog was full of shit. Tellin' everybody he saw his name in a *dream. L'Dog. Short for Love Dog, 'cause, like, I* am, *you know?* Uh-huh, right. Hang on now, I'll run and get a hammer, pound this nail in my forehead. Still, you got to admire how he made everybody go along with it, even Jabril. That shows, like, initiative.

And, hey, L'Dog was better than what they used to call him, right? Everybody walkin' around callin' him Rag, 'cause he always wore that stupid rag tied around his head. That's *hard,* man. People get to makin' jokes, you know?

He was wearing it now, a red bandanna tied with two knots at the back, so he had to keep his head tipped slightly forward as he drove to keep the knots from pressing into the back of his skull when he leaned against the seat. It made him look like he didn't *believe* the world out there beyond the windshield of his Camaro, looking out at it from under his raised eyebrows, his thumb tapping slowly on the top of the steering wheel as he drove, like *Uh-huh, what you want from me?* But you got used to that with L'Dog, the way he didn't say much after a while. In a way, James took it to mean that he didn't think of him as a kid who had to have everything explained to him. He'd taken a bust, hadn't he? No way they could call him a kid now.

They'd circled the same block three times, L'Dog takin' it slow, checkin' out the cars parked along Jabril's street. He lived in a shotgun back up off Josephine, kept his car parked down at the end of his drive, so you had to walk up between two other houses, open the wire gate to get into his yard. He had a set of intruder lights mounted on the edge of his roof, which lit up when you started up the drive. A bell rang in his kitchen when the lights went on, so by the time you made it to the door, somebody was looking at you from behind the door, tracking you with a shotgun as you came up the steps onto the porch. James always felt a shiver run down his back, standing there. Like they were takin' a minute to make up their minds, should they open the door, let you in, or should they pull the trigger, scatter your sorry ass all over the yard.

The kid they called AK opened the door, stepped back to let

141

them in. He nodded at L'Dog, looked at James for a moment, expressionless. Then he swung the door closed, headed toward the kitchen at the back of the house. James could see some people sitting around the kitchen table, eating fried catfish from a takeout bucket. Jabril Saunders sat hunched over his plate at one end of the table. He was wearing a Bob Marley T-shirt, black karate pants, and flip-flops. Except for the flecks of gray in his beard, you couldn't tell how old he was. Forties, James figured, at least. And for the street, that was *old*. When Jabril was younger, he'd started a gang called the Gangster Messengers, which ran two storefront day cares, a clinic, and a newspaper called *The Ghetto Blaster* on the profits they made selling hash to white teenagers from Metairie. After a police shootout, he'd beaten a murder rap, raising his fist in the courtroom after the verdict came in while the crowd in the spectator seats shouted, *Fight the Power! Fight the Power!*

Now he was a *Community Activist.* He collected "donations" from the Korean grocers, the Syrians who owned the liquor stores, even the crack dealers working the corners, mediated their disputes, and used the money to run a youth center in the basement of one of the buildings in St. Thomas. The boys who hung out there did his collections; in return, they got two pool tables, a speed bag in the corner, and two battered leather couches in front of a TV where they could watch a collection of old Bruce Lee videos, learning—Jabril liked to tell them, smiling—how to discipline their minds as well as their bodies. And two blocks away, in a boarded-up storefront, lay the prize for the true believers: a fully equipped thirty-two-track recording studio, watched over by an old man who'd once cut records with Alan Toussaint, Irma Thomas, and the funky Meters, where they could lay down demo tracks, try out the equipment, dream their way into a world of white limousines and sleek, unsmiling women.

Now James looked around the kitchen, seeing it like a revelation. Faded linoleum floor, table covered with a plastic sheet, a kid's drawings in crayon stuck to the front of the refrigerator. At the end of the table, a young woman sat holding a baby on her lap. She was smoking a cigarette, blowing the smoke up at the ceiling. She looked over at him briefly, then her eyes wandered away, bored.

Jabril finished off a piece of catfish, wiped his mouth on a paper napkin, looked up at them. "You hungry?" he asked L'Dog.

L'Dog shrugged. "Yeah, sure."

Jabril stood up, took his plate over to the sink, got another plate down from the cabinet and handed it to L'Dog. "You can have my seat. I'm done." He looked at James, his gaze curious. Then he raised one finger, motioned for him to follow. They went into the bedroom, which led off the back of the kitchen. The bed was neatly made, and there was a poster of some fat Chinese guy over the bed with the words THE PEOPLE'S REVOLUTION IS NEVER DONE! written across the bottom.

Jabril sat on the bed, reached over with his foot, and pulled a chair over to face him, about two feet away. Then he leaned over, tapped the chair lightly.

"Come on sit down, now."

James went over and sat down, his knees brushing against Jabril's. It was just a straight-backed chair, no arms, and he felt like he was on one of those rides, like at the fair, they strap you in, shoot you way up in the sky. Jabril sat back, crossed his legs, rubbed at his jaw with one hand. His eyes never left James's face.

"So you got busted, huh?"

"Yeah."

"They ask you where you got the gun?"

"Uh-huh. I told 'em I found it."

Jabril nodded, still rubbing at his jaw. "So where'd you *find* it?"

"In a trash can, over behind the hospital."

"They ask you what you doin' over behind the hospital?"

James shrugged, but that didn't feel right, so he shook his head. "I already told 'em my mama works over there."

Jabril stretched his arms out on the bed behind him, leaned back. He hooked a foot under James's chair, shoved it back so the kid yelled, grabbed at the air in front of him. But Jabril caught it with his foot, let it rock slightly, balanced there. He smiled at James, easy.

"You a big boy now, huh?"

James grabbed the seat of the chair with both hands, looked down at where Jabril's foot flexed slightly under the crossbar, making the chair rock gently. James looked up at Jabril, shrugged.

"I ain't said that."

Jabril pursed his lips, nodded. "No, I guess it was me said that. Wasn't it?"

James couldn't think of anything to say to that, so he looked up at the poster of the Chinese guy, little black cap on his head, smiling like he's your uncle. Jabril followed his gaze, leaning his head back so he was looking at the wall behind him. Then he swung his head back up, said, "You know who that is?"

James shook his head.

"Mao Tse-tung." Jabril smiled. "That mean anything to you?"

James hesitated. The guy's name sounded like *Mousie Dung,* and for a moment, he wondered if Jabril was joking. Then he shook his head.

Jabril sighed. "No, I guess not." He let the chair rock some more, studying James's face. "Say 'I'm a *man!*'"

"I'm a man."

Jabril shook his head, impatient. "No, that's not what I said. Say it, 'I'm a *man!*'"

"I'm a *man!*"

"You believe it?"

James thought about it for a second, went to nod, but Jabril raised a hand, stopped him. "Nah, see? You not sure."

He sat up, flexed his foot so that the chair rocked back suddenly. James swung his arms out, tried to catch his balance, but he felt it start to go over. Jabril reached out, caught the front of the chair with his hand, holding it there between James's legs.

"They want to keep you off balance, you know that?"

James swallowed, forced himself to meet Jabril's gaze. "Yeah, I know."

"That's good." Jabril nodded. "That's *real* important. You got to know that, 'cause it's the only way *any* of this . . ." He swept an arm out to one side, like he was taking in the whole neighborhood. "The only way *any* of this makes any sense. You see what I mean?"

James nodded quickly.

"Mao up there"—Jabril jerked a thumb over his shoulder at the poster—"he knew that. You know what he said?" He let the chair down so the front legs rested on the floor, leaned forward so his face was only inches away, and whispered, "He say, 'Justice comes from the barrel of a *gun.*'" Then he leaned back again. "You think that's right?"

James felt himself start to shrug, but Jabril raised a hand, said, "Now, hold on. You *think* about this one, 'cause I really want an answer, here."

James looked up at the fat Chinese guy, wondered what he knew about *justice,* the kinda guy who looked like he carried candy 'round in his pocket, handed it out to kids. Those little candy pistols they used to sell in the 7-Eleven, maybe, sweet little Uzis, you pop 'em in your mouth. Still, Jabril had the guy's picture on his wall, right? So he must figure it made sense. Cops carry guns. Guys on the street always talkin' *drive-by, gettin' back, even the score.* Then, James thought about the chair rocking under him, Jabril saying, *They want to keep you off balance, you know that?* He shook his head.

"No?" Jabril looked at him, curious. "You live 'round here, you don't believe justice comes out of a gun? Where you been, boy?"

"I been here," James said. "I been seein' it."

Jabril looked at him for a long moment, then nodded slowly. "That's right. I guess you have." He stood up, went over to the dresser next to the bed, started digging around in one of the drawers. "You know those two boys, got shot up over on Claiborne?"

"I seen 'em around a couple times."

Jabril nodded, his hands still feeling around in the drawer. "Couple hours after they got shot, I get a message on my pager, call this number." He looked back at James. "I only give my pager number to my *friends*, see?" He glanced up at the Chinese guy, *Meow*, then went back to digging in the drawer. "So I call the number, this guy say, 'You want the gun killed those two Conti Street boys?' I say, 'You got it?' He say, 'I know where it is.'" Jabril found what he was looking for in the drawer, a small white card with some writing on it. He shoved the drawer closed and came back to the bed, the card in his hand. "Now I'm thinkin', *Okay, how you know so much about this gun, and why you tellin' me?* But he's not gonna tell me that, now, is he? So I ask the guy, 'Okay, where is it?' He says, 'You know those green Dumpsters behind Charity Hospital? I saw the guy pull up in his car, pitch it in there.' Like that, 'I saw the guy *pitch* it,' see? You know any black man say that?"

James shook his head.

"So now I *know* it's a setup. Some white guy got my pager number, call me up, tells me where to find this gun. I figure I got a choice, right? I leave it where it is, let some white boy find it, he's lookin' for his dinner, or I send somebody to go get it, see what the deal is, here." He reached out, brushed something off James's shoulder. "Now I send L'Dog or AK, they both got police sheets, so that's no good. Anyway, they get picked up, I'll have cops 'round here twenty minutes later, talkin' about how they're my *known associates*. I mean, those two guys, they just about *live* here, right?" He smiled at James. "So that's why I sent you. Nice boy, good student. Worst they'll do you is a year, sus-

pended. And that's *if* they don't buy that you found the gun, seein'
how your mama works over there at the hospital."

He looked at James with his eyebrows raised, then he nodded,
smiling, so James nodded along with him.

"Can't let it slide, Bear. Somebody killed those boys, tryin' to set
me up, make it look like we all just niggers like to shoot cops. That's
not right, huh?"

"No."

"So that's why I sent you over there. And they busted you, right
off. Now we startin' to know what's the score." James watched Jabril
lean back on the bed again, his voice easing back into the way he usually talked, when it was just kids from the neighborhood. And with
that, James realized he hadn't noticed the moment when his voice had
changed, sounding for a while there like one of his teachers, or those
Muslim Brothers you hear yellin' at people on the street corner, you
got to give up *drugs.* James looked up at the Chinese guy in the poster,
wondered why he hadn't noticed that before. But Jabril was leaning
forward again, holding out the white card, saying, "I think you want
to get lost for a while, okay? This lady here," he tapped the name on
the card, "she's an old friend of mine, from way back. She live over in
Mobile, you can go stay with her a couple days." He grinned. "Lie on
the beach, get a *tan.*"

James looked at the card in his hand, then back up at Jabril, who
had leaned back on the bed again, raising one finger to point at him.
"But don't you go making her fall in love with you." Smiling at him,
now. "She's a sweet lady, and she take care 'a you. But you break her
heart, I have to kick your ass. You hear?"

James grinned, sheepishly. "Yeah, I hear."

"Good." Jabril put his foot on the seat of the chair, shoved it
back. "I'm glad we *understand* each other."

Somebody knocked on the bedroom door. Jabril stood up, went

to the door, opened it. L'Dog stuck his head in from the hallway, said, "Hey, Bear? Your brother's out front. Says some cops came 'round, lookin' for you."

Jabril turned, looked back at James, one eyebrow going up, like he was surprised.

"You still here?"

13

When Danny woke up, Maura was gone. She liked that, sneaking out while he was still sleeping. Once she'd taken all his shoes. When he had called her later that morning, she'd said, "Sorry, I just wanted to be the guy for once. Leave during the night, have you call up, hurt."

"So how's it feel?"

"Can't tell, yet. You don't sound pathetic enough."

"When do I get my shoes back?"

She laughed. "That's perfect."

But this morning, she'd simply vanished. Not even a coffee cup in the sink. He took a shower, got the newspaper off the steps, glanced at the headlines over breakfast. The shootings on Claiborne Avenue had slipped off the front page. Only a small article on an inside page, reporting on the victims' funerals. The article ended by noting that police had uncovered some new leads and were continuing their investigations.

Danny was putting his bowl in the sink when the phone rang. He picked it up, heard a man's voice say, "Danny?"

"Yeah. Who is this?"

"Marty Seagraves."

Danny leaned back against the counter, glanced over at a fly buzzing against the kitchen window. "I tried to call you, Saturday."

"Yeah? I was up in Shreveport, working on a case."

The fly kept bouncing off the glass, like it couldn't understand what was keeping it from escaping. Danny was silent for a moment, watching it.

Marty Seagraves was an FBI agent Danny'd gotten to know back when he worked over at the D.A.'s office. They'd worked on a couple cases together, although Seagraves reported back to the U.S. Attorney and Danny had to be careful not to let anything slip that might let the Feds move in on a case before his office could issue an indictment. But they got together for lunch every couple weeks, glad to put all the politics behind them for an hour. Mostly they talked about baseball. Both men had a secret passion for the Chicago Cubs. Discovering that about each other had sealed their friendship. In New Orleans, admitting that you were a Cubs fan was like confessing a secret taste for grand opera. Nothing but tragedy, and the fat lady always sings.

When Danny went to work for Jimmy, that all ended. From that moment on, they only met secretly. And they never got around to talking about baseball.

"You give some thought to what we talked about, Danny? Not much time left."

Danny smiled. *Jesus, if he only knew.*

"We can pull you out today," Seagraves went on. "We'd still have enough to get Jimmy on half a dozen different counts."

"You'd been in your office on Saturday, I was ready to go."

"So let's do it. Take me an hour to set it up."

"I got some things I want to find out."

Danny heard Seagraves sigh. For the last two years, they'd had the same conversation every couple weeks. When he thought about it, not much had changed, really. Instead of the Cubs, they talked about Danny's future: he figured it amounted to pretty much the same thing.

"Danny, the U.S. Attorney wants to move on this. He's putting pressure on me to produce my informant. The way he sees it, our whole case against Jimmy won't mean shit unless we can put you on the stand."

"Hey, my heart bleeds. The guy wants to go on TV, tell everybody how he's gonna nail Jimmy this time. Only he's scared he'll look like a jerk if Jimmy walks again." Danny watched the fly land on the window frame and fold up its wings, as if catching its breath in the sunlight that poured through the window. Then, suddenly, it took off again, flew out of the room. "I've been there, Marty. I know how it works. But we made a deal. I've spent three years helping you build a case against Jimmy, but it's my decision when I pull out. So you go tell the U.S. Attorney he's just gonna have to wait."

"Sure, Danny. Nobody's gonna *make* you back out, not as long as it's still safe. All I'm saying is, three years ago you came to me, told me you wanted to take Jimmy Boudrieux down. And you remember what I said?"

Danny smiled. "You tried to talk me out of it."

"You're damn right I did. I said, 'Look, you quit the D.A.'s office, go work for Jimmy, chances are all you're gonna accomplish is you fuck up your career. End of the day, Jimmy's probably gonna walk, same as always.' But you wouldn't listen. You're all charged up, ready to go. So, I figure if you're gonna do this thing anyway, you're gonna need somebody to keep an eye on you, make sure you don't do something stupid. I even let you make the rules. No direct contact, nobody knows the identity of my informant. Okay, so I can live with that. Last eighteen months, I've had the U.S. Attorney on my ass every day; the guy even called up the deputy director of the Bureau, tried to have me bounced off the case if I didn't give up the name of my informant. But I kept my promise. I told 'em if they wanted to prosecute based on the evidence you provided, they'd have to wait until you were ready to go public. And that's what I'll tell 'em again. But you made me a couple promises too. This thing doesn't go just one way."

Danny laughed. "C'mon, Marty. What'd I promise you?"

"You told me you wouldn't take any unnecessary chances, you'd only do this until we had enough to make a case, then you'd pull out.

Okay, so I'm telling you we've got enough. There's no reason for you to take any more risks."

Danny thought about his father, slumped over the steering wheel of his car as a summer rain beat against the windshield. Then his mind flashed on the scene in the restaurant, Phuong curled up on the floor, a pool of blood spreading beneath her. "There's a couple more things I still need to find out."

For a moment, Seagraves said nothing. When he spoke, his voice was quiet. "There something you're not telling me, Danny?"

"There's some stuff going on. It might be big. But I want to be sure."

"Maybe you'd better tell me what you've got."

"Give me a couple days. If I can't work it out by then, you can pull me out, and we'll go see the U.S. Attorney."

Seagraves hesitated. "I don't want you on my conscience, Danny."

"Yeah, no sweat. I'll give you a call in a couple days."

He hung up, stood there looking down at the newspaper spread out on the counter. *Jesus, three years.* When he'd left the D.A.'s office, taken the job with Jimmy, he'd figured it might take six months. He'd ride over the Lake Pontchartrain Causeway after making his pickups, meet Seagraves at a rest stop on the I-10 bypass up in St. Tammany Parish, and watch as he spread the money out on the front seat of his car, marked the bills carefully with an ink that only showed up under infrared light. Then Danny would get back in his car, drive on up to Baton Rouge, and hand the money over to Lucas Clay. Once, Seagraves told him that they'd tracked the bills as far as Las Vegas, where a state senator dropped $12,000 at blackjack, then flew home in time to vote in favor of a bill legalizing casino gambling. Danny'd smiled at the story. *Easy come, easy go.*

After the first year, Seagraves had offered to pull him out. Danny refused. At the time, he wasn't sure why. He just knew that—whether the prosecutors made their case against Jimmy or not—his own business with the man remained unfinished. So he stayed, kept his eyes open, until two more years had passed. And then, one day, Lucas Clay had taken him aside, asked him to make an extra stop, to pick up a package from a small-time hustler named Dewitt Foley . . .

They'd still be alive if you'd gotten out, Danny thought. *All those people dead, because you weren't satisfied.*

He pushed the thought away, grabbed his keys off the kitchen table, and went out to his car. The morning was bright, and hot enough to raise a blister on your brain, but Danny could see clouds piling up off to the west. He unlocked the Mustang, tossed his leather jacket on the passenger seat.

Just a couple more days, he thought as he started the Mustang up. *Then maybe you'll be able to look in a mirror again.*

14

Buddy Jeanrette knew the price of fear. Current market, it worked out to $240,000 on a twenty-year mortgage, one percent over prime. That's what it would cost you, if you act *now*, to get in on the initial phase of Beau Reve, a gated, fully secured community he was developing with partners down near English Turn. Eighteen-hole golf course, designed by Jack Nicklaus; tennis courts; gun range; clubhouse with bar, restaurant, and banqueting facilities; fifty-meter Olympic swimming pool; indoor lap and kiddie pools for the winter months; and plenty of waterfront along the Big Mar, with a deep-water marina so you can tie up your cabin cruiser fifty feet from the back door of your four-bedroom Cape Cod, half-acre-minimum lot, three-floor plans now available.

They'd broken earth on April 1, completed the first structure a week later: a paved entry road that led to a booth where a uniformed guard sat behind shatterproof glass, checking all vehicles that entered or left against a computerized log. Buddy's partners had questioned the expense of hiring twenty-four-hour guards to operate the gate during the initial construction phase, protecting 150 feet of paved road and a large pile of sedimentary gravel for the foundations, but Buddy told 'em, "Hell, it's the best advertising we can get. People ride by here, any hour of the night, they see the place is secured. Nine-foot brick wall along the whole front of the project. You drive your wife out here, she knows she'll be safe, you're out playing golf." The sign at the entrance read SOME UNITS STILL AVAILABLE!

That's where Ray Morrisey found him, out in front of the sign with a guy from the real estate office, arguing over the picture of a security guard leaning down to talk to a smiling family in their BMW, big old houses with bearded oak trees around them visible through the iron gate in the background.

"Let me get this straight," Buddy was saying to the real estate guy. "You're standing here tellin' me we're gonna lose business 'cause the fuckin' *gate's* not open in the picture?"

The real estate salesman looked like Rufus McPig, a guy in a pink suit, little pig ears on his hat, who used to come on between Saturday-morning cartoons to get hit with a pie when Morrisey was a kid, watching *Captain Eddie's Fun Parade.* The salesman wore a double-breasted suit with the jacket open, and had a long strand of hair carefully combed over his bald spot. He stood in the door of his Cadillac Seville, sweating heavily.

"It's not welcoming," he said, wiped at his forehead with a handkerchief. "We want them to see that it's just like home."

Morrisey got out of his St. Bernard sheriff's cruiser, rested one hand on the open door. He saw that the real estate guy's Cadillac had a vanity plate that said WIN-WIN.

"But that's the fucking point!" Buddy waved a hand at the sign. "This place, it's *better* than home, 'cause nobody gets in unless they own property or their name's on a list of registered guests." He shook his head wearily. "The guy who painted the sign, he brings me out here a couple weeks ago, shows it to me. I take one look at the thing, the gate's standing *wide* open, anybody could drive right in, back a truck up to your front door, walk out with your VCR. Change it, I tell him. 'But Mr. Wynn told me. . . .' I say, 'Look, who's payin' the bills here, me or Mr. Wynn?' Okay, fine, he'll change it. I finally get through yelling at the guy about that one, I notice the fucking guard's not even wearing a *weapon.* What kind of security we selling these people, the guard at the front gate's not even *armed*? 'You put a weapon on that man's hip,' I tell him. 'Big one, three-fifty-seven magnum. We ain't sellin' subtlety here.'"

Morrisey watched the real estate guy swipe the handkerchief across his face again and say, "Well, I don't want to tell you your business, but—"

"Then don't." Buddy glanced over at Morrisey. "You know how I got started? I was a state trooper, fifteen years. Drove a patrol car most of those years, just like that one. And you know what I learned, all that time?" He waved a hand at the sign. "People don't want to give up their fear. They *like* feeling scared. That's why I quit the patrol, 'cause it suddenly occurred to me that the whole way we police this country is wrong. Go ask a man what he wants. What he dreams about, he's sitting on the toilet, taking a crap. Does he dream about paying taxes so some guy can put on a uniform, protect his family? Or does he dream about buying himself a gun, standing in the dark next to his bedroom window, watching over his property?" He shook his head. "Deep down, every man wants to do it for himself. Cut down trees, build a wall around his land, get a dog who'll rip your throat out, he doesn't recognize your smell. *That's* what we're selling here. Underneath the whole thing—clubhouse, golf course, tennis courts—we're selling *fear.* We're selling 'em a high wall and a guard with a gun. Fort Apache. And I guarantee you, every guy who buys one of these houses is gonna go right out and get his own gun, keep it next to his bed. Not 'cause he *needs* one to feel safe, but because he loves that feeling of fear makes you sit there in the dark, gun in your hand."

The real estate guy wiped the handkerchief across the back of his neck, then shoved it in his pocket. "Okay, it's your project. I just sell 'em."

He raised a hand, then got back into his Cadillac, backed off the grass, and turned east on the highway, headed back toward the city.

Buddy grinned at Morrisey, shook his head. "You believe that guy? Wants me to promote a gated community with a picture, you can't see the gate."

Morrisey glanced up at the sign, shrugged. "Looks good to me."

"Yeah? Well, forget about it. Way they pay you boys, it'd take you forty years just to come up with a down payment."

Morrisey rubbed at his lower lip, like he was thinking about it, buy one 'a these places, put his boat in the marina on the river, play golf on Sundays. "I put some away, last couple years." Then he looked at Buddy, grinned. "Hell, maybe I'll do like you did. Quit the force, start my own business. Get rich as a pig in shit."

"Like it's that easy." Buddy waved to the guard to raise the gate, climbed into his Land Cruiser, then stuck his head out the window and said, "C'mon, I'll show you 'round."

Morrisey got back in the squad car, followed the Land Cruiser through the gate, then back into the woods where the road turned from paved to gravel, wound back through the trees past construction equipment plowing up the ground, knocking trees down, dragging 'em away to be burned. Not much to see, really. Buncha construction guys ripping shit out of some woods, that's about it. *Drive through here a year from now,* he thought, *the whole place'll be filled with rich folks.* He tried to imagine the expensive houses scattered along the road, fresh-cut lawns, tennis courts, but he couldn't. The place was a mud pit, and he almost cracked a tooth bouncing over the deep ruts in the road. Everything was covered by a thick haze of smoke and gravel dust.

The road wound back past the water, and Morrisey caught a glimpse of an old plantation house, set back from the water among a grove of ancient oak trees. Construction scaffolding rose up along the white columns, and a cement mixer was pouring a new foundation along one side of the house. Buddy pulled over on the grass shoulder, stuck his hand out the window, and waved for Morrisey to pull up beside him. He leaned across the passenger seat, rolled down the window, and called over, "You believe that place? Stood empty for thirty years. I used to see it from the bayou when I was a kid, way back in these trees. We'd bring girls back here, tell 'em ghost stories, see if we could get laid. Now we're gonna fix it up, make it the sales office." He sat back, pointed toward the woods up ahead, then put the Land Cruiser in gear, pulled out.

Morrisey followed, glancing up in the rearview at the plantation house vanishing among the trees. Impressed, even if he hated to admit it. The kind of place you'd see in the movies, some woman in a big skirt coming out on the porch to watch the niggers pick cotton.

He followed the Land Cruiser back into the woods, part of the property the bulldozers hadn't reached yet. The trees came right up to the road, thick with undergrowth, so you felt like you were driving between two high walls, snakes curled up under the bushes, watching you. That thought gave him a creepy feeling, like he always got when he was out in the woods, made him want to draw his service revolver, have it ready in case he heard that dry rattle. Man, he *hated* snakes.

The road swept back toward the water for about a quarter mile, and the woods opened up some so he could see the sun reflecting off the water, then they came to a fork, and the Land Cruiser made a sharp turn into an overgrown track that led away from the water. Morrisey glanced to his left as he made the turn, saw that the track led down to the water, where a line of thick oak posts stretching out into the bayou were all that was left of a crumbled pier. After that, he had to take it slow, the squad car bouncing in the deep ruts, scraping its oil pan against ridges of packed clay. He watched Buddy ease the Land Cruiser past a fallen tree then make a quick left, pulling into a clearing to stop, his rear bumper just visible beyond the thick bushes.

Morrisey felt the tree's branches scrape against the passenger door as he squeezed the car past. *Great. Try explaining that to the guys back at the garage.* Then he grinned, picturing it. *Well, see, I was drivin' along Judge Perez, and this tree . . .*

Buddy was standing in front of the Land Cruiser, waving him into the clearing like one of those guys who shows you where to park over at the Superdome. Morrisey pulled in next to him and got out, saying, "I hope you got a good reason, bring me all the way out here. I damn near ripped the bottom out my car, comin' over those humps."

Buddy just smiled, pointed back through the trees to where a crumbling building stood at the edge of the clearing. "Thought you might want to see this. See how they used to get things done around here."

Morrisey turned, looked over at the building. Three stories, with a broad balcony on the second floor, sweeping marble stairs leading up to an entrance with two stone lions on pillars. Arched windows like you'd see in a church, only with all the glass missing. A pair of high French doors stood open at one end, and he could see a large room beyond, with a large fireplace in one wall. Off to one side, there was an empty swimming pool among some pines.

"What is it?"

Buddy smiled. "C'mon inside. We'll see if you can guess."

They went up the stairs, walked down the front balcony to where the French doors stood half open. Buddy shoved the doors back far enough to squeeze through, and they went inside. It was a ballroom, with expensive gold fixtures on the walls and broad oak floors covered with blown leaves. A crystal chandelier lay on its side in the middle of the floor, spiderwebs strung between its arms.

Buddy pointed to a low stage at one end of the room. "They used to put a big band down there, have dancing. Serve champagne out of gold ice buckets. We found 'em down in the kitchen, a whole cabinet full of these gold ice buckets. Like something out of an old movie."

"People come all the way out here, go dancing?" Morrisey dug a pack of cigarettes out of his uniform pocket, lit one, tossed the match on the floor. He could see Buddy was waiting for him to look impressed, so he kept his face empty. *Gold ice buckets, huh? Big deal. Go down the Quarter, you can pick you up one 'a those in an antique store, thirty bucks.*

Buddy stared at him, then bent, picked up the burnt match. "You mind?"

"What?" Morrisey looked around at the leaves on the floor. "You just have the floors done? So, what? You pay some guy to come in here, scatter all these leaves around, give the place that natural look?"

Buddy sighed, shook his head. "Just put the fuckin' match in your pocket, okay? I don't want the place to burn down, I finally got the money to fix it up."

"Yeah? You're gonna fix this place up? Shit, what for? You got all the leaves you need right here."

But Buddy was already walking away, kicking the piles of leaves out of the way, shoving a door open at one end of the room. "C'mon, I'll show you the rest."

A broad corridor led out to the entry hall, where they climbed a curving staircase to the top floor. Buddy opened a door, went into a large room with a four-poster bed, marble fireplace, bay windows. "This is where the guests slept. Ten rooms like this up here. Two more on the floor below." He swung open another door, stepped back so Morrisey could see. "Bath with marble tiling, gold fixtures, in every bedroom."

Like he's tryin' to sell me the place, Morrisey thought. *Probably brings everybody he knows here, show the place off.*

They left the room, went on down the hall, Buddy swinging doors open so they could look in more bedrooms, every one of 'em just like the first one. At the end of the hall they came to a large dining room, about half the size of the ballroom below. The windows had been boarded up, and most of the floor had been ripped away.

"Watch your step in here," Buddy told him, kicked at a chunk of rotten wood. "Most of this flooring's rotten. Squirrels were coming in from the trees outside, shitting all over the place. So we had to rip out most of the floor. Used it to board up the windows, keep the little bastards out."

They picked their way along a narrow strip of floor beside the wall, came to a set of service stairs, which they took two flights down to the kitchen. Buddy swung some cabinets open, showed him the old refrigerators from back in the thirties, a big gas stove with twelve burners. Then he leaned on a counter, folded his arms across his chest, and said "So, you figure it out yet?"

"What's to figure out? Weird place to build a hotel, middle of the woods, but you run a couple gambling wheels, get some booze in here during prohibition, I guess you might want some privacy."

Buddy smiled, shook his head. "You got the time right, but it wasn't a hotel."

"Private club, then. Lawyers up from the city, do some hunting out in the woods."

"That's close." Buddy pushed himself up off the counter, went over to a door. "I figured the same as you until I saw this last part. We got our architect in here to look at it, he said it's custom-built. It's the reason for the whole place."

He swung the door open, waved Morrisey through. They crossed a small pantry, came out into a narrow, dark hall. Every few feet there was a pair of doors, each with a small window cut into it. Buddy reached up, opened one of the windows. The opening had bars and a wire mesh that slid up so you could shove in a tray of food. He stepped back, and Morrisey looked through the window into a tiny cell with a metal bunk, a sink, and a toilet. The only light came from a single tiny window, barred, in the opposite wall.

"Worked it out yet?"

Morrisey reached up, shut the window. "It's a whorehouse. They kept the girls in here."

Buddy smiled. "Actually, it was part of the state prison system.

The guy who ran the place would go up to the women's prison every couple months, check out the local talent. He liked a girl, the Department of Corrections would transfer her down here to serve her time." He waved a hand at the row of cells. "Eighteen girls, most of 'em in for whoring, so this must have seemed like home. Champagne every night, swimming pool. Not a bad way to do your time, right? They'd run a train down from Baton Rouge, practically empty out the Statehouse some weekends. Way I heard it, Huey Long had it built back in his first term so he could keep the legislature happy. Or maybe he'd invite his opponents down here, get somebody to take pictures."

Morrisey grinned. "So you going back into business? Get Jimmy Boudrieux down here to conduct the band?"

"Times change, Ray. Who needs a whorehouse, they got interns?" Buddy shrugged. "Anyway, it wouldn't fit in with the tone of the development."

Morrisey glanced at the heavy locks on the doors. "I don't know. Looks pretty secure to me." He pointed to a door that had a heavy padlock bolted across the door frame. "What's in that one?"

"That's the reason you're here." Buddy took out a set of keys, chose one, and opened the padlock. He laid it on the floor and lifted the security bar off the door, swung it open. Inside was the same tiny cell, the same barred window, except this one had a piece of hard plastic nailed over the window in place of the broken glass, and several large boxes stacked on the metal bed. Buddy went over to the boxes, opened one, and took out a semiautomatic handgun, vacuum wrapped in thick plastic. "I got a deal on these, a whole shipment, but no paper, so I can't keep 'em in my warehouse. ATF's got no idea about this place, so I'm storing 'em out here." He held it out to Morrisey. "ZCZ Model Seventy. Your basic Yugoslavian military pistol, holds eight rounds of nine-millimeter shot. Nice cheap weapon, could sell well as a street gun. Not for the top of the market, of course. Lawyers, they want a Beretta, maybe a Heckler and Koch. This is basically a nigger gun. But we could move a lot of 'em, we had the paper to get 'em on the market."

Morrisey reached out, took the pistol from him, unwrapped the plastic. "How many you got there?"

"Forty-eight. And more where these came from, if we can move 'em."

Morrisey hefted the gun, held it up toward the window, squinting along the barrel. Then he flicked the safety off, pulled back the slide to check the chamber, pointed it toward the hall, squeezed the trigger. "Same deal as last time?"

"Five percent on each sale. Provided the paper's good."

Morrisey shrugged. "Same as always. Might take a while to move all these guns through the evidence room, get 'em filed as old seizures. Have to rig up a case file, make it look like we've had 'em a while so they'll be cleared for the next auction." He passed the gun back to Buddy, watched him wrap it in plastic. "I could write it up as a suspected B and E. We get reports all the time from people out Paris Road, kids breaking into empty fishing camps during the winter. So the officer answered a call, found these stored in a back room. I sign it as the reporting officer, date it back in, say, January ninety-three, slip it in the files. No suspects, no arrest, so the guns are clear for resale. You put in a low bid, we lose all the others, you get your guns back with clean papers, ready to go."

"Terrific." Buddy laid the gun back in the box, closed it. "So how come we got all these problems?"

"We ain't got no problems. I got it all under control."

"Yeah? That what those two muscle boys of yours said before they went and got themselves killed?"

Morrisey shrugged. "Shit happens. That don't change nothing."

"That's great." Buddy gave a laugh. "Really, that's just fuckin' priceless. First you guys screw up the bids, let this fuckin' ankle-biter Foley walk off with four of my guns. I mean, I *know* this guy. You know what he is? He's what I wipe off my boots. But now he's got my guns, which means he's got a look into my business. Me, I see this as a problem. But when I tell you to clean it up, it's, 'Hey, relax. No big deal. This guy's an idiot. He don't know what he's got.' Okay, fine. It's only four guns. Easier at this point to let it slide. Only, next thing I know, I get a call from over at the federal building, turns out the guy's got a buddy over at Sixth Precinct, they ran the guns through the computer, got their whole history. Now he's cuttin' deals with the ATF, anybody else he can get to listen. This, even *you* got to see, is a problem. But I call you up, it's, 'Hey, no *problem,* Buddy. I'll send a couple 'a my guys to talk to him, they'll take care of it.' I figure, 'Okay, fine. At least he's taking it seriously now.' Then Saturday morning, I go out in my driveway, haven't even had my fuckin' coffee yet, I pick up the newspaper, what do I see? It's that shit-skimmer Foley, got his picture right there on the front page of the fuckin' *Times-Picayune.* These guys you sent down there, it ain't *enough* for them to just take the guy out, they got to spray the walls with blood. Now we got every cop in town on the case." He fixed his eyes on Morrisey, like two flat, scorched stones. "And now you're tellin' me not to worry?"

Morrisey grinned. "Damn, you should see your face. You look like you swallowed a nail gun." Then he raised both hands, quickly. "Hey, you're upset. I can see that. But you got to see this thing ain't simple no more. We ain't just dealing with Foley now. The cops, they got to have a shooter, motive, the whole bit. We got to feed 'em, or they'll go lookin' for food. Last thing any of us wants is for them to take a close look at Foley's business. Trust me, what everybody needs, this thing, is a nigger with a gun." He spread his hands. "And I got him."

"You got him how?"

"I got him right where I want him. He's hiding over in Mobile, where the locals can't find him."

"So? Get him back here, let's get this thing cleaned up."

Morrisey shook his head. "Nah, see, that's only half the answer. You got to think like a cop for a minute. They get their hands on this kid, first thing they do is throw him in an interrogation room, start askin' him questions. This kid, he's got all the wrong answers. We got to write those cops a script, give 'em something to *believe* in. See, I started out thinking we had two problems, the kid and the witness. Then I realized, Hey, no shit! You can *use* this situation, solve all your problems at once. Your boy, Chaisson, he ain't a problem. He's the *answer.*"

Buddy stared at him for a moment, then shook his head. "Now I'm really nervous."

"Yeah? So what's new? Everything makes you nervous."

"I got a lot at stake here." Buddy turned, waved a hand around him. "All this stuff I showed you, you know what it's built on? Confidence. Something goes wrong on this other deal, you watch how quick everything you saw today vanishes. Last thing I need right now is you writing the script."

"Hey, I understand. You a rich guy. Shit, own a place like this? I gotta tell you, I'm impressed." Morrisey nodded at the crates on the bed. "Only thing I can't figure out is, you so nervous, got all this on the line, how come you still dealing guns?"

Buddy smiled. "You think it's about money?"

"That's what it's usually about, ain't it?"

"Not in this case." Buddy glanced over at the cases, shook his head. "We sell all those, you know what my profit'll be? Somewhere 'bout two thousand, after all the overhead. That's small change."

"Shit, I'll take it."

"Yeah, I guess you would. But that ain't why I do it." Buddy went out in the hall, dug out his keys to lock the door behind him. "There's a principle for me."

"Gimme a break."

"I'm serious."

"Bullshit."

Buddy smiled. "You mind? I want to lock up." He waited for Morrisey to come out, shut the door behind him. "All right, you want to know the truth? I got people depend on me. Suppliers, guys who were with me when I got started. Some 'a those guys, they aren't as flexible as you got to be in business. Got into trouble with the ATF back when they put the Brady bill through, lost their licenses. So what do they do? They look around, see I got a healthy business here, they figure I owe 'em something now, for old time's sake. Every one of these guys, they got some deal cookin', they come to me, ask me do I want a piece of the action. 'Course, what they don't say is that if I say no, they'll pick up the phone, call up the ATF, tell 'em some stories about the good old days." He bent to pick up the padlock off the floor of the corridor. "That's how it is, Ray. This development, it's my future. Whole new business, got nothing to do with guns. But you try to rise, somebody's always there hangin' on, trying to pull you back down to earth. Nobody wants to let you forget what you were." He slipped the lock into the hasp, felt it snap shut. "And everybody's ready to cut a deal on somebody else. You can't trust nobody these days."

Morrisey grinned. "Now ain't that a hell of a thing. You got all this money, set to make a couple million more, and you still got to deal with guys like me."

"Man can't escape his past, Ray. Best he can do is keep it quiet for a while until the future comes along."

They walked back to the stairs. Morrisey took one last look at the row of cells. "What do you think happened to the girls?"

Buddy shrugged. "Somebody's grandma now, probably."

"No shit?" Morrisey grinned. "Hell, everybody's got something to hide, huh?"

15

Mickie Vega sat in Martelle Collette's kitchen, a cup of instant coffee between her hands, wondering how juvenile officers could stand it. The boy's mother was leaning on the kitchen table, shaking her head, tears streaming down her face. And all Mickie could think to do was look away, sip at her coffee, like it wasn't happening.

"He's just a boy," the mother said, rubbing her hand over her face. Her nose was running, and she wiped it with the back of her hand. "Just a sweet child, wouldn't hurt nobody."

Jesus, it was bad. Worse than Mickie could have imagined. The woman's younger son sat in the living room, watching a video. She hadn't let him out of the apartment to go to school, called his name out whenever he walked out of the room.

"Mama, I'm in *here,* okay?"

She had no idea where her son might be, hadn't known he was gone until the police woke her at 2:00 A.M., banging on her door. Like the doorbell don't work, just 'cause they live in St. Thomas? Two detectives, she told Mickie. A white man and a black woman, holding up those gold shields in the doorway, the way you see on TV. The white officer had moved forward slightly, so his foot was in the door, said, "Mrs. Collette?" His voice real polite, like he wanted to sell her some magazines or something, two o'clock in the morning, the middle of the projects. It took her a minute, rubbing at her eyes, to realize what was happening, and then she tried to shut the door on them, suddenly, but the white guy got a hand against it, stopped her.

"We need to talk to your son, Mrs. Collette."

Not even sounding upset that she'd tried to slam the door, like it happened all the time. Then he'd glanced past her into the dark apartment, and she thought for a minute that James might have come out of his bedroom. She turned to yell at him to go back to his room, but it was Rodney standing there in his pajamas with the cowboys on them, saying "Mama?" like he'd just had a bad dream, wanted her to come sit on the edge of his bed, stroke his hair, say, "It's okay, baby. It's just a dream."

But the cop pushed past her into the living room. "James?"

She reached out, grabbed his arm to stop him, yelling, "Rodney, go back to bed, you hear? *Now!*" But by then the black woman cop had pushed past her into the apartment, and there was a flash of metal in her hand, but so quick, in that darkness, that her mind couldn't really say what it was. The man turned, shoved her back against the door so she couldn't move, and she heard Rodney yell out, "James! Cops!"

The woman vanished down the dark hall, and she heard a door slam open. Then only a silence that stretched out like a bright wire in the darkness as she closed her eyes, praying, *Please God, oh please!* And then a moment later, like her prayer had been answered, the woman came back into the living room, shook her head.

In her hand she had a squat black gun, pointing at the floor.

The man had stepped back then, let her come away from the door, and Martelle wandered over to the couch, sat down heavily. She grabbed Rodney by the arm as he came over, pulled him down on the couch beside her.

The woman cop squatted down next to them, pushing her coat back off her hip to put the gun back in its holster. "Where's your son gone, Mrs. Collette?"

But all Martelle could do was shake her head, looking at the woman's face, her black skin, thinking, *Don't you know?*

As she told Mickie about it, she moved around the kitchen, running her hand across counters, pausing in front of the refrigerator like she was trying to decide what to make for dinner, then moving on past the sink, the cabinets full of dishes and canned foods, back along the table where Mickie sat, holding her coffee cup, before pausing at the door, from which she could see her younger son sitting on the couch in front of the TV. She fell silent for a moment, then moved on past the counters again, saying, "He's just a *boy.* Where could he go?"

Mickie was wondering the same thing. She'd driven down from Veterans Boulevard hoping that the boy's mother could see her way to picking up the phone, calling whatever cousin or aunt was hiding him up in Tangipahoa or Cheneyville, get him to come on home so they could talk it over. But it was looking like that wasn't going to happen. She could feel her knee starting to stiffen up on her. From climbing all those stairs, probably, the elevator broken. And the rain. She'd heard it beating on her bedroom window during the night, had to get up to take a couple aspirin about three o'clock so she could get back to sleep. It cleared for a while in the morning, and she'd thought maybe they were going to get a nice day, but now it was coming down again, splattering away on the sidewalks.

Mickie glanced at her watch, wondered if she'd recognize her Nova when she walked out to where she'd parked it on St. Andrews Street. If she left now, she thought, she might still get up to the ATF office in time to catch Jim Dubrow before he went into the weekly case review meeting, tell him that the boy had dropped from sight. Maybe suggest they put her on another assignment. *Anything,* she wanted to tell him. She'd even take license fraud over having to sit here and listen to this poor woman sobbing, watch her wander around the kitchen, wondering what it was that took her son from her, made him into one of those boys you see down on the corner, selling that dope, guns shoved in the waistband of their baggy jeans.

Mickie was just working up the nerve to get up from the table and say, "Perhaps I should come back at a better time," when the doorbell gave two sharp tones—*ping, pang*—like at a gas station. The woman froze. From the living room, Mickie heard the son yell out, "I'll get it!" His mother's face seemed to crumble; she took three quick steps to the kitchen door, screamed, "Don't you *answer* that!"

In the long silence that followed, they heard a man's voice, muffled by the metal door: "Mrs. Collette? My name's Danny Chaisson. I'm an attorney." And then, after a pause, "I wonder if I could have a minute of your time?"

Danny kept glancing over at the juvenile officer. She sat at the kitchen table, her hand wrapped around a coffee cup like it might fly up to the ceiling if she let go of it, shatter on the stained tiles. Mexican, he figured, with those high cheekbones, all that black hair pulled back into a braid. But it was her eyes that really struck him. Hard and bright as a pair of hollow-point bullets. She watched his face, silent, as he unzipped his leather jacket, brushed the rain off the shoulders.

Like it's something he takes care of, Mickie thought, *that leather jacket.* The guy didn't look much like a lawyer, at least not until he glanced over at the boy's mother, said, "Do you have any idea where your son might have gone?"

Danny saw the juvenile officer give a slight smile, raise the coffee cup to her lips. Stupid question, really. If the boy's mother knew, why would she tell *him*?

He glanced around the kitchen. The place was very clean, like Martelle Collette was the kind of woman who scrubbed the counters every night before she went to bed. When his eyes came back to the juvenile officer, he saw her watching him. *Mickie Vega,* she'd said when they introduced themselves. Standing up to shake his hand, looking him in the eye, like she knew exactly what he was thinking, was waiting to see if he'd say it—

Mickie Vega?

His mind flashed on the familiar faces—Mickey Mantle, Mickey Rooney, for Christ's sake, even Mickey *Rourke*—Irish guys soaked in whiskey, that flat look around the eyes like they'd spent some time in the ring, doing that slow white-boy shuffle, offering up their faces as target practice for some whip-quick black kid who'd go on to take a shot at the title. And where, in all that, was this woman, with her sun-lit eyes, this—who'd believe it?—*Mickie Vega?*

But the boy's mother was saying something now, quietly, like she was whispering it to herself, to the floor, to anybody except him—

"You *come* here, to my house, and ask me that?" Turning to look at him now, her face tight with anger. "You people got the nerve to come *here,* ask me where's my *boy?* You want to know where he is, go ask *Jabril.* You do, tell him to stay the *hell* away from my children, or I kill him *myself,* you hear me?"

From the corner of his eye, Danny saw the juvenile officer shift in her chair. He glanced over at her, raised his eyebrows as if to say *What?* But even as he did it, he heard the kid's mother give a sob, saw the juvenile officer look up at her and wince. He turned, felt the blow coming before it hit him. He tried to bring a hand up, but she caught him, hard, on the side of his face, came in with the other hand swinging right behind it.

He caught that one, heard her screaming something at him, but he couldn't see her face because his eyes had filled with tears. He grabbed her close, got both arms around her, hugging her tight. She kicked at his legs, but he stepped foward, pushed her against the cabinets and got his feet between hers, feeling her try to struggle against him. He felt a fingernail dig into the back of his right hand, peeling the flesh away, and heard himself telling her, "It's okay. It's all right."

Like they were dancing, a slow two-step. Like he'd swept her up off her feet, whirled her around, hearing her laughter in his ear. But then, suddenly, she stopped struggling, and he was cradling her head against his shoulder, one hand stroking her hair, his voice quiet now, saying, "I'll find him. It'll be okay. I'll find him."

Then she put a hand against his chest, and he let her push him away. She turned to lean her face against the cabinet, her shoulders shaking. Danny looked around, saw her younger son standing in the doorway, watching it all. The juvenile officer stood next to the boy, one hand resting on his arm, as if to hold him back. Their eyes met.

He raised a hand to rub at his sore jaw and thought, *Mickie Vega?*

16

"How's your jaw?"

Danny smiled, shook his head. "First time that ever happened."
They were standing in the hall just outside the Collettes' apartment,
waiting for an elevator that wasn't coming. "I guess she thought I was
trying to hurt her son."

"Are you?"

Danny glanced over at Mickie. "I'm a lawyer," he said. "Just
thought maybe I could help."

"The boy's already got a lawyer."

"Public defender, right?"

She nodded.

"You get what you pay for, this town."

She reached out, took his hand, turned it so she could see where
the woman had scratched him. "You're bleeding."

She dug in her bag, came out with a handkerchief, wiped away
the blood. There was a chunk of skin missing near his wrist, carved out
in a small half-moon. There were flecks of dark red nail polish stuck to
the skin, and she wrapped her finger in the handkerchief, tried to pick
them out. He liked the way her hand felt on his wrist, the way she
licked the corner of the handkerchief before dabbing at the cut.

"That sting?"

"No," he lied.

She looked up at him, smiled. "Hope you don't mind my germs."

He met her eyes, and something inside his chest seemed to peel apart, something dry and brittle, which she'd suddenly splashed with water.

"I can think of worse things."

She let go of his hand, stuffed the handkerchief back in her bag. "Come on," she said. "I'll drop you at your car."

They walked down the stairs together. The stairs stank of urine, and the cement-block walls were thick with layers of old graffiti, so you could trace several generations of kids claiming a street name, falling in love, taking up ancient feuds. On the first floor, there was a row of gang tags, each of them identical, dated, so you could see the territory being claimed, defended, and finally lost. The last tag was three years old. Someone had painted a bright red heart on a landing, with an arrow through it and the words *MJ & T, 4EVER.* Later, someone had come along and sprayed over it in black paint: *Fuck You, Bicth!!*

Danny saw Mickie glance at it as they went past. She smiled. "You think she dumped him for his spelling?"

It was pouring when they came out onto the front stoop. Two teenage girls were sitting on the iron railing, holding out their hands in the runoff. They looked at Danny, then at Mickie, went back to watching the rain splash against their palms.

"Jesus, look at it," Mickie said, moving past the girls to the steps. She held out her hand, and it occurred to Danny that he'd been watching people do that all his life. Standing at the edge of the porch, hand out, feeling the rain pour down. Like something they all shared, growing up in New Orleans.

Mickie sighed, wiped her hand on her trousers. "Can't stay here, I guess. We'll have to run for it."

They ran. Splashing through puddles on the playground, where the pavement had split and cracked, out to her car, parked at the curb. Mickie fumbled with her keys to get the passenger door open, then ran around the car to unlock the driver's side. When she got in, she reached down to rub at her knee, then caught herself doing it and sat back.

"Stiffens up on you, huh?"

She looked over at him, surprised. Like he'd caught her trying to get away with something. "Is it that obvious?"

"When you run. You wear a brace?"

"Only when the weather's bad."

They sat in her Nova, gazing out at the falling rain. The street was deserted. Even the benches where the teenage boys sold crack in tiny glass vials were empty. Danny could feel water trickling down the back of his neck, working its way down his spine. Mickie looked like she'd run through a car wash. He watched her reach over, dig in the glove box, and come out with a small box of tissues. She yanked at them until she had a wad in her hand, then wiped her forehead, the back of her neck.

"You ever hear of this guy she mentioned—Jabril?"

She shook her head. "Local dealer, maybe. A lot of them use young boys to carry drugs, 'cause they won't do any real time if they're busted."

"Shorties."

She looked over at him. "That's right." Her eyes curious, like she was starting to wonder just who he was. He could see his car, parked at the end of the block, and caught himself wondering why he'd accepted the invitation to wait it out in her car.

He glanced over at her. *Because she's beautiful, that's why.* They'd had a moment, he felt sure, as they left the mother's apartment. Now, sitting in her car, the silence growing thick, Danny wished he'd left it where it stood between them in the hallway, something they'd both think about later. He might have found a reason to stop by Broad Street in the next few days, look her up. Okay, so probably not, but at least he could have felt there was a *chance.* Now the moment had passed, replaced by this silence.

"I love the rain," she said suddenly. "Even when it gets to my knee, I still love just watching it."

Danny ran his fingers through his hair, trying to comb it back. "You must not have grown up around here."

"New Mexico."

He smiled. "This must look pretty different." Then found he didn't have much else to say about it. "How long you been in New Orleans?"

"A year and a half, end of this month." She shook her head, smiled. "I still can't get used to all the green, you know? I drive up Saint Charles, all I can think is, 'Who does all the watering?'" She waved a hand at the window. "But it just . . . falls from the sky."

"You should ride up to Saint Tammany. Mandeville. It's starting to get built up now, but a few years back, you'd ride along one of those little roads, think how they just cut all the trees back a couple feet when they built the road. A year later, they're starting to close in again." He saw the rain was starting to let up, but he wanted to keep her talking. "So how'd you get a name like Mickie out in New Mexico?"

She hesitated for a moment, then said, "My name's really Mercedes."

Her voice seemed to change when she said it, taking on a Spanish sound. Danny found himself shaping the name in his mouth, silently. *Mar-the-des.* He glanced over, saw her watching him. "So why'd you change it?"

"You try growing up as Mercedes Vega."

It took him a minute, but then he laughed. "Yeah, I see your point."

"My boyfriend back home liked to tell his buddies that I came with all the options, but I rattled when you got me up to speed."

This time Danny winced. "That's cold." He hesitated, then asked, "That why you came to New Orleans?"

She looked out the window. "Yeah, I guess."

They sat in silence for a few moments, watching the rain.

"So how'd it get to Mickie?"

She shrugged. "I changed it in high school. Told all my friends they had to call me Mickie, or I wouldn't talk to 'em. I figured it sounded cool. Like that mermaid Darryl Hannah plays in the movie, you know? She sees that street sign, tells everybody her name's Madison?"

"Great movie," he said. "Every guy I know went out and invested in fishing gear."

She smiled, looked back out at the rain.

"So I guess it worked, huh?"

"What?"

"Mickie."

She smiled. "I can be very determined."

Like she meant it as a *warning*. Danny thought about that for a few moments, but couldn't see why she'd be trying to scare him off. She seemed to play it pretty straight. Looking him in the eye. Making this chance for them to talk, but still holding back. Interested, maybe, but taking it slow. It made him feel flattered, but also a little nervous, like he had to play it close to the vest. Stay with her while she made up her mind.

She looked out the window at the slackening rain. Danny watched her eyes moving across the rows of low brick buildings, the wrought-iron balconies strung with laundry getting soaked in the rain, then down the block to the row of benches, where a white car had pulled up. A teenage boy came out on one of the stoops, pulled the hood of his sweatshirt up, ran down the steps into the rain. The passenger window on the car opened, and the boy leaned in. After a moment, he dug in the pocket of his sweatshirt, dropped something into the car's front seat, then turned and ran back up the steps until he was under the cover of the porch. He paused, shook himself like a dog, and disappeared into the building. The car pulled away from the curb, rounded the next corner, gone.

Mickie sat staring after it for a moment, then said, "You're not really a lawyer, are you?"

Danny looked over at her. "I'm a lawyer." He hesitated, then went on, drawn by something in her face. "But you're right. That's not why I'm here."

She was silent for a moment, thinking about it. "You know something about this boy's case?"

"I might. I have to talk to him to know for sure. But it could be important."

She nodded, looked over at Danny, thoughtful. Then she reached down, started her car. "Then I guess we better go see this guy Jabril."

17

Rodney Collette stood outside the Way-to-Go! grocery on St. Andrew Street, watching the kid they called Crew buy two cans of Dr. Pepper, then come away from the counter, stopping just inside the door to shake one of the cans up good. *Thinks I ain't watchin'.* Rodney smiled, turned away from the window. He leaned back against the metal security gate, hands shoved in his pockets, whistling softly through his teeth like dumb old Buckwheat, got nothin' better to do than watch the traffic. Crew came out, handed him one of the cans. "Here you go, man."

"Yeah, thanks." Rodney tapped on the lid three times, like he always did, something he'd seen Andre do with a can of beer. "You as thirsty as I am?"

Crew shrugged. "It's pretty hot." He eased back a step, his eyes on Rodney's can, waiting for it.

Rodney hooked a thumbnail under the pull tab, then made a show of hesitating, laying the cold can against his forehead. "Ah, man. That's *nice.*" He ran the can down the side of his face, let it rest on the back of his neck. "You know what I wish?"

"What?"

"Somebody'd open up one 'a these fire hydrants, spray us down. That'd feel *good,* huh?"

Crew grinned. "You like that, huh?"

"Sure. Don't you?"

"Yeah, I like it all right."

"Okay." Rodney brought the can down, pointed it at Crew as he yanked the pull tab open. It went off like a fire hose, squirting soda across Crew's face and chest.

"Shit!" Crew dropped his own can, jumped back. "What the fuck you do that for?"

Rodney grinned. "Ah, man. Sorry. These cans, they get all shook up sometimes." He squeezed his thumb over the can's top, shook it a couple more times, then dropped the can at Crew's feet and jumped back. Crew cursed, tried to dance away as the can spun wildly on the sidewalk, spraying foam across his new sneakers. He backed off to the edge of the sidewalk, shook each foot carefully over the gutter, muttering to himself. Then he leaned on a car, wiped each sneaker carefully on the opposite leg of his jeans.

"You're dead," he called back at Rodney. "You're fuckin' dead, man."

"Shit, you just too *obvious,* man."

Rodney turned away, laughing, and saw the car. Black Samurai, man. A seriously bad ride. Nigger had it painted solid black, even the windows tinted black and rolled up tight, so it looked like evil midnight comin' on as it turned on to St. Andrews down at the end of the block. He could feel the heavy bass line thumping from the speakers, *loud.*

"Hey, Crew. Check this out."

Crew looked up at it, stopped doing his duck dance long enough to shake his head and say, "Aw, man. I'm *havin'* one 'a those. That's a bad ride."

The Samurai rolled up on them, takin' its time, just prowling. The guys inside half deaf by now, Rodney figured, but too proud to turn it down, diggin' on the way everybody stopped to look as they went past, *Hey, check out those kids, man, over on the sidewalk. Starin' at us, bugs flyin' up in their mouths.* You buy a car like that, you're payin' for the *gaze,* man. Got no money for gas, shit, but everybody be lookin' at you while you sit there.

As it drew up beside them, the car seemed to pause, and Rodney half expected the door to open, one of the guys inside to jump out, run into the grocery for some beer, couple packs of Marlboros. Instead it just sat there for a long moment, engine idling, letting Rodney catch a glimpse of his own face in the dark glass, mouth open, staring. Then, suddenly, the throbbing music died away, and the window descended in one smooth movement, so Rodney found himself staring into a white man's face where his had just been, as if their two faces had crumbled into one, black vanishing into white, the man's grin a frightening secret within the dark hollow of his own skull. So he was not surprised when he saw the gun come up, heard the man say gently, "Say hello to your brother, kid."

He turned to run, heard Crew shouting something at him as if from far away, but suddenly it was all bright, too bright, and then slow settling dark.

Gregory Nowles sat back slowly in his chair, lifted his glass of Jameson's, and studied Danny over the rim. "You want what?"

They were sitting at a corner table in Nolo, under a framed copy of an 1837 decision by the circuit court granting an attorney named Raphael Squares "one day of labor each Sabboth by the slave known as William for the term of two years, in lieu of fees for legal services to his Master, Frederick Grant." Nowles liked to sit beneath this document, with his back to the wall so he could look out across the room, watching the corporate lawyers cut their deals on oil leases, real estate limited partnerships, insurance litigation. He watched them the way a man might watch a house burn to the ground, with expressionless eyes.

Danny shifted in his seat and glanced over at Mickie Vega, who was studying the document behind Nowles. "We want to talk to this guy Jabril."

"So you came to me." Nowles smiled. "Let me guess, I'm the only black man you know. You figure we all know each other, right?"

Danny looked down at his beer. His hand was wrapped around the glass, and he thought about taking a sip. But he raised his eyes, met Nowles's gaze instead, said, "Was I wrong?"

Nowles sipped at his whiskey, looked past Danny at the crowded room. It was early evening, and the fading light beyond the windows made it seem like a good place to sit very still and wait for your life to pass. The crowd was noisy, packed tight around the bar. But in the corner, you could feel the glass in your hand, the whiskey like a slow flame on your tongue, the way time swirled around you like a stone in a river, then past and away, gone.

"Yeah, I know Jabril." Nowles was still looking off across the room, but Danny watched his eyes take on a look like a man turning to gaze out across a desert he'd had to cross. "They had him up for murder, claimed he shot a cop." He smiled, shook his head. "Shows up for court the first day, he's wearing one of those T-shirts with the clenched fist on the front. Like he's Huey Newton, you know? I told him, 'Boy, you go in that courtroom lookin' like that, they're gonna put you in the *chair*.'" Nowles glanced over at Mickie and smiled again. "Had to send one of the legal assistants out to get him some clothes, fast. White boy from the legal aid clinic over at Tulane. He came back with all these Arrow dress shirts from over at Maison Blanche. Couple muted ties, one of those navy sport coats with the gold buttons. Jabril, he puts 'em on, now he looks like he's there to pick up your daughter, take her out to the country club for dinner. So we leave off the jacket, go for the 'nigger-who-knows-his-place' look. Shirt and tie, like it's Sunday morning, he's goin' to church with his mama." He let his eyes wander off across the room, sipped at his whiskey. "Anyway, they had almost no evidence, and what they did have was acquired in an illegal search. So I got him off."

Danny leaned forward. "You still in touch with him?"

Nowles was silent for a moment. He looked at Danny, making up his mind. "I see him around."

"Is he dealing?"

Nowles stared at Danny. "I don't know his business." Then he gazed off across the room at the lawyers crowded around the bar. "Hell, seems like everybody's dealing something these days."

"He deal guns?"

Danny glanced over at Mickie, surprised. She'd kept silent through most of the conversation, her eyes wandering over the room.

Nowles smiled. "Guns, huh?" He shook his head. "No, not Jabril. He might *use* a gun, if he thought it would change anything. But you want to know who's selling guns in the ghetto, you got to ride up to Metairie, ask a *white* man."

"This kid you're defending," Danny said quickly, "he's up on a gun charge. Claims he found it."

"That's right."

"His mother thinks Jabril gave it to him."

Nowles gave a sigh. "Yeah, well there's lotsa kids walking around with guns in that neighborhood. Trust me, ain't nobody *gave* those guns to 'em."

"So the mother's just wrong?"

"Maybe, maybe not. Listen, I see lots of these boys. Too many. And every one of 'em, their mama's got to tell me how it ain't her baby's fault. There's some guy in the neighborhood who gave 'em the drugs to hold, or put the gun in their hand. And, yeah, they're right. Except I got to take these boys into court, and all the court sees is one more nigger with a gun trying to tell 'em it's not his fault." He shrugged. "After a while, I start to see it that way myself. Yeah, okay, so some guy gave him the gun. But it's in his hand, so he's the one got to take the ride."

"You think Jabril might know where this kid is?"

Nowles gazed off across the room. "I think you better ask Jabril that."

Jabril Saunders kept a table for himself in the back room of Tug's Bar, three blocks from his house, on Magazine Street. There was a half-empty bottle of Baccardi Dark rum on the table, a bowl of limes, and a kitchen knife with a two-inch blade stuck into the table-top. To Greg Nowles, who had done eleven months as a gunnery sergeant outside Pleiku, it looked like one of those Buddhist shrines he'd sometimes see in a hooch before they'd torch it, couple flowers in a bowl, some food on a plate, incense burning. Nobody sat at the table, even on a Friday night when the bar was packed to bursting, and the bottle went untouched until the moment that Jabril pushed his way through the crowd, paused at the bar to get some fresh glasses and a bucket full of ice cubes, then settled into his chair and leaned to rest his hand lightly on its neck.

"You take the cure?"

Nowles smiled. "Do feel a touch of the fever, now you mention it."

Jabril glanced over at Danny, considered him for a moment, then raised an eyebrow. "You?"

"Yeah, thanks."

Jabril nodded slowly, then turned his head slightly until his eyes came to rest on Mickie Vega. She met his gaze, gave a tight smile. "I'll pass."

Jabril reached into the ice bucket, dropped some cubes into three glasses, then filled them about a third of the way up with rum. He grabbed the handle of the knife, worked it free from the table, quartered a lime. He used the tip of the knife to shove a slice to Nowles and Danny, then stuck the knife back in the table. Danny watched, expecting him to push the glasses across the table to them, but instead he reached across and picked up Mickie's hand from where it lay on the table, holding it just above the wrist. Before she could draw back, he turned it palm up, picked up one of the remaining slices of lime, and squeezed it gently over her wrist so a trickle of juice ran down. He raised her wrist to his nose, inhaled. Then he smiled. "Wasn't only Jesus could raise the dead."

Mickie stared at him. He opened his hand slowly, releasing her wrist. She didn't move. Her hand rested there, motionless, on his open palm. Then Nowles leaned across the table, picked up one of the glasses. "Count your fingers," he told Mickie.

She drew her hand back, wiped her wrist on the leg of her trousers. Jabril smiled, picked up his glass. He put a slice of lime between his teeth, sucked it, then took a long sip of the rum. He looked over at Danny. "You wanted to talk to me?"

He slid Danny's glass across the table, and it left a thin trail of water on the wood. The bar was crowded for a Thursday night, and Danny was aware of people looking over at him, the only white man in the room. He picked up his drink. Somebody squeezing past the table bumped his arm, and a little of the rum spilled on his jeans. He heard laughter behind him, over the thump of the music. There was a band in the front room, squeezed onto a tiny platform about three inches above the floor, opposite the bar. They were easing a slow blues number down, trading lines between the guitar and bass, while the woman singing leaned on the microphone, eyes closed, calling back at them each time they paused, "Uh-huh, yeah, uh-*huh*." And all Danny could think as he sipped at his glass, feeling Jabril's eyes on him, was how he'd heard a few years back that Irma Thomas used to come in here sometimes, get up on the stage, and shake the windows. The guy who'd told him that, a black ex-cop who worked the night desk at Danny's building, had smiled at him and said, "'Course, you hear that, we got to kill you."

Now Danny set his glass down on the table, shifted in his seat to glance back at the band, the singer swinging her hips back and forth slowly, in time with the slowing beat. When the song came to an end, there was scattered applause, a few shouts, and the band set their instruments down, left the stage for a break. Danny turned to face Jabril, leaned into the table so both hands were folded around his glass, said, "I'm looking for James Collette."

Jabril looked at him, expressionless. "Yeah?"

"His mother thinks you might know where he is."

Jabril sat back, sighed. He looked over at Nowles. "This is what you got me out here for?"

Nowles shrugged, lifted his glass. "And this."

Jabril grinned. "My man Nowles. Takes a *white* man to get you down here?"

Nowles glanced around at the crowd. His face hadn't registered it, but Danny could see he was looking to see if anyone had heard. "Took a white man to bring you to me."

"Yeah, but he was dead."

"You had a good look at this one?"

Danny gave a thin smile. One that let it go past, said, *Okay, joke's on me.* He felt Mickie glance over at him, but he avoided her eyes.

"A couple homicide detectives have been out to his house, lookin' for the boy," he told Jabril. "They want him on a shooting. The holdup in that Vietnamese restaurant last Friday over on Claiborne."

Jabril was silent for a moment. "You know why they want him?"

"They told the mother they got a ballistics match off the gun he was carrying."

Jabril sipped at his drink, let his gaze go off across the room. He raised a hand at a man near the bar, said to Nowles, "You seen the ballistics report?"

"I put in a request for a copy this afternoon," Nowles told him quietly. "Take a couple days."

Jabril looked at him for a moment, then nodded. He reached

over, dipped one long finger in his rum, stirred it a few times, and
stuck the finger in his mouth. "Gun's a thing. It's the man who used it
they want."

"The kid had the gun."

"That don't mean shit."

Danny raised his drink, watched Jabril over the glass. "You think
that, or you know it?"

Jabril laughed, glanced over at Nowles. "Listen to him. Mister
Lawyer." He turned back to Danny. "You ever use a gun?"

"I used to hunt."

"I mean a *hand*gun. You ever hold one in your hand, point it at a
man? So you know what it's *for*?"

Danny hesitated for a moment, then shook his head.

Jabril turned to Mickie Vega and smiled. "You?"

Mickie was tracing a smear of water on the wooden table with
her finger. She looked up at Jabril. "Yeah."

Jabril smiled. "Yeah, I guess you could." He sat back, looked
over at Danny. "So you can't imagine using a gun, but you think that
boy could. Why is that?"

Danny was silent, looking down at his drink.

Jabril leaned forward, aimed a finger at Danny. "You want to
know why that boy had a gun? Think about it. What's it get him?
Money? Drugs? Payback?" He smiled. "That's what counts down here,
right? You read the papers."

Danny looked up. "Yeah, I read 'em."

"You believe what you read?"

"Sometimes."

Jabril studied him for a moment, then nodded. "Things ain't always as simple as they look."

Danny smiled. "No, I guess not." He heard Nowles give a soft
laugh, glanced over. Nowles was looking away, watching the crowd.

"Tell me something," Jabril said. "You ever buy drugs?"

Danny looked at him. "Yeah, I have."

"Who you give your money to?"

"Guy who's selling."

"Uh-huh. Now, say you go over to McDonald's, get yourself a hamburger, who you give your money to? Some black kid works behind the counter?"

Danny smiled. "Yeah, I see your point."

Jabril shrugged. "Not hard to see. You got drugs in the ghetto, or guns, it's cause there's somebody makes it his *business* to get 'em there. So how come all I ever see in the newspaper is black *children* goin' to jail?"

"It's not the same," Nowles said quietly.

Jabril looked over at him, surprised. "Huh?"

"I said it's not the same." Nowles's eyes were still on the crowd. "I buy a hamburger, I eat it. Only harm I'm doing is to my own body." He shook his head. "I hear what you're saying, but somebody's got to teach these boys they got to think for them*selves*. You sell drugs, that's your choice. And the law can put you away. That's how it works in the real world. You use a gun, it's murder. Don't go blame nobody else. That just don't cut it with me."

Jabril stared at him for a moment, then looked over at Danny, grinned. "My lawyer. You believe it?"

Nowles smiled sadly. "Hey, I didn't say I wouldn't defend 'em. I just seen it too much, that's all."

Jabril's face became serious. He leaned forward, nodded. "I'm with you there, man," he said softly. "We just disagree about the cause."

Somebody in the crowd called out, "Yo, Ja*bril*," and he glanced over, raised a lazy hand. When he turned back, Mickie said quietly, "None of this helps the boy."

Jabril raised his eyebrows. "You want to *help* the boy?"

"I'm his juvenile officer. That's my job."

Jabril snorted. "Yeah, right. You hold his hand while they put on the cuffs." He shook his head. "You say they got a ballistics match on the gun. So they got the bullet in the gun, the gun in his hand, got his prints on the gun, probably. But I can *tell* you he didn't shoot cops."

"You know that?"

Jabril glanced over at Danny, shrugged. "Yeah, I know."

"You mind if I ask how?"

"Do I *mind?*" Jabril grinned. "You something else, man."

Danny watched him drain his glass, pick up a piece of lime, and suck at it. "It's a simple question."

"Yeah?" Jabril reached for the bottle, poured more rum over his ice. "Well, here's a question you can answer for me. What's it to you, anyway?"

"I want to help him."

"Why?"

Danny hesitated. "What do you mean?"

"How come you're interested, you're not his lawyer. How come you askin' the questions, and not my man Nowles here?" Jabril sat back, sipped at his glass.

Danny felt Mickie look over at him. Nowles raised his glass to his mouth, smiled into his drink.

"I was asked to look into the case," Danny said.

"By who?"

"I can't say."

Jabril looked at him for a long moment, then smiled slowly. "Looks like you the man with the answers, not me."

18

There was a strip of yellow crime scene tape lying in the gutter when L'Dog got to the scene, but the ambulance was gone, and the cops had finished asking their questions, left it to go back to the way it always looked—trash on the street, kids hanging out in front of the store, cars cruising past slow. Only somebody had come out of the store with a bucket of water, washed the blood off the patch of sidewalk in front of the door. You could see some still down near the edge of the sidewalk, and that's where the kids were standing, checking it out.

One of them spotted L'Dog as he got out of the car, watched him walk over. "Yo, man," he called out. "You hear 'bout Rodney?"

L'Dog didn't answer. He walked over to where they were standing, looked down at the smear of blood on the sidewalk. Then he looked at the yellow tape lying there, turned to gaze up the street at the passing cars. "Anybody see who done it?"

"Crew saw it," the kid said, his voice excited. "He was standing right over there, saw the whole thing."

"Where's he now?"

"He took off. 'Fraid the cops would take him."

"You know where?"

The kid shrugged. "Home, I guess."

"Where's that?"

"He live over on Saint Mary." The kid looked off down the street, trying to see what L'Dog was looking at. "You want me to show you?"

L'Dog glanced down at the bloodstain, frowned. "C'mon, then."

The kid's name was Nugget, and he hung out with some other

boys in the playground behind the benches on St. Andrew. L'Dog figured he was about twelve, a couple years too young to be useful, but
worth keeping an eye on. They walked over to St. Mary Street, where
Nugget went upstairs, then came back to tell him that Crew hadn't
come home. They stood there on the street for a moment, L'Dog looking up the street, thinking about it. The kid stood next to him, hoping L'Dog didn't think it was his fault. Then, as L'Dog was getting
ready to walk off, the kid flung out one arm like he was tossing something away and said "Ah, man. I just remembered. He got a sister, live
over by Saint James."

So they walked over there. The sister lived in a shotgun, with cement blocks where the porch steps used to be. L'Dog sat down on one
of the steps, spent a minute adjusting the bandanna on his head while
Nugget went up and knocked on the door. Somebody opened it a
crack, and L'Dog heard them whispering, then the door opened wider,
throwing light across the porch. He turned, saw a kid looking out at
him. He looked scared, kept one hand on the door like he was ready to
slam it shut if he didn't like what he saw.

L'Dog stood up, slowly, raised his hands, showing the kid they
were empty. "You Crew?"

"Uh-huh." The boy looked up and down the street, then stepped
back, held the door open. "Don't stand out here."

L'Dog came up onto the porch. "Wait here," he told Nugget, and
brushed past Crew into a narrow hall. Crew shut the door behind him,
pulled down a security bar. There was a bike against one wall, and a
folded-up baby stroller. A poster from the Jazz and Heritage Festival
hung next to the door, a crawfish, big grin on his face, holding a trum-
pet in one claw, a chef's hat in the other. Behind him, a bunch of gators
did a second line, waving umbrellas, dancing away so their knees
stuck out at funny angles. Big old teeth, smiling at you.

"My sister's sleepin'," the kid they called Crew told him when he
got the door locked. "She got a baby, so we got to be quiet."

"She know why you here?"

"Nah. I come here some nights."

L'Dog looked down the hall, rubbed at his jaw. "You tell anybody else?"

Crew shrugged. "Couple people, right after. Nugget and them, you know?"

"You tell 'em what you saw?"

"Just that Rodney got shot."

L'Dog looked at the kid, saw the fear around his eyes. He was trying to tough it out, make his face empty, like he was used to it, but he had that squint in his eyes told you he was deep inside the panic, staring out.

"You see who did it?"

The kid looked away, like something had caught his attention down the hall. He shook his head. "Guy in a black Samurai. Had those tinted windows, raised up."

"Yeah?" L'Dog leaned against the wall behind him, folded his arms. "Nugget told me you saw it."

The kid looked at him, and L'Dog saw something dark way down inside his eyes, like the place where a light used to be. Then he looked back down the hall and said, "I saw Rodney get shot, that's all. The car pulls up next to him, just sits there for a minute. Rodney, he's just standing there, man, like he's frozen. Then the guy rolls down the window, and I see the gun. Rodney's like three feet away from it, but he starts to turn, like he's gonna run, then it's like, *bang, bang, bang.* I see Rodney go down, looked like somebody shoved him, you know? There's, like, *blood* in the air where he was standing, just hangin' there, like a cloud. Then the Samurai takes off, the window going back up. And I'm standin' there, thinkin', like, 'Oh, power windows. You got to pay extra for that.'" The kid shook his head, and L'Dog saw that his cheeks were wet. "Rodney, he's lying there, and there's blood all over the sidewalk. He's got his legs crossed, but the wrong way, you know?

So his toes are pointing at each other. Man, I saw that, I thought, 'Okay, he's dead.' So I took off."

L'Dog waited a moment until the kid looked over at him, then said, "That's it?"

"Uh-huh."

"You never saw the guy?"

Crew looked away, shook his head.

"You see what kinda gun it was?"

"Looked like a nine."

L'Dog glanced up at the poster, all those gators doin' the nasty, sighed. "Rodney ain't dead. They got him up at the hospital."

"No shit?" The kid shook his head, surprised. "Man, he sure looked dead, you know? Guy shot him, like, three times."

L'Dog nodded. "I got to go." He watched the kid turn and lift the security bolt, unlock the door with a key on a string. "You got any more to say, you know where to find me?"

The kid stood there for a moment, facing away from him, his hand on the doorknob. "Won't be no more. I told you what I seen."

"Uh-huh." L'Dog reached past him, moved his hand off the doorknob, and opened the door. Outside, Nugget was sitting on the edge of the porch. He glanced around, stood up as L'Dog came out. L'Dog turned to put one hand on the door before Crew could swing it shut. "Maybe you'll think of something else. You do, come see me first."

Then he turned, walked down the concrete steps to the street. As he walked away, he heard the door close behind him, quietly.

L'Dog found Jabril at his table in the back room of Tugs. There were three empty glasses on the table, but he had an expression on his face that said he didn't want company. He sat with his chair shoved way back from the table, his legs stretched out in front of him, so he had to lean forward to pick up his glass. There was a crowd of people standing against the bar, and more against the back wall, listening to the band in the front room, but they'd left a wide space around him. His arms were folded tightly across his chest, his eyes closed. A few men nodded at L'Dog as he pushed through the crowd, then looked away as he pulled a chair away from the table, sat down.

Jabril opened his eyes for a moment, considered him. "Yeah?"

"Black Samurai, guy used a nine. That's all I got."

Jabril closed his eyes again, like he'd gone back to sleep. But L'Dog could see the muscles in Jabril's jaw tighten; L'Dog sat back, waited. Behind him, the band was churning it out, and L'Dog looked at the swaying bodies packed in tight beside him. He could have reached out and touched a woman's hip where it shimmied in a bright red dress. She swung it there, slowly, one beat off the band, so you knew she was *hearing* it, deep into it, not dancing, but following the music where it led her, down inside. He glanced up at her face. She was smiling, eyes raised to the ceiling, half closed. Coffee-dark, and old enough to be his mama. But, man, he felt it, watchin' her, get hard between his legs. *Real* hard. Wanting to *be* that beat, make her sway like that, little half smile on her face. But from inside. From way down low.

He felt Jabril's eyes on him, turned to see him smiling. He sat forward, called out over the music, "You ask her nice, you *might* get your eyes back."

L'Dog scowled.

Jabril tipped his glass, looked down at the wedge of dark rum that gathered at the bottom. He waited for the band to ease the song down, sat tight as they drew out the last three chords, then leaned into the silence that followed the crowd's shouts, and said quietly, "We got to know, Dog."

L'Dog shrugged. "Ask me, it's Conti Street. They got a Samurai."

"Yeah? Say you got a car like that, maybe you ride up to City

Park in it on Saturday, play the stereo loud. Let everybody see you, like those Conti Street boys. I *hope* you ain't gonna use it for no drive-by."

L'Dog looked away at the crowd. "Those Conti Street boys, they know me from, like, *business.*"

"Yeah?" Jabril leaned toward him across the table. "What kind of *business* we talkin' about here, Dog?"

L'Dog shrugged, his eyes still wandering around the room. "Ah, you know. I do a little sellin' sometimes."

Jabril was silent. L'Dog waited for him to say something, then snuck a glance. Jabril was looking down at the table, his finger drawing little pictures in the wet rings his glass had left on the wood. He didn't look surprised, just . . . tired. Then he looked up, and said, "You know, I knew your mama back about twenty years ago. She was real pretty then. *Real* pretty."

L'Dog grinned. "*My* mama?"

"Uh-huh. She could raise your hopes, man. Or break the heart in a heartless thing. Knew it, too."

"Damn." L'Dog shook his head, smiling. "My mama."

"Anyway, she made me promise to watch out for you. Make sure you stayed outa trouble." Jabril spread his hands. "Now you tell me you got those Conti Street boys on your ass." He folded his hands again, shook his head slowly. "Those boys are some bad niggers, Dog. That guy Blood? He's a stone killer. You got him in your shit, you might as well just go set your hair on fire, 'cause you got a *world* of troubles."

L'Dog sat stiffly, looking down at the table. "Yeah, well, it's tough all over."

Jabril sighed, thought, *Ain't that the fuckin' truth.* No big surprise, L'Dog talkin' about his problems with Conti Street. He hung out on the corner down at St. Andrews, sold to people who rode by in their cars, just small-time dealing, like a lot of these boys. Selling what's there to be sold, 'cause that's what they see, every day of their lives, people selling stuff—sneakers, cars, liquor, guns—so they got the money to pay for all the stuff some other guy's selling. *America, man.* Jabril shook his head. *A whole country, just flippin' coins.*

But those Conti Street boys, that was a different story. They ran a big operation, had spent the summer moving in on the little guys, grabbing new territory. A little muscle was all it took, mostly. A couple bullets through your window, a car burned during the night, maybe some guys come by, rough you up. Most guys got the message, closed up shop.

But not L'Dog. Nah, he's got to hang tough, show you he's a *man.* And here it came, the boy leaning across the table to whisper, "You still got those guns, man?"

Jabril studied his face. "Yeah, I got 'em. Don't mean we're gonna use 'em."

L'Dog sighed, shook his head. "Man, I knew you was gonna say that. So how come we bought 'em, we ain't gonna stand up?" *Nice guns, man.* Two .45s and a .38 revolver. Felt solid in your hand. He'd paid a white guy up in a coffee shop on Canal Street almost $500, cash, handed it to the guy and walked out with the guns, carried 'em home in a Nike gym bag. Just like Jabril had told him to. When he got back, Jabril had just glanced in the bag, nodded, then carried it away to hide someplace. Now L'Dog's hand felt hollow. He wanted those guns. "Those Conti Street boys, they think I'm not for real. But we could take 'em *down,* you know?"

"You cheat those Conti Street boys, Dog?"

L'Dog sat back and shook his head, both hands up. "Man, I don't cheat nobody. They just got their shit twisted, you hear what I'm sayin'?"

Jabril looked at him, silent.

"We got to show those niggers not to come 'round here, shoot up our people."

"Guns ain't enough, Dog. You got to know who to use 'em *on.*"
Jabril looked down at his glass, drained it, then set it down on the
table, pushed it away with the back of his hand. "We got enough dead
niggers, last couple years. You got to be *sure.*"

He raised his eyes to L'Dog's face. Their eyes met for a long moment, then L'Dog shrugged, sat back slowly, looked away. But in that
brief moment, Jabril had seen something in his eyes. An unspoken
thing, but Jabril recognized it. Like you see in young guys standing
around on a basketball court, hands on their hips, looking off into the
distance as the old guy gets up slow off the asphalt. Waiting, in silence. Your breath hot, burning within you. Jabril knew how it felt.
Back when you had that extra step to take you to the basket. Nothing
in your way, no doubt to hang at your heels, slowing you down. So you
look away as the old guy heaves himself up, wait till he gets to his feet,
then brush his hand with yours, say, *All right, man* to hide your impa-
tience, your embarassment . . .

Your contempt.

19

"You know your problem, Danny?"

Danny opened his eyes in the darkness, felt it lying on his skin like heat. "What's my problem?"

Maura pulled the pillow up behind her back, drew up her knees. "You don't engage."

"I was engaged to Helen. Before we got married."

She waved a hand around the room. "I mean with all this. Your life."

Danny was silent, looking up at the ceiling. Thinking about Mickie Vega, the way she'd looked at him when she dropped him back at his car and said, "Guess I'll see you around, huh?" Smiling, as she said it. Those dark eyes, looking up at him for a moment before she rolled up the window, put the car in gear, and pulled away.

Maura reached out, poked him in the chest with one sharp finger. "See? Lights on, nobody home." She shook her head sadly. "You're like a guy who goes to a psychiatrist, says, 'Doctor, I don't know what's wrong. I can't play the piano.' The doctor asks him, 'How long has this been going on?' And the guy says, 'All my life.'"

Danny smiled. "Send me a bill."

"I should," she said. "I really should."

He'd come home to find her sitting at his kitchen table, a cup of coffee in her hand, reading through his old letters from Helen, which he kept in a shoe box on the top shelf of his closet.

"I stole your extra key," she told him. She sipped her coffee, tossed the letter she was reading back into the shoe box. "She was crazy about you. You realize that?"

He reached over, picked up the box. "Stay out of my head, Maura."

"Don't worry, I intend to." She smiled. "No matter how much you fuck things up." She took a sip of her coffee. Danny carried the shoe box into the bedroom, put it away. When he came back into the kitchen, she said, "You ever wonder what your family did to keep busy before Jimmy showed up?"

"Drank, mostly."

She raised her eyebrows. "Old family tradition, huh?"

"Only the names change."

"You know Jimmy's setting you up, right?"

Danny looked at her for a long moment, then nodded. "Yeah, I know."

She glanced down at her coffee cup. "So my father fucks you, and you fuck me. Seems a crude justice in that."

"That what you think's happening here?"

She stood up, set her coffee cup in the sink. "Oh, you had a message." She smiled at him, her eyes dark. "Helen called. It's on your machine."

Danny stared at her. "Helen?"

"Just like old times, huh?"

Danny looked away, shook his head. "She must need something. Wants me to get Jimmy to talk to one of her clients."

"And she called you." Maura smiled. "I'm impressed." She reached out, tugged at Danny's sleeve. "C'mon, let's go to bed."

Later, when she was asleep, Danny got up, pulled on a pair of sweatpants, and went out on the porch. After Helen had moved out, Danny had stayed in their apartment for a few months, then stayed in a friend's place in the Quarter for a couple weeks until he found a second-floor walk-up on Lowerline, a couple blocks from the park. The apartment was small, but it had a porch overlooking the street. In the evenings, he liked to sit out there with a beer, his feet propped up on the railing, watching the kids race their bikes along the sidewalk opposite. There was an old oak tree that had split the sidewalk with its roots, and the kids liked to jump their bikes off the slab that jutted up, twisting sideways in midair, like they saw on television. He'd watched one kid break his arm on a bad landing the previous summer, but that didn't seem to slow it down much. And nine weeks later the same kid was back, racing through the late autumn leaves to get a good run at it, thrusting his fist in the air when he nailed the landing. Like he'd waited all that time to get it right, had lain awake at night thinking about it.

Danny identified.

It was two in the morning. He stood there for a while, watching a thin mist settle in the branches of the oak tree across the street. The air was damp, but cool against his skin. He closed his eyes, breathed it in. He could taste smoke and sweat, like wool on his tongue, from the crowded bar.

He went over to his desk, looked down at the light flashing on his answering machine, but didn't press the button. *Jesus. Helen.*

He wandered back onto the porch, settled into the chair, gazed down at the buckled sidewalk below. Sometimes, sitting there, he felt a secret desire to sneak off down the street one night, steal a bike from some kid's back porch, and take it out onto the sidewalk. Get some speed up coming down the block, raise up on the pedals as you come up on the broken slab, and just break free, man. Air under your tires, head in the sky.

But as soon as you're up, you got to think about coming down. The sidewalk rushing up at you before you're ready, making you give that freedom back too soon. So now you got to go back, do it again.

Danny knew that feeling too.

He got up and went over to the stereo, put the radio on softly. Flipped through the dial until he found WBLU, got Mo James and his Crescent City Classics show, four hours of black guys singing about lost love to ease you through the night. *Perfect.*

Forty minutes later Danny opened his eyes, realized he'd been sleeping. He got up out of his chair, shut off the radio, and glanced down at the street as he turned to go to bed.

At the end of the block, a man sat in a darkened car. As Danny watched, the car started up, headlights flaring, and pulled away from the curb. It drove past his house, slowly, turned at the next corner.

Danny stood there for a moment, thinking about it. Then he went inside, locked the porch door behind him. He dropped his clothes on a chair next to the bed and stood for a moment looking down at Maura, sleeping on her back with both arms across her chest, like she was warding off a thrust to the heart. He turned, caught a glimpse of himself in the mirror above his dresser as he drew the sheets back.

His face looked empty.

Like a glass somebody's drained.

Acorsi was leaning on a wall outside the emergency room entrance at Charity Hospital when Maya pulled up, his head tipped back against the cinder blocks, eyes closed. According to the clock on Maya's dashboard, it was 3:54 A.M., forty minutes since she'd woken to the phone ringing, heard Acorsi's voice say, "Maya? It's Tom."

"Jesus Christ, Tom. Don't you ever *sleep?*" She'd reached for the clock on her bedside table, brought it into focus. She'd been in bed less than two hours. "You at the office?"

"No. Why?"

"I need you to log in a homicide." She put the clock back on the bedside table, lay back against the pillow, and closed her eyes. "'Cause I'm really gonna kill you this time."

"They got the Collette kid over at Charity, Maya. Somebody shot him up. Looks like a drive-by."

"Shit." She sat up, rubbed at her face until she could get her eyes open. Then she slid her legs off the bed. "He gonna make it?"

"Not clear yet."

Her husband turned over, opened his eyes blearily. "What's the matter, baby?"

"Nothing, honey. It's just Tom." She reached over, touched his cheek gently. "Go back to sleep."

"You gotta go out again?"

"Sounds like it."

He reached out, grabbed for the phone. "Gimme that thing."

"Shhh." She pushed his hand away. "Go on, Tom."

"That Mike?"

"Yeah. He's mad at you, getting his wife out of bed, this hour."

"Tell him to go back to sleep before he wakes my kids."

"I heard that!" Mike grumbled, then he turned over and pulled the sheet over his head.

Maya stood up, slipped on her robe. "You want to come by here, or should I meet you at Charity?"

"Meet me down there. They got him in surgery right now. I want to be there, he regains consciousness."

Now, as she pulled up, got out of the car, her stomach sank. If Tom was out there, just leaning on the wall, it meant the kid hadn't survived the surgery. One more victim, the violence spreading out in all directions like a wind kicking up dust. They'd gotten the ballistics report that afternoon, matching the bullets taken from the victims' bodies to the guns found in the restaurant. They'd spent the rest of the day working out the implications, connecting each bullet to the gun that fired it, plotting out each shot on her hand-drawn map of the scene, until they could begin to make sense of what happened. A total of twelve shots had been fired. The crime scene technicians had pulled four bullets out of the restaurant's walls; the rest had come out of the bodies. The three guns recovered at the scene had accounted for eight shots, total. The bullets that killed the two Conti Street boys had come from a 9 mm SIG-Maremont P226 found lying next to Foley's hand. A Charter Arms Bulldog .44 revolver found next to one of the boys was unfired, while a 9 mm Smith & Wesson, .459 semiautomatic had been fired twice, both bullets ending up in the wall. The remaining six bullets, which included the four lethal shots that killed Foley and the restaurant's owners, had been matched by ballistics tests to the 9 mm Glock semiautomatic recovered from James Collette at the time of his arrest.

Acorsi had shoved the report aside wearily. "You see anything new here?"

"Looks like the Collette kid's the shooter."

"Pretty good shooting for a fourteen-year-old." Acorsi shook his head. "Must've been like Dodge City in there. This kid cleans the place out, like Wyatt Earp."

Maya shrugged. You got five people dead, over a couple hundred dollars. And their best suspect was a boy too young to drive. None of it made any sense to her, but that's just how it goes, you work homicide in New Orleans. The only answers, she figured, would come from the boy who'd disappeared, James Collette. And now he lay in the emergency ward, shot down on the street.

She walked over to Acorsi, saw him open his eyes, wearily.

"We lose him?"

Acorsi shook his head. "It's the wrong fucking kid," he said, his voice tired. "They shot the boy's little brother by mistake."

"Jesus." They were silent for a moment, both of them feeling their exhaustion. Then Acorsi angrily shoved himself up off the wall and said, "What a fucking waste."

"He say anything?"

"Hasn't regained consciousness. Doctors say it doesn't look good."

"Any witnesses?"

"Some people on the block say there was another kid with him, but he disappeared."

"So we got nothing."

Acorsi shrugged. "Couple people on the street ID'd the car. Black off-road vehicle. Jeep Cherokee, maybe. Suzuki Samurai. But customized, so it's a street car. You put that with the fact that it's a drive-by, starts to look like a gang thing. Revenge killing, maybe."

"Like maybe those Conti Street boys know more than they're saying."

"That's how it usually works." Acorsi rolled his head back, looked up at the night sky, rubbed at his neck with one hand. "Could turn out this whole thing's just the start of a gang war. Buncha kids fighting it out over territory. And everybody else just got in the way."

Maya sighed. "I guess we better get some patrol units down to Conti Street, start picking those boys up again." She rubbed at her eyes, hard. "Check out the DMV records on black Jeeps."

They were silent. The sky was starting to get pale over in the east. "Gonna be another long day."

Maya smiled. "I got home last night, Mike was waiting up. Lying there in bed, reading a book. You know what the title was? *Married to It.* Whole book on how to know if your partner's a workaholic."

"He wanted you to see it."

"Sure. Can't blame him, really. Last time we had a night out together was our anniversary, six months ago." She smiled again. "And when we got home, there was a message from you on our machine. Some new break in a case."

Acorsi laughed. "So I guess he thinks I'm trying to break up your marriage, huh?"

"You got to blame somebody."

He smiled. "That's our job."

Twenty minutes later, Acorsi was at the duty nurse's station, waiting for an update on Rodney Collette's condition. He glanced over at Maya, sitting on a plastic chair near the glass doors that led to the ER, with the case file open on her lap. She wore a pair of reading glasses, flipped through the pages slowly. He never got used to seeing her with glasses. Most of the time, she didn't bother with them, but she'd pull them out when she got tired. Wear them on the end of her nose, like a schoolteacher.

He realized he was staring, turned away. After a while a nurse came out, told him the boy's condition was unchanged. He wandered back to where Maya was sitting, dropped into a chair next to her, leaned over so his elbows rested on his knees, and rubbed at his face with both hands.

"Any news?"

He shook his head. "He's hangin' on."

"You think the shooter screwed up, took him for his brother?"

"Could be." He sat up, let his head rest against the wall behind him. "Any of those boys got shot last Friday have a brother? Maybe somebody's evening the score."

She flipped through the pages slowly, then shook her head. "Doesn't say. None of the kids we picked up has the same last name as the victims, but that doesn't rule it out these days." She closed the file and slid the glasses off. "Any reason we got to stick around here?"

"Only if the kid wakes up, we can get a statement." He stood up.

"I'll give them my pager number, they can call me if anything changes."

He went back to the nurse's station. Maya leaned her head back against the wall behind her, watching as an orderly wheeled a patient past on a gurney. She'd always hated hospitals, since she was a kid. Her mother had spent eight months in a hospital bed, cancer slowly eating her bones, when Maya was ten. Her father had brought her to the hospital every couple days, after school, until Maya felt as if the smell would never come out of her clothes, her hair. After her mother died, they'd buried her in a driving rain over in the black cemetery on Metairie Road. Three months later, her father remarried, a girl of nineteen who lived down the block. Within a year of her mother's death, Maya had a baby sister, and that awful year of her mother's dying had gradually slipped away into the past. But the smell of the hospital never left her. Like a ghost, always ready to stake its claim on her.

Now she barely noticed it. Eight years as a cop, she'd spent too many hours waiting outside hospital rooms for it to mean anything. Or maybe its meaning had just changed. Hospitals were where they brought the wounded, the dying. You leaned over their beds, waiting for them to whisper into your ear, hoping for a name, a description, something to get you started.

Every one of 'em giving you that same look your mother gave you, grabbing your hand, hanging on to you as the life leaves their eyes.

She jerked her head up suddenly, realized she'd dozed off. *Jesus, you got to get some sleep.* She stood up, laid the file on her chair, and stretched her arms up behind her head, feeling the joints in her shoulders and neck crack like old, dry sticks.

She could smell coffee brewing back in the nurse's station, wondered if they'd let her have a cup. But then Tom came back from the nurse's station, glancing at his watch.

"Almost six. Not much point going home, now." He looked at her. "You want some breakfast?"

"Point the way."

It was after seven when they got to the office. Acorsi sorted through a stack of interoffice envelopes on the front counter while Maya called home, spoke to her kids. At the bottom of the stack, he found an envelope with his name on it that somebody had dropped in the box before going home the night before. He tore it open, found a computer printout from the Automated Fingerprint Identification System, an on-line program with access to millions of fingerprints compiled from criminal, military, law enforcement, and civil service files across the country. The crime scene technicians had pulled several dozen different fingerprints from the restaurant's front door, counters, tables, and a stack of unwashed dishes beside the sink in the kitchen that the cook hadn't yet gotten around to soaking. Watching them, Acorsi figured most of it would lead nowhere; if they got a match on a print lifted from a table, it might turn up a customer who'd eaten there any time in the last couple days. The plates looked more promising, since they'd been used that night. But then he realized that if the owners had gotten around to clearing the dishes off a table, carrying them back into the kitchen to be washed, then they probably came from customers who'd left before the shootings took place. Not much chance the gunmen sat down and ordered up the Mekong chicken, then waited for the table to be cleared before opening fire. Still, maybe they'd get a witness who saw some black kids sitting in a car out front, waiting for the place to empty out. Acorsi had pointed out a couple of unwashed teacups stacked on a tray in a corner of the dining room, and an empty beer bottle in the garbage can, told the technicians to bag them when they'd finished lifting the prints.

On Saturday morning he had carried the print cards down to the print lab, filled out an AFIS search request form, checking off all the boxes so the operator would know to run the widest possible search—including all criminal, military, and civil service files nationwide. It took more computer time, but nobody behind the counter argued with him. You pull a multiple homicide, make the front pages of every newspaper in the state, it's like driving an express train through a crowded station; everybody knows to get out of the way.

It had taken almost forty-eight hours to run all the prints through the system, but now he had the results. He ran his eye down the page, a brief list of numbers and names, matching fingerprints in the national database to the card number of four sets of prints lifted at the scene. Jesus, all those prints, and what do they get? Four matches. All the rest were people who'd never been printed, or the print lifted by the technicians at the scene had been smudged, not clear enough for the system to pull up a match. Still, that gave them four more people to interview, maybe a few more bits of information to throw into the stew. That's what the job was about. Talk to everybody, ask the same couple questions over and over. You never knew when somebody you talked to might come out with a useful piece of information. Acorsi had broken a case once by tracking down a guy who walked his dog along the levee every day after work. The guy hadn't even realized that he'd witnessed a crime until Acorsi pointed out to him that the woman he'd seen getting into a blue Ford pickup truck outside a bar had turned up dead six hours later. When Acorsi pressed him, the man produced a detailed description of the truck, including a Texas Longhorns sticker on the back window. Two days later, they made an arrest.

Acorsi wandered back to his desk, his eyes on the sheet of paper in his hand. As he sat down, Maya wished her six-year-old daughter a good day at school and hung up the phone. She sat back, rubbing her hands over her face like she was trying to wipe something away, then looked over at Acorsi. "You get something?"

"Fingerprints." Acorsi leaned over, tossed the paper on her desk. "Four matches, none of them from the criminal files."

"So we struck out."

"Maybe."

She looked up at him, raised her eyebrows. "You see something here I don't?"

He smiled, reached over, and laid his finger beneath the final name on the list. "Small world. Turns out I know this guy."

Maura sat up in bed, reached out one hand, and gripped Danny's shoulder, her fingers digging into the flesh. "There's somebody here," she whispered. "Somebody at the door."

He opened his eyes, not moving. For a moment, he heard nothing. Then somebody banged on his front door. He glanced over at the clock next to the bed. Ten minutes past eight.

He sat up, reached for his jeans on the floor. "Stay here," he whispered to Maura. "I'll shut the door." He grabbed a T-shirt off the chair by the window, went out to the living room, pulling the bedroom door closed behind him. He heard Maura get out of bed and come over to lock it. Then she got back into bed. He turned on the lights in the living room, went over to the door, slid the Beretta out of the pocket of his leather jacket, which hung on the chair next to the door. "Yeah? Who is it?"

"Open up, Danny. It's Tom Acorsi."

It took him a moment, but then Danny had the face. Seeing him, for just a moment, as he used to look in high school, when they'd played ball together, a kid coming to the plate with his bat dangling lazily from one hand. He'd been a percentage hitter, planting his feet carefully, taking a few quick swings. But in his senior year, Tom Acorsi had hit more sacrifice flies than any kid in the state, long drives that either made the outfield wall or dropped into the right fielder's glove, giving the base runner time to tag third, sprint for home. He'd trot back across the infield toward the dugout, past Danny Chaisson, who'd nod at him and say, "Nice shot."

Lately, though, Danny'd seen him around town, dressed in a dark sport coat and gray slacks, a little tight across the ass where he'd put on weight. Like all of them, getting older. And, if you looked close, a faint glint of metal on one hip when the jacket swung open, where he wore his badge.

Shit. Danny slipped the gun back into the pocket of his jacket, then unlocked the door, swung it open. And there he was, Tom Acorsi, grinning as he held up that badge, said, "How you doing, Danny? Been a while, huh?"

Danny made coffee. While it brewed, he carried some mugs out, clearing a place on the coffee table for them.

"You know my partner, Danny?" Acorsi gestured to the black woman who'd followed him through the door. "Maya Thomas?"

Danny shook hands with her. "We've met."

"Yeah?" She studied his face, but she didn't recognize him. "You'll have to remind me."

"Fund-raiser for Moses Jackson a couple years ago. When he ran for state senate."

She raised her eyebrows. "You've got a good memory."

"Not really." Danny smiled. "Jimmy Boudrieux had me do some research on you. Thought you might make a good candidate some-day."

She stared at him. Acorsi glanced over at her and grinned. "You always learn something interesting, talkin' to this guy."

Danny shoved a stack of newspapers off the couch so Maya could sit down. Acorsi pulled a chair over and slumped into it, stretching his legs out in front of him like he'd been on his feet for hours.

"So how you been?"

"I'm okay. Hangin' in there." Danny jerked his head toward the kitchen. "Let me get the coffee."

He stood by the counter, waiting for it to finish brewing. *Stay cool. They're probably just sniffing.*

He picked up the coffeepot, carried it back into the living room, set it down on the table, then went back for a carton of milk and some sugar. Acorsi was pouring out three mugs and looked up at him.

"Spoons?"

Danny went back into the kitchen, got three spoons. As he passed the bedroom door, it opened a crack.

"What's going on?" Maura whispered.

"Some people came by. I made coffee."

"Jesus." The door closed.

Danny went into the living room, pulled another chair over, laid the spoons next to the milk. He poured some sugar into his coffee, stirring it slowly. Acorsi watched him, smiling.

"So what's new?"

Danny smiled. "Man, I hate that question. Everybody asks me that, I never know what to say."

"You say what everybody else says. 'Nothin' much. How 'bout you?'"

"That seem sad to you?"

Acorsi shrugged. "Never really thought about it." He sipped at his coffee, which was black and strong. "Anyway, it's New Orleans. What else can you say?"

"I guess you're right."

They sat in silence for a moment, the steam from the coffee rising in slow curls. Then Acorsi said, "You haven't asked why we're here."

Danny shrugged. "I figured you'd tell me when you're ready."

Acorsi reached over, picked up one of the newspapers lying on the table. It was open to the sports page, a story about a bicycle race over in France, with a photograph showing three guys bent way over their handlebars, pedaling up a mountain. Their faces were contorted in pain. Acorsi laughed. "Jesus. Look at these idiots."

"You identify?"

"Me?" He shook his head. "Nah, I take it pretty easy. Don't even play any ball anymore. You want to know my idea of a good sport these days? They got this place on a river up by Hammond, you stick an inner tube in the current, tie a six-pack of beer to it so it hangs down in the water, stays cold, then you just float away. Takes you, like, four hours to get downstream. You get to the end, you're laid out, sun-baked, not a care in the world."

"You get old, you get lazy. Happens to all of us."

"That's not what I heard."

Danny looked over at him, curious. "Yeah? What'd you hear?"

"I heard you're a busy guy. Run all over town, talk to all kinda people."

Danny looked at him over the rim of his coffee cup, said nothing. Acorsi sat back, folded his arms across his chest, met his gaze.

"Hell, you the only lawyer I ever met, don't spend a day in court. But I guess you done that, huh? Back when you was with the D.A.'s office. I remember you prosecuted a couple cases I worked on, put those guys away." Acorsi smiled, shrugged. "But that's a while back. Now you out there in the *world,* makin' things happen."

Danny put his cup down. "Cut the shit, Tom. What's on your mind?"

"Well, Danny, you remember when you went to work for the D.A.'s office? They took your fingerprints, ran a background check on you."

"Sure, they do that with everybody. So what?"

"Those fingerprints go into a computer file. We lift prints at a crime scene, we can check 'em against anybody who's been printed in the last twenty years. Which is how I got to wondering why your fingerprints turned up at the scene of a multiple homicide."

Danny sat back, slowly. "What homicide?"

Acorsi picked up the newspaper, flipped it to the second page, where a follow-up story on the Claiborne Avenue shootings described the weekend funerals of the victims and noted that police had spent the weekend questioning several suspects. He tossed the paper on the table, saw Danny's eye go to the headline.

"You eat out last Friday, Danny?"

Danny raised his eyes to meet Acorsi's gaze, then he reached over, picked up his coffee cup. "I was hoping to stay out of it."

"Well, you're in it now, so why don't you tell us about it?"

Danny shrugged. "Not much to tell. I was friends with Claude Raymond and his wife. Been eating there once a week since I was in law school. I stopped by Friday night, had a bowl of soup with Claude back in the kitchen, then I left."

"And a beer."

"What?"

"You left your prints on a beer bottle."

Danny nodded, sipped at his coffee. "Okay, I guess I had a beer."

"What time was this?" Maya had her notepad out, scribbling.

"Early evening. Seven-thirty, eight."

Maya's mouth tightened, and she shot Acorsi a quick glance. *Dead end.* But Acorsi ignored her, sipped at his coffee.

"You still work for Jimmy Boudrieux, Danny?"

Danny shot him a glance. "Last I heard."

"You ever run into a guy named Dewitt Foley? Used to sell guns up on Canal Street."

Danny studied him for a moment, then picked up the newspaper, glanced at the story on the shootings. "He's the guy who got killed?"

Acorsi reached over, took the newspaper out of his hands. "Yeah, Danny. He's the guy who got killed. You know him?"

Maya saw Danny's eyes narrow. Then he shrugged, said, "Maybe I saw him around. I run into a lot of people."

Acorsi nodded. "See, we got a witness says Foley spent the whole night in the restaurant. Got there around six, just sat around reading the papers. Like he was waiting for somebody."

Danny was silent. He sipped at his coffee.

"Might help us if you could confirm that Foley was there when you came in. Help us work out what happened."

Danny set his coffee down, sat back slowly. He spread his hands. "I'd like to help you, Tom . . ."

"But you can't."

Danny shook his head. He could feel the muscles in his face, like the frame around a photograph.

Acorsi looked at him, silent. Then he raised his coffee cup, drained it, and set it down on the table.

"Put some clothes on, Danny. There's something I want you to see."

20

Wednesday morning, Mickie Vega attended a weekly status conference in a small conference room at the offices of the Bureau of Alcohol, Tobacco and Firearms. Her boss, Jim Dubrow, caught up with her in the hallway, on her way to grab some coffee before the conference, pulled her aside.

"We got company today." He glanced down the hall at the door to the conference room, ran a hand across the back of his neck. "Seems the FBI has an interest in this guy Chaisson. They flagged our request for his file."

"Meaning what?"

"They want to know why we're interested in him. Then they'll decide if they want to let us see the file."

Mickie raised her eyebrows. "They'll *decide*?"

"That's how it works. It's their file, so we've got to make nice." He glanced up at her. "Don't give 'em too much in there, okay? Just the basics. These guys, the more they know about our interest in Chaisson, the less chance they'll let us see the file."

He rested a hand on her shoulder briefly, squeezed, then headed off down the corridor. She watched him go. He was in his fifties, with flecks of gray starting to emerge in his dark hair. He'd come up in the old days, before Waco and Ruby Ridge, when agents made cases by pulling on a pair of jeans and a T-shirt, riding out to some farmer's house to buy an unregistered shotgun, then showing up a couple hours later with a van full of agents to make the bust. But he'd ridden out the rough weather in recent years, learned to accept that a clean arrest meant taking it slow, isolating a suspect, avoiding confrontations that could only end under the TV lights.

"Watch your ass," he'd told her on her first day in the office. "Everybody else will."

Now, as the case group settled in around the conference table—Dubrow, Mickie, Jim Feldgate, who ran the computerized weapons tracking system, and Hal Timmons, who handled dealer licenses—Dubrow took a moment to make a quick series of announcements, then turned to a man on his left and said, "This is Special Agent Martin Seagraves from the FBI, and he's going to sit in this morning. I expect you all to extend him your cooperation."

Dark hair, cut short. Eyes like two copper pennies that some kids had rubbed smooth on the sidewalk. He wore a blue suit with a vest, which made him look like an insurance agent, the kind who works out of an office down at the mall, next door to Sears. Mickie watched him look around at them, a slight smile on his face, like he had a small animal in his mouth, was trying to keep it from escaping.

He's here to stonewall us, she realized. *He's got something to hide.*

Dubrow folded his hands across his notes and glanced over at her. "Mickie, you want to update us on how things stand?"

Mickie glanced down at the legal pad on the table in front of her, said, "Well, we've had some interesting developments." She spent a few minutes giving a summary of her contacts with James Collette and his mother, the police raid on the family's apartment, and the ballistics report that linked the boy to the killing of Dewitt Foley, then described her meeting with Danny Chaisson, Greg Nowles, and Jabril Saunders. "Saunders played it like he knows the kid, but he's staying clear of it. Wouldn't say if he knows where the kid is now." She looked up. "He asked Chaisson what his interest in the boy is."

"What'd Chaisson say?" Dubrow asked her.

"He wouldn't say."

The FBI guy leaned forward and touched Dubrow's sleeve. "Mind if I ask a question?"

Dubrow sat back, raised both hands. "Go ahead."

Seagraves turned to Mickie. "What's *your* interest in Chaisson, exactly?"

Mickie hesitated, then said carefully, "Well, he showed up, made a place for himself in the investigation. That caught my attention, so I did some asking around about him yesterday afternoon before our meeting with Saunders. Sounds like he's got some interesting contacts up in Baton Rouge."

"How interesting?"

"He works for Jimmy Boudrieux."

"And you see a connection?"

Mickie looked over at Dubrow, but he'd settled back in his chair, hands folded in front of his face, studying the table in front of him. "I made some calls up to Baton Rouge. Seems that Chaisson's father was a state legislator back in the seventies, then went to work for Jimmy Boudrieux. He shot himself up on River Road just before the first investigation into Boudrieux's fund-raising. When the cops found him, he was sitting in his car, a gun lying on the floor next to his foot, and a briefcase full of cash on the seat beside him." She paused, then said, "From what I'm hearing, the son's cut from the same cloth. He went to law school over at Tulane, did pretty well, got a job with the district attorney's office, then suddenly resigned. Sounds like there's a story there, but I couldn't get it. Anyway, that was a couple years back, and he's been working for Jimmy since then. Apparently, if you want to do business with Jimmy Boudrieux, you talk to Lucas Clay, but it's Chaisson who carries the money."

"So what's he doing in this case?"

"That's the question I'm hoping to answer."

Seagraves nodded, sat back. Mickie glanced over at Dubrow, who picked up his pen and scribbled a note on the pad in front of him. He put a box around it, underlined it twice, then dropped the pen on the table and looked up at the FBI man.

"Now seems like an appropriate time to ask what your people have on Chaisson."

Seagraves frowned, took a moment to stretch his legs out under the table, shifting his position as if he found the chair uncomfortable.

"We're in the middle of an ongoing investigation," he said. "Chaisson's a part of that investigation, but it extends beyond him." He paused, laid a hand on the table, like he'd decided it might be clean after all. "To be honest, I don't see anything in your current investigation that's likely to produce an indictment in the short term, and I'm concerned that your interest in Chaisson might jeopardize our investigation."

Dubrow waited a moment to see if he was going to say more, then glanced around the table. He ran the tip of his tongue across his bottom lip, said, "Well, I appreciate your candor, Agent Seagraves, but the fact is that Chaisson is trying to push his way into our case. So I'd say we're facing one of those moments when we could use some of that interagency cooperation I keep hearing about."

Mickie repressed a smile, hearing Dubrow's voice slip into its West Virginia drawl, the way it did when he was planning to stamp your ticket. Easing back in his chair now, lazily. Like he's reaching back behind him for a willow switch, getting ready to bring it down on your knuckles, *tsswik!*

Seagraves leaned forward, rested his elbows on the table, folded his hands. Mickie saw him steal a look at his watch. He wore it on the inside of his wrist, one of those guys who wants you to know he's got his own precise way of doing things. He looked thoughtful, then cleared his throat, as if he'd come to a decision.

"Let me put it this way, while Chaisson isn't our primary interest in this investigation . . ."

"You're after Boudrieux," Dubrow suggested.

Seagraves didn't answer, just rubbed his knuckles against his chin for a moment, then repeated, "While Chaisson isn't our *primary* interest, we are at the point where it makes sense for us to bring him in and apply some pressure. Let him see how cooperating with our investigation might be in his interest. If he goes along with that, we'd certainly pass on any information that seems pertinent to your investigation."

Mickie glanced over at Dubrow, alarmed. She opened her mouth to say something, but he raised one finger, stopped her.

"Any possibility that our investigations are connected?" he asked Seagraves.

"Hard to say. You haven't given me any real details."

Dubrow hesitated, shot a look at Mickie, then said, "We're tracing a series of illegal gun sales to minors. We've got a cooperation agreement with the NOPD gangs units. They supply us with serial numbers on all weapons they confiscate, and we try to track them back to the dealer." He gestured to Mickie. "Agent Vega is working the other end of the chain, in the public defender's office. She makes contact with the juveniles after they've been arrested, gathers information about their suppliers when that's possible, and where it seems appropriate, works with the local prosecutors to set up plea bargains in return for verifiable information." He paused. "Recently, we were able to connect several weapons confiscated in crimes in Orleans Parish to an unlicensed dealer named Dewitt Foley. We initiated a prosecution on Foley, through the U.S. Attorney's office, but in talking to Foley, it became clear to us that he was only one link in a much larger chain of illegal gun sales."

Seagraves smiled. "In other words, he cut a deal."

"He made it clear to us that he had information that would be useful to us." Dubrow paused, sat back in his chair. "Unfortunately, Foley was one of the victims killed in the shootings last Friday night over on Claiborne."

"Somebody got to him?"

"That's one theory we're exploring."

Seagraves leaned forward, rubbed at a mark on the table with the tip of his thumb, thoughtfully. "So where does Danny Chaisson come into it?"

Dubrow glanced over at Mickie. "Do we have an answer to that yet?"

"Not clear," she said. "The New Orleans cops arrested a boy named James Collette for weapons possession early Saturday morning. Unfortunately, the kid was bailed on Monday morning, before they ran ballistics tests on the gun he was carrying. Once the tests were run, they got a match with the gun that killed Foley. But by that time, the boy had vanished. Yesterday, Danny Chaisson turned up at the boy's home while I was there, and made it clear that he was interested in finding the boy."

Seagraves smiled. "So Danny's on the case, huh? That's interesting." He was silent for a moment, then sat back, spread his hands. "But I'm afraid I don't see any obvious connection to our investigation."

Mickie, watching his eyes, thought, *Bullshit.*

"Any precedent for Chaisson doing criminal defense work?" Dubrow asked.

"Danny?" Seagraves gave a laugh. "Let me tell you, this is not your idealistic young attorney. Not for the last couple years, anyway."

"So it's a favor."

He shrugged. "New Orleans politics."

"You know anybody who'd want this kid bad enough to call in a favor like that?"

Seagraves started to answer, then hesitated. "We're talking Danny *Chaisson,* here. He hasn't been in a courtroom in three, four years. He's a bagman, that's it. He carries money from point A to point B. If he doesn't get too obvious about it, or drop a handful of cash on the street, he's a success." He smiled. "I'm not sure you'd be doing anybody a favor, putting Danny on the case."

Mickie leaned forward. "He was an assistant district attorney a couple years back. Could have some useful contacts around town."

"Danny was a political appointee. When he'd served his purpose, he left."

Mickie picked up her coffee cup, gazed at him over the rim. "Just out of curiosity, what *could* you see somebody using Chaisson for? Besides carrying cash."

Seagraves smiled. "You remember that Bugs Bunny cartoon, he's got a stick of dynamite instead of a carrot? Goes up to Elmer Fudd, says, 'Here, hold this a minute.' Couple seconds later, it explodes in his face. That's about Danny's speed." He glanced at his watch. "Well, if you'll excuse me, I've got a meeting with the U.S. Attorney at eleven."

As he stood up, Mickie said, "Agent Seagraves, it would help a great deal if I could look at Chaisson's file."

He paused, smiled down at her. "Trust me, it's not exciting reading."

"Is that a no?"

"Let me check with my superiors. I'll get back to you." He reached down to pick up his briefcase. Mickie got up, came around the table to stand in front of him.

"I'd like you to leave him on the street."

He took a step back, looked over at the men seated at the table, and raised his eyebrows. "Well, I wish I could help you there, but that's out of my control."

"Is this your operation?"

Dubrow said, "Mickie—"

"That's right, it's my operation. But I work with a team."

"I'd like your personal assurance that—"

Dubrow stood up and took Mickie's arm. "Sit down, Mickie." He turned to Seagraves, extended his hand. "Thank you for your cooperation, Agent Seagraves."

Seagraves shook his hand. "My pleasure." He nodded to Feldgate and Timmons. Then he looked at Mickie and smiled. "I'll consider what you've said, Agent Vega."

She looked up into his smile, waited a moment too long before smiling back at him. "That's all I ask, Agent Seagraves."

After he left, she went back to her seat, her face tight as Dubrow drew the meeting to a close. Her knee throbbed. When he'd finished, she gathered up her notes, slipped them into the file folder. As she got up from the table, Dubrow glanced over at her and said, "Just a minute, Mickie. I'd like to talk to you."

She sat down again, waited as Feldgate and Timmons left the room. Dubrow scribbled some notes on his pad, went on writing for a few moments after they'd closed the door. Then he tossed his pen down, reached back behind his neck with both hands, closed his eyes, and stretched.

"I got to start getting some exercise."

She remained silent, waiting. He opened his eyes, let his arms down, rolling his shoulders a few times to loosen them. Like a ballplayer, she thought. Getting ready to take a swing.

"You want to tell me what that was all about?"

"I wanted him to know my concerns."

Dubrow raised his eyebrows. "Your *concerns?* Mickie, the way you went after him, you told him everything he needs to know." He rubbed his face with both hands, then let his head rest there in his hands as he said wearily, "All right, stay with it. Let me know if you come up with anything solid enough to cut a deal with these guys when they move on Chaisson. I'll try to get you in the room when they talk to him."

She nodded, left him sitting there, his head in his hands. But as she dropped the file on her desk, she caught herself thinking of Danny Chaisson's eyes, the way he looked at her as she wiped at the cut on his hand.

Just do your job, she told herself. *Work the case.*

But something inside her wouldn't let it go. She sat down at her desk, peeled her sheet of notes off the legal pad, and started transcribing them into the case file, her mind drifting to the moment at the kid's apartment when she'd glanced up, caught Danny watching her. She was used to men staring at her; it was something all the women she knew lived with, every day of their lives. Men stared at her in the street, at the grocery store, right there in the office. But somehow, the way he'd looked at her was different. Not laying a claim on her, the way most men stared, but . . .

More like a drowning man, looking toward the shore.

She closed the file, shoved it into the top drawer of the small file cabinet next to her desk. She gathered up her jacket and briefcase, signed out at the desk, and drove downtown. It was a hot morning, the air heavy on her skin. She turned the air-conditioning in the Nova on high, felt the engine strain under the extra burden, but all it did was blow the heat around.

She parked in her usual lot, near the courthouse. On her way into the public defender's office, she stopped in the D.A.'s office, grabbed three pink slips from the box on the secretary's desk. She dumped her briefcase next to the chair, glanced at the messages as she stripped off her suit jacket. Two calls from the clerk of juvenile court's office telling her to pick up some case files she'd requested, and—half buried underneath—a message that read: *9:08 A.M., Danny Chaisson.* Below that, the subject line read simply, *Collette,* and the receptionist had made a neat check in the box marked URGENT.

Mickie felt a hollow place in her chest as she picked up the phone, dialed the number.

Rodney Collette lay motionless in a bed on the intensive care ward at Charity Hospital. He had tubes running into both arms and an oxygen hose taped under his nose. There was no movement beneath his eyelids, and his skin was the color of wax. A wad of bandages was taped to the base of his neck, where one bullet had shattered his collarbone, punched a hole through his left shoulder blade on its way out. Mickie could see a second wad of bandages beneath the sheet, where the emergency room surgeons had split his chest open to restart his heart. In the narrow hospital bed, he looked like an eight-year-old.

His mother sat in a plastic chair next to his bed, her head slumped against the metal railing. She was dressed in the blue uniform of a nurse's aide. Three hours had passed from the moment her son was wheeled through the doors of the ER until they'd tracked her down, working her usual shift behind the night desk on the pediatric ward. By that time, the surgeons had replaced nearly half his blood, dug two bullets out of the pulp of his left lung, and closed him up, feeling it was safer to let him take his chances on a night in the IC unit than to risk more surgery.

"He made the first night, so that's a good sign," the duty nurse told Mickie as they stood outside the glass, looking in at the row of beds. "They'll have to go in again later today, try to clean up his lung. But they want to see him stabilize first. No point putting him back on the table, if . . ." She trailed off. Danny nodded. The nurse shrugged, left them standing at the glass while she went off to finish her rounds.

"What did the cops say?" Mickie asked.

"Not much. One of the detectives told me they got some kids who remember seeing a black Jeep cruising around the neighborhood before the shooting." Danny gazed through the glass at the boy, tried to think of something else he should say, then gave up. They stood there in silence for a while, until Mickie shifted the strap of her briefcase on her shoulder, reached out to touch his arm.

"You okay?"

He nodded. "Makes my eyes hurt just to look at him. All those tubes in his arms."

She waited to see if he would say more, but he just shook his head, looked away.

"Come on," she said. "I'd like to show you something."

He followed her downstairs to the doors of the ER, where she told him to wait, went over to the duty desk to talk to a nurse. The woman looked up at her with tired eyes, like she'd spent the night carrying rocks and Mickie was asking her for a hand with her groceries. But then she shrugged, reached over and picked up a phone, dialed an extension.

Danny turned, looked through the window in the ER's doors. Patients were slumped in plastic chairs, or wandering around with that dazed look of people who didn't expect the party to end this way, coming down *hard.* One man stood against a wall, a wad of bloody paper towels pressed to his forehead, rocking slowly, his eyes closed. As Danny watched, he leaned forward and threw up onto the floor between his feet.

Danny looked away. At the desk, the nurse was hanging up the phone, pointing Mickie toward a door at the end of the hall. Mickie nodded, waved him over.

"Don't touch anything, okay?" she said as they moved away from the desk. Then, as they reached the door, she smiled at him apologetically and said quietly, "Sorry. Had to say that."

She held the door for him, then led him down a set of metal stairs into a basement, where stacks of supply boxes, gurneys, and plastic chairs lined the hall. She paused at a door, opened it a crack, and glanced in.

"Okay, this is us." She swung the door open, stepped back to let him pass. He took a few steps into the room, stopped abruptly.

"Jesus."

It was a tiny room, a supply closet. But somebody had cleared it out. Now the walls were lined—from floor to ceiling—with photographs of gunshot victims. Autopsy shots, surgical photos, even a few of minor wounds, the victims lifting their bandages to display the wound, grinning at the camera.

"They call it the gun club," Mickie told him, her voice quiet. "One of the ER guys showed it to me when I started the job."

Danny shook his head, moving around the room slowly, his eyes drifting over the images of chest wounds, shattered skulls, the fixed eyes of the dead. There was almost no blood, just torn flesh and splintered bone. The wounds had been cleaned for the camera, exposed.

"A surgeon started it a couple years ago." Mickie leaned against the door, arms folded, watching him. "Took pictures of chest wounds for teaching new residents. They bring them down here on their first day, make 'em sit here until they can identify all the different kinds of wounds."

"I guess this is how they see it, huh? Doctors."

"Every day." She pushed off the door, came into the middle of the room, looking around. "I'd like to bring some of those boys I work with down here, let 'em see how it all ends."

Danny had paused in front of a shot of a head wound, a young black kid, eyes fixed, mouth slightly open like he was trying to think of something to say. He'd been shot in the back of the head, Danny figured, because the bullet had blown a chunk of his skull out just above the hairline. A small bulb of brains protruded from the hole, like a piece of cauliflower.

Danny felt something rise in his throat, swallowed it down. He took a deep breath, let it out slow. Then he turned to look at Mickie, waved a hand at the photographs around him, weakly.

"Why are you showing me?"

She laid a hand on his arm and said, "C'mon. I'll buy you a coffee."

Neither of them spoke as they rode the elevator up to the cafeteria. They got in line at the coffee machine, then Danny went in search of a table while Mickie stopped at the cash register, found a dollar and some change in the inside pocket of her briefcase to pay for the coffee.

She found him sitting by the window, stirring his coffee. His face looked pale. There were two packets of sugar torn open next to his cup, and an empty container of creamer. He glanced up, caught her watching.

"I got some bad habits." He nodded at her cup. "Black, right?"

"As death."

He winced, and she felt the blood rush into her face. "Sorry."

They sat in silence, watching the steam rise from their coffee. Behind them, a group of nurses sat over the remains of their breakfast. One of them told a joke, leaning forward to whisper the punch line, just out of Mickie's hearing. The table erupted with laughter. Mickie glanced over, wondering how people could laugh in a hospital, then realized, *What else can they do?* She looked away.

"The kid, Rodney, you figure he was mistaken for his brother?"

Danny nodded. "Makes sense. That, or it's a warning."

"What about revenge?"

"Only if they think James did the shooting last time around."

Mickie looked up at him sharply. "What makes you think he didn't?"

Danny hesitated. "He's a fourteen-year-old kid. I can't picture it."

Mickie sat back, her eyes on his face. "What's your interest in this kid, Danny?"

Danny was silent. He looked down at his coffee. He started to pick up his cup, then set it down and shook his head. He looked up at her, his eyes hard.

"You saw his brother just now. Nobody deserves that."

Mickie held his gaze. She leaned forward. "Who's paying you, Danny?"

He stared at her for a moment. Then he looked away.

"Is it Jimmy Boudrieux?"

Danny pushed his coffee cup away and stood up. "I gotta go."

Mickie shoved her chair back, followed him out of the cafeteria, caught him by the arm in the hallway. "Where are you going?"

He met her gaze for a moment, his lips parting slightly as if he was about to say something. Then he looked down at the floor, shook his head. "This isn't the way it looks, you understand?"

She nodded. "I know, Danny. We'll talk when you're ready."

He glanced up at her for a moment, his eyes narrowing. Then he turned, walked away.

21

"Hold up a minute."

The music faded, like somebody had pulled a plug. Gregory Nowles watched Jabril slip a pair of earphones off his head, wearily. He turned to a boy sitting next to him at the soundboard, waved a hand at the rows of controls and lights on the panel in front of them, said, "What's this called?"

The kid looked down at the controls, shrugged. "Mixing board."

"Uh-huh, that's right." Jabril sat back, folded his arms. "So what's that tell you it's for?"

"Mixing."

"All right. Now tell me, you got six guys in your group, so how come I only hear *your* voice coming outta there?"

The kid scowled. "You can hear them other guys."

"Where? You talkin' about those little *squeaking* sounds come in whenever you take a breath?"

The kid sighed, reached up to get his Chicago Bulls cap resettled on his head. "That's the *way*, man. Go listen to Snoop or Biggie, they sound just like that. You got to hear the *words*, you know?"

Nowles watched Jabril lean on the mixing board and bury his head in his hands. They were sitting in a storefront on Jackson Avenue, heavy metal security grilles over all the windows, the walls of a small storage room in the back lined with acoustic tiles to make a recording studio. The control room was built along one wall where the cash registers used to stand when the place had been a late-night grocery selling liquor and Chore-Boys. They'd cut a window into the storeroom, installed a heavy sheet of glass and an intercom so the guy behind the mixing board could look in at his buddies, watch 'em put their best moves on, like they'd seen in the videos. Spending the first couple days just grinning at each other, Nowles figured, like, *Check us out!*

Jabril had hung Bob Marley posters on the walls of the control room, plus a few signed photographs of New Orleans stars—Irma Thomas, Fats, the Meters, even Louis Armstrong. But the kids got in there, wearing hooded sweatshirts and sunglasses at the soundboard, laid down track after track of gangsta, knockin' back their bitches, whippin' out their nines. "Fourteen-year-old boys," Jabril told him, shaking his head. "You listen to 'em, they all got six bitches and a homicide."

Nowles shrugged. "Better you hear it than me." Thinking, *Let 'em work it out. The style won't change until everybody does it.*

He watched Jabril lift his head out of his hands, rub at his eyes. "You know what I hear comin' outta there?"

"What?"

Jabril leaned back, made a fist with one hand, and moved it back and forth over his lap, lazily. The kid folded his arms, looked off at a photograph of Ellis Marsalis that Jabril had taken during one of the gigs down at Lu and Charlie's on Rampart, shook his head.

"Look't this," Jabril said, resting his hand on the board. "You got what I call a one-track mind. Pump one track way up, all the others down here at the bottom." He took a moment to reset the board, bringing the volume settings closer together. "What happens, you try it like this? You scared you gonna get lost in there? If you got something *real* to say, we'll hear it. And you get all those other voices in there with it, that's a sign of *strength*." He reached up, tore a sheet of paper off a pad resting on the top of the soundboard, held it out to the kid. "Tear that."

The kid looked at the paper for a moment, then reached out with one hand, took it, tore it slowly in half.

"Okay, good." Jabril took one of the torn halves from him, folded it twice. "Now tear that." The kid took the paper again, tore it. Jabril took the other half of the sheet, folded it five times, then laid it on the edge of the soundboard and folded it one last time. "Now try."

The kid took the wadded-up paper, tried to tear it. Nowles saw the muscles in his shoulders and neck straining, then he relaxed, handed it back to Jabril. "Yeah, okay."

"You see what I'm sayin'? You got one voice, it's just some punk sayin' 'Yo! I'm bad!' But you mix it up, you know what you got? You got *power.*" He leaned back, tossed the paper across the room into a trash can. "Man sits up in his house, locks his doors up tight, watches TV, it's 'cause he's weak, and he knows it. You go out on the street, you got to mix with the people. That's where it all happens, right? But you got to *give* a little to *get* a lot, see? Man on his own, he's all rights, no responsibilities. Selfish. Got to hear *my* voice. Got to have it *my* way. You want to mix with the people, you got to give up some of those rights, say '*Our* way.' Means you get in your car, you can't drive like no fool, 'cause there's kids that play up here. You don't steal from that store down the street, 'cause we *all* gonna pay for that. And that guy owns the store, he's got to deal right with the people who come in there, treat 'em with respect. Got to find a balance, you know?" He waved a hand over the control board. "Yeah, I want to hear the words, but I want to hear some 'a that *gui*tar, too. You get that right, man, it comes out smooth, like Marvin Gaye. You put that shit on for your lady, makes her want to roll over on her back, get her belly scratched. And *that's* power, little man. You hear what I'm sayin'?"

The kid grinned. "Hey, you know what Marvin Gaye's daddy said after he shot him?"

Jabril stared at him. *"Huh?"*

"He said, 'Boy, that's the last forty-five you ever hear.'"

Jabril glanced over at Nowles wearily. "You see what I'm dealin' with, here?"

"Uh-huh."

The kid looked offended. "Yo, ease up. It's a joke!"

Jabril picked up the earphones on his lap, dropped them on the soundboard. "Your tape," he said. "You got a choice. You can mix it up, or you can be a punk, shootin' off your mouth. But I want you to think about one thing, okay? Who we gonna remember twenty years from now, Marvin or his daddy?" He stood up, slid out from behind the board. "Mix it up, man. That's my advice. Mix it *up*."

Out on the street, he shook his head, looked out at the traffic. "These kids, they're gettin' eaten alive," he said to Nowles. "They look around 'em, all they see is stuff their mamas can't afford to buy. Like you don't have to *be* a man, you can go out and *buy* it."

Nowles smiled. "When'd you become a preacher?"

Jabril looked over at him, surprised. Then he grinned. "I always was one. You just forgot."

"I got to get back to the office, man. What's on your mind?"

"This guy Chaisson. You think he's straight?"

Nowles grinned. "Nobody's straight. This guy, he's bought and paid for."

"You think he's setting me up?"

"Sure looks like somebody is."

Jabril dug in his shirt pocket, came out with a pair of RayBans, put them on. "That ain't new."

Nowles nodded, walked over to his car. He unlocked the door, then looked back at Jabril and grinned. "Mix it up, huh?"

"Mix it *up*."

It took L'Dog two hours to find the house. All he had was the bitch's name, from hearin' Jabril walk around his kitchen, barefoot, that little phone pressed to his ear as he cooked up that Thai food he liked to eat, sayin', *Hey baby . . . Listen, baby . . . Now, don't talk like that, Janelle!* Shaking his head as he put the phone down, then going into his bedroom and coming out with a wad of bills and an envelope, leanin' on the table to scribble her address on it before stuffing the money inside, licking the envelope, then shoving it across the table to L'Dog to go stick in the mail.

"Sorry I ever got involved with that bitch."

Just saying it, L'Dog knew, 'cause that's what you said, right? L'Dog could tell by the way he talked to her when he got her calmed down on the phone, all sweet, like, he wasn't *no* way sorry. *Janelle Quart.* L'Dog hadn't looked at the address, just that she lived in Mobile, but the name had stuck with him, all right. Jabril laughing about it, "Yeah, and she *take* a quart, too. Every time I see the bitch."

So how hard could it be, find a woman lives in Mobile named *Janelle Quart?*

Two hours. Bad enough tryin' to find a phone book he could look at, then it turned out, hey, no shit, she wasn't in the damn thing. So then he was stuck, standin' there at the counter of a Texaco station, white guy watchin' him from behind the register like he was just *waitin'* for him to whip out a gun, try to stick his ass up. L'Dog closed the phone book, passed it across the counter, said, "Thanks, man." Then just walked out, the guy starin' after him, wiping his hand on his grease-stained overalls after he put the phone book back under the counter.

L'Dog hated Mobile. White beaches, waves rollin' in from the Gulf. Yeah, *right.* His old man'd grown up in a little town just up the road, didn't even have a name, man, unless it was *Niggertown.* He'd told L'Dog everything he ever wanted to know about *Al'bama,* before he took off. Jabril, he liked to call it *Al-banana.* But then, he'd had some trouble once, drivin' through.

So L'Dog, he felt scared even before he'd hit the state line. Mississippi was bad enough, man, but when he saw that sign sayin' WEL-COME TO ALABAMA, he almost turned around, right there, drove back to New Orleans. But that ain't how you get things done, huh? You want to be a man, you got to put it on the line, even when you're bleedin' inside. So he drove on into Mobile, worked his way through the back roads that led away from the beach, kept going until he saw black faces, startin' to feel better then. He drove around for a while, tryin' to think how he could find a bitch named Janelle Quart, until he pulled up at a light, looked across the road at a sign over a storefront, said, LADY BE GOOD! BEAUTY SALON.

Boy, now you thinkin,' he told himself, pulling the car over to the side of the road. Bein' *resourceful,* like Jabril always said.

Still, it took four tries before he got lucky, goin' into beauty salons all over town, sayin' to the woman behind the counter, "Hey, you know my aunt? Her name Janelle Quart. My mama sent me down here to see her, but, like, I forgot where she said she lived at."

Smiling at 'em, even when the woman behind the counter in the last place looked at him with that face, all pinched up 'round her eyes, tells you she thinks you just *nasty,* put her hands on her hips, and said, "Child, you go 'round with that *rag* on your head, people think you a field nigger. You hear me?"

Big woman, like she got sick 'a all that pick, pick, pick, just sat down one day and ate the whole damn refrigerator. But L'Dog just grinned, gave a shrug like he knew she was right, told her, "Yes, ma'am. I hear you."

"Janelle *Quart,* you say?"

"Uh-huh, that's right."

And she stuck one arm out, big old sacks of chicken fat wigglin' back and forth under it, like she hung 'em up there to dry, told him, "She live back up the road, by the laundromat. Green shutters on the house, need paint."

Callin' after him as he went out the door, "And I *know* that ho' ain't your aunt!"

He rode back up the street until he saw the laundromat, the

house two doors past it with green shutters, the wood showing through where the paint had peeled away. There were long weeds in the front yard. L'Dog walked up the driveway, opened the screen door, and knocked. A few moments passed with no sound from inside the house, so he leaned in, used his open palm to bang on the door.

He heard footsteps, somebody fooling with a chain on the opposite side of the door. It opened a crack, and Sugar Bear, wearing only his underwear and a New Orleans Saints T-shirt, looked out at him, rubbing at his eyes.

"Damn, Bear! You always sleep this late?" L'Dog pushed past him into the house, paused before he let the door swing closed. He jerked his head at the weeds in the front lawn. "How come you don't get off your lazy ass, cut the lady's grass?"

22

Danny's hands shook. Just like that first night, when he'd sat there in the darkness outside Jimmy's house, his hands trembling on the steering wheel, waiting for his heart to stop pounding. But this time it wasn't fear. It was anger.

He drove across town, the image of the boy in the hospital bed, tubes coming out of his nose, rising up on the windshield in front of him every few seconds, like somebody was sitting behind him, showing slides. When he turned onto Audubon Place, he realized that he was headed for Jimmy's house.

Like a dog with a stick.

There was a line of cars in the driveway, and as he got out, he could hear the sound of voices from the back garden. He walked up the drive, past Jimmy's office, and ducked through the hedge.

They were sitting at a pair of tables beside the pool, Jimmy reaching across to pour drinks from a large pitcher as a grill smoked behind them. Danny's eyes took it all in as he crossed the grass toward them: Buddy Jeanrette leaning over to whisper something to Helen, then sitting back, laughing, as Jimmy topped off their glasses, swung the pitcher over to refill the other man's glass at the table. Danny recognized him as Helen's date at the party, Richard Brooks, from the U.S. Attorney's office.

Lucas Clay sat off to one side, watching in silence. When he saw Danny, he stood up, came across the lawn to meet him. One hand coming up, like a traffic cop's, to stop him.

"You shouldn't be here, Danny."

Danny swung from behind, caught Lucas solidly on the jaw, knocked him backward over a lawn chair. His phone flew out of his hand, skittered across the patio tiles, and vanished into the swimming pool.

Danny bent over, got a handful of Lucas's shirt, said, "I ought to take you in to the cops myself."

Lucas coughed, twisted his face away, and spat blood onto the grass beside him. Danny felt a hand grasp his arm, then somebody pulled him away. He caught a brief glimpse of Jimmy's face, pale and tight, heard him say, "Get him out of here!"

Then Helen was hustling him across the lawn, back toward his car.

In the car, he looked down at his hands, found that they'd stopped shaking. Helen was driving him, her hands gripping the wheel tightly, eyes fixed on the road. But for a moment, as he looked at her, it seemed as if he'd woken from a dream, found that three years could vanish into nothing, a bright flicker in the dark.

Then she glanced over at him, said, "You never change, do you, Danny?"

And suddenly, his right hand began to hurt, blood swelling slowly out of one knuckle where he'd split it on Lucas's jaw, and those three years came rushing back at him like a hot wind off an empty desert. "What were you doing there?" he asked her, his voice hoarse. "With them?"

"My *job.*"

He turned, looked out the window at the traffic passing on St. Charles. "You sure it wasn't *my* job?"

She flashed him a look, then had to hit the brake, hard, to keep from rear-ending a motorbike. The Mustang stalled. For a moment he thought she might reach over and slap him. But then she fixed her eyes back on the road, got the car started again, put it in gear.

She drove on for a few blocks in silence. Then she said, her voice tight, "You know me better than that, Danny."

She was silent for a while. When he glanced over at her, he saw her hands were trembling.

"I'm sorry," he said. "I didn't mean it."

She nodded, her mouth tight. They made the turn onto his street, and she pulled to the curb in front of his house. They sat there in silence, both of them staring out at the car in front of them. It was a Volvo.

"What happened to you, Danny?"

"I woke up."

She shook her head. "That's not good enough. Not this time."

"You think I shouldn't have hit Lucas?"

She slammed her hand down on the steering wheel. "Fuck Lucas! You should've punched him out three years ago."

He looked at her, surprised. Then he laughed. "You're right. That's what I should have done."

"But you didn't." She turned her eyes on him, angry. "And now we're all in it too deep for that to solve anything."

He invited her in for coffee.

"I should use your phone, call Richard to come pick me up."

"What happened to your car phone?"

"It got stolen last week. Right out in front of my house."

He watched her look up at the house as she got out of the car. It was an old house, the paint cracked and faded. But it stood in the shade of a large oak tree, so the porch looked shady and cool.

"I've got the second floor." He dug his keys out of his pocket, re-

C o l d
S t e e l
R a i n

alizing he felt nervous. "It might be pretty messy." Then he saw her look. *Jesus. You punch Lucas out, your ex-wife has to pull you off him, and you're worried that she'll see your apartment's messy?*

"I think I can handle it, Danny."

She locked the car, followed him up the steps. She looked out at the street while he unlocked the door. "Looks like the place where you lived in college."

"Who says you don't get a second chance?" He held the door for her. "Up the stairs."

She waited at the top of the stairs for him to unlock the apartment door, smiled at him as she stepped inside. "Like old times."

He followed her into the apartment, dropped his keys on the table next to the door, watching her move around slowly, looking. She stopped in front of a table next to the window, picked up a photograph of the two of them at their graduation, standing on the steps of the law school, her father grinning between them with his arms across their shoulders. "So that's where that got to. I wondered if you had it."

"You want it?"

She shook her head, set it down on the table. "It's so weird, seeing all these things here."

"C'mon. Some of it's new." He looked around the room, panicked briefly, then his eyes settled on a leather chair in front of his desk. "That chair. I got it last year."

"Nice try, Danny." She looked up at him, smiled. "Did I really let you keep all this stuff? You got off easy."

"No." He smiled. "I really didn't."

Their eyes met, and then she looked away, her hand trailing across the things they'd owned as she moved around the room. "No, I guess not."

"The phone's on the desk. I'll make some coffee."

He ground some beans, kept the grinder running longer than he needed to, trying not to hear her voice in the next room. When the coffee was brewing, he went out into the living room, found her standing by the French doors, looking out.

"Everything okay?"

"I called my office. My secretary went home sick. So even if there's a crisis, I won't know about it until tomorrow."

He looked at her standing there and suddenly found he couldn't swallow. She was wearing a linen dress, with her hair pulled back so he could see the faint trace of tiny hairs at the back of her neck. He turned, went back into the kitchen, and stood by the coffeepot with his eyes closed, waiting for it to finish brewing.

When he came back out with two mugs of coffee, she had opened the French doors, was standing on the porch, one hand resting on the railing. He went to stand beside her, handed her one of the mugs.

"Feels like a museum in there, Danny."

He sipped at his coffee. "I read somewhere that a museum is a place where you save all the things that don't really matter."

"You believe that?"

"I do now."

She met his gaze. "That's nice." She paused, glanced out at the branches of the oak tree, and said, "When we separated, the thing that hurt me most was that you didn't seem to have lost anything. You kept smiling, like none of it made any difference to you."

"I lost everything."

She leaned one hip against the rail, the cup held in the palms of both hands. "I couldn't tell."

"Neither could I." He smiled.

She reached up, touched his face with two fingers. "Don't."

Her fingertips were warm from where she'd been holding the coffee. He could smell the sun on her skin. He didn't move, and she took her hand away, turned back to the oak tree.

"You must get squirrels."

"I used to. The kid next door got a twenty-two for Christmas."

She shook her head, raised the coffee cup to her lips. He could see the hairs at the back of her neck moving slightly in the breeze. He reached up, touched them lightly with the tips of his fingers. She closed her eyes, and a shiver ran down her back.

"Oh, Jesus."

Later, she sat on the edge of his bed, resting her forehead on the palms of both hands. "God, I promised myself this wouldn't happen."

He reached out, ran a finger down the curve of her back. "I'm flattered that you even thought it was possible."

She straightened as his finger came to the base of her spine, then reached back and caught his hand. "Don't start something you can't finish."

"Who said I can't finish it?"

She lay back on the bed, turned to face him. "I used to see these headlines on the women's magazines in the supermarket, like SEX AFTER DIVORCE: THE LAST TEMPTATION? You read the articles, they make it sound like everybody does it."

He ran his finger along the narrow ridge of her collarbone, fascinated by how familiar her body seemed, and yet strange at the same time, like a childhood home. "I must have been reading the wrong magazines."

"My favorite was ANGRY SEX. All these wives whose husbands had left them for younger women, talking about how they'd seduced him again for revenge. You know, get him to cheat on the new wife, then dump him. They all said the sex was the best of their lives."

"You feeling angry?"

She smiled. "You wish." Then she leaned in, kissed him gently. "It was nice."

"I've missed the way you taste."

"Yeah, I could tell." Then her eyes became serious, and she

touched the side of his face in a way that told him she was thinking of other things. He laid his head on the pillow, and watched her face, waiting.

"What are you into, Danny?"

He turned on his back, looked up at the ceiling. There were faint water stains in the plasterwork, and he'd spent many nights staring up at them in the pale glow from the streetlight beyond his window, seeing, at different times, a pattern of clouds in a windy sky, a woman's face, a bird perched on a branch. Now it looked to him like smoke, rising.

"I don't know."

"Are you in trouble?"

He thought about the boy lying in the hospital, then the two deputies, dead in a ditch. "I'm being set up to take a fall."

She turned on her side, rested her head on one arm, looking at him. "Why?"

"I guess they think it's what I do best."

She was silent for a while, then asked, "And Jimmy's part of it?"

"Jimmy's part of everything. What worries me is who's behind him."

"You have no idea?"

He hesitated. "I want to be sure."

She sat up, looked over at the window. The sky was streaked with a last blue light, so deep it looked like you could drown in it. "Oh God. What time is it?"

He reached over, found his watch on the bedside table. "Eight twenty-five."

"Shit." She got up, started looking around on the floor for her clothes. "I've got to go."

He sat up, turned on the light next to the bed, watched her gather up her things. "Got a date?"

She paused, stood looking down at him, a shoe dangling from one hand. "I'm having Richard over for dinner."

He looked away. She stood there for a moment, like she was trying to think of something to say, then slowly began to get dressed. When she'd finished, she crossed to the mirror on his dresser, wincing as she caught a glimpse of herself. "Terrific."

She turned to face him, leaned against the end of the bed to slip her shoes on. "Danny, I'm sorry. It's work."

He nodded, brought his eyes up to meet hers. "You don't have to apologize."

"I feel like I do."

He shrugged. "It's not like we're married, right?"

She stood there for a moment, very still, then said, "No, it isn't." She turned back to the mirror, ran her fingers through her hair, pushing it back. Then she straightened, said, "I should go."

He nodded. Their eyes met in the mirror. She used his phone to call a cab. Then she turned, came over to the bed, and leaned over to kiss him. He raised a hand to stop her.

"Can I call you?"

Something in her face seemed to relax, as if she'd been waiting for the question. "Would you understand if I said no?"

He shook his head. "No way. I'm a catch."

She smiled, kissed him gently on the mouth, turned to pick up her jacket from the chair where she'd dropped it. She paused, reached into her pocket, took out an envelope, held it out to Danny. "I almost forgot. Jimmy asked me to give this to you."

He looked at her, then at the envelope, feeling something heavy settle over his heart. After a moment, he reached out slowly, took it. He slid a finger under the flap, slit it open, glanced inside. It contained a bundle of cash, wrapped with a rubber band. Fifty thousand, he guessed.

He looked up at Helen. She had her back to him, slipping her jacket on in front of the mirror.

"When did he give it to you?"

"This morning." She picked up her briefcase, slung it over her shoulder, then turned to gaze at him for a moment, silent. "He said you'd know what to do with that."

Danny tossed the envelope on the bed. "Yeah, I know."

She nodded, turned to go. As she left the room, he called out, "Helen?"

She turned. He reached over, picked up the envelope, and tossed it to her.

"Keep it. You earned it."

Helen came down the steps, pausing to lean on the railing for a moment, eyes closed, like she was catching her breath. Then she opened her eyes, looked up at the sky briefly, as if feeling its weight, before crossing the sidewalk to the waiting cab.

Maura, watching from her car parked at the end of the block, smiled.

"You know your problem, Helen?" she said softly as Helen got into the cab, leaned forward to give the driver her address. "You always believed in fairy tales."

Maura sat in silence, watching as the cab pulled out into the street, moved past her to the corner, where it turned right, toward St. Charles. She kept her eyes fixed on Danny's house, curious to find that she felt nothing. An empty shell. Like you find on the beach. Hold it up before a candle, it goes transparent, like glass.

The light went off in Danny's apartment. She pictured him lying in the dark, his eyes open. She smiled. "You hurting, Danny? Somebody mess with your heart?"

Then she reached down, started the car, pulled away from the curb.

23

L'Dog sat in the passenger seat of a red Corolla that AK had picked up from a tourist lot down in the Quarter, watching the street. They were parked on Galvez, two blocks down from the playground where the Conti Street boys hung out. Five of 'em tonight, standing 'round some benches at the edge of the playground, passing a bottle wrapped in a paper bag. Not even watchin' the street, or they would've seen the Corolla swing past, come 'round the block, and pull into a space where its passengers could sit for a minute, get their heads together. Lights off, stereo on low, just a murmur from the backseat. The guy who owned the car had a bunch of tapes in the glove box, heavy metal shit. So AK flipped through the radio dial, found the Word on WJAX, the quiet storm. L'Dog sighed, shook his head. Not what they needed, a job like this. Makes you want to turn the lights way down, ease back with your lady, whisper in her ear like Barry White. This kinda job, you need Death Row, straight up. Can't get too re*laxed,* you know? Gotta keep your eye on the kid.

L'Dog turned and looked at him, slumped in the backseat, staring out the open window beside him. "You okay, Bear?"

Sugar Bear looked up at him, his face hidden in the shadows. "Yeah. I'm cool."

His hand rested on a 9 mm Glock semiautomatic that lay across his lap. It was a big gun, and when L'Dog had bought it off a guy he knew in Westwego, it looked like the answer to every man's prayers. But now, seeing it there in the kid's hand, he worried that he'd miss the shot when the time came, tryin' to be like those guys in the movies, hold it one-handed or sideways, wantin' to look *bad.* They'd stopped up in Slidell on their way back into the city, turned off the highway, and rode back up into some country roads until L'Dog found a little dirt track that led off through the pine trees, drove his car up in there to where it opened up into an old cow field, fences all tore up now. L'Dog dug under his seat, brought out the paper bag with the gun in it, said, "Okay, Bear. Time somebody taught you how to shoot."

He'd shown him how to hold it two-handed, brace his arms on the door of the car so you get a steady shot. Then he'd pointed out an old junked refrigerator lying on its side among the trees and said, "Think you can hit that, or you need somethin' bigger?"

Sugar Bear didn't say nothin', just slumped down in the seat like L'Dog told him while they drove up on it, then when the car stopped, he jumped up on his knees, stuck the gun out the window, and banged off like ten shots, *pop pop pop pop pop pop pop . . .*

L'Dog had to reach over, grab the gun out of his hands, laughing. "Damn, Bear! What you think this is, man? *Die Hard?*"

But the kid just looked over at him, his face serious, and said quietly, "I never done this before."

"Man, I can *see* that." L'Dog shook his head, stuck the gun back in the bag, and shoved it under his seat. "You just think 'bout what they did to your brother. Keep your mind on that, you'll do what's got to be done."

But lookin' back at him now, starin' out the window of the car at the soft rain comin' down in the yellow streetlights, L'Dog had his doubts.

"You sure you up to this?"

The kid looked down at the gun in his lap, his hand curled around it like he couldn't quite figure out how it got there, but he knew he had to hold on to it, tight. "They the ones shot up Rodney, right?"

"That's right."

Sugar Bear looked out the window. "So let's do it."

"Okay," L'Dog said, turning to AK. "Let's go."

"Yo, 'bout fuckin' time." AK started the Corolla, pulled away from the curb. He ground the gears going into second, cursed, then stomped the clutch and jammed it into gear. The tires squealed as they made the corner, comin' up on the benches, fast, and L'Dog saw the Conti Street boys glance up, their faces frozen with that look says, *Ah fuck . . .*

Martelle Collette was dozing in an armchair that a nurse had dragged into the IC ward for her, caught up in a dream about the afternoon last summer when her brother Andre had taken her and the boys out to the lakefront, laid out a picnic of boiled crabs, fresh-picked tomatoes, and ice-cold Cokes. The sun had melted into tiny flames on the water, and she had watched the boys scrambling on the rocks while Andre walked back to his car, dug in the trunk, and came out with a half-pint bottle of Absolut. He settled onto the blanket beside her, poured some vodka into their Cokes, then passed her can across to her.

"How come it ain't always like this?"

He'd shrugged, lain back, holding the can on his chest. "I got no answer to that one."

So she'd sipped at her drink and squinted into the light, one hand raised to shield her eyes so she could see the boys down at the water's edge . . .

She heard a cough, opened her eyes. Rodney had his eyes open, looking around him slowly at the respirator, the IV tubes hanging from their stand, the curtain the nurse had drawn around his bed after her last rounds. Martelle leaned forward, laid her hand on his arm.

"I'm here, baby."

His eyes came around to her, studied her face for a moment. He opened his mouth like he was starting to say something, then closed it, swallowed painfully. "I'm thirsty," he whispered. His voice sounded like somebody'd grabbed it on both sides, torn it right down the middle.

Martelle reached for the pitcher of water the nurse had left, took a plastic cup off the tray, and filled it. She leaned forward, lifted Rodney's head slightly with one hand, and held the cup to his lips. He closed his eyes as she let a gentle trickle of water into his mouth, waited for him to swallow, then gave him a bit more.

"How's that? That feel better, honey?"

He opened his eyes, looked up at her. His mouth opened, then he seemed to hesitate, his eyes focusing on something behind her head.

And she realized he was dead.

Jabril was asleep when his beeper went off. He fumbled on the bedside table, heard Sandrine mutter something to herself before he managed to find it, shut it off, glance at the message on the display. He sat up on the edge of the bed, rubbed at his face, looked over at the clock: *3:20. Jesus.*

He heaved himself up off the bed, found his pants on the chair, dug his phone out of the pocket, and went into the kitchen to make the call. He could hear his baby daughter snuffling in her Portacrib in the next room, making little whimpering noises as she shifted position. He leaned in to take a look at her while he dialed the number on the pager, then pulled the door halfway closed so he could switch on the light. He went over to the refrigerator, phone pressed to his ear, took out a carton of orange juice, and shook it over the sink while the number connected. It rang once, then there was a click, and he heard a man's voice say, "Yeah?"

"It's Jabril."

He heard the man take a slow breath, like he was getting ready to lift something heavy. "You got it coming, man."

Jabril paused, the carton halfway to his lips. "Who *is* this?"

"Don't fuck with me, Jabril. I got two boys dead already, two more over in Truro, one of 'em fixin' to die. You want to play *games,* man?"

Jabril took a long drink from the carton, wiped his mouth on the back of his hand. "I hear you angry, but you got the wrong man."

"Yeah? Well, bull*shit*! My boys *saw* who done it, and I'm just callin' you, Ja*bril,* to tell you it's just gettin' started between us. You hear me?"

Jabril set the carton down on the table, looked out the kitchen window into the darkness beyond. "You sayin' it was my boys?"

"Fuck you, Jabril! It's on *your* head now!"

The phone went dead in his hand. Jabril set it down on the table, slowly. He stood there for a moment, thinking. Then he went into the bedroom to get his clothes.

By the time that Tom Acorsi pulled the Ford to the curb behind the TV4 news van, the yellow tape was already up, and the scene was lit by the bright glare of the news crew's high-intensity spots. A crowd had gathered along the tape, watching.

Acorsi sighed, shook his head. "Three A.M., there's people out here looking at a murder scene. Don't they ever sleep?"

Maya looked over at him, and he saw her lips tighten. *"They?"*

Ah, shit. Acorsi raised both hands hurriedly, like he was surrendering. "Hey, same thing where I live."

She stared at him for a moment, then shook her head, opened the car door. "Uh-huh. Right."

He watched her get out and go over to duck under the yellow

tape in the glare of the headlights. He shut off the car, sat there for a moment, rubbing his fingers on the steering wheel. "Terrific."

He got out, paused to adjust the .38 on his hip, and followed her under the tape.

Maya stood near the EMS van, talking to a uniformed cop. A white guy who kept reaching up to scratch at the back of his neck while he talked. She had her notebook out, but she was listening to him closely, nodding as he spoke. She had a way with uniforms. She looked them in the eye, took no notes until they were finished, letting them see she was listening carefully to what they told her. It helped deflect their hostility, even among the old-style white patrolmen from cop families in Metairie and the Irish Channel. They started out suspicious, but by the time they'd finished, she'd gotten more information out of them than Acorsi could have.

So he stood a few feet away, hands on his hips, letting his eyes scan the scene. Drive-by, no question about it. He'd learned to recognize it from one glance at the crime scene. Car pulls up, guy in the passenger seat sticks a gun out the window, starts shooting. Twenty minutes later, you pull up in a police car, find the victims scattered in all directions, the way you toss seeds on your lawn. Sometimes the guy pulls out an Uzi, you could see which way he swung the gun by how far the victims got, then match it up to where the shell casings fell.

But these guys hadn't gotten very far. Two bodies sprawled on the pavement next to some benches, white plastic sheets draped over them. The EMS guys had rushed two more to Truro, Acorsi heard the uniform say, one of them unlikely to make the trip, a head shot. All four victims were teenage boys, hanging out on a street corner at two in the morning.

"You know 'em?" Acorsi heard Maya ask the beat cop.

"Yeah, they're Conti Street. The kid who took the head shot? You had him up in your office two days ago." He grinned. "Not like you'd recognize him now."

Maya nodded, made a note in her book. "Any witnesses?"

The cop laughed, waved a hand at the crowd. "Hey, you think they'd tell *me?*"

Acorsi turned to see Maya smile, looking down at her notebook now. One survivor, Acorsi thought. Maybe they'd get lucky, the kid would talk. More likely, he'd lie there in his hospital bed, watching Vanna White on the TV, tell them, *I didn't see nothing, man.*

Acorsi went back to the car, got the metal forensics case out of the trunk of the Ford. He carried it back to the bodies, set it down on the sidewalk beside one of them. Then he reached down, lifted the plastic sheet.

The kid looked about fifteen. He lay on his back, both arms flung out, like the impact had thrown him back violently. His eyes were fixed, and his mouth hung open, making him look like he wanted to say something. *Same thing they all try to say,* Acorsi thought. *"Shit!"* Like when you stumble on the sidewalk, go down flat on your face. Another thing he'd never gotten used to, working homicide, how so many murder victims looked *embarrassed.*

He felt Maya come up to stand beside him, looking down at the boy in silence.

"Looks like two entrance wounds," Acorsi said, pointing at two ragged holes in the sweatshirt, high up on the kid's chest. He glanced up at her, and she nodded, silent. He let the plastic sheet drop, walked over to the other body, lifted the sheet. "Jesus."

One bullet had struck the victim at an upward angle just above his mouth, destroyed his nose and left eye, then exited from the top of his head just above the hairline. Bits of brain and bone were scattered across the pavement behind him, and someone had used a piece of notebook paper to mark a hunk of flesh and cartilage that lay in the grass a few feet away. Acorsi realized it was the kid's nose.

He felt a wave of nausea seize him, let the sheet drop. Maya had already turned away, going over to the yellow tape to talk to someone she recognized in the crowd. Acorsi went over to the forensics case, took out a Nikon camera with a heavy flash attached to one side. He returned to the first body, pulled the sheet back and dropped it to one side. He raised the camera, heard somebody in the crowd call out, "Smile, Gap!"

Acorsi took a series of shots from different angles, then moved in close, got some tight shots of the entrance wounds. He stepped back, looked around him at the street, squatted down to take a couple shots over the body at the spot where he guessed the car had stopped. He set the camera down on the pavement, took out his notepad, and sketched the intersection, where the body lay in relation to the benches. At the top of the page, he wrote *Gap.*

Then he picked up the camera, went over to the second body. When he tossed the sheet aside, he heard a sigh from the crowd, like this was what they'd been waiting for. He heard somebody start to retch, and a woman turned, pushed her way out of the crowd, hurried away. Acorsi turned to the uniformed cop and pointed after her. "Go stop her. I'll want to talk to her."

The cop looked over at where she'd disappeared into the darkness between the buildings, his face skeptical. "You sure?"

Acorsi felt the anger rise up within him. "You heard me! Do it!"

The cop shrugged, walked over to the tape, lifted it so he could duck under, then pushed through the crowd to follow her. Acorsi turned back to the body, took his photographs, then set the camera aside, dug a measuring tape out of the metal case, and noted the distance between each body and the edge of the street, the benches, a metal trash can that stood nearby. He sketched the position of the second body on a new sheet of his notebook, used the tape to measure the distance from the body to the last bit of splattered blood he could find. The kid's nose lay exactly seven feet from his body. The fact struck him as bizarre. Years later, he would still remember it.

He pulled on a pair of rubber gloves, squatted next to the body, and searched it quickly. He found a roll of cash in the kid's left pants pocket, wrapped in a rubber band. He riffled through it, making a quick count. Almost three hundred dollars, small bills. He dropped the money in a plastic evidence bag, set it aside. Then he opened the kid's clothes, ran his hands over his body, feeling for entrance wounds. He flipped the kid over, checked his back, but found nothing. One shot, head wound. Tough luck, kid.

He went back to the first body, pulled the sweatshirt up so he could see the entrance wounds, then heaved the body onto one side, found the exit wounds close together above the left shoulder blade, near the spine. There was a lot of blood under the body, and early signs of heavy lividity where blood had settled in the body. He figured one of the bullets must have hit an artery; otherwise, they didn't look like lethal wounds to him. Too high to hit the heart. He felt around for other wounds, found nothing.

He stood up, pulled off the gloves, wondering how long it had taken the EMS ambulance to arrive. They'd called the kid dead on scene, but after his quick inspection of the body, he'd lay money down that the coroner would write up the cause of death as massive internal bleeding. Slow fade to black. So was he still alive when they got there? He made a note to check with the paramedics, find out if he'd been conscious.

Two shots, he thought, looking down at the body. Close together in the chest, blew him straight back. This kid had been the first target, then, had taken it face-on. The car pulls up, he jumps up off the bench and gets shot twice in the chest, quickly. No chance to move, or the wounds wouldn't have been so close together. If he'd tried to run, you'd get entrance wounds on the back. Maybe he tried to talk, hands out to his sides, easy. Or maybe it went down too fast, the shooter nervous, pulling the shots high. Whatever happened, Acorsi realized, this kid had seen it coming, the nightmare come true. He'd stood there, looked his killer in the eye.

Acorsi opened his notebook to the page titled *Gap* and scrawled *EMS: statement?* He paused, then underlined the words twice. He walked back to the second victim, studied the position of the body, the way the kid had landed on his back, his feet crossed at the ankles, his arms thrown back over his head. He'd tried to run, Acorsi figured. Backing away, probably, got hit before he could get more than a few steps.

He squatted beside the body, studied the upward angle of the bullet track through the bloody pulp of his face, easier to look at now that he saw it as a problem to be solved. He glanced up at the street, then back down at the body. So why the weird angle?

He stood up, moved a few feet away from the body, studying the pavement between where the kid lay and the street. No sign of a deflection mark on the pavement, where the bullet might have bounced off, caught the kid on the rise. He glanced back at the body, crossed feet toward the street, his head almost hidden by the mound of his chest. He turned, and walked back to the street, stood where the car might have stopped. Maybe the kid was on the ground already, looking up at the gunman, Jesus, *watching* him bring the gun around, taking his time to line up the shot. He crouched slightly, trying to imagine the height of a car window. He brought his arm up, made a gun with his hand, put the kid in his sights.

But the angle was still wrong. He couldn't get a clear shot at the kid's head, not without getting out of the car and walking over to him. He straightened up, moved toward the kid's body until he stood almost over him, raised his hand so he was gazing down the length of his arm, over his outstretched thumb and finger, to the kid's destroyed face staring up at him. *Christ.* He took a deep breath, tried to imagine it: the gunman standing there, looking down into the kid's eyes, seeing the terror there like a bright bead of light, then . . . pulling the trigger.

He let his arm fall, suddenly aware of the crowd watching him.

Pretty cool gunman. Or some serious bad blood.

A paramedic came over to him, carrying a plastic body bag. "You almost done here?"

Acorsi looked up at him. "Huh?"

The paramedic nodded to the body. "You ready for us to bag 'em?"

Acorsi rubbed a hand across his face, then nodded. "Yeah, soon as I do the hands." He went over to the forensics case, took out a box of plastic sandwich bags and a jumble of rubber bands, peeled off four of each. Then he went over to the first body, squatted beside it, and fitted a bag over each hand, slipping a rubber band up around the wrist. He got to his feet, nodded to the paramedic, and moved over to the second body to repeat the process.

When he'd finished, he looked up at the kid's face one last time. *Last chance,* he thought. *Anything you got to tell me, say it now.*

But it was hard to imagine this kid had ever said anything. He wasn't just dead now; looking at him, it was impossible to believe that he'd ever lived. A broken thing, like the shattered glass where a window had been. Nothing changes, the view's still there. You just call some guy in to clean it up, start over.

Acorsi got to his feet. *That's me. Guy who cleans up the mess.*

24

Mickie Vega caught the phone on the third ring, brought it over to her ear, and rubbed her face with one hand to wake up a little before she said, "Yeah?"

She heard street noise, traffic passing in the background, then Jabril said, "You lied to me."

Her eyes opened, and she looked over at the clock. *4:37.* She sat up, tugged at her T-shirt where it had bunched up under her. "What are you talking about?"

"I just drove by Conti Street. There's two dead boys lyin' on the sidewalk over there, and this whole place is 'bout to go up in flames." He paused, traffic noises behind him. Mickie wondered where he could be, so many cars on the road at this time of night. The warehouse district, maybe. Or down by the French market, trucks bringing in the produce. "You *hear* what I'm sayin'?"

"Where are you?"

He made a sound like blowing air through his teeth. "You not *listening,* huh? I got a problem here, and I want to know what you people gonna do about it!"

"Look," she told him, reaching over to grab her watch off the night table, then struggling to get the leather band buckled around her wrist. "You just woke me up. I've got no idea what you're talking about, here—"

"What I'm *talkin'* about is them Conti Street boys just got shot up, and I'm hearing how it's my boys did it."

Mickie pressed a hand to her forehead, her head starting to throb. "Okay, I can hear you're upset—"

"You damn *right* I'm upset!"

"Just take it easy for a minute, all right?" She tossed the sheet back, feeling it damp to the touch, the heat still hanging in the room, even at this hour. "You tell me where I can find you, give me twenty minutes to get dressed, we'll sit down, work this out, okay?"

She heard him take a deep breath, let it out slow. "I'm down on Front Street."

"Where you want to meet?"

"You just come on over here, I'll get in the car."

She hesitated for a moment, picturing it, the street dark, Jabril coming out of the shadows to jump in her car. Then she let the thought go, said, "Twenty minutes," and hung up the phone.

"You sure it was them?"

Jabril stared out the window of the car, a light rain falling now as the sky began to take on an edge of blue out over the river.

"I'm not sure of nothing. Guy calls me, says he's gonna take me down. So I ride over to my boy L'Dog's house, ask him what's goin' on, only he ain't home. His mama says she ain't seen him. I'm thinkin', where's he gonna be, he ain't with me?" He looked over at Mickie, his face hidden in the shadows. "I told him we was buyin' guns in case we had trouble with Conti Street. Next thing I know, somebody's tryin' to plant a gun on me. Now my boy Collette's brother is lyin' up in the hospital, all shot up, and L'Dog, he's hot to go take *care* of it. I tried to cool him down, but now I don't know." He was silent for a moment, then turned to look out the window again. "What it comes down to, there's a buncha boys lyin' on the pavement over there on Conti Street, and they got *me* down for it."

Mickie felt her stomach growling. She'd grabbed a cup of coffee at Dunkin' Donuts on the way downtown, but now she was starting to feel weak with hunger. She glanced at her watch; it was after six. They'd been sitting in her car, parked along the railroad tracks next to the river for almost an hour.

"Maybe it's time we brought you in."

He shook his head, not even looking at her. "Not a chance. I got to think about my boys."

"If they shot up those boys . . ."

She felt him look over at her, left the sentence unfinished. When he spoke his voice was tight with anger.

"If they *did,* it's 'cause I told 'em some shit about Conti Street comin' after us. Sent L'Dog up to Canal Street to buy those guns. Like you *told* me. Okay, we did that. Got you people the evidence you wanted so *you* could shut those motherfuckers down, sellin' them guns up here. So what's it got me, huh? How come I don't see you makin' any arrests?"

"It's become . . . complicated."

He raised his eyebrows. "Complicated?" He gave a laugh, shook his head. "Man, that's perfect. Buncha dead niggers lyin' on the street, that's *simple.* But you gotta go bust some *white* guys, put the guns in their hands, now that's a *complicated* situation." He turned to look at her, not angry, as she'd expected, but something in the way he looked at her making her turn, meet his eyes. "You came to me, right? Sat there across the table from me, told me you could shut down the guns, stop the killing down here. You know what I thought, you said that?"

Mickie hesitated, shook her head.

Jabril smiled. "I thought, 'Here's this pretty white girl . . .'"

"I'm Chicana."

Jabril paused, stared at her for a moment. "Here's this pretty *Chicana* girl, comes down to *my* neighborhood, tells me she can stop

the killing. Teach us black folk how to keep our children from killin'
each other."

Mickie started to say something, but he raised a hand, stopped her.

"I'm sitting there, listening to you talk about gun deals, dirty
cops, how you can shut 'em down, and all I can think is 'Bull*shit*!' You
people don't know *nothin'* about where I live, about what makes those
boys go out and shoot some kid lives two blocks down the street. Just
'cause you got shit don't mean you won't fight to defend it. Fight *hard,*
'cause it's all you got. Only these boys, all they see is some guy just
like them, got nothing, and thinks somebody's gonna come along,
take it away. I tell my boys, 'Go look in the mirror. That's who you
killing.' Then I tell 'em, 'You want to carry that gun *up*town, have a
talk with the people who put you here, that's a different story.'" He
smiled, his teeth bright in the early morning light. "But you don't
want to hear that, huh? You got your heart set on saving us, take the
guns out of our hands."

"Nobody twisted your arm."

Jabril spread his hands. "Yeah, you're right. I signed up, let you
talk me into it. Sent my boy James to pick up a gun, even when I *knew*
they was tryin' to set me up. All so you can get the people selling those
guns down here. And now look where we at. Won't be no children left
to save, we keep on like this."

"Bring your boys in. We'll get it straightened out."

Jabril sighed, looked out the window. "Uh-huh. Straight for
who?"

"You leave 'em on the street, they'll be the next target."

Jabril was silent. Then he nodded. "You right there."

"So what do you want from me?"

Jabril looked over at her, studied her face. "You don't get it, huh?"

"What?"

"We tried it your way. Now we got to do it *mine.*"

25

"They had it coming."

Sugar Bear didn't say anything, just kept staring out the window at the trees going past. Scrub pine, red clay hills. L'Dog could start to make it out now, the light coming up in the sky ahead of them. He caught a quick glimpse of a road sign: twenty-three miles to Mobile. Drop the kid, get back into New Orleans before Jabril got out of bed. No problem.

Except now L'Dog was worried about the kid. Three hours, he hadn't said a word, just stared out the window at the darkness. L'Dog talkin' to him, telling him how they'd done what had to get done, how he'd handled the gun like a pro, took those assholes *down,* man, but getting nothing back. The kid just staring off, sinking into it.

"Go easy on yourself, Bear. It's over, right? So let it *be* over. Hear what I'm sayin'?"

L'Dog glanced over at him, quick looks, the highway still empty, except for a couple trucks. He kept pushing it up to ninety, then catching himself, easing back down to sixty so he didn't get pulled over, two niggers in a Camaro, Mississippi state patrolman shining a flashlight in on them, yelling for them to keep their hands where he could see 'em. They'd gotten rid of the gun, rode up Chef Menteur and dropped it in the canal before they got on the highway, but he still felt jumpy. All he needed was some cop pullin' 'em over, puttin' his flashlight on the kid, seeing that look on his face, sayin' *Whoa, now. What you boys been up to, huh?*

L'Dog smiled. *Ah, nothin', officer. We just been out killin' people.*

Yeah, but for *real.* The kid up on his knees in the backseat of the Corolla, holding the gun in both hands, *pop pop pop pop . . .* The gun *loud,* man, two feet from L'Dog's ear, and those Conti Street boys stumblin' all over the place, two of 'em down on the ground, not moving, blood hanging in the air like a cloud over 'em, until AK punched the gas, got 'em out of there, fast. Twenty seconds, L'Dog figured, and they were flyin' up the street, makin' the corner at Broad, headed up toward the Fairgrounds, where he'd left his car. AK glancin' over at him, eyes wide, sayin', "Man, you *see* that?"

Like it was a movie, they could run it back.

They dumped the Corolla, got rid of the gun, and AK went on home. L'Dog put the kid back in his car, and they took off for Mobile. Now he could feel the tiredness behind his eyes, realized that his jaw ached from clenching it. He rubbed at the muscles with one hand, moving his jaw to loosen it. Weird, how it felt. Just like a hinge, his body a machine under the skin.

He glanced over at the kid. "I know how you feel, man. You want to go back, make it like it was before. Maybe go crawl up in your mama's bed, let her hold you in her arms, huh?"

He saw the kid look over at him, expressionless.

"That's normal, man. You feel that way 'cause it's hard to think of yourself doin' something like, you know, we just done. Know what I mean? That's something, like, *other* guys do, guys in movies and shit. You still a baby, in your mind. Look at the world like you don't really belong here, got to go ask your mama, you want to do something." He shook his head. "Well, you a *man,* now. And you got to live with that. Put your hand out, say, 'I'll take that car, that money, that lady over there with the nice ass.'" Looking over at the kid, grinning. "Got to say, 'Give it up, bitch! 'Cause I'm a *man.*'"

The kid staring at him, not saying a word. Empty, like.

L'Dog tried to think of something else to say, but there wasn't nothing else. You kill a man, Jabril had told him once, it's in your head. Nothing you can do to wipe it clean, get it out of there. You go to sleep that first night, you see it, man, feel the gun in your hand, the way it jumped back at you when you pulled the trigger, like one 'a those mean-ass dogs you got to watch close, so they don't go for your throat. You dream it every night for a while, fighting your sheets, until you think you can't take it no more. Then one night, it's gone. You wake up, realize that you slept through the night, first time in months. Like somebody erased the tape. So a couple weeks later, when the cops pick you up, take you into that little room, nothing but a table and a plastic chair, start askin' you about it, you look at 'em like you can't *believe* it, man. *Who, me?*

It's just waiting it out, L'Dog wanted to tell the kid. Hangin' in there until you can look that cop in the eye and tell him the flat truth, man, what you feel in your bones: *No way, man! I don't do that shit!*

Then you're clean. Say it, *believe* it, you can make it true.

He wanted to tell the kid that, get him nodding, see that look in his face like he's grateful, so you can feel okay that he won't go off and do something stupid. Like get busted. Let some cop see it in his eyes, rub at that spot till it's raw.

L'Dog glanced over at him, every few minutes. But the kid just stared out at the trees going by, pine trees, for Christ's sake, every fuckin' one of 'em looks the same, until L'Dog couldn't take it anymore said, "What the *fuck* you lookin' at, anyway?"

The kid turned his head slowly, looking over at him. He shrugged. "Nothin'."

"Don't go losin' it on me, Bear."

And the kid seemed to think about it for a while, then shrugged again, like, *Okay.* Went back to staring out the window. For a moment L'Dog thought about reaching under his seat right then, whip out his .38 and just put one behind his ear, take care of the whole problem. Pull off into the woods somewhere, dump the body.

But it wasn't just the cops he had to worry about now. Jabril, man, he'd know for sure what went down if the kid disappeared. Start giving him that look, like he sees right through you, makes you think he's just deciding what to do about the problem. And then what?

Same problem, same answer.

L'Dog ran a hand across his forehead, the muscles tight up there. It was a bitch, this whole fuckin' deal. Fuckin' Jabril, man. Wouldn't be none 'a this happening, he'd taken care of the situation. Can't let it slide, somebody takes out one of your boys. He wants to be the *man*, he's got to handle it. So now he's gonna sit there, give you that look, like you're some kinda mess he's got to clean up?

L'Dog glanced over at the kid, thought about the gun under his seat. *Maybe it wouldn't be such a bad thing. Get it out in the open, huh? Jabril, he's got to look it in the eye, see how maybe it's time to step back, enjoy his old age.*

Get off the highway, tell the kid you got to take a piss. Find a spot out in the woods, pull over, grab the gun from under the seat as you get out. The kid, he's so busy lookin' at the fuckin' *pine* trees, he'd never even notice. Walk around the back, like you lookin' for a nice bush to piss on, only you come up behind him, jerk the door open, lay the gun right up behind his ear, *pop*. Then just grab his arm, pull him out of the car real quick, so he doesn't bleed all over the seats.

Only, L'Dog saw the trees were giving way, now, to houses, shopping centers, gas stations, as they came into Mobile. L'Dog sighed, let the thought go.

"Just a couple more minutes," he told the kid, "we get you back to your *lady*."

Grinning over at him, easy like. He saw the kid bite his lip, turn his face away, but not before L'Dog had caught a quick glimpse of it, not quite believing what he'd seen until he reached over, grabbed the kid's jaw, turned his head toward him so he could get a better look. *Ah, Jesus.*

Tears streaming down his face.

26

Danny sat in his office, the morning edition of the *Times-Picayune* spread out on the desk in front of him. The lead story was a drive-by shooting over on Conti Street, two dead. Below it, another story described an incident at a junior high school in a town outside Chicago, some kid walking into the lunchroom, opening up with a 9 mm Glock. Three dead, seven wounded. Afterward, the kid told the cops he'd been pissed off 'cause other kids were teasing him.

Danny shoved the paper away. *Some fucking world.* He sat back, glanced at the the strip of plastic he'd picked up off the desk, his hand playing with it idly. He turned it over, saw it was the badge that Jimmy had handed him at the middle school, *Jesus,* only a couple *days* ago—I DID MY PART!

He laid the badge down on the desk carefully, closed his eyes. *Christ.* He'd woken up early, from a dream in which he was adrift in a boat on a sea of marsh grass, no engine, no oars, no land within sight. Now, it was still dark out, hours from dawn, but he got out of bed, his mouth dry as a salt flat, went into the kitchen, and drank down three glasses of water from the sink without pausing. When he put the glass down on the counter and turned away from the sink, he saw the envelope he'd tossed to Helen lying on his kitchen table.

He got up, went over to the window, looked down at the half block of St. Charles he could see from his office window. A streetcar rolled past, crowded with tourists, the driver hauling on the brake lever to slow it down as a car stopped abruptly in front of him. You live in a city for a while, you get used to its rhythms, the way its muscular heart beats out the days, a steady pulse drawing in every morning, flowing out at night. Watch those skycam shots of the commuter traffic on the evening news, it starts to look like blood flowing, a circulation of desire, money, *blood.* All things hunger, feed, then hunger again. And a city, it feeds and bleeds, man, you better fuckin' believe it.

He'd put the envelope in the empty safe, locked it. *Probably where it came from.* Money in, money out. Like a pulse. Think about it enough, you could start to see it that way, as if this beat-up Mosler safe in an empty office was the heart of everything, what kept the whole city going when it should have just laid down and died. Payoffs, kickbacks. A little cash under the table, just to keep everyone happy. So nobody has to worry about paying the cops a decent wage, putting money in the schools. Things are fine, right? *Laissez le bon temps rouler, son.* Everybody got enough to drink? Havin' you a real good time?

Hell, boy, why you think they call it *Dixie?* From a ten-dollar bill they used to print up in New Orleans. *What you pay for dat, mon? Dix.*

So take the money. Shit, nobody cares what happens to some black kid, got himself shot on the street. Happens all the time.

Danny leaned his forehead against the window, closed his eyes. *And what've you done about it?* Nothing. Unless you count punching out Lucas Clay, and that didn't solve anything. Just a way of getting the bad taste out of his mouth.

He couldn't shake the feeling that all this was happening because of him. Because he'd wanted answers. Not just about the shootings that killed five people down on Claiborne Avenue, but about Jimmy Boudrieux. And about his father.

Bullshit. What you really wanted to know about was you.

He'd left his job with the D.A.'s office because he couldn't stand the knowledge that it wasn't real, that Jimmy'd pulled some strings to get him there just so he could get a case thrown out of court when it threatened his power. And yeah, if he was honest about it, the reason he'd gone to see Marty Seagraves, agreed to become an FBI informant, was not because he believed in justice or honest government. He'd done it because he was *mad.* Because his whole life had suddenly become somebody else's game.

And now he'd kept quiet about what he'd seen in that restaurant, told Seagraves to stall the U.S. Attorney, because it wasn't enough to see Jimmy go to jail for political corruption. He wanted to take him down personally, to look him in the eye when they came to make the arrest, and know that there was no way he'd walk away from it this time. So he went looking for the kid, like some guy in the movies who's gonna solve the mystery, catch the bad guys. And where had that led?

He opened his eyes, looked out the window. Below, a woman started to cross the street, pausing at the edge of the sidewalk to wait for the traffic to clear. When she got a break, she ran across.

She had a slight limp.

He turned from the window, sat down behind his desk. A moment later, he heard footsteps on the stairs. He waited, heard them reach the landing, come toward him across the corridor. She tapped on the glass.

"Danny? It's Mickie Vega. I need to talk to you."

He looked up at the light through the window blinds striping the wall, felt something grab at his chest. And then he smiled.

You're a popular guy, Danny.

Mickie sat across the desk from Danny, glanced around the office. He could see her eyes taking it all in—the scarred desk, the air conditioner with its slow drip, the safe over in the corner. She glanced at the badge on the desk beside him, then up at his face.

"Long night?"

He shrugged, picked up the badge, opened a drawer, and dropped it inside, then slid the drawer closed. "I saw this TV show once, on these monks in Ethiopia or someplace. They live in these little stone huts on a mountain, freezing in winter . . ."

"In Ethiopia."

"I guess it gets cold in the mountains." He eased back in his chair, watching her face. She looked tired. "Anyway, one of the rules of their order is they can't sleep, ever. It's part of their vows. They sit up all night, praying. One guy starts to nod off, they hit him with a stick. They talked to one old guy, he hadn't slept in thirty years. The reporter asks him, 'Don't you miss it?' He just shrugs, says, 'My body will sleep in the grave. But my soul will dance.'"

"So you thinking about signing up?"

Danny laughed. "Yeah, right. Poverty, chastity, and insomnia. I'm all set."

He saw Mickie's eyes wander over to the safe against the wall, but she just smiled.

"The great thing was, they put this show on at three in the morning, so all over the city, people are watching it, thinking, 'Yeah, *so?*'"

"I usually end up watching a video," Mickie said. "I've got the complete Fred Astaire boxed set."

"Yeah? I like the one where they dance on roller skates."

"Swing Time."

"Right. He's a compulsive gambler, but he keeps trying to lose because he promised some girl he'd marry her when he made enough money. Only now he loves Ginger."

She laughed. "A classic plot."

"At the end he dances with a whole chorus line, fifty girls wearing Ginger masks. Shows her he can only think of her."

"Every woman's dream. I always wonder how the fifty girls felt."

"Probably tell their grandchildren, 'I danced with Fred Astaire!'"
He smiled. "You think he ever stepped on their toes?"

She gave him a curious look. Like she'd just found his collection
of baseball cards all boxed up in the bottom of his closet. *Seeing* him,
for the first time, getting the whole picture in that one moment.

He turned his chair, looked out the window. "You had breakfast?"

"Danny," she said, leaning forward to rest one hand on his desk.
"Two boys were shot dead over on Conti Street last night. I think
James Collette was part of it."

He let his eyes close for a moment, feeling the exhaustion sweep
over him. "What a fuckin' waste."

She was silent, waiting until she saw him open his eyes and look
out at the morning traffic on St. Charles. "Danny, we need to get some
things clear."

He didn't answer, his fingers picking at the cracked leather on
one arm of his chair.

"Did Jimmy Boudrieux ask you to find Collette?"

He brought the chair back around, looked at her. "Let me ask
you something. Before you were a juvenile officer, what did you do?"

She hesitated. "I did some social work back in New Mexico. Before that, I was in college."

He nodded slowly.

"You're not answering my question, Danny."

"No, but you haven't really answered mine." He smiled.
"Right?"

She stared at him.

"You had breakfast or not?"

He took her to the Hummingbird Café down the street, got two
coffees at the counter, brought them back to the table. She watched

him stop to talk to a cop at one of the other tables, glancing over at her while the guy launched into some kind of story, gesturing angrily. Catching her watching him. *Okay,* she thought, *so he knows.* The thought made her feel strangely excited. She pictured them talking about it when he came back to the table, but not like they'd talked up until now: talking, instead, the way Fred and Ginger danced, wary but flirtatious, both of them holding back what they knew about each other, making it up as they went along.

Danny said something to the cop, gesturing with the coffee cups, then came over to the table. He grinned, shook his head. "Guy runs a Mister Softee truck in his spare time. So now he owes two years of back taxes to the state, and he thinks I can fix it for him."

"Can you?"

Danny pulled out a chair, sat down. "Yeah, I can. But not for that asshole. When I was in high school, he used to sit outside the parking lot after football games, pull guys over, make 'em take a sobriety test in front of their dates." He picked up his coffee cup, steam rising in front of his face. "You ever try to walk a straight line when you've just spent three hours under the bleachers, necking?"

"Sounds painful."

He smiled. "So's taxes." He sipped his coffee, then sat back, shook his head. "Anyway, I'm not sure I can do it now."

"Lost your magic wand?"

"Let's just say I seem to be out of the loop on some things."

She set her cup down on the table and looked at him. "You're being set up, Danny."

He didn't respond, his eyes going off across the room, squinting slightly against the steam as he raised the cup to his lips.

"You see it, don't you?"

His eyes came back to her, and he studied her face. "Are you wired?"

"What?"

"Somebody send you in here, figure you'd get me to start crying on your shoulder?"

She sat back, slowly. Blood coming up in her face like she'd been slapped. For a moment, her mind flashed on Fred and Ginger, dancing in the gazebo in *Top Hat,* the rain falling around them. Except now Ginger was stepping back, changing the choreography, a little smile on her face as she turned, kicked him in the balls.

He looked away. "I'm sorry."

"You know what it's like, talking to you? Watching a guy burn his own house down, but he locks all the doors first, make sure the firemen don't try to rescue him."

He smiled. "You should talk to my ex-wife."

She looked away, her eyes moving across the restaurant. "You gotta talk to somebody, Danny. Might as well be me."

He cradled his coffee cup in both hands, looked up at her. "So what are you? IRS?"

"Oh, thanks." She reached over, took the cup out of his hands, set it on the table. "Look at me, Danny. Straight question, straight answer. Jimmy Boudrieux asked you to find the kid, right?"

He met her eyes, hesitated, then shrugged.

"C'mon, Danny!"

"Hey, it's New Orleans. That's as close to an answer as it gets."

She held up both hands. "Okay, fine. Next question. Who's he asking for?"

Danny glanced down at his coffee cup. "Can I have my cup back?"

"If it makes you feel better." She watched him pick it up, take a sip. "So what's this all about, Danny?"

He smiled at her. "You know what kills me about those Fred Astaire movies? They got the same plot, every time. He's in love with her, but she's not interested."

Mickie looked down at her coffee. "She's interested."

"Okay, maybe. But every time he tries to get to know her, he ends up looking like an idiot. Then they dance, and suddenly it's all reversed. Like he's driving a car, she's just along for the ride." He smiled. "When I got married, we got up to do the first dance, Helen starts counting. In this little stage whisper, you know? *One, two, three . . .*" He grinned, shook his head. "Three weeks, she had me practicing. She was sure I'd screw it up."

"Yeah? So did you?"

"We're up there, she's counting, I'm whispering, 'Let me lead! Will you let me *lead?*'" He took a sip of his coffee, smiled. "Our first fight, it's on the dance floor at our wedding."

"That was really your first fight?"

"Figure of speech."

She drank off the last of her coffee, said, "So I guess you're not into dancing, huh?" Trying to keep the disappointment out of her voice as she said it.

"Hey, I love dancing. Turn on some music, I'll start dancing. I'm just not much good at team sports."

She smiled. "Is that a warning?"

They were leaving the café, coming out into the morning rush hour on St. Charles, Danny thinking, *Okay, now what?,* when he looked up, saw Tom Acorsi getting out of his Ford at the corner across from Danny's office. Acorsi leaned in the window, said something to his partner, who nodded, then the car pulled away and he straightened, ran a hand across the back of his neck as he gazed up at the morning sky.

He turned, saw them, and his expression changed, his face going hard, angry. He came toward them. Danny caught his eye, gave him a look that said, *Cut me a break, okay?* He saw Acorsi's eyes glance over at Mickie then come back to him, and something in his face seemed to ease back, one of those moments of silent understanding they'd worked out in high school—*Go easy on me, I like this one.*

"Hey, Danny. I was just coming to see you." Acorsi held out his hand, and they shook. Danny nodded to Mickie, said, "You know Mickie Vega?"

"Yeah, we've met." Acorsi shook hands with her. "You're with . . ."

"Juvenile office," Mickie said, quickly.

Acorsi stared at her for a moment, then nodded. He turned, pointed at a thick bank of clouds rising over the Gulf, narrow shafts of sunlight piercing the top layer like knife blades. "You believe that sky? We're gonna have one hell of a storm this afternoon." He grinned at them. "You know what I love about storms? Makes my job a lot easier. All the crackheads, they move inside, off the street. Sit there drinking beer, hitting the pipe while they wait for the rain to end, get back to business. You get a big one like this, they've been inside for three, four hours. Their brains get melted down, and they start killing each other. Two hours after every big storm, we start getting calls. Knifings, shootings, you name it. One guy beat his buddy to death with a broken toilet seat. Only they do it right there in their living rooms, so I get a nice compact crime scene. All the evidence, right there in the room. A couple times we get there, find the killer sitting there on his couch, watching cartoons on TV. Too stoned to get up and walk away. Easy." He turned, looked back up at the sky. "Only problem, with this heat, you don't get a call pretty quick, those apartments turn into ovens. You find the body, you can't tell if it's been shot or stabbed or *what.* Cockroaches crawling all over it, feasting away. I've seen guys, twenty years on the job, lose it when they got to go into one of those rooms."

Danny said, "But not you."

"No, not me." Acorsi turned, smiled at Mickie. "So how come you're hangin' out with this guy?"

"He's helping me with one of my cases."

Acorsi's face got serious. "Collette?" She nodded. He looked at Danny, and his eyes narrowed. "You got an interest in this kid, Danny?"

Danny flushed. "I just hate to see him end up in prison. I hear he's a smart kid."

"Yeah, I heard that too. Math genius. Now I don't know. We got three dead, drive-by over on Conti Street."

"You think it was him?"

"Maya showed the kid's picture to a witness, she starts screaming, 'That's him! That's the one killed my brother!'" He smiled thinly. "Not that it'll ever go to trial. Those Conti Street guys, they'll put some money on the street. Couple days, we'll get a call, come pick up his body."

Danny saw a few raindrops hit the sidewalk. He held out his hand, palm up. "I guess you got to live where you live."

Acorsi laughed. "That what you've learned, Danny? Twenty years' worth of experience?"

"Yeah, that's about it." Danny shrugged. "We expect these kids to rise above it, you know? Smart kid like Collette, he could be anything. That's what we tell him. All he's got to do is keep his head above water, stay away from the drugs, the gangs. Go to school in the morning, come straight home in the afternoon, sit at the kitchen table, do his homework. Get up the next day, do it again. Don't look around when you're walking home, don't go over to the playground, 'cause that's where the drug dealers hang out, just keep your eyes on the prize. Do that for ten, fifteen years, you're home free." He looked over at Acorsi. "You put this kid in prison, he'll feel right at home."

"You ever been up to Parish Prison?" Acorsi smiled. "Trust me, he won't feel at home."

Mickie looked over at Danny, watched him shake his head slightly, his eyes going back up to the sky.

"He's talking about himself," she said quietly.

"Yeah?" Acorsi grinned. "That true, Danny? You worried about the condition of your soul? Been too long since your last confession?" He gave a laugh, opened the door to the café, paused.

"Tell you what," he said to Danny. "You come talk to me, anytime. I'll be happy to hear your confession."

27

Danny walked Mickie back to her car, raindrops spattering the sidewalk around them. She dug in her bag for her keys, unlocked the door, then turned to smile at him.

"We always seem to get caught in the rain."

"It's New Orleans. I'd say that improves our chances."

She glanced up at the sky, closed her eyes, feeling the drops landing on her face. "I must be the only one in this town who loves when it rains on the weekends. I just lie in bed, read the paper, watch a movie. If it's coming down hard, I go for a walk. Makes me feel like the Morton Salt girl."

"When it rains, it pours."

She laughed. "I never knew what they meant, living in New Mexico. I get here, all my salt shakers turn into glue sticks."

"Put some rice in them."

"Yeah, somebody at work told me that."

They were both silent for a moment, looking at the drops hitting the sidewalk, both of them starting to feel a little wet. Then Danny said, "I used to like to walk up into Audubon Park, sit under an oak tree. You get this mist rising off the ground all around you, rain coming down through the branches. After a while, you can't see more than a few feet beyond the tree. Makes you feel like the world's just been created, you're the only person alive."

"Sounds nice." She glanced at her watch, got into her car. She reached out to pull the door closed, looked up at him. "Maybe you could show me sometime."

"That would be nice."

She smiled. "I'm in the book. Call me the next time you feel like getting wet." Then she paused, closed her eyes. "Oh, God. I didn't really say that, did I?"

"What?"

She looked up at him, smiled. "Thanks." She pulled the door closed, started the car. He stood there, hands in his pockets, watched her drive away. When she reached the end of the block, he saw her glance up at the rearview. He raised his hand. Then she turned the corner, and he looked up at the sky, rain falling toward him, hitting his face.

Beautiful.

Mickie glanced up at the mirror, saw him lift his hand, give a little wave. She smiled, then reached down to switch on the wipers before making the corner. She fumbled for the headlights, got them on as the rain started coming down hard. Then she sat back, ran a hand across her forehead, wiping away the dampness.

Jesus.

She ran back over what they'd said in her mind, trying to figure out exactly where the conversation had turned. She'd felt bad, watching the cop go after Danny, his eyes getting that distant look, like if he tried hard enough, he might just vanish. She recognized it. Her brother was a cop out in Albuquerque whose wife had left him, taking the children. For a year afterward, he'd called himself "the Disappearing Man." There, but *not* there. Like he'd go away somewhere in the middle of a conversation, find himself a hole in the silences between the words, curl up inside it. Safe.

Watching it happen with Danny, she'd felt the anger well up inside her. The cop jumping in there between them, like she'd just finished raking a field of fresh soil, getting it all smoothed out, ready to plant, and he'd walked right across it, left his footprints everywhere. She'd wanted to bring Danny back from wherever he'd gone in his mind, rebuild the trust between them . . .

She winced. Yeah, right. What was it she'd said to him? *Call me the next time you feel like getting wet.*

Now, as she watched the headlights of the oncoming cars appear out of the mist, she took a deep breath, blew it out hard enough to make the windshield fog up. *Okay, so you're playing the guy, even flirting a little, just to bring him along. If that's all it is, how come you're feeling so . . . twitchy?* Her stomach full of that empty feeling, hands moving around on the steering wheel like she's scared it might get away from her. Let's face it, the way she felt when she *liked* a guy.

So, let's say you go walking in the rain with him, find yourself an old oak tree to hide under when it starts to pour. You really think the two of you are gonna sit there, talk about the kid?

She smiled to herself. The sad thing was, they just might.

Hard to picture it any other way, really. He didn't seem the type to wrap her up against the rain in his beat-up leather jacket, so she'd feel like a little girl inside it, then put his arm around her, and lean in with that little moment of hesitation most guys used, like asking permission before kissing her. This guy, he'd probably sit there and just . . . *talk.* Pick up an acorn to play with, keep his hands busy while he stared off into the rain, told her some story about when he was a kid.

But then, that was what she liked about him. He hung back, didn't try to knock her over. Walked around with that empty look in his eyes like he didn't think he had a *right* to everything. Most men, they came at you like knife throwers. This guy had no expectations. Which, as she thought about it, seemed a little weird for a guy who spent his days riding around town, people handing him money.

Or maybe it was perfect. That sad look, so people *wanted* to give him the money. She could see how it might work. Maybe he put it on, used it to get people off their guard. She let the idea grow in her head for a while, starting to feel angry as she imagined him pulling it on her. Like one of those beggars you see down in Mexico sometimes, sitting there on the sidewalk with a starving kid in their arms. You start to reach into your pocket, then you notice the kid's wearing a brand new pair of Baby Reeboks under his filthy blanket, forty bucks a pair.

She kept having to remind herself that Danny was dirty. Guys like him, they fed the corruption that kept New Orleans the way it was. Not so bad, maybe, if you lived up on St. Charles. But when you got down in the neighborhoods where kids played with crack bottles on the street corner, you could smell the filth, the blood, like a bitter scent hanging in the air. When she'd just arrived in the city, first day on the job, Jim Dubrow had taken her into his office, shown her a map of the country on his wall. "See this?" he'd asked her, his finger tracing the Mississippi River down from its source near the Canadian border. "This river feeds the whole country, right? You got snow melt running down off the Rockies out west, rain off the Appalachians, all of it spilling down into the Mississippi, feeding all this farmland here in the Midwest." He swept his hand across the middle of the map, then came back to the river and ran his finger down its length again. "I like to see it as a big digestive system: feeds the country, carries away what's not needed. Small intestine, large intestine . . ." His finger moved past Memphis, along the border of Arkansas and Mississippi, finally came to rest on New Orleans. "And ends up right here." He looked at her. "We're living in the asshole of the country, here. We got every kind of shit, Mickie. Drugs, violence, political corruption. You name it, it's worse here. Our job is to wipe the country's ass." He smiled. "Can't get it all. There's always more shit, right? So we just clean up what we can, try not to let it stink so bad that everybody else starts to notice."

Mickie laughed. "So why do people put up with it?"

Dubrow crooked a finger and led her over to the window, raised the blinds so she could look out from his office window way up on the twelfth floor of a building near the eastern end of Veterans Highway, looking southeast across I-10 and the cemetery toward the skyline of the central business district. He waved a hand, said, "Say what you like, it's a nice piece of ass."

Mickie winced, remembering it. She'd lived in New Orleans for six months now, and she was starting to see what he'd meant. The whole city like some worn-out whore, spending her night shaking her ass for the tourists down on Bourbon Street; she wants to put her feet up during the day, not think about it. Look at it that way, it's not so hard to understand a guy like Danny Chaisson. Okay, so the city's drowning in shit, but he's just doing what men like him have always done, keeping his head above the surface. These guys, they played the game the way their fathers taught it to them. Chase the whore or pimp her. Either way, you got to play her as she lay.

Mickie drove up to Metairie, watched the morning rush hour start to build up on the downtown side of the Pontchartrain Expressway. She had an apartment in a complex a block off West Esplanade, two blocks from the lakefront. Most of the other tenants were singles, some secretaries, a couple nurses who worked at City Hospital, and four car salesmen who liked to set up lawn chairs next to their grills on summer evenings, cooking steaks, drinking Mexican beer from the bottles, and giving her the eye when she pulled in. Still, the place was cheap, and her apartment had a small balcony that caught the late-afternoon sun. She'd managed to fend off the car salesmen so far, telling them she was vegetarian. That seemed to have put them off, for the moment, but she could see one of them working himself up to take another run at it. *Probably run down to the Greenfields,* she thought. *Bring home some veggie burgers.*

She parked her car and ran in to grab some work clothes, laying them across the bed while she slipped into the shower. When she came out, she tossed her towel across the back of a chair, caught a glimpse of herself in the full-length mirror on the closet door as she reached for her underwear. She paused, looking at herself in the mirror, the bed behind her, morning light spilling in through the sheer curtains beyond. She needed a haircut, more time at the gym. But, for the moment, everything seemed to be staying where it belonged.

She let her mind imagine a man stretched out on the bed behind her, seeing her like this. Reaching out to run the tips of his finger over the damp skin on her hip, gently. Danny Chaisson, she realized without surprise, looking up at her from the bed with his sad smile, telling her, "I don't deserve this."

"No, you don't."

But then giving it to him anyway. Not holding back, surprising him. Seeing the pleasure in his eyes. Not that triumphant look some guys got in bed, or—*Jesus*—that *straining* expression, like they were lifting something heavy. No, what she imagined was like a dense fog breaking, light filling the sky.

Mickie's eyes came back up to her face, and she grinned, shook her head. *Get a grip, girl!* She turned away from the mirror, got dressed. Pausing, as she zipped up her skirt, to shake her head again and laugh. *Jesus.*

Still, her body was trembling slightly. Like it felt when she'd just come in from running. Like she'd gone farther than she'd planned.

28

Lucas Clay drove out St. Bernard Highway, past the strip malls and low-end motels, the old Domino Sugar plant, oil refineries. *Jesus, you're really out in it now. The real New Orleans.* He reached over, locked the doors on his Lexus.

At Paris Road, he made a right, past the carnival of razor wire that was the St. Bernard Parish Prison toward the chemical plants along the levee. He caught a whiff of the river. Thick and heavy, like a slow-moving animal. Above the buildings, he could see a freighter gliding past, headed east past the ferry landing toward English Turn and the channel to the sea.

A block from the river, he pulled into the gravel parking lot in front of a large tin-roofed building, as big and plain as a warehouse. There were windows at one end with a display of fishing gear, Coleman tents, and a double row of shotguns. A sign over the entrance said RAGIN' CAJUN SPORTS. At the other end of the building, there was a metal door, a sign attached to a security grate: CAJUN RANGES.

He got out of the car, went around to the trunk, unlocked it. A briefcase lay next to the spare tire. He lifted it out, shut the trunk, hit the button on his key chain to set the car's alarm. Then he walked over to the metal door, went inside. A man stood behind the desk, reading a gun magazine. He wore a Marine Corps T-shirt and a semiautomatic pistol in a holster attached to the belt of his jeans. Behind his head, a sign read HANDGUN CERTIFICATION COURSES NOW AVAILABLE. A glass display case next to the desk contained two shelves of handguns, as well as a selection of holsters, ammunition, and gun-care kits. On the desk was a leather-bound ledger, turned toward the customers, ready for them to sign in.

The man behind the desk glanced up from his magazine, looked Lucas over carefully. "Help you?"

"Buddy around?"

"He expecting you?"

"Lucas Clay. He called me this morning, asked me to come out."

The man nodded, picked up the phone on the desk, dialed two numbers, his eyes still fixed on Lucas's face.

Lucas reached up, touched his lower lip gently. All day, he kept feeling like it was bleeding. He could still taste blood in his mouth. He turned his back on the guy behind the counter, wandered over to one of the display cases. Two rows of handguns laid out on velvet. Holsters, cleaning kits. Beside the case was a cardboard cutout of a man in a business suit, carrying a briefcase, a slogan printed across the top: *What you can't see CAN hurt you!* Next to the display was a full-length mirror where customers could check that their concealed weapons didn't screw up the cut of their sports jackets. Lucas edged over toward it, stole a quick glance at his face.

No blood, just a split lip. A dark bruise along the right side of his jaw.

"Mr. Clay?"

Lucas turned, looked back at the man behind the counter.

"Buddy's in the warehouse." He nodded toward a door at the back, reached under the counter. "Just give the door a shove. I'll buzz you in."

Buddy Jeanrette stood at the end of a row of large wooden shipping crates, using a crowbar to pry one of them open. As Lucas walked down the row toward him, Buddy laid the crowbar aside,

picked up a clipboard, and flipped through a stack of shipping re-
ceipts, checking them against the contents of the crate. He glanced
up, holding his place in the papers with his thumb.

"Hey, Lucas. We finally got you out into the *real* world." He
looked at the briefcase in Lucas's hand. "That what I think it is?"

Lucas set the briefcase down on the concrete, slid it across to
Buddy with his foot. "Expensive lesson. You should choose your
friends more carefully."

"Yeah, well, you can't always pick your friends." He opened the
briefcase's clasps, glanced inside at the four guns. "But these boys,
they won't let you down."

Lucas looked around at the pile of crates. "Looks like you could
use some more help back here. You unload the trucks yourself, too?"

Buddy straightened, picked up his clipboard. "Nah, I hire guys
to do the *real* work. But I got a secretary out with the flu, over two
million dollars of new stock sittin' over in the warehouse, and I can't
get a decent temp in here to record these deliveries. I don't even know
what I got here." He turned back to the crate, dug through it, checking off items on his form as he spoke. "Anyway, I enjoy this part. My
first job, I worked in a warehouse. Furniture distributor over on the
West Bank. The guy who ran the place used to make me go out back,
burn all the shipping cartons in the incinerator. I'm talking the middle of summer, right? It's a hundred degrees in the shade, I'm out
there tossing boxes into a furnace all day. I lost twenty pounds that
summer." He laid the clipboard on a crate, picked up the crowbar,
worked the narrow end under the lid of the next crate. "Still, I come
out here every chance I get." He threw his weight against the crowbar,
pried up the lid. Inside, Lucas saw a row of handguns, each wrapped in
plastic. Buddy reached in, brushed aside some of the Styrofoam pack-
ing pellets, picked up one of the guns. "This is what it's all about, you
know? This is the real thing."

Lucas glanced at an open crate next to him. A delivery receipt lay on top of the shipping pellets. The form had the words *ARMA-TECH INC.* printed across the top margin, and recorded the delivery of twelve 9 mm semiautomatic handguns to Ragin' Cajun Sports, payment on account.

"Lucas, you know Ray Morrisey?"

Lucas looked up to see a heavyset man in a St. Bernard sheriff's deputy uniform come toward them from the back of the warehouse, wiping his hands on his trousers. "Damn, Buddy," Morrisey said as he came up to them. "You *ever* clean them toilets back there?"

Buddy grinned. "We been savin' it up for you, Ray. Knew you'd be the man to appreciate it."

Morrisey reached past Lucas, picked up one of the guns from the crate, a small, black semiautomatic. It looked like a toy in his hand. "What the hell is this?"

"Bauer twenty-five, six-shot magazine. Purse gun, mainly. I'm thinking about running a special, calling it the *Little Miss.*"

Morrisey shook his head in disgust. "Good name. They buy one, that's what they'll do."

"Ray, you know the average distance at which a woman uses a gun in self-defense?" Buddy reached over, took the gun out of Morrisey's hands, put it back in the crate. "Four feet. Guys use a gun, they're protecting their house, their business. Women, they're defending their body. Four feet, Ray, you got six shots? Trust me, it'll do the job. Women want a gun they can carry in their purse, whip it out to blow some guy's balls off, he gets too close."

Morrisey glanced over at Lucas, shook his head. "Listen to this guy. Jesus, no wonder he can't get nobody to come out here, do his inventory."

Lucas smiled. "You should ask for a raise."

"Hey, fuck you too." Morrisey looked at the briefcase on the floor. "That our guns?"

Buddy sighed, shook his head. "You hear that? *Our* guns." He

shoved the briefcase over to Ray with his foot. "They're *your* guns now,
Ray. You're the one who sold 'em to Foley. Hell, they're useless to me.
I try to move 'em now, somebody gets picked up with one, I'd have the
ATF all over my ass. They'd run it through the computer, trace it right
back to Foley. Then we're *all* fucked. So you take 'em back to the evidence room, get some clean paper established, and then we'll talk
about how to unload 'em."

"Jesus." Morrisey bent over, picked up the briefcase. "You really
gotta chill out, Buddy. One 'a these days, you're gonna bust a vein."

"I ever do, I'm sure you'll be there to see it, Ray."

"Yeah? Well shit, now I got a reason to live." Morrisey turned,
walked away down the aisle.

Buddy shook his head, turned back to his clipboard. "Talk about
your inaccurate weapons."

"You wanted to talk to me, Buddy?"

Buddy ignored him, his lips moving slightly as he read off the
serial numbers on the shipping form, compared them to the contents
of the crate. Then he took a pen from his pocket, initialed the form,
picked up the crowbar, and moved a few cases down the row. "How's
your jaw?"

Lucas watched him fit the crowbar under the lid of the next
crate, pry it off. "Why do I get the feeling that you're not really concerned with my health, Buddy?"

"That was quite a show your boy Danny put on."

Lucas smiled. "Danny's got a dramatic streak. Likes to think he's
a tragic figure."

Buddy shoved the lid of the crate back, flipped through his forms
until he found the right one, glanced in at a row of large revolvers.
"Runs in the family. Danny's father used to have a couple drinks, tell
everybody what an idealistic guy he was back when he got started.
'Course, what that leads to, you got to tell 'em how screwed up your
life is now. Guy had some *real* indiscreet conversations."

"So you knew Danny's father?" Lucas reached into the crate, ran his finger across one of the guns. It had been vacuum-wrapped, the plastic stretched taut from the barrel down across the trigger guard to the grip. It felt smooth, but oddly soft, as if he were touching the idea of the gun, not the gun itself. A gun you'd see in a dream, lying on a table in an abandoned house, draped in pale light, waiting for you.

"Yeah." Buddy made a note on his clipboard. "Back when I was with the state police. I was head of Jimmy's personal security detail for eighteen months." He looked up at Lucas, smiled. "You didn't know that?"

"I heard a few things."

"Keep your ear to the ground, huh?" Buddy flipped a page on the clipboard, ran his thumb down a column of numbers until he found the one he wanted, put a check beside it. "Yeah, me and Jimmy, we go way back. I saved his ass a couple times, got him out of some real messes. Jimmy never forgot that."

Lucas nodded but kept silent. Watching him.

Buddy laid the clipboard on the edge of the crate. "'Course, the thing about Jimmy is, there's always another mess. Gets like washing the bugs off your car in the summer. You go for a ride, it's covered again."

"So you figured you'd open your own business."

Buddy shrugged. "I saw an opportunity, I took it." He reached into the crate, took out one of the pistols, hefted it. "Look at this. Forty-four Ruger Redhawk. This is a man's gun, not like that other one. You pick this up, you *know* you got a gun in your hand." He reversed it, held it out to Lucas by the barrel. "Feel it."

Lucas took the gun, held it up to sight down the barrel. The front sight seemed halfway to the target.

Buddy grinned, watching him. "You don't know shit about guns, do you, Lucas?"

"No."

"Fact is, you don't give a shit. Ain't that right?"

Lucas smiled. "Not really, no."

"It's all just politics for you, huh?"

"You're saying it wrong. It's not *just* politics. It's *all* politics. Everything."

Buddy grinned, shook his head. "A man with a vision." He took the gun from Lucas's hand, laid it back in the crate. "Fact is, I agree with you. A gun like that Ruger, it's not just a product I sell. It's a whole way of thinking. A man gets one of those in his hand, he knows he don't have to take no shit from nobody. No more living in fear. Somebody gives you a problem, you can *solve* it." He waved a hand at the rows of crates stacked up across the warehouse. "That's what I'm selling here, Lucas. Self-knowledge. A man buys a gun, he's got that power. You put a gun in every man's hand, you've got a society where every man can protect his own interests." Buddy smiled. "But you ask me, that isn't even the most important thing. What matters is that you'd have a society where every man knows his own nature. A gun's just a piece of metal. It's the man *behind* the gun who's got the power, 'cause he's the one has to answer the hard questions. No morals, no choice. No choice, no power. That's what the Jesuits taught me, anyway. And they should know, huh?"

"You trying to sell me a gun, Buddy?"

Buddy laughed. "I guess it's a habit." He picked up the crowbar, pried open another crate. "But you're right. That's not why you're here." He laid the crowbar on the floor. "My point is we got a problem that won't go away."

"You mean Danny."

Buddy nodded. "But we might have to think about more than that, son. Your whole operation's lookin' pretty shaky right now. There's a point where you got to cut your losses, look to the future."

"That could get messy."

"You look at your face this morning? We *already* got a mess."

Buddy glanced back at Morrisey, who was trying on a shoulder holster from a rack at the end of the aisle. "Anyway, there's nothing wrong with a mess, you got someplace to dump it all when you're done."

Lucas followed his gaze. "Sounds like you speak from experience."

"Yeah, life's a bitch." Buddy grinned. "But you play it right, you can fuck her blind."

Jabril rode by L'Dog's building, circled the block twice, checking the parked cars, the faces on the women coming out of the neighboring buildings on their way to work. All of 'em with that first-thing-in-the-morning look in their eyes, says they got to lift the load one more time. *So where's the men?* Jabril thought to himself, though he knew. *Jail, dead, or lyin' in bed.* All those boys he'd said it to over the last couple years—*Say it, "I'm a man!"*—hearin' 'em yell it back at him, like if they said it loud enough, it might be true. *So where they now?*

He looked out the window as he drove past, saw women glancing over at him as they made their way to the bus stop. Seeing him, he knew, as one more man didn't have nowhere to be at eight in the morning, out ridin' around in his car. Like his mama, shakin' her head, tellin' him that his daddy never done nothing but "steal, deal, or get under my heel."

"This got to stop," he said, right out loud. "This got to *end.* We got too many enemies, don't need *no* damn help from us."

No respect, that was the problem. Man don't respect himself, then his woman don't respect him either. Young kid goes out, shoots some boy just like himself over nothing, it's 'cause he looks in the mirror, hates what he sees. Can't wait for the world to give you what it owes you, no way. Got to respect your*self,* make 'em see that you do.

Be a hero, work a job. Be a hero, raise your kids. Be a hero, don't pick
up no gun.

Respect.

Jabril grinned, shook his head. "Shit, listen to you, boy. You be
soundin' like Jesse pretty soon."

He circled one last time, then pulled the car up on the sidewalk
in front of L'Dog's building. He got out, glanced up and down the
block. Empty. He swung the car door closed, left it unlocked. *Respect.*
Nobody should have to lock their car in a *black* neighborhood. Got to
show a man you trust him, make him *act* like a man. He climbed the
steps to the porch, went inside, three flights of steps, that piss smell on
every landing. *Respect.* On the third floor, he stopped in front of L'Dog's
door, used his fist to pound it out, three quick beats, pause, three slow
beats. He waited a moment, did it again.

Now he heard footsteps, shuffling. They paused on the other side
of the door, silence. Jabril smiled, picturing both of them leaning in
close to the door, listening to each other.

"Hey, Dog!" he called out. "Open your damn door!"

There was a pause, like he was thinking about it, then Jabril
heard him start to open the locks. Three of them, top, bottom, and—
slowly now—middle. Then the door swung open a crack, and L'Dog
peered out at him.

"I guess you got something worth stealing, huh?" Jabril put his
hand on the middle of the door, pushed it open. L'Dog backed up a few
steps then let go of the door, stood looking at him, rubbing his eyes
like he just woke up.

"What's up, man?" L'Dog was wearing a *Shaq Attack!* T-shirt,
white underpants. He scratched at his leg absently, like his hand happened to be there.

Jabril glanced around the apartment. "Your mama home?"

"Nah, she's at work."

Jabril looked over at him, raised his eyebrows. "So how come you still in bed?"

L'Dog shrugged, turned, and walked down a hall, disappeared into one of the rooms down there. Jabril heard him urinating into the toilet, loudly, for almost a minute. He grinned, shook his head. *Young man.* Then the toilet flushed, and L'Dog came back out, one hand under his T-shirt, scratching his ribs.

"You wash your hands?"

L'Dog stared at him. "Huh?"

"I asked you did you wash your hands."

L'Dog started to say something, then just shook his head. "Damn, man. What's your *problem?*"

"My *problem* is you come by my house, like, every day, shake hands with me. Now I'm standing here, I just saw you come out of the bathroom, and all I can think is you *want* me to have some 'a your piss, 'cause it looks like you been handin' it right *to* me."

L'Dog sighed, went back into the bathroom. Jabril heard water running, then L'Dog came out, sat down on the couch, rubbed his face with both hands.

"You gonna tell me what's up?"

"Get dressed. We're takin' a ride."

L'Dog looked up at him, and Jabril saw a flicker of anxiety in his eyes. Then he shrugged, got up from the couch, and went back down the hall. Jabril looked around him at the apartment, the place clean, breakfast dishes stacked neatly on a drain board in the kitchen. There was a bookcase in the living room with some Toni Morrison, Maya Angelou, a couple Chester Himes novels in beat-up paperbacks. On the bottom shelf was a row of old *National Geographic* magazines. Jabril smiled. Only place, back when he was growing up, you could see a picture of a naked black woman. All his friends going down to the library, look at those African women, in there with pictures of monkeys and zebras. Trying to figure out how come they never had pictures from, like, Finland.

L'Dog came down the hall, pulling a T-shirt over his head. He was wearing black nylon sweatpants, a pair of black BK Knights, and a black T-shirt, about three sizes too large for him, with the words *Black Man* on the front in white letters. Jabril looked at him. "Who died?"

L'Dog glanced up at him, real quick, then made himself look away. He took a minute to tug at his shirt, getting it to lie right over his sweatpants. "What you mean?"

Jabril let his eyes travel down the length of his body. L'Dog glanced down at his clothes. He came up grinning. "Hey, shirt says it all, right?"

"Maybe." Jabril crossed to the door, opened it. "I guess we'll see."

L'Dog followed him down the stairs, hesitating in the entrance-way, giving the street a quick scan. Then he trotted down the steps, slid into the passenger seat of Jabril's car.

Jabril took his time getting in, hitching up his karate pants, then took a moment to adjust the rearview, dig in his pocket for his keys. He saw L'Dog glance around at the street, one knee jiggling like he was jazzed up.

"You in a hurry?"

L'Dog looked over at him, shrugged. "Don't know where we goin'."

Jabril started the car, eased it down off the sidewalk, then twisted around in his seat, unhurried, to check the traffic before pulling out. "Yeah, well. We all end up the same place, you know? Tag on your toe, no place to go."

"Yeah, I hear that."

Jabril glanced over at him. "You do, huh?" He reached over,

grabbed L'Dog at the waistband. L'Dog, surprised, caught his hands. "Hey, man!" But Jabril flicked his hands aside, jerked up the bottom of L'Dog's shirt, and held it there, looking down at the gun stuck in his waistband. A little black semiautomatic, .25-caliber, by the look of it. Like a woman buys to carry in her purse.

He let the shirt drop, his eyes going back to the road. They rode in silence for a while, then L'Dog said, his voice quiet, "Man's got to defend himself."

Jabril took a deep breath, let it whistle out between his teeth, slowly. "That what you think?" He turned onto St. Charles, heading down toward Canal.

"That's what I *know*."

"So you a man now, huh?"

L'Dog looked over at him, and Jabril saw anger come into his eyes. "Shit, I guess. Somebody got to be."

Jabril raised his eyebrows. He swung around Lee Circle, kept on toward Canal. "Man, oh man. They grow up *so* fast."

L'Dog looked out the window, said nothing. Jabril drove on in silence, then said, "So I guess you a *killer* now, huh?"

L'Dog looked over at him, lifted his shoulders, easy. "That's what it takes."

Jabril nodded, slowly. "Got you that little gun in your pants. Gonna whip it out, put some guy *down*."

He came up on Canal Street and eased out into the intersection, waiting his chance to make a left. L'Dog was staring out the window again, his lips moving silently, like he was talking it out to himself.

"First time I held a gun, you know what I remember thinking?" Jabril made the turn onto Canal, took it slow in the right lane, leaning forward to check out the numbers on the buildings. Then he sat back, picked up his speed. Two more blocks. "How heavy it was. Know what I mean? It's a *solid* thing, got some weight to it. Makes you feel like you got the real thing, right there in your hand. Ain't that right?"

L'Dog kept his eyes on the window, shrugged.

"That's why there's no such thing as a gun don't get used. You feel all that power in your hand, ain't a man in the world can say no to that. That bullet, it's got to *go,* only question is where." He shook his head. "Like pussy, you know? You start thinkin' 'bout it, man, that's all she wrote. You got to have it. Do anything for it. And then that woman *owns* you, man. Gun's the same way. You don't own no gun. It owns you." He slowed to check the building numbers, then sped up again. "But when I was a kid, hell, every fool had a gun." He grinned. "White man, he used to come 'round, say, 'You want a gun, boy? Hey, no problem.' Eighteen years old, man, they *made* you take a gun. Put that gun in your hands, ship your ass off to the jungle. Take you out there, snakes and bugs and shit everywhere, tell you, 'This here is your *weapon,* it will save your life.' They never call it a gun, right? It's a *weapon.* 'Your *weapon* is not a toy. Treat it with respect.' Got to clean it, oil it, polish it, carry it every day for a year, man. You out in the jungle, sun beating down on your head, it's like a hundred-fifty degrees, and you got this fuckin' *rifle* you got to carry, feels like it weighs thirty pounds. Like it's your baby, man. Don't set it down, don't let it get dirty, 'cause it *owns* you. You just a slave, man. You just a pair of legs to take that gun where it needs to go, do what those white guys up in Washington sent it there to do." He glanced over, saw that L'Dog wasn't listening, off in his head somewhere.

"You know the first time I realized that?" Jabril went on. "First week of boot camp, they take us out to the shooting range, there's this DI—that's what they call 'em, drill instructors. But I always figured it's a hint, you know? Like that's what they're there to teach you how to do, D-I." He laughed, shook his head. "But I never was much of a student, you know? Anyway, they take us out to the range with our *weapons,* there's this DI carrying an M-sixteen walkin' back and forth out there in front of the firing line, not even looking at us. For a minute, I thought he was, like, the *target.* Like one 'a those ducks in the shooting gallery, you know? But we finally get all lined up, he looks over at us, says, 'Ladies, let me introduce you to your new best friend.' And he holds up that M-sixteen in both hands, like it's this beautiful thing. Careful, you know? These guys, they get all *serious* when they touch a gun, like they want you to see how it's a big responsibility. You watch a guy work on a car, really knows what he's doing, it's all casual, right? The way he holds his tools. Or, you know, guy who plays in the NBA, holds that ball like he's easy with it, don't even hardly know it's there. Guns, they make a guy all stiff." He pulled over to the curb, next to a bus stop, waited until L'Dog looked over at him. "That's how I knew you were carrying. You all stiff. Cop takes one look at you, profiling? He's gonna slap your ass against a wall, take that gun away from you. You got that *weight*, Dog." He leaned across, touched L'Dog's forehead gently. "Right here. And it ain't you, so it must be a gun. Like some little boy, wants you to think he's a *man*."

Then he reached down, lifted L'Dog's shirt, and slid the gun out of his waistband. L'Dog watched not moving, as Jabril racked the slide, then raised the gun, leaned across the front seat, and put it against L'Dog's forehead, pushing his head back against the seat.

"Look at it," Jabril said, his voice suddenly quiet. He twisted the gun sideways, so L'Dog was looking up at it, his finger curled around the trigger. "Easy thing, huh? Just point and squeeze, game over." He reached over with his other hand, grabbed L'Dog's jaw, twisted his head so he was looking at Jabril, the gun still pressed against his forehead. "So you got a *gun*, guess that means you the *man*, huh?"

L'Dog swallowed, whispered, "No."

Jabril pursed his lips, considered him. Then he let go of L'Dog's jaw, lowered the gun. "Shit, I guess not."

L'Dog watched as Jabril ejected the magazine, racked the slide again to empty the chamber. He opened the glove box, tossed the gun inside, slipped the magazine into his pocket.

"Get out," he told L'Dog.

"What?"

"This as far as you going."

L'Dog looked out the window, frowned. A bus stop, some old ladies sitting on the bench, waiting for the bus to take 'em to work. Not one of them looking over at the car.

"What, here?"

Jabril leaned across him, opened his door. "That's right."

"You drove me up here to get a *bus?*"

Jabril shook his head, sadly. "See, that's what I'm talking about. You so busy thinkin' about that *gun* you carryin', watchin' out those Conti Street boys don't come after you for some *payback* . . ."

L'Dog looked up at him sharply, and Jabril nodded. "Uh-huh, that's right. What you think we're *talkin'* 'bout, here?" L'Dog looked down at his feet, his face tight now. "You so busy there with your little gun and your *Black Man* T-shirt, like you got to *tell* me who you are, you got no idea where we are, right?"

He reached out, rested one hand on the dashboard, pointing up the block at a storefront, a sign on the door that said—U.S. MARINE CORPS, RECRUITMENT CENTER.

L'Dog read the sign, moving his lips slightly, then looked back at Jabril. "You're shittin' me."

Jabril smiled, spread his hands. "Hey, you want to be a *killer,* man? Well, there it is."

"No way, man." L'Dog shook his head. "I ain't gonna sign up for no fuckin' Marines."

Jabril reached over, rested a hand on the glove box latch. "Okay, so you want me to drive you over to Conti Street, get it over quick?" Jabril watched L'Dog close his eyes, lay his head back against the seat like he just wanted to go to sleep, wake up when it was over. Jabril sat back. "Time to be a man, Dog. Get out of the car."

L'Dog opened his eyes, slowly. He looked over at the window, shook his head. Then he glanced back at Jabril, asked, "So what is it? Like two years?"

"That's what they tell you. But I got to warn you, man, it feels like more."

L'Dog slid out of the car, stood up. He stood there for a moment, looking over at the posters in the window, some white guy standing at attention, his chin tucked down so hard you could see the muscles like twisted wire in his neck. L'Dog turned back to lean on the car, one arm resting on the door, looking in at Jabril. "You know, I thought you was *righteous*. All that bullshit about how we got to stand up for ourselves, respect our brothers. I thought you knew the score." He glanced over at the recruitment center, shook his head. "Turns out, you just choppin' cane like the rest of 'em. Got to send me off to the *Marines*."

"You the one got to decide, Dog."

"Yeah? How you figure?"

"You the one with the gun."

"Nah." L'Dog straightened. "You got it now."

He swung the door closed, walked away. Jabril sat there for a moment, then started the engine, leaned across the seat to roll the window down. "Hey, Dog!" he called out. L'Dog turned to glance back at him. "One piece of advice?"

L'Dog turned, spread his hands wide. *Whatever.*

"Lose the shirt. You come back, we'll get you one that fits."

29

Mickie had the file on James Collette spread out on the desk in front of her, entering her notes on the events of the last two days, when she glanced up and saw Jim Dubrow come out of his office, coffee mug in his hand. He went into the coffee room, stood there for a moment, looking at the empty pot. Then he turned, glanced over at her, caught her watching.

She smiled, went back to her file. There was a silence, then she heard water running, being poured into the coffee machine, the slight *whoomp* as it hit the heating unit, began to steam. She heard him open the cabinet, take out the package of filters, put one into the machine. Then a slow trickle as the pot began to fill.

Good boy, she thought. *Just like loading your gun, isn't it?*

As the coffee dripped into the pot, Dubrow came out, walked over to Mickie's desk, stood looking down at her. "Got a minute?"

She looked up at him. "Sure. What's up?"

He pulled a chair over, sat down, then glanced down at his empty coffee mug, leaned forward to set it on her desk. "I had a talk with the FBI this morning." He looked down at the file in front of her. "About the Collette case."

"Yeah? They gonna let us see their file on Chaisson?"

He rubbed at his jaw. "You want the simple answer?"

"Shit."

He nodded. "Turns out they've got a confidential informant to protect. Somebody close to Jimmy Boudrieux. They've never been able to get this close before. Looks like they might get him this time, only the informant's getting nervous. Sounds like all this business with Chaisson, it's got them scared. Informant's worried somebody could get hurt."

Mickie sat back, looked at him. "So they've asked you to back off."

He glanced down at his coffee mug, then reached over and picked it up. Rested it on his thigh like he needed something to hang on to. It had a picture of a guy in plaid pants holding a stack of papers, his face all sad. Underneath, it said, *I'd rather be GOLFING!*

"We've got no real claim on Chaisson, Mickie. Far as I can see, he's not part of our investigation. And without Foley, we're right back where we started."

"That's why they killed Foley." Mickie leaned forward and laid a hand on the file in front of her. "We're on to something much bigger than one gun dealer here. Danny Chaisson isn't interested in this kid because he's a nice guy. He's representing Boudrieux, which means there's some serious political muscle behind this thing. We pull back now, that's exactly what they want."

Dubrow smiled. "I think you may be overestimating Chaisson's importance, Mickie. The guy over at the FBI told me they got a report from their informant that Danny's lost his place in the inner circle. Seems he showed up at one of Jimmy's garden parties yesterday, took a swing at Lucas Clay."

She looked at him, surprised. "No shit?"

Dubrow nodded. "Sounds like the guy's coming apart at the seams. He's angry, unstable. Might explain why Jimmy cut him loose."

"I saw him this morning. He looked perfectly calm." Mickie glanced down at the file, frowned. "Anyway, that still doesn't explain why he's looking for the kid."

Dubrow sighed, stood up wearily. "He's out of a job, Mickie.

Maybe he's just looking for something to do." He gave a slight smile. "Or maybe he's got other interests."

She felt the blood come into her face, looked away toward the window. Christ, raining again.

He picked up his chair and slid it back against the wall. "At any rate, I'm pulling you off this matter. There's better ways for you to spend your time. Let's get you back down to the courthouse, see if we can start getting a line on some of the other dealers selling to these kids." He glanced down at the empty mug in his hand, then over at the coffee room. "You think that coffeemaker's finished brewing by now?"

She looked at the file spread before her. "Shake the basket," she told him numbly. "Or it'll drip when you take the pot out to pour it."

"Thanks, I'll do that."

She watched him walk away, then glanced over at the agent at the next desk, who cleared his throat and picked up his phone as if he hadn't heard a word. She watched him dial, then glanced at her watch, and said, "It's ten-fourteen, Dave. And it's raining."

He looked over at her, then slowly reached over, hung up the phone. "Never hurts to stay on top of these things."

"I'll remember that." She closed the file, slid it into a bottom drawer, shoved it closed with her knee. Then she stood up and picked up her mug. "Guess I'll get some coffee."

She stood beside the sink, stirring the powdered creamer into her coffee, watching it swirl into a smooth brown. *So how come you can't stir it backward, make it come apart?* She could remember her physics teacher talking about that in high school. Some law. Burnt toast doesn't unburn, it just cools. And that's why the universe will end up cold and dead.

She'd gotten a B+ on her physics final, then gone out and gotten drunk, lost her virginity in the backseat of a Camaro to a football player named Jim Fallows. The next morning her neck was so stiff that she couldn't turn her head, and the only physics she could remember was something about not eating burnt toast. The last she'd heard, Jim Fallows had gotten fat and sold industrial refrigeration units in Phoenix.

Maybe he's right, she told herself. *Maybe there's just no case.* She laid the spoon in the sink, carried her coffee back to her desk. *You're disappointed because you thought you could break a big one, show 'em what you can do.* She pictured Danny's face as he watched her drive away. *Hell, you can't even figure out if you're interested in the guy. Maybe you were just excited about making the case.*

She looked over at the window, watched the rain coming down. Tried to imagine herself standing under an oak tree in Audubon Park, shivering, hair stuck flat to her forehead. *Crazy.*

When her phone rang, she was almost relieved. She reached over, picked it up, and said, "Vega."

"Mickie? It's Danny Chaisson. You free?"

She looked at the phone, its tangle of cord and one unblinking light. "How'd you get this number?"

There was a pause, and she could almost see his smile. "I called up all the federal law enforcement agencies in town and asked for you. When I got to ATF, they transferred me."

She rubbed at her eyes. "So what's on your mind, Danny?"

"You look outside lately?"

"Yeah, it's raining."

"Feel like taking that walk?"

She was silent for a moment, glanced up at Dubrow's office. The door was closed. She took a sip of her coffee. It was already getting cold.

"Tell me where to meet you."

Five left, back through zero to twenty-four right. Then just a flick of the wrist to seventeen left, and . . .

C o l d
S t e e l
R a i n

"Shit." Maura crouched in front of the safe in the closet of her father's study, checked the slip of paper in her hand. She'd found it taped to the back of the top drawer of Danny's dresser, peeled it off, then waited to see if he'd notice. When he didn't, she figured it was only there for an emergency. Like the day the FBI came, and somebody had to empty the safe. So she put it in her wallet, hung on to it. *For a rainy day.*

Only, every day is a rainy day in New Orleans. And men are shits. And it wasn't *fucking* working. She spun the dial back to the right a few times and tried it again, more slowly. Then she slammed her hand down on the safe in frustration, stood up.

Fucking Danny. Figures nobody'd trust him with the combination, she thought, bitterly. *Probably just give it away, first time Helen smiled at him.*

Once she'd watched her father take six thick packs of bills out of the safe, toss them on his desk for Danny to pack into a gym bag. Danny counted it out, $120,000, like it was no big deal. And she'd seen more in the safe. Enough for a girl to just fly away, find a windy beach in Morocco, turn into one of those strange American women with a bitter mouth and tangled hair who scare the local children. She smiled. *A girl's gotta have a dream.* And there was nothing here to stop her. Not now.

Except she couldn't get the fucking safe open.

She looked at her father's desk, then went over to it, tried the drawers. Locked. She grabbed a silver letter opener from his desk set, jabbed it into the crack between the top drawer and the frame, splintering the wood. *Sorry, Dad. Take it out of my fucking allowance.*

She slid the blade along the center of the drawer until she found the lock, then worked it back and forth, leaning her weight on the drawer, until she felt the lock give. She jerked the drawer out. Paper clips, pens, a pocket calculator, an extra set of house keys, an address book, loose papers. She dug around in the drawer, then said, "Fuck this," and pulled it out, dumped it on top of the desk. Sorted through all the junk, getting a sudden flash of what it would be like when her father died, a whole house full of secrets to dig through, his stuff *and* her mother's, all those sealed boxes he'd shoved into storage after she'd died, locked the door like she'd just gone away for a while, would be coming back from the hospital someday to unpack her things. As if the whole house had just been waiting for her to come back, waiting for its life to start up again.

Jesus, she thought. *Not me. I'm gone.*

Then she froze, looking down at the pile of junk in front of her. She reached down, moved some papers aside, and picked up a photograph in a metal frame. Her mother stood at the center of a group, smiling in soft sunlight. Next to her, Maura saw herself, wearing a black graduation robe, her own smile wary. Then Danny and Helen, Danny dressed in street clothes, his own graduation over, there to watch the girls' high school go through the same ceremony, except they each carried a candle, like they were taking vows as nuns. She turned, carried the photograph over to the window, held it up to the light. Jesus, so *young.* Just three kids, smiling those embarrassed smiles, like they knew this one would go into the photo albums, come back to haunt them someday. Only her mother's smile was real. Her eyes looked so happy, so full of hope.

Six months later she was dead.

Maura lowered the photograph, looked out the window. Her father sat at one of the tables under the glass roof of the pool house. Rain dripped from the trees, splattered on the patio tiles, but Jimmy always went outside when he wanted to talk these days, so he'd carry his coffee out to one of the metal tables he'd had set up out there, listen to the rain pounding on the glass roof, hoping that no federal law enforcement agencies could pick up what he was saying over the noise. Now he had a guy in a St. Bernard sheriff's deputy uniform out there, sitting there with his arms folded across his chest, listening as Jimmy explained something to him. A briefcase lay on the table between them.

Maura turned and went back over to the desk, dropped the photograph on top of the pile of junk from the drawer. She pulled open the bottom drawers, but they were full of files; each file had the name of a state legislator typed neatly on the tab. She shoved the drawers closed, angrily. *Just fly, girl. Fly far, far away.*

She looked over at the safe. *But first you've got to feather your nest.*

"It's a matter of trust," Jimmy Boudrieux was saying, leaning forward to stab the air with his finger. "A man's got to know he can trust the people around him. Without that, he's got nothing."

Uh-huh, Ray Morrisey thought, smiling. *Only some of us got more nothing than others.*

What he had today was a briefcase. And, he'd realized as he drove away from Buddy's warehouse, that meant he had something else, something rare in his experience: a choice. He could carry it back to the evidence room, sign the guns in as unclaimed property, like Buddy told him, or he could find a way to *use* them. And one thing he was beginning to figure out, hanging around with Buddy, was there was more than one way to use a gun.

"See, your pal Buddy's a real ambitious guy," Jimmy was telling him. Sitting back now, sipping at his coffee, like they were just killing time until the rain quit. "Last couple years, he's into this property development. That's his big thing now. He wants out of guns, sees the business as peaking. We passed these concealed weapons laws, everybody ran out, bought a handgun, so Buddy figures they're approaching market saturation. Nowhere to go but down. And then there's the product liability suits. You imagine what could happen, the liability lawyers ever win one of those? Hell, if you can get five billion dollars from a car company, just 'cause it might explode in an accident? Imagine what you could get, you put some guy makes handguns in front of a jury, line up a couple kids in wheelchairs to talk about how it felt when they got shot." Jimmy grinned, shook his head. "Can't blame Buddy, he wants to get out. Only he needs somebody to buy him out. He's going public in November, can't afford any bad publicity. This whole business, it makes him nervous. He's looking around for a way out, somebody to take the fall." Jimmy looked down at the briefcase, raised his eyebrows. "Could be that's you, Ray."

"Yeah, that thought occurred to me, too." Morrisey shifted in his chair, glanced back at the house. "Your boy Lucas brought those guns back, I figured we'd just go out, toss 'em in the river. Make sure nobody gets their hands on 'em, ties us to Foley. But Buddy, he wants me to take 'em back to the evidence room, get the paper cleaned up. Shit, I take these back to the evidence room, they got to run 'em through the computer. Take a couple days, but they'll trace 'em back to Foley. Next thing I know, they got some questions for me." He shrugged. "Not like I couldn't bullshit my way out of it. Tell 'em I pulled into a minimart, saw some jigs standing around, they took off running, left the briefcase behind. Hell, they'd believe that, my record. Only, do I want my name in this thing, I can help it? And anyway, I figure I'm dead by then. Buddy gets me to put the guns back in the evidence room, so it's my name on the papers, then drives me out in the woods, puts a bullet in my head. Anybody comes looking for me, they'll think I got nervous, took off. End of story."

Jimmy nodded. "Sounds like Buddy's got his own ideas about who walks away clean on this one."

"Uh-huh." Morrisey leaned forward. "See, but then I got to thinking about this whole deal. Like why did Foley call *you* to try and cut a deal on this thing. That don't make much sense to me. Hell, everybody in town knows you and Buddy are tight."

Jimmy studied him for a moment, then shrugged. "I guess he thought I could straighten things out for him with Buddy."

"Yeah, maybe. But that got me to thinking. How come Foley put in a bid on those guns, anyway? The guy never bought guns from us. You gotta have a federal dealer's license to move 'em, and Foley, his business was strictly under the table. He buys guns at a public auction, it's only a matter of time until the ATF shows up, asks to see his license. That's something a guy like Foley don't need. Only, I did some asking around, and what I hear, he *already* had the ATF on his ass, some colored boys ready to testify he sold 'em guns. So how come this guy who's got trouble with the ATF goes out of his way to dig himself in deeper? And if he's gonna buy guns at auction, why's he put in a bid on those four guns? Most dealers, they put in bids on forty, fifty guns. What's the point buying *four?*" Morrisey sat back, spread his hands. "You see why I'm confused?"

Jimmy was silent for a moment, looked over at the rain falling out on the patio. "Interesting questions. You come up with any answers?"

"Just the obvious ones. Like somebody *told* him to go buy those guns, so he'd have something to cut a deal with. But that'd mean somebody got this whole fuckin' mess started just to put a squeeze on Buddy." Morrisey grinned. "Not that I'd mind, if it wasn't me got stuck cleaning it up. But I guess this guy, he'd need a pretty damn good reason to do something like that, huh? Get all these people killed? Must be a *damn* good reason."

Jimmy sipped at his coffee. "Let me tell you a story. When I was a kid, up in Abita Springs? We used to go swim in the river out back of my house. My dad hung a tire swing from a tree out there. You had to climb up on a branch, get a good swing off it to get out to the deep water. Drop off it too soon, you'd land on a sandbank, break your leg. Anyway, one day, this kid from down the street, Rickie Avery, he's ten years old, weighs like two hundred pounds, gets up there on the branch. Only kid I ever knew who *flossed*. Anyway, he's up there, got the tire between his legs, he's getting ready to swing, and suddenly the branch he's standing on breaks. Just snaps right off. Sounds like a rifle going off. Rickie, he's not ready to jump yet, up there trying to get the tire just right under his butt. So he's only hanging on with one hand, and when the branch goes, we see his feet fly straight up, the tire starts spinning like crazy, and Rickie, he loses his grip. Next thing we know, he's way out there over the water, hanging upside down from the tire, spinning." Jimmy paused, took another sip of his coffee. "So now he's stuck. He's too fat, so he can't pull himself up. And he didn't get a good swing, so he's hanging out there over the shallow water. He drops off, he's gonna land on his fuckin' head. You see the problem?"

"Uh-huh." Morrisey grinned. "So how'd he get down?"

"Didn't. Just hung there, screaming. My cousin ran over to his house, got his father. He came out with a ladder, got Rickie down. Then he took out his knife, cut the rope. No more tire swing."

Morrisey waited for him to say more, but he didn't, just sat there drinking his coffee, looking out at the rain. "So, Buddy's the fat kid?"

Jimmy looked over at him, frowned. "No, you're the fat kid."

"*I'm* the fat kid?"

"That's right."

Morrisey sat back, confused. "How am I the fat kid?"

"You're out there, dangling. Can't make up your mind. You got a feeling Buddy's setting you up, so you start sniffing around, come over here, see if you can cut a deal with me." Jimmy shrugged. "It's up to you, Ray. Hang on where you are, or let go. Swing or drop. You got to make the call."

Morrisey glanced down at the briefcase, then back up at Jimmy. He smiled. "Just tryin' to make sure I don't land on my head."

"That's all any of us are trying to do, Ray. We're all hanging by our ankles, here. Takes a smart guy to figure out how to get down

without cracking his skull." He leaned forward, set his coffee cup
down on the table.

Then he smiled. "Are you smart, Ray?"

"You sure about this?"

Maya nodded. "It's okay. He just wants to talk."

Acorsi leaned forward, looked down the row of cars parked along
the breakwater at the West End boat launch. At the far end, Jabril
Saunders sat behind the wheel of a dark blue Acura, gazing out across
the marina at some sailboats tied up along the pier, barely visible
through the falling rain.

"We could haul him downtown, he could talk there."

"He called me, Tom. That's because he trusts me to handle this
right. If he's got something to tell us, he's only going to say it here."
She reached out, laid a hand on his arm. "Just sit tight. It won't take
long."

Acorsi watched her get out of the car, pull her raincoat tighter,
and walk down to the Acura. Jabril reached over, unlocked her door,
and she got in beside him.

"Shit." Acorsi leaned across the front seat, rolled the window
down. He couldn't hear a thing over the rain beating on the roof.
Jabril had the windows rolled up, and the windows quickly began to
fog. Acorsi saw him reach forward, turn on the air-conditioning, but
it didn't help much. He could just make out Maya's face, turned
slightly this way as she listened. Every few minutes she'd nod, and
then Jabril would go on, looking out at the sailboats every now and
then, as if checking to make sure they were still there. Maya's eyes
never left his face.

She doesn't look like a cop, Acorsi realized. *More like a lawyer, somebody on his side.*

He'd heard about Jabril Saunders, knew some cops who'd give

their right nut to come up with something on the guy they could make stick. White cops, mostly. Guys in their fifties who remembered how he'd walked away from a murder rap back in the seventies, a *cop* killing, for Christ's sake, but also a case so circumstantial that even the conservative white judge who heard it finally lost patience, chewing out the prosecutors in full view of a room full of reporters. In the end, Jabril Saunders had walked, and three homicide detectives lost their shields in the internal investigations that followed. But that didn't stop the cops from watching him *damn* close. Not guilty ain't the same as innocent, right? All you had to do was look closely at Jabril's new car, his recording studio, and his entourage of young black boys, you could *see* that the guy was dirty. The only trouble was proving it. Twenty years, they'd been watching him, and they still hadn't worked up a case that a judge wouldn't laugh out of court.

Ghost chasers, Acorsi thought. *Every cop's got a case he can't drop. After a while, the past starts to eat you alive.*

Only now Jabril was pushing his way into a gang killing. Calling Maya at home, claiming he had information he'd give only to her. And Maya'd taken it seriously, treated the guy like somebody they should listen to carefully.

He saw Maya get out of the car, come over to him. She leaned in the open window, rain dripping off the hood of her raincoat. "He's going to give us the boy."

Acorsi raised his eyebrows. "Just like that?"

She looked over at the rain speckling the surface of the water. "He claims the gun was planted. Somebody called him the night of the killings over on Claiborne, late, told him where to find it. Only he got suspicious, sent the boy instead."

"You buy it?"

She shrugged. "We get the kid, that's what counts."

Acorsi glanced over at Jabril. He was staring out at the rain, not moving. "Any chance this guy's the shooter? Made the boy take the rap for him?"

"He was at Tug's when the shooting happened. About eighty people saw him."

Acorsi was silent for a moment. Then he reached down, started the car. "Okay, let's go."

"He said just me, Tom."

Acorsi shook his head. "No way. You don't go anywhere with this guy without backup. Don't even think about it."

"He's right, Tom." Maya looked down at her hands. "This boy, he'll be scared enough if it's just me. But with you there, he'll do what he's learned to do around white men his whole life. He'll keep his mouth shut, eyes on the floor. I've got a chance of getting him to talk to me. But only if I go alone."

Acorsi looked over at Jabril, who hadn't moved. "You really trust this guy?"

She raised her eyes, met his gaze. "I believe him when he says he'll take me to the boy." Then she smiled. "We grew up in the same part of town, Tom. That's why he called me. You understand?"

He was silent for a moment, then he nodded. She reached across the seat, touched his arm, gently. Then she turned, walked away through the rain.

L'Dog sat in a chair across the desk from the Marine recruiting sergeant, a white guy with a face like a half ton of gravel falling out of a truck, staring at a glossy brochure with pictures of Marines standing at attention, the brass on their uniforms shining, wading through a swamp in combat gear, gathered around a computer screen in a classroom, as the guy told him about all the educational opportunities available in the Corps, job training, electronics or computers, maybe, not to mention a sense of achievement and self-discipline that would make him attractive to any employer. L'Dog stared at the men in the pictures, the pride in their faces, thought, *Not me, man. No fuckin' way.*

He realized that the sergeant had finished what he was saying and was staring at him, waiting for him to respond. L'Dog nodded, shrugged. "Yeah, sounds good."

"Maybe you have some questions I could answer."

L'Dog tried to think of a question. Nothing much came to mind, but the guy seemed to expect it, so he said, "So, I join up, am I, like, *in?* Do I have to take a test, or something?"

The guy shifted in his chair. "There's a basic literacy test, yes. But that's nothing you need to worry about. What I tell people is, if you can read the posters, you can handle the test."

L'Dog looked up at the posters, nodded. "But that takes a while, right? I mean, it's not like I sign up today, I'm on the bus."

"Well, no. Normally, once I've processed the paperwork, we assign recruits an induction date. Could be a few weeks, or as much as a couple months." He smiled. "You could have the rest of the summer to hang out with your friends, if that's what you mean."

"Yeah, that's what I mean." L'Dog stood up, the brochure still in his hand. He looked down at it, then folded it once, stuffed it into his pocket. "Listen, I got to think about this, you know?"

The recruiter sat back and smiled, spread his hands. "Hey, I understand. It's a big decision. You've got to ask yourself, 'Can I handle it? Am I man enough to be a Marine?'"

"Uh-huh. So, you know, thanks."

"No problem. Come back when you've made up your mind. We'll see if there's a Marine in you."

Outside, L'Dog paused on the sidewalk, pulled the brochure out of his pocket, dropped it into a trash can. *Man, they don't let up. Sell you Nikes, sell you Miller time when you want to kick back. You let 'em, they sell you your own dick.* He shook his head, walking away. *Guy look at you, his*

mouth say "Pride," but his eyes say "Nigger." Be a Marine! We show you how
to walk like a white man!

He caught a bus downtown, got off on Canal, walked into a couple stores, then back out again, thinking. *Can't go home, right? Can't*
stay in town. He had a couple cousins in Chicago, came down sometimes for Mardi Gras. Maybe he could stay with them a while till
things cooled down. He stepped into the doorway of a store, dug his
wallet out of his back pocket, thumbed through the bills. Eighteen
dollars. Go pick up your car, drive straight through, you'd need, what?
Like three tanks of gas, maybe? Plus food. He had about 400 bucks
wrapped in a pair of socks in a drawer back in his room, and his mama
kept two twenty-dollar bills folded up in the toe of a shoe in her closet
for emergencies. *So, this is an emergency, right?* He'd leave her a note, say
he'd pay her back when he got to Chicago, made a little cash. Okay, so
she'd cry. That's what mamas do. Couple months, she'd understand.

He walked up to his bus stop, sat on a bench, waiting. *Get in*
there, grab your stuff, toss it in the car, and you're gone. He tried to imagine how he'd feel when he drove out of New Orleans, city streets turning to bayou when you cross the parish line, then up past Lake
Maurepaus, swamp grass spreading out on either side of you, like the
whole city was just a dream, birds and alligators out there waiting to
come take it all back. It always gave him a weird feeling, driving up
there, a twist of fear in his stomach, seeing all that empty bayou right
there, so close. Animals, man. Dumb-ass Cajuns with shotguns, no
teeth.

But the road? Beautiful. Strung out there ahead of the car,
rolling away up north, to places he'd never even *imagined.* Man, that's
freedom. Get away from Jabril, those Conti Street boys, all that shit,
start a whole different life. Or damn, just turn west on I-10 up there
by Hammond, head on out to California, see what that's like. He
started smiling at the thought of it, looking forward to it, even. Finding out which life he'd grab for, not thinking about it as he drove out

of the city, just get up there where the highway splits off, see which way the car wants to go.

The bus came and he got on, grabbed a seat in the back. Always made Jabril laugh, the way he liked to sit back there. "All that fightin' for your *rights* we done," he'd say, shaking his head. "Rosa Parks got herself thrown in *jail.* Now you want to go sit in the *back* of the bus? Hell, grab you a seat right up front, show 'em you know where you belong."

L'Dog, shrugging, had told him, "Man, I *like* sittin' in the back." Spread out, lay your arms across the whole backseat, nobody behind you, lookin' at you. Hey, back's okay. Go check out a school bus, see which seats the kids fight over. Back's cool. Back's the place to be.

He started feeling nervous when he made the transfer, the bus rolling down Jackson, people he knew out on the street, hangin' on street corners, shootin' hoops up at the playground. How could he expect to get out of there without being seen? And then, next moment, he'd wonder if he really wanted to. Stick around, keep your head down, what's the big deal? These are your people, right?

Then he remembered Jabril pointing that gun at his head, his mind goin' from that to Sugar Bear stickin' that gun out the car's window, those Conti Street boys stumbling as the bullets blew their bodies apart. *Nah, man, you got to go.* He got up, eased along the aisle to the door as the bus came to his stop. He glanced up the street as he got off, wishing he had his gun. Fuckin' Jabril, man. He kept his head down, eyes movin', checkin' everything out, and walked the last two blocks *fast,* man. Like Carl Lewis, he got the runs and no place to go.

He started to relax when he reached his building, sayin' to himself, *Be quick, now. Just go in, grab the money, some clothes, and get the fuck out of here.* Wondering, now, if he could afford the time to call up one of his boys, get him to come over, check out his car before he left the apartment, make sure nobody's waiting for him there.

He stole a last glance over his shoulder at the playground behind him, jerked the metal fire door open, and slid into the stairway. Held up there, in the shadows, for a minute, listening. But there wasn't nothing to hear, just old Mr. Rawlings's TV goin', like usual. Some game show, where you got to solve a puzzle, win a new car. *Shit.* Only puzzle you got to solve, this world, is out there on the street. Win you more than a new car, too. And you lose, man, that's it. You out the game for good.

He started up the stairs, thinking about should he leave his mama a note, tell her where he's goin', or just call her when he gets there. Deciding, yeah, he'd wait. Have to start actin' like a *man,* do things his own way. Call your mama every couple weeks, tell her the good stuff. All that other shit, she don't need to know it, right? Digging his keys out of his pocket as he came up on the landing, started up the last flight to his floor, where a kid was sitting on the step, playin' on a GameBoy. L'Dog squeezed past him and went over to his door, started to unlock it when he heard the kid stand up and say, "You L'Dog?"

L'Dog turned, looked over at him. Little kid, eight or nine, wearing a T-shirt with a picture of the Tasmanian Devil, and the words *I'M A LITTLE DEVIL!* printed across the chest. L'Dog grinned, shook his head. He'd had the same shirt when he was little. Loved that shirt, too. Wore it *out,* man. 'Cause that's what he was, a little devil, always gettin' up to all manner of hell. Just like Taz.

"Who wants to know?"

"I got a message. Guy told me to give it to L'Dog, not nobody else."

"What's the message?"

"You L'Dog?"

L'Dog sighed, nodded. "Ain't nobody else. Now what you got to say to me?"

The kid reached back, pulled a .38 revolver from the back of his sweatpants, pointed it at L'Dog's chest. "This for my brother."

And he squeezed the trigger.

30

"You sure know how to show a girl a good time."

Danny glanced over at Mickie, gave a tight smile. They were standing under an oak tree, watching as a heavy rain fell on a small crowd gathered around an open grave. Mickie recognized Martelle Collette standing between two men who held on to her arms, supporting her. The men held their black umbrellas over her so the rain dripped around her, a woman swallowed up in darkness. Someone wailed as the small coffin was lowered into the grave, but Martelle stood silently, watching it happen, as if she'd simply turned to stone.

Like a fly caught in a web, Mickie thought. *Eventually it just stops struggling.*

They were standing about thirty yards away, back by the road with its row of parked cars. A police car stood nearby, two uniformed officers like shadows behind the glass, watching.

"So James didn't come."

Danny shook his head. His face looked empty, as if all the life had been drained out of it. Seeing him that way gave her a desperate feeling, like she had to keep talking, stop him from vanishing on her completely. But then she'd glance over at the crowd around the graves and the words died in her mouth.

So they stood there, silent, as the black preacher finished sending the boy to God, and the men each took a turn tossing a shovel full of dirt into the grave. Then the crowd broke up, everybody trying not to look like they were hurrying to get out of the rain as they made their way back to the cars. But the boy's mother wouldn't leave; she stood there next to the grave, refusing to be coaxed away. The preacher put his arm around her shoulders, whispering in her ear, but when he tried gently to turn her away from the grave, she shook her head violently, broke free. The preacher spoke quietly to one of the men, who hurried away to the cars. He opened the rear door of one, spoke briefly with someone inside, and a tiny old woman got out, hobbled back across the wet grass. She grasped Martelle's shoulders roughly, spoke to her with shrill words Mickie couldn't make out, and with a quick shove, turned her away from the grave. The men caught Martelle's arms, led her away. But as they approached the cars she suddenly gave a cry, broke away from them, tried to turn back. One of the men bent down and gathered her up in his arms, carried her sobbing to the car.

Danny stood there, not moving until the last car had driven away. At last Mickie reached out, touched his arm.

"You okay?"

He was silent for a moment, then nodded slightly. "You ever feel like you spend your life doing the right thing for the wrong reason?"

"You mean coming here?"

"Among other things."

They walked back to his car. Her knee was stiff, and she limped slightly. She felt him slow down, waiting for her. The rain was hitting the street so hard it bounced.

For a moment, after they got in the car, Mickie remembered the first time they'd sat together in her car outside the boy's apartment, talking as the rain beat on the windshield. She'd felt a connection between them that time, like a spark jumping between two copper wires. Feeling, as she realized it, like there was something bright and sharp coiled in her belly, something that had been there for a while without her knowing it, getting tighter, until—suddenly—it was ready to unwind.

It wasn't like that now. Danny sat looking at his hands resting on the wheel, like they were strange to him. Rain dripped from his face, but he didn't wipe it away. Just sat there staring at his hands. She kept quiet, figured he'd say something when he was ready. But after a few minutes, he just shook his head and reached down to start the car.

"Where should I drop you?"

"You sure you want to be alone right now?"

He looked over at her. "This part of your job? You waiting around for me to crack, tell you everything I know?"

"That's not fair."

He was silent for a moment, gazing out at the rain. "You're right. I'm sorry." He put the car in gear. "You want to get some coffee?"

She reached up and shoved her wet hair back off her face. "Sure, you don't mind being seen with me like this."

That got a smile. He looked over at her and started to say something. Then he caught himself, shook his head.

"What?"

"Nothing. Let's go get that coffee."

She reached over, pulled the emergency brake. "You're not getting off that easy. What were you going to say?"

"You really want to know?" He raised his eyes, met her gaze. "I was going to say, 'You make the rain look beautiful.'"

She was silent. Neither of them moved. Then, slowly, he reached over, took her face in his hands. Like he was framing it. For a moment, he just looked at her. And then, just when she'd started thinking he was going to let the moment pass, he kissed her. Gently, taking his time with it. Something they'd both been waiting for, were in no hurry to get past. He tasted like tears.

He sat back, smiled; his face clearer now, something bright there. "I've changed my mind."

"Yeah?" She wiped the rain from her forehead. Her skin felt hot. "About what?"

"Let's not go out for coffee." He reached down, released the emergency brake. "I've got a better idea."

"You did all this?"

Jabril shrugged. "Got some help. Lotta people in the business made donations, we got most of the work done at night, off the books. You get people workin' together, they can make things happen."

They were standing in the sound booth of the recording studio on St. Andrew Street, Maya reaching down to run her hand over the rows of switches on the soundboard. Beyond the glass, Greg Nowles sat on a folding chair with a guitar on his lap, trying to show James Collette some basic chords. The boy sat beside him, watching his hands. When Nowles passed the guitar over to him, he took a minute getting his fingers set, then strummed at it tentatively. The guitar looked huge in his hands.

Jabril reached down, hit a switch, and said, "Greg, we here. You ready?"

Nowles looked up at the window, saw Maya standing beside him. "It's just the two of you?"

"Yeah, no problem."

Nowles glanced over at the boy. He was still trying to get his fingers into the right position, like Nowles had shown him, so the strings wouldn't buzz. Caught up in it, something new he was learning. His forehead all wrinkled up, concentrating.

"Okay, c'mon in."

The boy looked up from the guitar when they came in, watched Jabril get two more chairs from the stack over by the wall, bring them over. His eyes came to rest on Maya's face, watchful.

"Bear, this is Detective Thomas," Jabril said. "She'll treat you fair, but you got to be straight with her. You know what I'm sayin'?"

He nodded, once. Both hands resting on top of the guitar, like he was getting ready to sing them a song.

Jabril sat back, looked at Maya. "Let's get this done."

She nodded, turned to the boy. "James, I've got to ask you some questions. Okay?"

"Yeah, I guess."

"How 'bout we start with what happened to those boys over on Conti Street the other night. Think you could tell me about that?"

She saw the boy shoot a glance over at Jabril, then at Nowles, the two men sitting there silently, watching him. Then Jabril leaned forward, and said softly, "Time to stand up, Bear, take responsibility for what you done." Nowles nodding now, slightly, as the boy's eyes went back and forth between them. "Time to be a man."

"Don't ever ask me to marry you."

Danny made the turn onto St. Charles. He glanced over at her. "Yeah? Why not?"

Mickie dug a crumpled handkerchief out of her bag, used it to wipe her face. "What would we tell the kids, they ask about our first date?"

He smiled. "You never made out in a graveyard when you were a kid?"

"That what kids do in New Orleans?"

"I know a couple guys got laid in a graveyard. We like to take good care of our dead. Gives 'em something to think about."

Talking about it, she realized, to keep herself from thinking about what she was doing. *Your job,* she thought. But even that wasn't true anymore. Dubrow had pulled her off the case. She looked out the window, wanting the car to keep moving so she wouldn't have to decide what to do when they got there. Looking at the trees, the unbelievable green. Then she heard herself say, "So where was your first time?"

He looked over at her. "We're really gonna talk about this now?"

"Breaks the ice."

"Yeah?" He grinned, shook his head. "Can't be much ice left, the way we're going."

"So? Let's hear it."

He pulled up at a light, opened a window slightly to let some fresh air in. "Her dad's boat. We spread out some cushions on the deck."

"Sounds romantic."

"Not really. It was parked in their driveway."

She laughed. "Perfect."

"So what about you?"

She smiled, nodded toward the windshield. "You got a green light."

He took a moment to get the car in gear, but finally got them moving again, out along St. Charles, past the big old houses. A streetcar rattled past them, heading the other way. Tourists wiping at the windows to clear the fog, get a look at old New Orleans. He glanced over at her.

"So? Your turn."

"Backseat of a Camaro."

He smiled. "Sounds painful."

"Would've been fine, except there was no place to put my head."

"Probably just as well. You're doing it in the backseat of a Camaro, your head just gets in the way." He looked over at her. "So what's the first time you enjoyed?"

"The girls' shower room, in high school."

He looked at her, raised his eyebrows. "Yeah?"

"Don't get excited. It's not how it sounds. I ran cross-country, and my boyfriend was on the basketball team. He used to stay behind after practice and wait for me to come back from these eight-mile runs. I'd grab a shower, get changed, then we'd walk home together. One night I got lost on some roads out in the country, ended up running like twelve miles. By the time I got back, everybody else had left."

"Except your boyfriend."

"He was shooting baskets in the gym. Anyway, when we realized we were alone . . ."

"One thing led to another?"

"So to speak."

"You weren't tired, you just ran twelve miles?"

She laughed. "I was sixteen. Anyway, I ran every day. I was in great shape."

Danny took a deep breath, let it out slow. "Jesus." He gave a laugh. "You better buckle up, 'cause we may have an accident any minute."

She smiled at him, pulled the belt across her lap, snapped it into the latch. "I'm ready."

Tom Acorsi watched the Mustang pull up outside Danny's house. Mickie Vega got out and came around to stand next to Danny as he locked it up. She let her hand rest on his arm, then they started up the walk toward the front door.

Undercover work, Acorsi thought, smiled. *ATF's come a long way since Waco.*

He got out of his car, saw Danny start to unlock the door as Acorsi crossed the street and called out, "Hey, Danny!"

They turned to look at him, and he smiled, seeing the same look on both their faces. Like kids, when you walk in the room, trying to shove the beer cans behind the couch. Neither of them said a word. Acorsi walked up the sidewalk, taking his time, no hurry in the world. Car keys dangling from his fingers.

"You got a minute, Danny? There's something I want to show you."

31

The car stood in mud up to its doors in an empty lot under the approach ramp for the Mississippi River Bridge. Several police cars and an ambulance had pulled up as close as they could get, and the area around the car was strung with yellow tape. An overturned grocery cart lay a short distance away, and a sheet of plastic spread out across two wooden chairs to make a crude tent. The ground was covered with broken wine bottles. Acorsi held the tape for Danny and Mickie to duck under, and they walked over to where a group of men stood around the car. Danny saw Marty Seagraves among them. They all turned to watch as Danny approached.

Wendell Keyes lay stretched out across the front seat of the car. He'd been shot once in the head. A handgun lay in a puddle of blood on the floor beside his hand. His wallet lay open in the mud a few feet away, marked by a strip of yellow tape.

"There's some homeless guys who hang out down here. We think they found him this morning, emptied out his wallet." Acorsi squatted, gesturing to the entry wound in the right side of Keyes's head. "One gunshot in his right temple so it looks like suicide. " He looked up at Danny. "You recognize him?"

Danny looked down at Keyes's face, his eyes staring off toward the river. "Yeah, I recognize him." He straightened up, looked away across the field of mud, broken glass sparkling faintly. Traffic whined on the roadway above his head. "It's my father."

Acorsi stared at him. "What is that? A *joke*?"

"He means they found his father like this," Mickie said quietly. Her eyes never left Danny's face. "Somebody's got a sense of humor."

Nobody said anything for a moment, then Acorsi took a pair of rubber gloves from his pocket and slid them on. He reached in the passenger door, lifted the gun out of the puddle of blood on the floor. He straightened up, wiped the blood off the slide. *STAR,* it said, the words etched into the dark metal. *B. Echeverria, Eibar, Espana.* There was a scar across the base of the grip, like somebody had slipped with a screwdriver.

Danny turned, walked away a few steps back toward the cop's car. He looked at the plastic tent that the homeless guys who lived under here had set up. It didn't look like it would keep the rain out for long.

This town, nothing does.

Danny heard the door to the interrogation room open behind him, stood unmoving as it swung slowly shut. He stood before a large window, watching Jimmy Boudrieux lean back in his chair, have a good laugh at something the assistant commissioner of police had just said. Danny had shut the sound off ten minutes ago, when the assistant commissioner had taken over from Acorsi, and now he simply watched. Beyond the glass, Helen smiled, glanced down at the legal pad on the table in front of her, staying focused even now.

"You hear?" Acorsi came over to stand beside him. "He just asked would we be done in time for him to make some fund-raiser he's got scheduled out in Saint Bernard."

Danny nodded, said nothing.

"We've got no evidence, Danny. He never touched the briefcase, so we can't connect him to the guns." Acorsi shrugged. "Maybe the FBI can get him on corruption, if you testify. But there's no homicide case."

Danny's face was tight. "What about Lucas."

"We got him in the other room. Hasn't said a word."

"He had the briefcase in his hand. You can prove that."

Acorsi was silent for a moment, slid his hands in his pockets. "Well, we've got your testimony . . ."

Danny looked over at him. "But that's not enough."

"Danny, I don't make the rules. I've got to take the case to the D.A. Something like this, you're going after Jimmy Boudrieux, they won't touch it without some corroborating evidence." He looked at Danny. "You know how it works, Danny. They get you on the stand, they'll go after your credibility."

Danny looked at Jimmy beyond the window. He was leaning forward with one hand on the table, his face serious as he eased up to the big finish of his story. Then he sat back and grinned, and Danny watched in silence as the assistant commissioner burst out laughing.

"So they walk."

Acorsi shrugged. "We'll hold Lucas overnight. We got enough for that. Give the guy some time to think, see if we can put some pressure on him to give up Jimmy."

"And if he doesn't?"

Acorsi turned to the window, his eyes expressionless as he watched Jimmy fold his arms across his chest and laugh.

"Then they walk."

Mickie was standing beside Acorsi's desk, on the phone to her office, when she saw Danny come out of the interrogation room and walk quickly across the homicide squad room toward the door, his face flushed and angry. She put a hand over the receiver, called out, "Danny?" But he kept walking, brushing past the FBI man, Seagraves, who turned and called after him, but Danny pushed through the door, vanished into the hall beyond.

"Look, I've gotta go," she told Dubrow. "Something's happened."

She hung up, went after Danny. She'd been waiting to talk to
him most of the afternoon, from the moment they brought him back
to police headquarters, put him into an interrogation room with
Acorsi, and she stood behind the one-way glass, listening as he described to the detective how he'd been an FBI informant for almost
three years. Now what she wanted to say to him, more than anything
else, was what she knew she couldn't—*Why didn't you tell me?* Instead,
she'd have to keep it official, work the case, ask him about Foley. Both
of them getting that sinking feeling as their eyes shifted away, avoided
each other's gaze. But now even that was slipping away.

She got to the elevators just in time to see the doors close, then
had to wait, *damn,* almost four minutes, leaning on the button, before
she could get another one. It was full, but she shoved her way in, ignored the angry looks from the pair of civilian secretaries crowded together at the front. She touched the door gently as the elevator
descended, as if she could hurry it up, make it open to find Danny
waiting there in the lobby.

He was gone. In the lobby, she saw a crowd gathered off to one
side, TV lights shining against the marble walls like a bright water-
fall. The crowd of reporters had showed up just before Jimmy arrived
to give a "voluntary statement" to homicide investigators on the death
of one of his former campaign workers, Wendell Keyes. He'd paused
in the lobby, spoke into the cameras, telling the voters that everybody
had to give the police their cooperation if they wanted to make New
Orleans a safer city. Then he'd waved and headed toward the elevators.
The reporters had hung around, waiting to see if anything interesting
happened, ready to jump on a story if it developed. And now, as she
went past, she caught a glimpse of Gregory Nowles, pushing his way
through the crowd. Beside him, she saw Maya Thomas, Acorsi's partner, and a young boy, his face frightened in the bright glare of the TV

lights. She stopped to watch them push through the crowd to one of the elevators, caught another quick glimpse of the boy's face as the doors closed. James Collette.

She hesitated for a moment. *Why are they bringing him in if Danny's told them Collette wasn't even at the restaurant?* But the thing had spun way out beyond any easy answers now. Like when she was a little girl and she'd watched a spider build a web in a bush outside her window. When it was finished, it hung there, motionless, an answer to that faint, gleaming mystery. But no answer is ever complete. A few days later she watched the spider lay eggs, and when they hatched, she saw the baby spiders swarm over their mother, hungry for blood.

She went out through the glass doors at the front of the lobby into a small concrete plaza where a fountain splashed weakly. When they'd built it, the water had sprayed high, cooling the hot afternoon air, rainbows drifting in the mist. Local politicians had gathered to have their photograph taken standing in front of it for the newspapers, a symbol of the campaign to clean up the city's law enforcement and renew people's faith in city government. Over the years the fountain had shrunk to a trickle, like somebody'd left a hose on. *Dirt in the jets,* she thought. *Blocking it up. That's what happens, you don't clean it out.* She crossed the plaza to the concrete steps, looked down at the street below. Danny stood at the edge of the street, talking to a black man who stood beside the open door of a car. *Just like Jabril drives,* she thought, then realized, *Jesus, 'cause it's his car.* She watched Danny brush past Jabril, start to walk away, but Jabril reached out and grabbed Danny's arm, saying something that made him stop and listen.

"Shit," Mickie whispered and started down the steps at a run.

Danny walked quickly along the sidewalk, his anger coiling in the muscles of his legs. He saw a car parked illegally in the yellow zone just ahead, a blue Acura with a black man behind the wheel, saw the man glance back at him in the driver's side mirror, watching him approach. Then, as he came alongside the car, he saw the window descend.

"The man with the answers," Jabril said, looking up at him from behind the wheel. "You still looking for my boy James? 'Cause he's upstairs right now. They got his ass on a *homicide* charge." He smiled thinly. "But then, you the man with the answers, so maybe you knew that."

Danny stopped, looked down at him. He could feel his hands clenched tightly into fists, feel the anger in the muscles behind his face.

Jabril studied him for a moment, then said, "Damn, son. Somebody sure put the fire up inside *your* head." Jabril opened his door and got out slowly, leaned one elbow on the car's roof. Calmly, glancing up at the police building behind Danny. "They pretty good at that, huh?"

Danny stared at him for a moment, then looked off across the street at the ruins of the old Jax brewery behind the public parking lot. Crumbling brick walls, smashed windows, open sky where the roof should have been. *Like a mirror,* Danny thought. *Cops look out their window, see those empty windows looking back at them.*

And then, without his quite realizing it, he was talking, telling Jabril the whole story. His voice felt like broken glass in his throat. It took only a few minutes, but when he was done, he felt exhausted, like somebody'd stuck a tube in his vein, drained all the life out of him.

"You angry, huh? Can't get no justice?" Jabril laughed. "Now you know what it's like for a *black* man. They got my boy James upstairs right now. Got to be there, 'cause he picked up a gun. But your people, they gonna walk, huh?"

Danny looked at him, surprised. Then suddenly he felt the anger return, like a bright flame rising within him. He pushed past Jabril, felt him grab his arm. But what stopped him was the way Jabril's voice went quiet, like he'd let the whole angry black man thing drop away for a moment, to get right to the heart of the matter, saying, "So what you say we cut all the bullshit and go do something *about* it?"

Danny stared at him. Somebody called his name. He turned to see Mickie hurrying down the steps toward them. She'd hung her ATF badge from her belt, and Danny saw it flash with the light from the setting sun.

He turned back to Jabril, said, "Let's go."

Ray Morrisey sat behind the wheel of his cruiser, watching as Danny got into the car with the nigger, drove away. A woman with long dark hair, looked Mexican, came down the concrete steps at a run, reaching the street just as the car pulled away. She stood there for a moment, gazing after it.

Morrisey started his car and swung out past the woman, got a good look at her face. Not bad, you like it spicy, order of beans on the side. Morrisey made a left onto Broad Street, caught a glimpse of the Acura up ahead in the traffic, but hung back, taking his time. He thought about the woman on the sidewalk, the hot tamale, wondered if Danny was getting any of that.

Maybe he'd ask him before he died.

32

Buddy Jeanrette sat forward, watched Jimmy talking to the reporters on the steps of the police headquarters, shaking hands with a couple before he waved Helen down the steps toward the rented limo. He made a show of opening the door for Helen, then climbed in beside her, swung the door shut, and reached over to grip her arm, hard.

"You know Danny was cutting a deal?"

Helen looked surprised. "No."

Buddy tapped on the glass partition, then sat back as the driver pulled out. He said, "How bad is it?"

"Danny gave me up." Jimmy sat back, disgusted. "They're lookin' to hang an accessory murder charge on me for Keyes."

"They've got no case," Helen said. "And we can't be sure that it's Danny who sold you out. All we know is that they've got a witness who can tie the gun that killed Keyes to this briefcase Danny picked up from the gun dealer in the restaurant. They might be able to make a case against Lucas, since he took the briefcase from Danny, but if he doesn't implicate you directly, the worst they could do is bring a conspiracy case. And even that probably wouldn't stand up before a jury."

Buddy stared at her. "That's all, huh?" He looked over at Jimmy. "So where's Lucas now?"

"They're holding him overnight," Jimmy said. "Probably file some bullshit weapons charge against him in the morning, then try to get him to testify against me." He looked out the window at the passing traffic. "Anyway, if they've got Danny, they don't need a murder charge. I'm looking at six to ten in Lewisburg on racketeering, he tes- tifies."

"Do they have the guns?"

Jimmy looked over at Buddy. "What?"

"The guns. They have 'em or not?"

Jimmy glanced at Helen, hesitated, then said, "Just the one they found with Keyes."

Buddy followed his gaze. Then he tapped on the glass again. The driver lowered the partition a few inches, and Buddy said, "There's a cab stand up on the next block. Pull up there, okay?" Then he sat back and glanced at his watch. "Helen, I've got to get Jimmy out to the party. You mind grabbing a cab back to your office?"

Her eyes narrowed. She looked over at Jimmy. He nodded. "I'll see you later tonight."

The car pulled up next to a cab stand and the driver got out, opened the door for her. She didn't move, her eyes fixed on Jimmy. Then she shook her head, grabbed her bag off the floor beside her. "This is serious, Jimmy. They're not screwing around this time. You better make sure your hands are clean."

She got out of the car, walked away toward the cab stand. The driver closed the door, got back behind the wheel, and raised the par- tition. Then he pulled out into traffic, and they headed out Claiborne Avenue.

"Nice lady," Buddy said. "Got a mouth on her, though."

"Tell me about it." Jimmy shifted in his seat, like something was digging into his back. "Everybody's got a fucking opinion, this town."

"So what's the story on the gun?"

"You tell me. Last I heard, you had 'em."

"I gave 'em to Ray, told him to take 'em back to the evidence room. Get some clean paper."

"Looks like Ray's got his own ideas."

Buddy considered him for a moment, then rubbed at his jaw. "Jesus. Ray *Morrisey?* This guy, it's load and fire. That's it."

"He know that?"

"If he don't, he will. *Real* soon."

Jimmy gazed out the window at the setting sun. "Danny's the real problem. He's the one who can take us all down. Unless Lucas decides to cut a deal. Then we're truly fucked."

Buddy took out his cellular, punched up a number, stared out the window as he waited for it to connect. Jimmy watched him, curious.

"What are you doing?"

Buddy looked over at him. "Calling in a favor. But it's gonna cost you."

"For what?"

"To make sure Lucas doesn't cut any deals." Buddy looked over at Jimmy and smiled. "Then we'll have a little talk with your boy Danny."

"So you figure this guy Buddy's got the guns?" Jabril drove out St. Claude toward the St. Bernard Parish line, taking his time, listening to Danny tell his story.

"The guys who did the shooting were from up in Saint Bernard. Buddy's in the gun business over there, and he's tight with Jimmy. It adds up."

Jabril shrugged. "Okay, we'll go take a look. Personally, if those motherfuckers want to kill each other, I got no problem with that. But they get my people involved, that's a different story altogether. You know what I'm sayin'?"

Danny watched the traffic flow past like a river, carrying them along. When they came up on the turn for Buddy's store, he said,

"Make a right up here." A freighter was gliding past beyond the levee as Jabril steered the Acura gently over the potholes, heading for the gravel lot at the end of the street, where the setting sun reflected off the metal roof of Buddy's building like fire on water.

Jabril pulled into the lot and swung the car around so it faced the store's entrance. There was a rusty brown Chevrolet Caprice parked nearby, and the metal security grate was still up. Jabril glanced at his watch. "Stays open late. Got to catch all them people comin' home from work, want to stop off and buy a gun."

He leaned across Danny, opened the glove compartment, took out a 9 mm Glock semiautomatic. He sat back and racked the slide, looked over at Danny. "I got a thirty-eight in the trunk, you need it."

"I'm okay." Danny slid the Beretta out of his pocket. He'd been carrying it around for a week, had started getting used to the feel of it in the pocket of his leather jacket. Now it felt strange in his hand.

He got out, shoved the gun back in his pocket, and followed Jabril to the door. "Let me go in first. They know me in here."

"And that's a *good* thing?"

"Depends. You want to get shot, you walk in the door?"

Jabril raised his eyebrows. "Not today, man." He stepped back, waved Danny ahead.

The guy behind the counter glanced up as Danny came through the door. He was ringing out the cash register, leaning on the counter with his arms folded across his chest, watching as the register spewed out a long strip of paper. He wore a T-shirt with a picture of Oliver North on it and *American Hero* printed below. His pistol was in a holster on his belt.

"You lookin' for Buddy, he's not here," he said. "He's out at the project. Some kind of fund-raiser." Then his eyes narrowed as Jabril came through the door. He jerked his head at the gun in Jabril's hand. "Hey, pal. We keep 'em holstered here until you get in the range."

"I'm not your pal." Jabril raised the Glock, pointed it at his head. "And I don't *need* no fuckin' range."

Ray Morrisey watched from his cruiser near the end of the block, as Danny walked the counter guy out of the building at gunpoint, took him over to the beat-up Chevy parked by the door. Danny motioned toward the car's trunk with the gun, and the counter guy dug out a set of keys, opened it. Then Danny waved him back against the wall, glanced into the trunk. When he was satisfied, he stepped away from the car and gestured for the counter guy to climb into the trunk. Danny closed it, went back inside.

"Jesus." Morrisey laughed. "Looks like our boy Danny's found himself some balls."

Jabril hit the buzzer behind the counter, and Danny pushed open the door at the back of the store. He led the way down the narrow corridor, past the silent gun range to Buddy's office, felt around on the wall next to the door until he found a light switch.

Jabril glanced around the office. Navajo rugs on the walls, glass gun case, stone fireplace, huge oak desk. "Nice setup. Built it with his own hands, huh?"

Danny went behind the desk. "I'll need a few minutes here."

"No problem. You want me to check out the warehouse?"

Danny glanced at a door to the right of the desk. "Through there." Jabril crossed the thick carpet, turned the deadbolt, and opened the door. The office lights carved a small patch of concrete floor from the darkness. He found a light switch, flicked it on. Three rows of industrial fluorescents blinked on across the broad metal ceiling of the warehouse. Jabril saw rows of wooden crates, stacked high. At the far end of the warehouse, there were racks of canoes, sleeping bags, shotguns. He went over to an open crate, lifted the clipboard resting on it. The crate was full of handguns.

"Jesus." He shook his head in amazement. "We at the fucking source, huh?" He disappeared among the rows of crates.

Danny got up, shut the door, then searched the office carefully. The briefcase wasn't there. He figured the FBI would do a better job, maybe pull up the floorboards, check that the concrete slab underneath didn't have any secret hiding places, but after ten minutes, he'd seen enough to know that the guns weren't there. The gun cabinet was locked, but Danny studied the handguns hanging on hooks beside the rows of rifles and shotguns. They looked expensive; a few were antiques. Nothing you'd toss in a briefcase with a sheet of paper showing somebody'd used it to rob a liquor store. The closet was unlocked. It contained a couple sports jackets, a pair of expensive sneakers still in the box, and a beat-up pair of work boots. An autographed Louisville Slugger leaned in the corner. Danny picked it up, looked at the signature. *Joe DiMaggio.*

Rich man's toys, he thought as he put it back. The whole place was laid out so Buddy could just open the closet, take out the bat, show it to some guy he wanted to impress. Same with the guns. Buddy'd shown them to him once, when he came to make a collection: "You like guns, Danny?"

Danny'd shrugged. "Not really my thing."

"Not like that old car you drive, huh?" Buddy grinned and got up from his desk, went over to the gun case. "But you appreciate when something's beautiful, right? Like Helen. She's one beautiful woman. Elegant." He dug out a set of keys, chose one, unlocked the glass doors, and lifted out an old rifle. "But look at this. Remington Civil War contract rifle. Manufactured in eighteen sixty-two. Fifty-eight-caliber muzzle loader. Beautiful weapon." He handed it to Danny, who stood up and raised it to his shoulder for a moment, then lowered it, handed it back.

"Heavy."

"You ever see any statistics on the average height of a Civil War soldier? They ran about three inches shorter than we do now. This was a lot of gun to carry, especially when you're charging up a hill under fire." He put it back, took down a shotgun. "Lefaucheaux pinfire gun, eighteen thirty-six. First breech-loading double-barrel shotgun. I love the metalwork on this gun. Look at the trigger guard. Like something you'd see on a balcony down in the French Quarter. Always makes me think of a bird, walking."

Now Danny turned away from the gun case, looked over at the file cabinet. He was wasting time. The guns weren't here. But sometimes the real weapons aren't the ones you can hold in your hands.

He went over to the file cabinet, opened it. In the top drawer, he found copies of the incorporation papers for Ragin' Cajun Sports. He flipped through them, saw that the company was a limited partnership, and was surprised to see that Buddy Jeanrette was actually a minority shareholder, with only 28 percent of the total shares. The bulk of the company's shares were held by something called River Road Partners, which listed as its mailing address a bank in the Cayman Islands. Danny paused over that for a while, then pulled out the file, tossed it on the desk. He dug through the remaining files in the drawer, mostly back invoices from suppliers and legal forms, including a federal firearms license renewal application filled out in Buddy's name. Near the back of the drawer, he came to a file labeled *River Road.* He pulled it out, opened it. It contained a series of shareholder statements, which showed quarterly payments to Buddy from River Road Partners on a 32 percent holding in the partnership.

Danny did some quick math, worked out that if Buddy held 28 percent of the company's shares directly, and 32 percent of the partnership holding the remainder of the shares, that gave him a slight majority of the total shares. Enough to exert daily control over the company, but an effective split on the profits. There was somebody behind the scenes, taking almost half the money.

Danny tossed that file on the desk and kept digging. The next drawer down contained files on a real estate project Buddy was fronting out near English Turn. Danny glanced up at a map on the wall over Buddy's desk. It showed miles of curving roads, a golf course, a marina, clubhouse, tennis courts, two pools. Some place. He went back to the files, dug through them until he found one labeled *Financing.* He pulled it out, opened it on top of the drawer, and was studying the legal agreements it contained when Jabril came in and sat down in one of the leather chairs that faced the desk.

"Lotsa guns back there, but nothing like you said. You find anything?"

Danny looked up from the papers. "Yeah. Money stuff."

"Like the guy in the movie."

"Huh?"

"The guy in the movie, hangs out in the parking garage. Tells Robert Redford how to break the story."

Danny smiled. "Follow the money."

"Always leads you home. Guy like you should know that better than anyone." Jabril sighed, got up. "There a bathroom in here? Lookin' at all them guns, I gotta go take a leak."

"Back through the warehouse."

Morrisey sat in his car, watching the entrance to the store. When twenty minutes had passed, nothing happening, he said, "Fuck it," got out, and walked across the street. He drew his gun as he eased into the gravel parking lot, moving along the fence, out of the light. When he reached the Chevy, he eased down one side to the trunk,

keeping his gun on the door just beyond. The keys hung in the trunk
lock, and he could hear the counter guy moving around inside. Hearing his steps on the gravel, probably. Starting to get nervous.

Morrisey turned the key and lifted the trunk a few inches. The
light came on, and he saw the guy look up at him, eyes wide.

"Hey, Jerry. You okay in there?"

"Shit, Ray. You scared the fuck outta me. I thought it was—"

Morrisey raised a finger to his lips, silencing him. "Back in a
minute." And he closed the trunk. As he moved away, he heard a muffled curse from inside the trunk, then a series of loud thumps as Jerry
started kicking at the lock.

Morrisey eased up on the entrance door, thought for a moment
about just pulling the security grate down, snapping the padlock
closed. Be pretty funny, just lock the guys in there, wait till they try
to get out. *Hey, sorry. Looks like you're stuck.* He could picture the look
on their faces. Or even better, Buddy's face, when he showed up, found
him standing there with two armed guys locked inside like animals in
a zoo.

Then he thought, *Jesus, maybe not. Lock 'em in there, they'd have
enough firepower to blow away half the city.*

He pressed his back against the wall next to the door, reached
down with his free hand, and opened the door a few inches, carefully,
just to make sure it wasn't locked. Then, abruptly, he jerked it open
wide, went in low and fast, swinging his gun across the shop in a wide
arc as he ducked behind a counter, making sure the place was empty.
Must be in the back. He took a moment to picture the building's layout.
Hallway, gun range off to the left, Buddy's office on the right, then the
warehouse in the back. Just take it slow, keep quiet. Check one room
at a time.

He glanced at the button under the counter that unlocked the
door, then stood up, went over to the door, and ripped out the wire
that led from the door up to the buzzer mounted on the wall. He went

back to the register, dug around under the counter until he found a roll of duct tape, peeled off a strip and taped it over the button, heard the lock on the door click open. Then he picked up his gun off the counter, went over to the door, swung it open gently. The corridor beyond was dark, but there was a narrow strip of light under the door of Buddy's office.

Morrisey grinned. *Fucking lawyers, man. Whole warehouse full of guns to choose from, this guy's interested in what Buddy keeps in his fucking file cabinet.*

He eased down the hall quietly, listened for a moment at the door, then reached down, turned the knob silently. Danny didn't even look up as Morrisey swung the door open.

"Man, you wouldn't believe what Buddy's making off this place," Danny said, his eyes still on the file in his hands. His gun lay on the desk. "We're in the wrong fucking business."

"Hey, speak for yourself, asshole." Morrisey grinned as Danny glanced up, his face going tight when he saw the gun. "'Cause I love my work."

Morrisey went over to the desk, picked up Danny's gun, slipped it into his pocket. "Where's your partner?"

Danny was silent. His eyes looked like two coins that somebody'd tossed in a fire until all the color was scorched out of them.

"Look, I saw you two come in here, so I know he's around somewhere." Morrisey gestured toward the door to the warehouse. "You want, we can go look for him. But he gets nervous, starts shooting, first thing I'm gonna do is put a bullet in your fucking head." He shrugged. "Your call, son."

Danny looked up at him. "You're going to kill me anyway."

"Yeah? What makes you think so?"

Danny nodded at his uniform. "You sent the last two guys."

Morrisey grinned. "Shit, I guess you got me there." Then his face went serious, and he reached over, pressed his gun against the side of

Danny's head. "So you're a smart guy. What you think Buddy'd say if I blew your brains all over his desk?" He took a step back, waved Danny out of the chair. "Now get the fuck up, and let's go find your friend."

He opened the warehouse door, shoved Danny through ahead of him. Just inside, he caught the back of Danny's shirt collar and held him there, the gun pressed against his ribs. Near the door, the warehouse was brightly lit, but the back of the building was dark. Long rows of crates stacked high off the floor vanished into the darkness, and Danny could see a forest of tents and sleeping bags hanging on racks near the back. Outboard engines lay on pallets against one wall, next to a display of Coleman stoves and fuel cans.

Morrisey was silent for a moment, listening. Then he called out, "Sheriff's department! Come on out, now. I got your friend here." His voice echoed across the warehouse briefly, and then the building fell silent.

He's not calling for backup, Danny thought. *Doesn't want any witnesses.*

For a moment, he wondered if Jabril had found a back way out. Then he heard him call out from the darkness at the back of the warehouse, "This guy for real, Danny?"

Danny felt Morrisey press the gun tightly against his ribs, yelled back, "He works for Buddy."

Morrisey raised the gun, clubbed Danny across the back of the head. Danny cried out, fell to his knees, but Morrisey hauled him back to his feet. "That was stupid, boy. You give me a hard time, I'll make sure you get hurt." He saw movement in the shadows at the back of the building, raised his gun, fired once.

"Don't make me come down there and haul your ass out," he called to Jabril. "You can walk or get dragged, it don't matter shit to me."

For a moment there was only silence, then Danny heard Jabril laugh. "You got the balls to walk back here, we'll talk about it. How's that?"

Morrisey looked around, saw a stack of boxes next to the door. The label on the top box read EMERGENCY FLARES. Morrisey dragged Danny over to the stack and said, "Grab that top box."

Danny lifted the box down, set it on the floor.

"Now open it."

Danny tore the box open, then Morrisey shoved him aside, took out a flare, snapped it in half so it ignited, then threw it down the center aisle. It bounced off some boxes, skidded across the concrete floor, and came to rest against a stack of cinder blocks near the back of the building. A harsh light spread across the back wall of the warehouse, white as shattered bone. Danny saw Jabril move quickly between two stacks of boxes over by the stack of fuel cans. Morrisey fired twice, and Danny heard one of the bullets hit the cans. Fuel began to pour out, spreading across the concrete floor toward the burning flare.

"Shit," Morrisey said, grabbed Danny's arm, shoved him back into the office. Behind him, Danny heard a *whump* as the fuel ignited. The flames raced across the floor toward the stack of fuel cans, and then, one by one, they began to explode. Bright red flames shot across the warehouse as if somebody had pulled a curtain. Then Morrisey pulled him away from the door, kicked it closed. He went over to the desk, grabbed the files Danny'd been reading, then waved him toward the door with his gun. "Let's go."

"Buddy's gonna be pretty pissed, you burn his place down."

Morrisey smiled. "I'll just tell him you did it. That ought to make things pretty simple."

33

"What is this shit?"

Danny sat in the back of the squad car, his wrists cuffed behind him. Morrisey had the files open on the front seat beside him. He looked up at Danny, raised his eyebrows.

"You broke in Buddy's warehouse for *this*?"

Danny said nothing. His throat felt tight. He glanced over at the warehouse, where flames rose behind the front windows of the gun shop.

Morrisey shone the flashlight in Danny's face. "You gonna tell me what's so interesting about these papers, or I got to guess?"

Danny turned his head away from the light. "Those guys at the restaurant, were they friends of yours?"

"Friends?" Morrisey shrugged. "Nah, I wouldn't call 'em that. We got along okay, had a couple beers, but that's about it." He studied Danny's face. "So now we know where we're at, huh? I know what you know, and you know what I know. We don't have to play no games, right? You might even say we got some mutual friends."

"I doubt it."

Morrisey raised his eyebrows. "Yeah? That's too bad. I was hoping we'd get along. So let's say we've got mutual *interests*. Like we both know Buddy's got a partner, wouldn't be too happy, this stuff got too public." He picked up the files, held them up. "That's what this means, right?"

Danny hesitated, then nodded. "That's what it means."

"You thought I didn't understand it, huh?" Morrisey grinned.

"So I'm reading this stuff on the real estate project right? Buddy's got to pay off a loan to this partner or the partner gets the whole thing?"

"Something like that."

Morrisey tossed the files on the seat beside him and started the car. He said nothing as he put the car in gear and pulled out of the parking lot, swinging it around so they were headed back up toward the highway. They'd gone a few yards when Danny heard an explosion behind them, twisted around to see the back windows of the warehouse shatter, flames shoot out like blood from a wound.

"Damn!" Morrisey hit the brakes, turned to watch it. "You see that?" He watched for a moment, then shook his head. "Shit, I wouldn't want to be you, Buddy finds out about this."

He drove on. When they reached St. Bernard Highway, he made a right, headed east out of town. Danny looked out the window and thought about the papers on the seat beside Morrisey. According to Buddy, Helen had done the legal work on the real estate deal. So that meant she'd probably drafted the contracts for the financing.

He closed his eyes. *Jesus, Helen.* How much did she really know about Buddy's business? Enough to know that she'd helped set him up?

Not that any of it mattered anymore. He looked up at Morrisey. Beyond him, the car's headlights led into the darkness. They'd kill him, dump his body out in the swamp somewhere, then go back to cutting their deals.

Then he remembered Jabril and winced. *There's worse things than dying quick.*

Jabril stood in the shadows behind the loading dock, watching the squad car drive away. *Stupid fucker didn't even wait to make sure you're dead. Shit, that's basic. You gonna kill a man, make sure you finish the job.*

When the fire started, he was crouched behind a stack of boxes near the loading dock at the back of the warehouse. He watched as the fuel cans exploded just a few feet from where he'd been standing only moments ago, flames shooting out across the warehouse. The cop dragged Danny away, slammed the door behind them. For a moment he didn't move, listening. But all he could hear was the flames. He stood up, went back out to the loading dock. It had a heavy steel door that rolled up across the ceiling; a security bar locked into a metal frame on both sides. All he had to do was pull a lever to disengage the security bar and hit the switch on the wall beside it to raise the door a few feet. He felt cool air rush past him toward the flames as he dropped down and rolled under the door, then jumped off the loading dock onto the gravel.

He caught a glimpse of the squad car pulling out of the parking lot and eased back into the shadows close to the building. Then the windows exploded. The squad car stopped for a moment, and Jabril saw the cop behind the wheel look back. Jabril raised his gun, waiting for the guy to get out or reach down and pick up the radio. But after a moment the car just drove away slowly. Like the cop was worried about tearing up his tires in a pothole.

Jabril could hear the fire spreading through the building behind him. He walked over to the Chevy parked near the shop door, took the keys out of the trunk, the guy thumping away in there, and got behind the wheel. He started it up and pulled about twenty yards away from the building, right up against the chain-link fence. Then he got out, left the door open and the keys in the ignition, walked around back, and banged on the trunk to get the guy's attention.

"Hey, listen up in there. Cops'll be here in a couple minutes to let you out. ATF'll be right behind. You think you could give 'em a message for me?"

The guy in the trunk said something Jabril couldn't make out. But his tone was clear. Jabril put his foot on the bumper, rocked the car a couple times.

"Be nice, now, or I'll snap the key off in the lock, they'll have to break your trunk open with a crowbar." The guy shut up. "That's better. You see a little Hispanic girl, works for the ATF? You tell her I said she don't need no fuckin' warrant now. " Behind him, a window shattered. Jabril turned, saw flames pouring out of the warehouse. "And I hate to be the one to break it to you, man, but it looks like you out of a job."

Lucas Clay felt naked without his telephone. They'd taken it from him, along with his wallet, keys, pocket change, Rolex, and a gold Cross fountain pen, before escorting him upstairs to a holding cell for the night. For the last two hours, he'd sat on the edge of his bunk, listening to the prisoners shouting to one another in the main part of the jail. The noise never ceased. It was like the time his Boy Scout troup had spent a night at Audubon Zoo. He'd been fourteen and had found the experience terrifying. They'd pitched their tents across from the monkey house, and that night none of them had slept, just lay in their sleeping bags, listening to the monkeys screaming and fighting. Lucas could smell the fear. Shortly after that, he'd quit the Boy Scouts, got a summer job at his uncle's law office. He became silent, watchful.

Only here he was, back in the monkey house. He closed his eyes, made himself breathe slowly. *Don't panic. Jimmy'll get you out of this thing. He's probably on the phone right now, taking care of the whole deal.*

Except it was *him* who usually got on the phone, worked out the problems. What he needed, right now, was his phone. Make a couple quick calls, they'd have somebody from the D.A.'s office down here unlocking the cell door in twenty . . .

"You Lucas Clay?"

Lucas opened his eyes, saw a guard standing at the door of the cell. "That's right."

The guard glanced back up the corridor, then dug in his pocket, came out with a ring of keys, slid one into the door. He swung the door open, grinned at Lucas.

"You got some important friends." Then he stepped into the cell, pulled the door closed behind him. "They asked me to give you a message."

Mickie flashed her badge at a St. Bernard sheriff's deputy and pulled into the gravel lot, swung wide around the fire trucks to where an ATF arson investigation team in blue fatigues was gathered around a mobile headquarters truck. *Early for anybody to call in an arson team,* she thought. Thick smoke rose from the warehouse into the night sky, and she could see flames beyond the windows. Firefighters kept a safe distance, pouring water into the flames. *Must have a witness. That or somebody called it in. Maybe the arsonist, claiming it.*

She spotted Jim Dubrow standing near the front of the ATF truck, talking with the team leader. She managed to squeeze her Nova into an empty spot near the chain-link fence and walked over. Dubrow glanced over at her as she came toward them, nodding at something that the arson team leader said. He held up a finger to Mickie, and she stopped a few feet away, waited as they finished talking. Then the team leader went back to brief his men, and Dubrow came over to her, said, "Sorry to call you out, Vega, but it looks like you're in on this one."

She raised her eyebrows. "You're assigning me to the arson team?"

"Not today." He turned, nodded to a heavily muscled man in jeans and a T-shirt who was leaning on a beat-up Chevy Caprice, talking to a couple of plainclothes cops. "We've got a witness, guy who worked the counter, who says the two guys who set it left you a message."

She felt something settle on her chest, like somebody'd just dropped a weight on her from a great height. "What message?"

Dubrow was watching her closely. "Now you won't need a warrant."

She winced, looked over at the flames rising from the building. "He get a look at them?"

"White guy and a black guy. They locked him in the trunk of his car, then they torched the place. Took the time to move his car away from the building before they took off. Local cops rolled on the first call within three minutes. Probably just missed 'em." Dubrow glanced over at where the counter man was telling his story for the sixth time, showing the cops with elaborate hand gestures how the pair had held guns to his head. "He also said a local deputy showed up while they were inside. Took one of 'em away."

Mickie looked at him and her eyes narrowed. "Locals know anything about that?"

"That's what those guys from the sheriff's office are talking to him about right now. Not only don't they have any record of an arrest, nobody's seen this guy he said was here for a couple days." Dubrow took a small notebook out of his shirt pocket, glanced at it. "Deputy's name is Ray Morrisey. He's done some private security work for Buddy Jeanrette over the years. Sounds like they're tight. He's got a patrol car signed out, but he's been calling in sick on his shifts for the last three days." He stuffed the notebook back in his pocket, looked up at her. "There's something else, Mickie. We got a call from your guy Acorsi down at NOPD. He wants to talk to you about Danny. He took off on them, nobody knows where he went." Dubrow looked over at the fire, said quietly, "They're worried he might do something stupid, Mickie."

Mickie followed his gaze. "Danny's not an arsonist."

"I hope you're right. But he's a crucial witness." Dubrow looked at her. "They just found Lucas Clay dead in his cell forty minutes ago. Looks like he hanged himself."

She stared at him. "You buy that?"

"It's not our case, Mickie."

She looked over at the detectives interviewing the counter man. He had the trunk open, showing the cops how the men had made him climb inside and locked him in there. "Danny used to make collections from Buddy Jeanrette. If that guy worked behind the counter, he'd recognize Danny."

"So?"

She hesitated. "Could be he figures Buddy doesn't want Danny in jail. This deputy, Morrisey, he might be the connection between Jeanrette and the two men Danny saw at the restaurant. That could explain why he's calling in sick. They're trying to clean up the mess before anybody figures out that they're behind it." She looked at Dubrow, her face tight. "If he's got Danny, he's not taking him to jail."

Dubrow rubbed at his jaw, looked over at the witness. "That's pretty speculative, Mickie."

"Let me talk to this guy. If Danny came out here, he was looking for something."

Dubrow raised his eyebrows, looked over at the burning building. "Well, he didn't bother to cover his tracks." Then he saw the expression on her face, her eyes like nail points, and he raised both hands in surrender. "Okay, fine. Talk to the guy. See if you can find out where they might have taken Chaisson. You get anything, you've got my authorization to go after it." He looked over at the fire crews spraying water on the blaze. "Looks like the rest of us are gonna be here a while."

The counter guy leaned against his Chevy with his arms folded across his chest, ran his eyes over Mickie's body slowly. "You really with the ATF?" He grinned. "You wanna check my weapon?"

Enjoying it, she thought, watching him ease himself up on the car's hood like a guy at a high school party, getting ready to hit on her. *Gets off on telling his story, everybody nodding.*

She met his gaze, her eyes cool. "Don't waste your time," she told him. "I've heard 'em all." Then she walked back to the car's trunk, opened it. "So how'd it feel, being locked up in here?"

He turned to stare at her. "Jesus, how you think it felt? Like being in a coffin. I thought they were gonna *do* me, you know?"

She nodded. "You're probably gonna hate jail, then."

He came off the car, fast, like he'd suddenly realized it was *real* hot. "What do you mean, jail? I'm the fucking *victim* here."

She ran her hand along the edge of the trunk, shrugged. "Depends how you look at it. Arson's a funny crime. They find any kind of accelerant on the floor in there, they'll start looking at anybody who had something to gain from burning the place down. I'm guessing your boss is insured, which means the insurance company gets involved. And they *hate* paying out on claims where there's evidence of arson. First question they ask is who's making money on the deal. So what they'll do is take a real close look at your boss, his business, everything. Then they'll start checking out the statements you've given the officers investigating the fire. If you've held anything back, they might start wondering why. Like how come these guys went so easy on you. Even moved your car so it wouldn't get damaged?" She smiled, shook her head. "Looks funny, you got to admit."

He started to say something, but she held up a hand to stop him. "See, that's not even the worst thing. A fire like this, it makes the whole place a crime scene. That means anything we find in there once the fire's out can be taken into evidence, even if it has nothing to do with the fire." She smiled at him. "That's what your guy meant by saying we didn't need a warrant now. So if we find any evidence that suggests this place was used for illegal activity before the fire, you could find yourself choosing between a conspiracy charge and having to testify against Buddy Jeanrette. I guess you know him better than I do, but that's not a choice I'd enjoy, myself."

He looked at her for a long moment, and she could see hatred in his eyes. When he finally spoke, his voice was quiet, almost a whisper. "What the fuck do you want from me?"

"The white guy, it was Danny Chaisson, right?"

He shrugged. "Yeah, sure. That's all you want? You people can fuckin' have him."

"Where'd Morrisey take him?"

"Hey, how the fuck should I know? Ray Morrisey, he's not a guy you go ask his business. Maybe they went to the zoo."

"You said Morrisey works for Buddy sometimes. Say he was taking him to Buddy, where would that be?"

The guy hesitated. "You never heard this from me."

"Fine."

"Buddy's having some kind of party tonight. At his property out by English Turn. Some kind of political thing."

Mickie felt the excitement start to grow within her. "For Jimmy Boudrieux?"

"Yeah." He shrugged. "Whatever."

"Tell me how to get there."

34

Ray Morrisey pulled up at the gate, waited for the uniformed guard to come out of his booth and lean down to glance in the window, looking at Danny behind the wire screen. His eyebrows went up, and he said, "Got you one, huh?"

"Yeah." Morrisey grinned. "Thought Buddy might want to have a talk with this one before I take him in."

The guard rubbed at his jaw carefully. "Have to call up to the house. Big party up there tonight. Somebody's not on the list, I'm not supposed to let 'em past."

"So go make the call. Tell him I got Danny Chaisson here."

The guard glanced back at Danny, nodded. Then he straightened up, went back into the booth, picked up the phone.

"Fucking security guards," Morrisey said. "Guy was gonna stand there and argue with me, all he's gotta do is pick up the phone."

"He'll remember you brought me here," Danny said. "You kill me, he's a witness."

Morrisey turned, looked back at him. "Did I *ask* for your opinion? No? So what do you say you just shut the fuck up, okay?"

The guard hung up the phone, hit a button to raise the gate. "Take your first left after the pavement ends," he called out to Morrisey. "You'll see the lights."

Morrisey raised a hand, drove on through the gate. The road quickly turned to gravel, and he swung onto a road that led off to the left through a thick stand of trees. They passed a patch of cleared ground, construction equipment parked along the edge of the road. Then more trees, and suddenly Danny saw an old plantation house, brightly lit, with a long line of expensive cars parked under the row of oaks leading up the driveway. There was scaffolding along one side of the house, but in the darkness of the unbuilt development, it looked like a swan gliding across a lake at night. Danny could hear music as Morrisey pulled around the back, past a long row of BMWs, Mercedeses, and Cadillacs. A black man in an antebellum servant's costume, his face wooden, was waiting on the cobbled walk that ran down the side of the house.

"Witness," Danny said.

Morrisey turned in his seat to glare at him. "What if I fucking *want* witnesses. Did you ever think about that?"

"Then you're an idiot. Guys like Buddy and Jimmy, they always need somebody to take the fall. You're just making it easy for them."

Morrisey smiled. "You think so, huh?" He slid Danny's gun into his pocket, picked up the files off the seat beside him, and got out. Then he opened the rear door, dragged Danny out by the elbow. "People always underestimate me."

"You ever wonder why?"

Morrisey shoved him toward the sidewalk. "Shut the fuck up."

They followed the guy in the servant's outfit around the side of the house past a row of high, brightly lit windows. Danny caught a glimpse of a crowd holding champagne glasses. Jimmy Boudrieux was standing near one of the windows, surrounded by a crowd of guests in evening clothes.

They turned the corner, went along a dark sidewalk toward the back of the house. When the sidewalk ended, the guy in the butler's outfit picked his way through the weeds carefully; Danny saw that he was wearing flat cloth slippers with tiny bows on them. "I hope you're getting paid a lot for this."

The man looked at him, expressionless. "It ain't enough."

Morrisey grabbed the back of Danny's neck, dug his fingers in. "Didn't I tell you to shut up?"

Danny jerked free. "So shoot me."

The butler stared at them for a moment, then continued around behind the building. They followed, finding their way across the uneven ground. The back of the place was covered by scaffolding; sheets of clear plastic hung from the roof, and Danny could see where they'd torn away part of the wall, the lights in the front rooms shining through. Somewhere back across the lawn, he could hear water lapping against a pier.

A light came on over a narrow door, and Danny saw that they were walking past piles of construction debris, old boards, cracked bricks, a pair of ancient metal sinks. They went in the door, back through a narrow hall, past a large kitchen where a chef was hurriedly arranging hors d'oeuvres on small trays for the waiters to carry out to the crowd. The butler stopped beside a door, knocked softly, then swung it open. "You're supposed to wait in here."

Morrisey shoved Danny past him and closed the door. It was an office with floor-to-ceiling French windows, two sofas, and a large oak desk, covered with site plans. Maura sat behind the desk, cutting a line of coke on a glass picture frame she'd laid flat on the desk. She looked up at them, said, "You mind? I need some privacy here."

Morrisey shoved Danny down on one of the sofas, went over to the desk. He tossed the files on the desk, picked up the picture frame. "This what it looks like, I could send your butt to jail, sweetheart." He wet the tip of his finger, touched it to the cocaine, then rubbed it on the gum beneath his upper lip. "So how 'bout you just go back to the party, like a good girl."

Maura sat back, folded her arms across her chest, looked over at Danny. "This guy a friend of yours, Danny?"

"I'm wearing handcuffs, Maura. Does it *look* like he's a friend of mine?"

She shrugged. "Haven't seen you in a couple days. Could be a whole new scene."

Morrisey picked up the rolled dollar bill Maura had laid out on the desk. Then he set the picture frame down on the edge of the desk, bent over, and snorted the line she'd cut. When he straightened up, his face was flushed and his eyes glittered. "You know this broad, Danny?"

"She's Jimmy Boudrieux's daughter."

"Yeah?" He looked at Maura. "Your daddy know you're back here choking the monkey?"

She kept her eyes fixed on Danny. "Jimmy caught me trying to bust his safe open. I was gonna take off, go live on the beach in Morocco. Like in that Hendrix song."

He gave a smile. "Castles in the sand."

She nodded. "My punishment is I've got to go to all his parties. He doesn't trust me alone." Her eyes moved down to the handcuffs. "So what's your excuse?"

"They're going to kill me."

The door opened behind him and Buddy came in, looked at Maura. "What's she doing here?"

Morrisey shrugged. "She was already in here when we got here."

"Jesus." Buddy pointed a finger at Maura. "You, *out!*"

She stood up, and Danny saw that she was wearing a tight black evening gown. A faint trace of white powder clung to the front of her dress. "You know your problem, Danny?" She picked up a small black handbag. "You've got lousy taste in friends." Then she walked past him, out the door.

Buddy shut the door behind her, glanced over at Danny. "Get those cuffs off him. They leave marks." Then he went over to the desk and sat down. He was wearing evening clothes. They looked good on him, like fur on a cat.

"Listen to this shit," he said to Danny, while Morrisey unlocked the handcuffs. "Last week, I call up the caterer, tell him we got sixty people coming, I want enough of those little oysters in filo things so each guest can have four. I mean, we got shrimp skewers, those cheese and endive rolls, Thai fish cakes, plenty of food, right? But I specifically *told* the guy I want plenty of the oysters, 'cause I know people like 'em. So what happens? I see a waiter come by a couple minutes ago, he's got a whole tray full of fish cakes, nothing else. I tell him, 'Wait a second. Go back in the kitchen, get 'em to give you some more of the oyster things.' 'Cause I've seen, like, two trays of them go around, and that's it. You know what he tells me? 'We're all out of oysters.' After I *told* the guy and everything. So I go back in the kitchen, you want to guess what I see? They've got a plate of oysters sitting on the counter for the *waiters*. I walk in there, one of 'em is just getting ready to stuff one in his mouth. I say, 'You eat that, boy, you're fired.'"

He shook his head, picked up the picture frame Maura'd been using, brushed it off, and put it back in its place on the desk. "Now what I *should* do, this point in the evening, is find that caterer, show him an easy way to get his head out of his ass." He sat back, looked at Danny. "But instead I got to come in here, deal with this shit."

Morrisey clipped the handcuffs back on his belt, took Danny's gun from his pocket, tossed it on the desk in front of Buddy. "I took this off him. Might be useful." Then he went over to a cabinet that held a row of whiskey bottles, chose a single malt Scotch, and poured a few fingers into a glass.

Buddy picked up the gun. "A guy from your office called me about twenty minutes ago, Ray, told me my warehouse just burned to the ground." He laid the gun down on the desk, glanced over at Morrisey. "He also asked me if I'd seen you in the last couple days. You been busy?"

"Just covering my ass." Morrisey took a seat on the couch, sipped at his drink.

Buddy raised his eyebrows, looked from one to the other. "So? Somebody planning to explain to me how my place got torched?"

Danny rubbed at his wrists where the handcuffs had chafed the skin and stared at Buddy. "You don't look too cut up about it. Maybe somebody did you a favor."

"Yeah?" Buddy sat back, smiled at him. "How you figure?"

Danny nodded to the files on the desk. "You're cash poor. And you've got a loan payment coming up on this project. You don't make it, your partner can assume control of the whole project."

Buddy was silent for a moment. He reached over, picked up a 9 mm bullet that he kept on his desk, started rolling it gently between his fingers. "Go on."

"Insurance payment could take care of it." Danny smiled. "Only problem is, your partner might not go for it." He sat back, put his feet up on the coffee table in front of the couch. "You should have had an independent lawyer look over that loan agreement, Buddy. You've been set up."

Buddy watched him, playing with the bullet idly. "Yeah? How?"

"You financed this place by taking a loan from your partner's profit shares from the gun business. There's a repayment schedule, first payment thirty days after the public stock offering on the gun business, second payment ninety days after you've sold the first half of the units in Phase One of the real estate development, final payment on completion of Phase One sales. Sounds like a pretty good deal. You've got your payments scheduled on expectation of income, rather than on a fixed date. All you've got to do is make sure you complete the stock sale within a year of when you've planned. That's a generous schedule. Makes it hard for you to default." He smiled. "But you've got all the real financial exposure. Your partner loans you his share of the profits on the gun business so you can get initial financing on the project. By

the time your first payment comes up, you've begun construction."
Danny waved a hand at the window. "You've got all the environmen-
tal approvals now, you've cleared the land, got roads built in here, sold
the first couple units. So the value of the project's gone *way* up before
you even make your first payment. You make the payments on time,
you get rich. But if anything happens so you can't make that first payment, you go under, and your partner steps in, takes over the project,
collects the profits." Danny sat back, spread his hands. "That means
your partner's got a serious interest in seeing you default. You go under, he gets rich. Simple as that."

"Not bad," Jimmy said behind him. "You could've been a pretty
good lawyer, you'd stuck with it."

Danny turned to look at him, standing in the open door of the
office. "Maybe. But I guess you had other plans for me."

Jimmy smiled, shut the door behind him. "So everything's my
fault, huh? Sounds like something Maura would say." He came over,
sat down on the sofa opposite Danny. "You got to stop living in the
past, Danny. Now's all we've got."

Morrisey laughed. "And there ain't much of that left either."

"You know, I'd like to do that. Only the past keeps coming
back."

Jimmy raised his eyebrows. "Yeah? How's that?"

"Wendell Keyes. Funny how he'd just take a notion to blow his
brains out like that. A guy who survived cancer. But then I've seen it
before."

Jimmy looked off at the window and the darkness beyond.

"Back when you were still with the state police," Danny said,
looking over at Buddy. "Jimmy wasn't Speaker yet. But he was on his
way up. Chair of Appropriations, with a highway job coming up. So
they cut some deals, and everybody got a piece. Only, the way I heard it,
somebody wasn't happy. One of the construction contractors, probably,

C o l d
S t e e l
R a i n

who didn't put up enough when the collection plate came around, got cut out of the bidding. So this guy made a couple calls, and pretty soon the FBI was sniffing around. Nobody took it too seriously at first, just figured it was the price of doing business. But then they got hold of some papers somebody had been careless enough to hang on to, started issuing subpoenas. That's when people started getting nervous. Everybody looking for somebody to take the fall. But, see, the problem with a deal like that is everybody's hooked into somebody else. One guy goes down, the whole chain goes with him. So the only way out is to break the chain. You find the guy who carried the money, take him out of the picture. That way, even if the Feds *know* there were payoffs, they can't get up in court, show the money moving from here to there. No proof, no case. Everybody keeps their mouth shut, they don't start talkin' about it on the phone, they're safe." He looked over at Jimmy, who sat there watching him, his face expressionless. "So somebody got to the guy. Two nights before he was supposed to testify, he goes for a ride, ends up in a gravel parking lot, some club on River Road up by Baton Rouge, his brains splattered all over the backseat of his car. State trooper found him there, called it in. The FBI took a look at it, but they couldn't find anything wrong with it. So it went down as a suicide. Tough luck for the guy's family, but everybody else was happy."

Jimmy glanced at his watch. "This is fascinating. But I should get back to the party." He stood up. "You know how it is, Danny. Let 'em get bored, they don't write the check."

Danny smiled. "Just tell 'em to make it out to River Road Partners. You can throw in a membership at the tennis club when you own this place."

Jimmy shot a glance at him, then looked over at Buddy. "Can I trust you to take care of this?"

"Can you *trust* me?" Buddy laughed. "Jimmy, I've been wiping up your shit for twenty years."

Jimmy raised his eyebrows. "You haven't done badly for yourself, either."

"That's true." Buddy looked over at Danny, grinned. "We started out, I didn't have a pot to piss in. Now, I own the pot, and he pisses in it." He shifted his eyes back to Jimmy, and Danny saw them glitter, like bits of broken glass. "You want something done here, I want to hear you say it straight out."

Jimmy was silent for a moment. His eyes came over to Danny, and something seemed to fall away, like a light going out in an empty room.

"Kill him," Jimmy said. Then he turned and left the room.

For a moment, nobody moved. Then Buddy stood up, tossed the bullet to Danny. "Smart guy. You win the prize." He picked up Danny's gun off the desk, gestured toward the door. "Let's go."

They took him out the back way, walked him back along the cobbled path that ran along the side of the building to where the cars were parked. Buddy unlocked a Toyota Land Cruiser, motioned for Danny to get in. Danny glanced back at the house as he climbed in, saw Maura standing at the office window, watching as they took him away.

"Sorry, ma'am. You're not on this list, I can't let you in."

Mickie reached over to dig in her handbag on the seat beside her. The guard stepped out of his booth, let his hand rest on the gun on his hip. Little Mexican chick, ready to argue with him. No *way* was she getting past him.

His eyes widened with surprise when she came out with a badge, held it up in the light. *Bureau of Alcohol, Tobacco and Firearms.* He lifted his hand off his gun, very slowly. "I'll have to call up to the house."

"Then do it."

He went back inside the booth, picked up the phone. Mickie watched him speak to somebody, then he got put on hold, glanced over at her while he waited. After a while he spoke into the phone again, listened, and hung up. He came out, shaking his head.

"Sorry, but Mr. Jeanrette isn't available at the moment. He's the person who'd have to approve you being let past. So I'm afraid you'll have to get in touch with him."

"How?"

The guard looked puzzled. "I'm sorry?"

"How should I get in touch with him if he's not available?"

"I guess you'll have to wait until he *is* available." The guard pointed back down the driveway. "Now, if I could ask you to back your car up . . ."

Mickie reached back, drew the gun from her hip, racked the slide, and pointed it at his chest. "Step back from the car, please."

The guard froze, one arm stuck out like somebody'd just whipped away the wall he'd been leaning against. His eyes widened as he looked at the gun in her hand, then he raised his other hand slowly and stepped back.

"Take your gun out of the holster, very slowly, and lay it on the ground."

He did as she told him, holding the gun with two fingers, laying it on the ground next to the car.

"Now step back inside the booth." Mickie kept her eye on him, watching him do it as she reached over with her free hand and opened the glove compartment. She felt around in there until her hand closed on a pair of handcuffs. Then she opened her door and got out. "Get down on the floor."

She pressed the gun against his head while she cuffed his hands behind his back, looping the cuffs around one leg of the stool he sat on when traffic was slow. Then she straightened up, holstered her gun, and pressed the button that raised the gate.

"I'll leave the key outside," she told him. He refused to look at her. "When I get up to the house, I'll send somebody down to unlock you."

She got back into her car and drove on through the gate.

35

"You know the secret of a successful residential development?" Buddy was behind the wheel of the Land Cruiser, taking it fast along the unlit roads, swinging the wheel hard to avoid ruts in the gravel. "Two things, trees and roads. You got to limit people's vision. Everywhere they look, they should see a bunch of trees. They drive up a street, you make 'em turn every fifty yards. That way they go slow, look around. People come to a place like this to look at a house, they want to feel like they're on a little country road up in New England. That's everybody's secret fantasy, a farmhouse in Vermont. You see it in all those books they give you when you're a kid, it stays with you. Only who wants to spend their life shoveling snow, right? So we bring that image here, add a premium security environment, armed guards at the gate, you got a recipe for gracious living." The Land Cruiser's headlights swept across woods, gravel road, long stretches of cleared ground that Danny figured were part of the golf course.

"Anyway, you see all these trees? How the road bends every fifty yards? That's an investment in quality. A lot of developers, they buy a piece of land, bring in the bulldozers, plow it all under: trees, bushes, the whole thing. Then they lay a grid over it, put in roads that run straight back from the entrance. Cross street every quarter mile. You buy a house there, you get a square piece of dirt. You got to go out, buy your own trees to plant in the front yard. Hang on to the house for twenty years, you *might* have a tree that'll give you some shade. You know why they do it that way? 'Cause it's quick and cheap. Buy it, build it, sell it. Then go do it again somewhere else. That's how you get rich, this business." He made a hard left onto a narrow road Danny hadn't seen coming; the Land Cruiser slid on the loose gravel. "But for me, this is more than just a business. I look at this place, I see the next stage of our development as a species. Human growth. We come out of the jungle, we impose our will on the world around us, we fight each other for land, for food, for respect. And only when we've achieved *mutual* respect can we learn to live together in a community based on common understanding, shared dreams." He waved a hand at the darkness beyond the window. "It's the story of my life. I started out in law enforcement, spent fifteen years as a state trooper. That's the jungle, son. You see all the animals, watch 'em feed on each other. Then I sold guns. Building a society based on *mutual* respect. God might not have created all men equal, but Smith and Wesson sure as shit did. Now I'm taking the next step up the ladder. Creating a real community from the ground up. Carving it out of the wilderness, the way our grandfathers built this country." He glanced over at Danny. "And I'm not gonna let *anybody* get in the way of that. You understand what I'm saying?"

Danny kept his eyes on the window, gazing out into the darkness. "Jimmy know that?"

Buddy laughed. "Shit, Jimmy's got his uses. Next year, he's gonna put through a highway bill, get the Belle Chasse Highway expanded, and he's talkin' to some people in Washington about getting a new bridge put up, right down the road by the ferry. You want to imagine what all this out here is gonna be worth, you could get to the Central Business District in twenty-five minutes?" He smiled. "Yeah, Jimmy's a good man to know. But he ain't *half* as smart as he thinks he is." He swung the Land Cruiser hard to the right, slowed as they squeezed past a fallen tree that lay across the road. Then he gave it some gas, made an abrupt left between some bushes, and bounced over the grass into a meadow. The headlights caught some glass glittering between the branches of a low-hanging tree, and then Danny saw a building appear straight ahead of them, like something out of a boy's dream. High windows, like a church, but with all the glass smashed, scattered across the ground below. Vines growing up the outside walls, old graffiti sprayed along the ground floor—*Shark wuz here!* Caught in the headlights, it looked ghostly.

"C'mon," Buddy said, getting out. "You won't fuckin' believe this place."

Mickie left her car at the end of a long row of cars, next to a Mercedes, glanced over at it as she walked up the drive toward the house. Like a bad joke at her expense. When she was a girl, she'd complained to her mother that they'd stolen her name. For a while, in junior high school, the boys had started going out at night to steal the hood ornaments, wore them on chains around their necks. A couple different boys had offered to steal her one, but she'd turned them down. She already knew who she was.

Weird, that memory coming back now. She glanced through the windows as she went up the front steps of the house. Rich people, talking with other rich people. The women in their expensive dresses, with their hair sculpted and sprayed, looked like a flock of exotic birds. The men looked like well-fed dogs getting ready to mark their territory.

Nobody stopped her at the door. There was a table in the entryway where people could leave checks. She walked past it, glanced through the door into the main room, where a jazz combo was playing quietly in one corner, ignored by the guests. Jimmy Boudrieux stood in the center of the room surrounded by people. He was telling a story, and when he got to the punch line, he threw his head back and laughed loudly. The people around him smiled.

Mickie pushed her way through the crowd, slid her badge out of her pocket, held it up where Jimmy could see it. "Representative Boudrieux, I'm Special Agent Vega of the ATF. I wonder if I could speak with you for a . . ."

She felt a hand close on her elbow, gripping it hard. Mickie looked over, surprised; she recognized the lawyer who'd accompanied Jimmy to the police station, Helen Whelan. *Danny's ex-wife.* She looked elegant in her pale silk dress. Standing next to her, Mickie felt like just what she was—a working-class Mexican girl from Albuquerque. Cop family, cop dreams.

"This is outrageous," Helen said. "This is a private party. If you have anything to discuss with my client, I suggest you contact my office in the—"

Mickie cut her off: "I'm looking for Danny Chaisson. I have reason to believe he's here, and he could be in serious trouble."

Helen shot a look at Jimmy. Then she turned to Mickie and said, "This isn't the place. Come with me."

Mickie followed her back along the hall. She could smell food cooking, hear the sounds of dishes being stacked. Near the back of the building, Helen opened a door to an office and stepped back to allow Mickie to pass. Mickie saw a desk, two couches, a bar built into the far wall.

"Wait here," Helen told her, reaching for the door. "I'll be with you in a minute."

"If Danny's here, we may not have a minute. I think there's a good chance he'll be killed."

Helen turned to stare at her. "Why would they want to kill Danny?"

Mickie hesitated, then looked at her eyes closely. "Because he can destroy them. He's been an FBI informant for three years." She saw Helen stiffen, and the surprise on her face was real. "You really didn't know."

Helen looked away, then closed her eyes wearily. "No."

Jesus, they were probably still married then, Mickie realized. *He didn't even tell his wife.* She suddenly felt an odd sympathy for this woman, learning that she'd spent the last three years caught up in somebody else's secret. Like waking up one day to discover your husband's a gambler, and he's just lost your house on Ole Miss vs. Louisiana Tech.

Then Helen spoiled it, looking up at her with a tight face that Mickie figured was the closest she ever came to anger. "I'm sorry. I want to help you, but you'll have to wait here. I have to speak to Jimmy first."

Mickie reached out and caught her arm as she started to close the door. "This is a lousy time to start thinking like a lawyer. Danny's life is at stake."

Helen shook her off angrily. "You want to know where Danny is? I'm going to find out. Nobody's told me anything." Then she looked at Mickie; her eyes were tired. "It's all just boys and their games. That's all it's ever been. And it never ends."

She pulled the door closed, walked away quickly. Mickie stood looking at the door, thinking that maybe it wasn't always a blessing to be beautiful. Behind her, somebody said, "Now you know why Danny didn't tell her."

Mickie turned, saw a woman lying on the nearest couch. She had short dark hair and very pale skin, with that aging-child look Mickie'd seen on chronic drug abusers. Like a strange innocence, the look of somebody who'd spent her life turning her eyes away from an unpleasant world. The woman got up and wandered over to the desk, looked at some large rolls of paper lying there. "Jimmy won't tell her anything."

"How do you know?"

She looked up at Mickie, gave a faint smile. "'Cause he's my father. And he's a lying piece of shit." She reached down, spread out one of the rolls of paper on the desk. "You want to know where they took Danny?"

Mickie went over to the desk. The roll of paper was a construction plan for the whole development. Most of it just empty lots, plenty of woods where you could dump a body. But who'd kill a guy, leave the body where one of your own construction crews could stumble on it? The property was bordered by water on three sides. Easier to just take him down there, shoot him, and roll the body into the water. Let the gators take care of the rest. Then she saw a building site near the rear of the property, an existing structure marked for renovation in Phase II of the project. It looked close to the water, and an old building like that would have thick walls. Thick enough to muffle a gunshot.

She looked at the faint, twisting lines that marked the roads, thinking, *No lights, no road signs.* Christ, no way to know if all those roads marked on the map had even been built yet. She grabbed the map off the table and started to turn away, then hesitated, dug one of her ATF business cards out of her pocket, tossed it on the desk.

"You think you could call the number on this card, tell 'em Special Agent Vega could use some backup out here?"

Maura picked up the card, looked at it. "That's you?"

"Uh-huh. Can I count on you to do that?"

Maura looked up at her. "You're asking me to call the cops on my father."

"That a problem?"

Maura smiled and reached for the phone. "You kidding? I've been waiting for this all my life."

Jimmy saw Helen standing in the doorway, signaling to him. He was in the middle of a story he was trying out on the young wife of a wealthy owner of a concrete manufacturing plant up on the north shore, and he'd just gotten to the part where he could tell, just from the way she looked at him—blushed, maybe, or smiled, looked him right in the eye—exactly what kind of gal his rich friend had found

himself. So he waved Helen off and started to turn back to the concrete
lady when he caught a look at the expression on Helen's face, like she'd
just swallowed the business end of a scorpion and was getting ready to
cough it back up.

"You know," he said, resting one hand on the concrete lady's elbow, "it just occurred to me that this story isn't *appropriate* in mixed
company." He grinned at her, saw her eyebrows go up as if he'd caught
her interest now. "So if you'll excuse me a minute, I'm just gonna go
take my snake for a walk before he goes and bites someone." And he
winked at her, walked away as she stared after him, openmouthed. *Always leave 'em with something,* he'd learned, twenty years in politics.
Don't matter what, just so long as they can't wash it off.

He crossed the room toward Helen, pausing to shake hands with
the president of a bank up in Jefferson Parish, thinking how Lucas
would have briefed him on the guy in a whisper as they came toward
him—name, company, spouse's name, issues the guy would pay to
have resolved. Amazing, really. Like watching a guy walk through a
room, striking matches on his teeth.

Damn shame, Lucas.

But at the moment he had Helen to deal with, and judging by
the look on her face, she wasn't going to be happy until she had most
of his skin under her fingernails. From talking to the ATF woman,
probably. Jimmy snuck a quick glance at his watch. A couple minutes
and the whole thing would be over. He'd be out clean, or clean enough
to retire from politics while the string was still tight on his bow, spend
some time on *other interests.* He liked the way that sounded. Lets people
know you're getting out at the top of your game, that you're still
somebody with a few cards to play. 'Cause in New Orleans, if you're
not a player, you're nobody. No, it's worse than that. You're what gets
played.

Jimmy smiled. Hell, that's what Buddy was just about to
find out.

He eased past the last group in the room with a smile and a nod, caught Helen's elbow, and drew her out into the hall. "Okay, Helen. I can see you're angry, so spare me the performance. What's going on?"

Her eyes flared, and she jerked her arm away from him. "Where's Danny?"

"I have no idea. Why?"

"You haven't seen him?"

"Here?" Jimmy shook his head. "The guy'd have to be an idiot to show up here, he just sold me out."

Helen looked at his face closely. "You're lying."

"Come on, Helen. You've known me your whole life. You really think I'd . . ."

She took a step back from him, shaking her head. "It's all a game to you, isn't it? People are *dead.*"

He grabbed her arm, pulled her down the hall, away from the crowd. "And you think *I* killed 'em?" He pointed back down the hall, his voice a harsh whisper. "Honey, go take a look in that room. All those people want something from me. They didn't, they wouldn't be here. I don't have *time* to go killing people."

"I won't be part of this shit."

He looked at her, and suddenly he smiled. "You won't, huh? It's a mean old world out there, ain't it? But you're too pure to get involved. I guess that's what Danny found out. Things get messy, you hit the fuckin' road."

She stared at him, then turned abruptly and walked out. Jimmy stood there, watched her vanish into the darkness outside. A moment later, he heard a car start up, toss some gravel up as it pulled away. *Terrific.*

He glanced at his watch. No time to worry about it now. He had one more card to play, and then it was time to collect his winnings, walk away from the table. And if he played it right, there'd be nobody to accuse him.

Send her some flowers, he thought, as he slipped out the back, headed for his car. *Or, even better, send her some business.* He knew most of the partners at her firm. They'd bring her around. With guys like that, money doesn't just talk, it *sings.*

He opened the trunk of his car, used his handkerchief to lift out the briefcase Morrisey had left with him. Then he turned and walked back toward the house. *Hell, son, you handle this one right, you'll have a whole fucking choir singin' sweet songs of praise.*

"So? You figure it out yet?"

They stood in a narrow corridor on the ground floor, a row of doors on each side. Buddy swung one of the doors open and shone his flashlight into the tiny cell.

"Give you one more clue." He pointed the flashlight at the wall above the metal sink. The reflection made Danny look away. "They put mirrors in every cell."

Danny glanced over at Morrisey, saw him grin. Like he was getting a kick out of it. For the last twenty minutes, they'd followed Buddy's flashlight through the abandoned building, Morrisey pointing his gun at Danny while they listened to Buddy: "Check out those fixtures. That's real gold." And "You see those moldings, over the windows? You got any idea what those would cost today?" Danny stood there, his hands shoved deep in his pockets, his fingers gently touching the bullet Buddy'd tossed to him back at the house. *Won't be long now.*

"C'mon, take a guess." Buddy arced the flashlight across the interior of the cell. "Hell, you shouldn't have any trouble figuring it out, Danny. This one's right up your fuckin' alley."

Danny kept silent. What was there to say? When Buddy finished showing off his property, they'd get down to business. So he kept his mouth shut, watching for a moment when Morrisey's eyes wandered.

Like that would help. You can't outrun a bullet.

His mind kept flashing on a scene from a movie he'd seen, a guy who'd been marched out into the woods at gunpoint, down on his knees, begging for his life. The two soldiers who'd been sent to kill him just looked at him with contempt, and when he broke down, started sobbing, one of them reached down and shot him in the head. Watching it, Danny'd felt queasy. He wondered if he'd beg when the moment came, soon now. He wondered if he'd even have time, or if Morrisey would casually raise his gun like the guy in Saigon and blow his brains out. He'd read somewhere that the last words of most soldiers who'd suffered mortal wounds were "I want my mama." Suddenly that seemed unbearably sad to him, as if their lives had come full circle in that last moment. But Mama wasn't there; she couldn't help you. There was only the pain, like a bright fire in your chest, and the endless darkness settling over you.

He looked up, realized Buddy had stopped talking, was watching him. "What's the matter, Danny? You not enjoying the tour?"

Morrisey grinned. "I don't think he's too impressed by your place, Buddy."

"That right, Danny? You think I wasted my money?" Buddy slid his hand into his jacket pocket, drew out Danny's gun. He racked the slide, chambering a round, then raised the gun, drew the barrel lightly across Danny's cheek. "You know, you look just like your father?" He smiled. "First time you walked into my office, I almost thought it *was* him. Like seeing a ghost. Only this time you were collecting money, and your father, he used to come 'round, pay *me*."

Danny swallowed, feeling the gun move down along his jaw and come to rest under his chin. He felt it push against his throat, lifting his head slightly, then turning it gently to one side, as if Buddy were studying his face. "Then why'd you kill him?"

Buddy smiled. "Guess you could say I bit the hand that fed me." He shrugged, let the gun slide down Danny's throat to the zipper on his leather jacket and pushed it down, slowly, until the gun came to rest just over Danny's heart. "Wasn't like he gave us much choice, really. He was like you. Things get going too good, you figure it's time to stick your finger in the socket."

"I'm not the one who killed all those people."

"No, that's true." Buddy gave a smile. "You just showed up, picked up the briefcase like they told you. I got Ray to thank for the rest."

"Ah, Christ." Morrisey shook his head. "We got to go through that shit again? Just shoot the guy, let's get this thing finished."

Buddy raised his eyebrows. "Hear that, Danny? Ray thinks I'm taking too long."

Danny stood very still. "I'm in no hurry."

"No, I guess you aren't." Buddy raised the gun, pressed it against Danny's forehead. "Maybe you should be."

Danny met his gaze. "You'll kill me when you're ready. There's nothing I can do about that."

"And that doesn't scare you?"

"Yeah, it scares me. But I got what I came for."

Buddy's eyes narrowed. He studied Danny's face.

"And what's that?"

"Jimmy's going down this time." Danny gave a thin smile. "And you'll be dead before morning."

36

"Get your things. We're leaving."

Maura watched Jimmy carry the briefcase over to the desk and set it down next to Buddy's chair. He took out a handkerchief, wiped off the handle carefully. Then he straightened up, tucked the handkerchief into his pocket, and looked over at Maura on the sofa.

"You hear me?"

"I'm staying here."

He rubbed at his eyes wearily. "The police will be here in a few minutes. It would be better if we weren't here when they arrive."

She looked toward the window. "So leave."

He studied her for a moment, then shrugged. "Okay, suit yourself." He reached up to straighten his tie, then glanced around the office, as if to make sure he hadn't left anything important behind. "I'm going to say good night to my guests, collect their checks, and call it a night." He opened the door. "Try not to do anything stupid, okay?"

He closed the door behind him. *Asshole,* Maura thought. She looked over at the briefcase he'd left beside the desk. Then she got up, went over and picked it up, laid it on the desk. She popped the clasps, opened it. "Fuck."

There was no money. Only three handguns, each with a sheet of paper folded under it. *Face it, girl. You just got no luck.*

She closed it, started to put it back. Then she paused, looked out the window at the rows of expensive cars parked in the driveway. Her father's Seville gleamed in the faint light from the window.

She picked up the briefcase off the desk, walked out of the room.

Mickie drove way too fast for the narrow gravel roads that wound across the back of the property, glancing down every couple seconds at the project plans spread out on the seat beside her. She could feel her tires sliding on the gravel every time the road took a sudden bend, felt herself start to lose it once before she spun the wheel back and took her foot off the gas, caught the car as it started to slide the other way.

Like driving the back roads out in the desert when she was in high school, racing with the boys in their low-slung Toyotas, gravel snapping against the frame. Trying hard, Jesus, *hard,* to go easy on her father's car. But then one of those boys would grin at her as he went past, and her foot would stomp the gas to the floor, she'd feel that V-6 kick in, and there'd be no time for thinking, just the road spinning it-self out in front of her headlights, white dust, black sky. When the cops showed up, you'd shut your lights off, make a run for it up those back roads, or cut out across the fields, wire fences twanging across the front of your car as you went through. Just follow the taillights, they'll lead you home.

There were no lights to follow now. The roads twisted and turned like snakes trying to crawl out of their skins. Several times she thought she was lost, until the road suddenly came to a dead end in front of her, just like on the map, and she made a hard right back away from the wa-ter, thinking, *Should be right up ahead on the left.* She didn't see the tree that lay partway across the narrow road until it was too late and she had to cut the wheel hard to the left to avoid it; she felt the car slide right, then left, as she hit the brake, swung it back to avoid the ditch.

She almost made it.

The car spun, clipped the fallen tree, and she felt the wheel go loose in her hands as her front wheels swung out over the edge of the ditch, hung there. The engine stalled. She sat there, feeling the car rock slightly as the gravel slid away, shifted the car's weight. After a moment, she opened the door carefully. The car moved slightly, and she saw rocks slide away under the frame just below the front of her seat. *Jesus.* Like something in a movie. Only, it was a movie, they'd have her stuck on the edge of a cliff, waves crashing below.

Louisiana cliff-hanger, she thought. *How long it takes you to fall into a ditch.*

She swung her feet out sideways, got them on the rocks. When she stood up, the car tilted forward and slid slowly down the gravel into the ditch, came to rest with its front end in several inches of sludge. *Terrific. Let's hope that's not an omen.*

She reached back, drew her gun, eased a round into the chamber. Then she turned and walked up the road into the trees.

"*I'm* gonna be dead?"

Danny kept his eyes on Buddy's face, away from where his finger curled around the trigger. "That's what I said."

Buddy grinned. "You read the tea leaves, Danny?"

"Don't have to. I read your files."

"My *files?*" Buddy laughed, shook his head. "You believe this guy, Ray? He looks at my tax returns, I'll find out I've got cancer."

"He's just stalling. Do it, and let's go."

"No, this I gotta hear." He grinned at Danny. "So? Let's have it. How do you get all that just from reading my files?"

Danny smiled. "It's right there in the contract, Buddy. You're in somebody's way. Foley didn't know what he had with those guns. He was scared when I talked to him. That's not how a guy acts who's holding all the cards. Somebody *told* him to get his hands on those guns so he could cut a deal with the ATF. But it had to be somebody who knew your business. Somebody who could see where you'd cut corners, where you'd be vulnerable. And this guy, he'd have to have a serious interest in seeing you take a fall. Enough to justify getting people killed. See, that's where I made my mistake. I figured Jimmy only cared about covering his ass. He's been doing it so long it's like breathing for him. So he'd help you set up Foley if he thought it was the only way to handle it. That's what I thought was going on, until I looked at your files. River Road Partners. That wasn't too subtle, Buddy. But I guess you figured every time Jimmy got a check you'd remind him what he owed you."

Buddy smiled. "Thing like that, you're partners for life."

"That ain't the same as forever, Buddy. You set up this real estate deal, you put a lot of money on the table."

Buddy studied his face. "You got to do better than that, Danny. Sounds to me like you're just trying to shove a spike in the gears. Get us killing each other." He grinned. "That what you want, Danny? Payback for your father?"

Danny spread his hands. "It's out of my hands now. You guys are gonna do it for me."

"Don't be so sure. I can handle Jimmy."

Danny glanced over at Morrisey. "Maybe it's not Jimmy you got to worry about."

Buddy followed his gaze. "What, *Ray?*" He swung Danny's gun around and shot Morrisey in the face. The sound of the shot was like a bone snapping behind Danny's eyes. He saw the back of Morrisey's head explode, blood splattering the wall behind him. Then his body simply crumpled, became a heap of wet clothing on the floor. Buddy swung the gun back to point it at Danny's head.

"Problem solved."

Mickie stood at the edge of a clearing, studying the crumbling building. Broken windows, vines climbing up the walls, leaves blown into drifts against the corner of the balcony. *Jesus,* she thought. *All it needs is a ghost.*

The sound of the shot made her heart jump, and she felt fear race through her. *You're too late,* she thought. But she made herself move forward, to cross the moonlit clearing to the steps, where she saw a row of tiny windows that ran along the front wall under the balcony. Hearing the instructor back in Glynco, Georgia, telling the class, "Assume they know you're coming. Every window is an open eye. Every door is a trap. Choose your point of entry to minimize your exposure."

So what's your entry plan? Straight up the front steps, push the door open a couple inches. Not too clever, but quick. She stole a quick glance through the door, then let her gun lead her into the dark. Her body armor, she realized as she slipped inside, was back in the trunk of her Nova. *Doing it all as wrong as it can be done.* But she didn't hesitate, just eased in there, found a wall to follow with her hand, trying to step lightly on the boards that creaked under her feet.

But Jesus, it was dark in there. No moonlight through the broken windows, no way to tell a wall from a door. She paused when her feet touched a staircase leading up, wondered if she should go back to the Nova, get her flashlight out of the trunk. Get the body armor while she was there. But shine a flashlight in a dark room, you might as well paint a target on your chest. Better to take your time, move quietly in the darkness, count on the other guy to light up his area while you used the darkness. Only problem was, she saw no lights on this floor, didn't trust the stairs to take her up to the next one without giving way under her feet, sending her crashing into the basement. She paused, listening. For a moment, she thought she heard voices, then they were gone. Off to her right somewhere. She skirted the staircase, moved in that direction, one hand waving in front of her, feeling for the opposite wall. A board creaked underfoot as she stepped on it, then even louder as she lifted her weight off. *Christ, you better hope they're not expecting you.*

She took a few more steps, and found the wall with her hand. Then she paused, listening. Her knee had begun to ache. She could hear rain begin to fall beyond the windows. She slid along the wall until her hand found an opening, then shuffled forward carefully until the floor dropped away under her feet. A flight of stairs, going down. Below there was only darkness and silence.

She shifted her gun to her left hand, wiped her sweaty palm against her jeans. Then she transferred the gun back, took a deep breath, and started down.

"Look at him." Buddy pointed the flashlight at Morrisey's crumpled body. "Stupid fucker."

Danny glanced over, then looked quickly away. There were bits of bone and brain stuck to the wall above Morrisey's body.

"You know Ray's problem? He figured everybody must be as stupid as he was." Buddy sighed, shook his head. "Jimmy told me they'd found one of my guns with Keyes, I figured Ray was trying to carve himself off a piece. Dump the whole thing back in my lap, make sure I wasn't around to point the finger at him. He must've cut his own deal with Jimmy. They get me to kill you, then Ray kills me. Everybody shakes their heads, figures I was the guy behind those two deputies who got killed in the car wreck, and Ray walks away as the cop who broke the case. Couple months later, he retires from the department, Jimmy sets him up as his new front man in the gun stores."

"So he kills you, then he becomes you."

"That's how it works." Buddy smiled. "You know, Danny, all these years, you've been angry about your father. You ever wonder why Jimmy was so hot to get you to come work for him? Went to all that trouble to get you to quit the D.A.'s office?" He laughed. "You scared the fuck out of Jimmy. He figured it was only a matter of time until you figured out what happened to your father, better to get you where he could keep an eye on you."

Danny stared at him. "What are you talking about?"

"You think he didn't know you were gonna testify someday?

Why do you think he had you and Lucas go through that whole act over in your office, like you were his lawyer? You testify, he can claim you were his attorney, so everything's privileged. Judge'll throw out the whole case." He saw Danny's expression and grinned. "Look't you. Locked and loaded. You been thinking about getting Jimmy all these years, that's all you got. Now you find out he's been playing you the whole time. Wasn't so funny, I'd be crying."

A board creaked softly just above them. There was a pause, then Danny heard it again. Buddy glanced up at the ceiling. He reached up, not looking, and pressed his forearm against Danny's throat, shoved him back against the wall. The flashlight clicked off, and Danny blinked against the darkness. A faint streak of moonlight came in at the window of the cell across from them, spread across the floor toward him. He could smell rain.

They stood there, listening. A stair creaked to Danny's right. Buddy pressed his arm tighter against Danny's throat and moved the gun away from his head, swung it over toward the steps. Then, abruptly, he pulled Danny off the wall, back into the doorway of the closest cell, and held him there as a shield, one arm curled around his throat.

Mickie could feel the air get cooler as she reached the bottom of the stairs. The place smelled like mold and rotting leaves. *Root cellar,* she thought. *Keeps your vegetables fresh.* She paused, listening. If anybody was there, they weren't moving. Not even breathing. Her mind was spinning webs in the darkness, that's all. Making the silence around her into a spider, poised and waiting.

So move, she thought. *Don't freeze up, here.*

She took a step slowly. Her hand waved blindly in the darkness ahead of her, then touched a wall opposite. It was a hallway, running off into the darkness on each side of her. The stairs were behind her, so if she kept moving along one wall, she'd be able to find her way back. Seeing building plans in her mind as she turned, slid her hand along the wall, large rolls of blue paper spread out on the table at Glynco, an instructor running his finger over the page, showing them where to expect structural walls, concrete slabs that could stop a bullet, power lines, gas. Stairs were blue piano keys making a *Z* down the paper, one flight going up, one going down. Find the stairs, you've found the building's hollow heart. Its point of mobility and danger. Thirty-eight percent of police officers are killed in doorways, another 15 percent on stairs. Everybody fights to control the stairs.

Then her hand touched a metal door and pushed gently. The door gave way, opened with a faint creak. From a few yards down the hall, a light came on suddenly, blinding her. She cried out and swung her gun toward the light, stumbling against the metal door. She heard a gun go off somewhere behind her as she fell into the narrow darkness, felt a bullet go past her, flicking dust off the stone wall of the corridor. And then she was lying on her back on the damp stone floor, her gun pointed back at the doorway. In the faint light, she could make out a metal bunk hung on the wall to her left, a toilet and sink in the corner, and a cracked mirror on the wall. Like a jail cell after all the prisoners had been released.

She rolled to her right, out of the light from the corridor, then got to her feet, feeling a sharp pain in her hip where she'd hit the floor. She ignored it, got her back against the metal door, the gun held out low in both hands, ready.

"Federal officer," she shouted. "Put your weapon down and step into the middle of the hall."

She heard a scuffle in the hall, and the light abruptly went out.

Danny felt Buddy's arm tighten around his throat as the footsteps reached the bottom of the stairs, then a faint creak of rusty hinges as one of the doors swung open. Suddenly the pressure on his throat was gone as Buddy swung the flashlight toward the sound, flicked it on. Danny caught a brief glimpse of Mickie Vega, startled, swinging her gun toward them. Danny grabbed Buddy's gun just as he fired, saw the bullet spark off the stone wall a few inches from her left hip. Then she plunged through the open door of one of the cells and vanished.

Danny felt Buddy try to shove him away, but he clung to his gun hand, kept him from bringing it around. He swung his left elbow wildly, felt it connect with Buddy's head. Buddy grunted, staggered back against the corridor wall, then raised the flashlight in his left hand and swung it at Danny's head. It caught Danny high on the shoulder, made him cry out in pain. He saw the flashlight fly out of Buddy's hand, hit the opposite wall.

Everything went black.

Danny swung wildly in the dark. His forearm caught the side of Buddy's head, awkwardly, but he felt Buddy stumble, off balance. Danny lost his grip on the gun, and it went off, a bright tongue of flame erupting out of the end of the gun. Danny turned to run and stumbled over Morrisey's outstretched feet, landed hard on his hip. The gun roared above him as he hit the floor. He rolled to his right, felt the gun crack again just behind him. He kicked out blindly, felt his foot catch Buddy solidly on one thigh. Buddy stumbled over him, fell hard, the gun clattering away across the floor. Danny punched at the dark shape above him, felt his knuckle split on Buddy's face. He heard Buddy curse, then roll away, one hand grabbing for the other gun holstered on his hip. "You fuck. Ah, you *fuck*!"

"ATF!" he heard Mickie shout. "Put your weapons *down*!"

But he knew she couldn't see them, could only point her gun into the darkness, wait for the flash from Buddy's gun. Danny heard metal scrape against leather as Buddy got the weapon clear of its holster, then heard him rack the slide.

And then Danny was on his feet, stumbling into the open door of a cell. His leg hit something hard in the darkness, and he fell against the metal bunk. He grabbed the edge and pulled himself under it just as Buddy rose up in the doorway and began firing.

Later, they figured he must have emptied the gun. Mickie found it next to Buddy's body, the breech locked open on the empty clip. But what stuck in Danny's mind was the way the dark cell had seemed to erupt with light and wild music, bullets singing off the concrete walls, the floor, the metal bed. And then, in the sudden silence that followed, the sound of an empty cartridge spinning crazily on the floor, and the slow, wet sound of someone gasping for breath. Danny heard the sound slow, then stop.

Mickie kicked the gun away from Buddy's hand, stood over him with her gun pointed down at his body. "Danny?" she called out into the darkness. He heard the despair in her voice, the fear that nobody could have survived that bitter storm she'd watched erupt in the darkness when Buddy emptied his gun.

Danny lay there beneath the metal bunk, not moving. He wondered if he was still alive. Then he felt his leg hurting where he'd stumbled over the metal bunk, and he knew that if anything could hurt that bad, he must be alive.

He swallowed. "I'm here." His voice sounded strange to him, as if somebody else had spoken the words. Mickie came into the cell, shuffling forward in the darkness, and he reached out, touched her leg gently as she passed the bunk. He felt her jump, then she went down on her knees, grabbed his hand.

"Are you shot?"

He reached up, touched the metal bunk an inch above his face. "No." Then he slid out from under the bunk, and she stood up, helped him to his feet. He stood close to her, her hand grasping his in the darkness, and he could smell her hair, feel her breath on his cheek. He touched her face gently. She stepped back suddenly, then turned, felt her way back to the door.

Buddy lay slumped against the wall of the corridor, where he'd collapsed when Mickie shot him. She went out to her car, got her flashlight from the trunk, carried it back to squat beside the body, point the light at Buddy's shattered face and chest. She found where she'd hit him, high on the right side of his chest. But he had four other wounds across the front of his body, including a lethal head wound where the bullets he'd fired started coming back at him off those hard concrete walls. One bullet had blown away most of the left side of his face. His left eye socket gaped.

Danny had to look away. "Jesus."

Mickie stood up, pointed the light over at Morrisey. "I guess it's like they say. Everything comes back at you sometime."

They took Buddy's Land Cruiser, left her car tilted in the ditch for the tow truck to pull out in the morning. Neither of them said much as Mickie drove them back out the winding gravel roads.

Danny watched the windshield wipers smear the rain across the glass, trying to figure out how to feel. "What happens now?"

She glanced over at him. "I go back to my office, file a report. You go home and get some sleep."

He nodded, let his head rest against the window, looked up at the rain falling out of the night sky. "You ever wonder where birds go when it rains?"

"They don't go anywhere. They get wet."

And that seemed to be all there was to say. They drove on in silence until they came to the main road that led back to the development's entrance, where Mickie made a left, then suddenly hit the brakes.

Up ahead, near the subdivision's entrance, Danny saw three cars blocking the road, the red emergency lights mounted on their roofs knifing through the dark. A heavily armed ATF team in blue fatigues stood behind the cover of the cars, gazing up the road at a car that had slid into a shallow ditch a short distance away, as if the driver had come around the corner, slammed on the brakes when he saw the road-block, then been unable to hold the car on the road. Spotlights mounted on the squad cars lit up the car, and Danny saw that it was a Cadillac Seville. Jimmy Boudrieux sat behind the wheel. He was talking into a cellular telephone pressed to his ear. His other hand held a gun to his head.

An ATF agent left the group, walked back toward them with his hands raised, motioning them to back up. A compact assault rifle was slung from his shoulder. As he came up to Mickie's window, she took out her badge and held it up where he could see it. He glanced at it, then up at her face. "You're Vega, right?"

"Yeah, I called you out." She looked up at the scene ahead of them. "What's going on?"

The ATF agent hitched the weapon on his shoulder slightly, glanced back at the cars blocking the road. "We get here, there're about thirty cars trying to pull out. Whole place emptying out. So we set up a checkpoint, start searching the cars as they're leaving. We've pretty much cleared them out when this guy comes up the road, gets one look at us, and slams on the brakes. Next thing we know, he's got the car in reverse, trying to back up, get turned around. Only he cuts it too close, gets his back wheels in the ditch. So he's stuck. When we walk over there to talk to him, the guy puts a gun to his head, tells us to get back or he'll blow his brains out. We're running the plate now, try to figure out what we got here."

"It's Jimmy Boudrieux," Danny said, watching him in the pale glare of the spotlights. "That your people on the phone with him?"

"No, he's been on there the whole time. Made four calls already."

Danny smiled. "He's trying to get hold of the U.S. Attorney, somebody who'll pull you off him." He opened his door, got out. "He'll talk to me."

Mickie leaned across the seat, grabbed his arm. "Danny, that's a real bad idea."

He looked over at her and smiled. "Jimmy's not stupid. He won't do anything like that. All he wants is a way out."

"It's not up to you to give it to him."

He gently slipped her hand off his arm. "Who said I was?" Then he walked up the road, raising his hands carefully as he approached the car to show the ATF agents that he was unarmed. Jimmy took the phone away from his ear, used it to shade his eyes against the spotlights, watching him approach. When Danny got to the car, he rested both hands against the passenger door, looked in at Jimmy.

"Looks like you fucked up, Jimmy."

"Tell me about it." Jimmy tossed the phone down on the seat beside him in disgust. "Can't get anybody on the phone. All I get is their fucking answering machines."

"You think anybody's gonna want to talk to you right now? You're sitting here with a gun to your head."

"You got a better idea?" Jimmy sighed. "Fucking gun's empty, anyway." He jerked his head toward the backseat. "Came out of there."

Danny bent down, looked in the back. Foley's briefcase lay open on the backseat; the two remaining guns lay on the floor in front of it, as if they'd fallen out. "Looks like you ended up holding the bag."

"I put it in Buddy's office, figuring that's where they belong. Then I get in my car, ride out here, and when I hit my brakes, I hear this thump from the backseat. I look back there, it's the fucking briefcase. Like the goddamn thing's following me."

Danny smiled. "Maura."

Jimmy rubbed his eyes wearily. "Fucking bitch has been waiting her whole life to do this to me. Only thing she's ever done is give me a pain in the ass." He looked up at the ATF agents watching them. "They find these with me, I'm fucked."

"So you grab one, hold it to your head." Danny smiled. "Kind of gives away the whole secret, Jimmy."

"What else was I gonna do? I'm stuck in the fucking ditch, they're walking up to the car. It was the only way I could think to keep 'em away while I made some calls." He sighed, lowered the gun, looked at it. "I never liked these fucking things. That's where Buddy and I were different. You got a brain, that's where real power comes from. Not some stupid piece of metal."

"Maybe it's power that's the problem."

Jimmy looked at him in disgust. "Jesus, Danny. Ain't you learned anything, this life?"

"So call Lucas. He's the guy with all the answers."

"Lucas is dead." Jimmy looked out at the dark trees around them. "Hanged himself in his cell a couple hours ago."

Danny straightened up and stared at him. "Whose idea was that?"

"Buddy's." Jimmy sighed. "I never wanted anybody to get hurt, Danny. I wish you could believe that. It's just, I let guys like Buddy . . . help me. Like with your father." He shrugged. "After that, it's like you can't stop. Every day you worry about something from the past coming back at you." He looked at the gun in his hands. "And it always does."

"Cut the shit, Jimmy. It's too late for that."

Jimmy looked up at him, surprised. "It's true, Danny. I never got into politics to make money. It's just money you want, you can make a shitload more doing something else."

"You did all right."

"Yeah, I did fine. But you know what happened to most of that money you carried. It got spread around." He shook his head sadly. "I really believed I could do some good, you know? Work the system, get things done. Only, after a while, it's like you forget all that shit, and all you can think about is the process. Who you got to pay off, who you can threaten. Where you can get the money. It's like you're so busy *doing* it, you got no time to think about *why*." He looked at the gun. "Then the next thing you know, some guy like Buddy shows up, tells you he can solve all your problems."

"Buddy's dead," Danny told him. "It's just you now."

"Yeah, I figured that when I saw you walk up here." He looked up at Danny. "So I guess there's no way out, huh?"

Danny looked at the ATF roadblock, shook his head. "Doesn't look like it."

"Any chance you'd help me out here?"

"Me?" Danny smiled, shoved his hands in his pockets. "I'm just the guy who carries the money." Then his fingers brushed against something hard and cold, and he stiffened slightly. He drew his hand out of his pocket, looked at the small copper bullet that lay in his palm.

Then he smiled. "Seems I've got something for you after all." He reached in the window, tossed the bullet into Jimmy's lap. Then he turned, walked away.

He could feel a light rain against his face. Up ahead, Mickie stood beside the Land Cruiser, watching him. Her face was wet with rain, her hair plastered to her forehead. She looked beautiful.

"Let's go," he said and got into the passenger seat. He rolled his window down, leaned his face out into the falling rain. She got behind the wheel, looked over at him.

"What happened?"

"I gave him a way out."

She stared at him. "You did *what?*"

He closed his eyes, felt the rain against his skin. The gunshot, when it came, was just an echo among the trees.